Advance pra[...]
JERI SMITH-R[...]

EYES OF CROW

"Jeri Smith-Ready's lyrical prose brings to life unforgettable characters and a poignant story that haunted me long after I finished the novel. She has a remarkable gift for making the reader care about her world and its people. Highly recommended."
—Catherine Asaro, bestselling and Nebula Award-winning author of *The Dawn Star*

"Fantasy and romance blend together to create a wonderfully organic novel.... Neither element is predictable, the story woven with a deftness that enhances the power of Smith-Ready's gentle take-no-prisoners style in both love and war. *Eyes of Crow* draws the reader in one subtle thread at a time, catching them in a complex, beautiful world they may never want to retreat from."
—C.E. Murphy, author of *Urban Shaman*

"*Eyes of Crow* lured me into its clutches by page two. By the end of the first chapter I felt like I was walking around in Jeri Smith-Ready's world—and had no desire to depart. Ms. Smith-Ready has woven an exquisite tapestry of a world filled with texture and richness. Beware reader! You may never want to return."
—P.C. Cast, bestselling author of *Goddess of the Rose*

EYES OF CROW

JERI SMITH-READY

LUNA™
www.LUNA-Books.com

LUNA™

EYES OF CROW

ISBN-13: 978-0-373-80258-6
ISBN-10:   0-373-80258-7

Copyright © 2006 by Jeri Smith-Ready

First trade printing November 2006

Author Photo © 2006 by Szemere Photography

This edition published by arrangement with Harlequin Books S.A.

® and TM are trademarks of Harlequin Books S.A., used under license.
Trademarks indicated with ® are registered in the United States Patent
and Trademark Office, the Canadian Trade Marks Office and in other
countries.

www.LUNA-Books.com

Printed in U.S.A.

Acknowledgments

Many thanks to my family, for encouraging
my love of nature and love of writing.

Much gratitude goes out to my "first readers," who spied
gaffes big and small that I couldn't see: Danell Andrichak,
Catherine Asaro, Sharon Galbraith-Ryer, Cecilia Ready,
Terri Prizzi, Tricia Schwaab, and Rob Staeger. Kudos to the
hardworking folks behind the scenes at LUNA who helped
bring the book to life: Mary-Theresa Hussey, Adam Wilson,
Tara Parsons, Karen Valentine, Marleah Stout,
Kathleen Oudit, as well as artist Chad Michael Ward
of Digital Apocalypse Studios.

Thanks to my phenomenal editor Stacy Boyd, who gave
intrepid support and insightful feedback from Day One.
This novel wouldn't exist without her care and vision.
My agent, Ginger Clark of Curtis Brown, Ltd., "gets" me
like no one else; she's the best ally an author could ask for.

Thanks most of all to my husband, Christian Ready,
for his love and patience, and for answering bizarre
questions on seemingly random subjects.

To Mom, for her faith

Beloved, gaze in thine own heart,
The holy tree is growing there;
From joy the holy branches start,
And all the trembling flowers they bear.

—William Butler Yeats
"The Two Trees"

The dog would not die.

Surely he was ill, and had been a puppy before the dawn of Rhia's earliest memory, more than five winters ago. He lay before the fire with his thick gray head in her lap, staring dully into the flames. She stroked the wiry hair along his side. His flesh felt cold, and she could fit her fingers between the ridges his ribs made in his skin. Even his halting breath smelled stale, like a half-open grave.

All her senses told Rhia that Boreas would not see tomorrow's sun. And yet…

Her mother Mayra turned from the table and crossed the room, feet whispering over the wolfskin rug. Holding an earthen bowl and a pale green cloth, she knelt beside Rhia.

"This will take away his pain and help him on his journey home." She showed Rhia the bowl's contents—a tiny amount of liquid, no more than what the child could cup in her palm. It wasn't enough.

Mayra covered the bowl with the cloth and began to chant, low and soft, calling upon her Otter Guardian Spirit to augment the medicine. Rhia closed her eyes and tried to clear her mind of fear and grief. The Spirits worked best when those present stayed out of their way.

Through her eyelids Rhia saw a golden light flare, the color of the sun on an autumn afternoon. A swish of liquid and Mayra's whispered gratitude told her that Otter had hearkened to the plea for help. When the light faded, Rhia opened her eyes and locked her gaze onto the dog's. Two tears, then another, plopped onto his muzzle.

Mayra dipped the cloth in the half-full bowl to let it soak. They sat listening to the only two sounds in the room—the dog's labored puffing and the snapping of sparks in the stone fireplace.

Rhia heard the cloth drip into the bowl as her mother squeezed it. The drops must not be wasted, but enough medicine needed to reach the dog's throat to give him release. Even in his withered old age, Boreas was much larger than Rhia—on his hind legs he could rest his paws on her head. A year ago, while Rhia was recovering from a muscle-wasting illness that sapped all strength from her limbs, Boreas had lent her his sturdy back and legs as a crutch. Now on cold nights like this one, when the wind and the wolves howled in harmony outside these log walls, she would curl up within his furry frame, one forepaw over her shoulder, and sleep warm and safe.

"Hold his head, dear."

Rhia reached under Boreas's snout and tilted it up. All at once he exhaled hard, almost a cough, and a weight lifted from him. In the back of her head she heard a sound like the hurried flapping of heavy wings. Her breath caught, and she craned her neck to peer behind her.

"What is it?" her mother asked.

Rhia turned to the worn face reddened by the wind and the firelight.

"It's not time," she said.

"Time for what?"

"For him to go."

Mayra cast a tender glance over her daughter's face. "I know you wish it were not his time, but—"

"He's not ready." She swallowed a sob and steadied her voice. "The world's not ready."

Mayra's gentle eyes narrowed. "Why do you speak of this?"

Rhia tilted her head to the northwest, from where the wind blew. "He'll take a wolf with him when he goes."

Her mother's whisper shook. "How do you know?"

"I just know." She blinked, and her last tear fell, this time on her own wrist. To stop now would be to waste her mother's magic—magic she herself hoped to carry one day. But something not entirely inside her begged for the dog's life. "Please don't make him die, Mama. Wait until morning, and you'll see. I promise."

Mayra's eyes glistened in the firelight as she gazed at Rhia with something more complicated than sympathy. The look held more pain than her mother's face had shown since Rhia's sickness—which, the girl now realized, was the first time she had heard those wings rush over the landscape of her mind.

Finally Mayra reached out and retucked one of her daughter's red-brown curls behind her ear, then brushed the back of her hand against Rhia's cheek. Without a word she stood and placed the cloth and bowl on the table, then shuffled over to climb the ladder to the sleeping loft she shared with her husband, Tereus.

Rhia dragged a thick log across the hearth and heaved it into the flames. It spit and hissed like a cornered wildcat. She blinked at it with near-pleasure as she remembered how even a few months ago she could no more have lifted the log than raise the house itself. Though her limbs would never regain normal strength, they no longer betrayed her, no longer pretended not to hear what her mind ordered them to do. They obeyed grudgingly, with the reluctance of sullen children.

She turned away from the fire and lay on the floor behind Boreas, her front to his back. Reaching around him, she pulled the wolf skin rug over both their bodies. The hound groaned deep in his throat.

"Go to sleep," she murmured into the knobby ridge on the back of his head. "You'll wake tomorrow."

The dog would not die, not for another two and a half years, when Rhia was nearly eleven. A wolf pack tried to drive the ponies from her family's farm into the surrounding forest. Though far into old age, Boreas was the first of the dogs to attack, killing the lead wolf. Moments later, his body crumpled from the effort. Because the summer soil was too dry and hard to dig a grave, Rhia and her family made a cairn of rocks for the dog and wolf together, then said a prayer to Crow to guide them safely home.

A rumor of Rhia's vision must have escaped, for the villagers began to invite the girl to observe their sick hounds or lame ponies. She wanted to help, but the animals' suffering saddened her, and their journeys toward the Other Side reminded her of the one she had almost taken as a child.

The bitterest blow came when Mayra, a village healer, no longer brought her along to patients' homes. During Rhia's childhood, they had both hoped that the sweet, playful Otter would touch her, too. A different Spirit had chosen her—one that courted not life but its dreaded opposite.

One day, after Rhia had just turned fifteen, Galen the village Council leader came to her family's horse and dog farm with his son Arcas. It was a brisk late afternoon in early spring, when the leaf buds were still only in the trees' imagination. Rhia was cleaning the hounds' pens when she saw the man and boy trudge up the steep hill to her home. She hurried to smooth her long hair and wipe the sweat from below her eyes. Mustn't look slovenly for Galen, she told herself, then smiled at her feeble attempt at self-deception. It was the sight of Arcas, not his imposing father, that made her pulse jump and her hands twitch and wonder what to do with themselves.

She couldn't put a pin in the moment when she first saw Arcas as something other than a childhood playmate. Most likely it happened either an instant before or an instant after he had kissed her behind the stables the month before. Since then, the smell of manure made her swoon with joy.

Rhia trotted toward the house to call her parents, then stopped to regard the two men again, for something was different about them today. Their steps were heavy, tan faces set in unusual grimness, heads bowed so that the sunlight glinted off their hair, the color of freshly tilled soil. Arcas's hair fell halfway down his back, but Galen's swept the top of his shoulders; it had been cut short last year to mourn the death of his mother.

As always, a single brown hawk feather, black-streaked and red-tipped, hung around Galen's neck. Everyone she knew who possessed animal magic—which was every adult she'd ever met—wore some fetish of their Guardian Spirit to signal their powers. It was not to boast but rather a courtesy to let others know what they were dealing with. For instance, no one could be tricked into trying to deceive Owl people, who saw through a lie as if it were made of air.

When they were about ten steps away, Galen's sharp gaze finally found Rhia. Something in it made her want to draw a thick cloak around herself, both for warmth and conceal-ment. She sensed he knew more about her than she cared to confront on this til-now-tranquil day.

Rhia greeted them with a bow, which they returned. "Welcome," she said, then looked at Galen. "How is your brother's health?"

"Not good, Rhia. Thank you for asking." He managed a slight smile, tempering her unease. "May I speak with your parents?"

She nodded and reached for the front door, which opened before she touched it.

"Galen, greetings." Her father was dressed for company, in clean shoes and a russet shirt that matched his hair, which looked freshly combed and plaited into a long braid down his back. A single white Swan feather, dust-fringed from long days on the farm, swung from a leather cord around his neck as he bowed. "We've been expecting you."

Mayra appeared at Tereus's side and took his arm. Her thin lips trembled as she glanced between Rhia and the Council leader. "Please, come in."

Galen crossed the threshold, turned and held out his palm in an unambiguous gesture that told Rhia and Arcas, "stay outside."

The door closed, and Rhia turned to her friend.

"Why didn't they tell me you and your father were coming?" They could have at least given her the chance to wash her face and comb the hay out of her hair. But she realized now that all day Mayra and Tereus had behaved as if they were both monitoring and avoiding her. "And why can't we hear?"

Arcas hunched his shoulders. "My uncle's very sick. Father probably wants some of your mother's healing wisdom."

"But he didn't ask for my mother. He asked for my parents. Don't you think that's mysterious?"

A slow smile spread across Arcas's face. "When you've lived with my father for sixteen years, you get used to mysteries."

She turned away at the sight of his grin, which warmed her toes. "I have to water the dogs."

Arcas followed her into the hounds' pen. The tall gray beasts swarmed him as if he were dinner itself. He patted his broad chest with both hands, and two of the dogs propped their paws against him and licked his face. Rhia noticed that for the first time, he was taller than they were.

"It's hard on their backs to stand like that." She picked up the two dirty pails of water.

"Sorry. Off!" he told the hounds in a tone too playful for them to heed.

They left the pen and headed for Mayra's herb garden, where Rhia splashed the leftover water from the pails.

"Besides," Arcas said, "I shouldn't teach your dogs bad manners. If they ever jumped on you that way, your little bones would be crushed to a fine powder."

Rhia tried to glare at him, though she preferred being taunted rather than pitied for her lack of physical prowess. Arcas was one of the few people who didn't treat her like she was made of eggshells.

"For that remark, you get to pump." She tossed him one of the buckets.

"You're a big girl now, you can do it."

"I can, but I'd rather watch you."

Arcas actually blushed as he knelt beside the well pump next to the garden. The lever squeaked in protest when he lifted it.

"Before you know it," he said in a teasing voice, turning the attention back on her, "you'll head into the forest for your Bestowing."

She suppressed a shudder at the thought of entering the dark woods. "I'm too busy. If my Guardian Spirit wants to bestow my Aspect, It can bring it here."

"Spirits don't grant powers to those who hide from them." He pumped water into the bucket with a slow, steady rhythm. "Except maybe for Mouse."

"I'm not a Mouse!" Rhia almost slung the other pail at Arcas's head.

He raised a defensive arm in front of his face and laughed, but then his voice sobered. "Everyone knows what you are."

She drew in a sharp breath. "Don't say it."

They stared at each other for a long moment. *Everyone knows?* She wondered if this consensus made it true. But they were right. Denial wouldn't change destiny's course, any more than turning one's back on a wolf could make it retreat. But she was young, with time to pretend her future was as open as a meadow instead of narrow as a forest path.

She knelt beside him to rinse her pail, then scrubbed its interior with a horsehair brush. If only she could cleanse her mind as easily of its troubling thoughts. "You'll probably go first, since you're older."

"That's one mystery Father doesn't keep." Arcas sat back on his heels and gazed toward the distant woods. "If anyone but Bear comes to me that night in the forest, I'll die of shock."

"Just don't be a Wolverine. Useless troublemakers." She tossed the brush aside and jerked the pump handle with extra force. Her older half brothers Nilo and Lycas—twin Wolverines—had tormented her from the time she could walk until the day they moved to their own house when they were sixteen and she was eleven. She and her parents had quickly grown accustomed to the peace her brothers left behind, although at times she missed the way they made her laugh.

"We'll need Wolverines if there's ever another war," Arcas said.

The handle slipped from her fingers, and the metal clanged into the silence. She spoke without facing him. "Bears, too."

He scoffed. "Don't worry about me. Bears plan wars. We don't fight them." To her suspicious look he replied, "Usually. Besides, it's not your concern."

"It is, because—" She stood and chose her words with care. "Because so many Bears and Wolverines have been called. It's odd, Papa says. It means a war is coming to Asermos."

"Not necessarily."

His nonchalance made her fists clench. "The Spirits do everything for a reason," she said. "If no one were ever sick, we wouldn't need healers, the Otters and Turtles. If no one ever had dreams, we wouldn't need Swans like Papa to interpret them. And if we didn't have wars, we wouldn't need you. Or my stupid brothers."

Arcas picked up both pails and turned toward the dog pen. "You worry about things you can't even see. It makes no sense."

"Sense has nothing to do with it." She followed him. "You know I'm right."

He chuckled at her over his shoulder. "You're always right."

Feigning surrender was his signal to change the subject. She searched her mind for a casual topic, but she was curious about his upcoming Bear-ness.

"Are there any bear paws for you to wear as a fetish?" She had never seen one up close.

"Not until the next bear kill, which could be years." He lowered the pails over the edge of the pen. "I'll wear a carved claw for now."

"Will your cousin Jano make it for you? His fetishes are lovely."

"They should be. He's the artist of the family. The Spider, of course." Arcas looked around, as if to make sure they were alone. "Can I show you something?"

She nodded and waited. He reached into the pocket of his trousers, then withdrew his hand.

"Come closer." His warm voice held a slight tremor, and his eyes looked strangely vulnerable.

Rhia drew near him. The top of her head barely reached his chin, and she swore she felt his breath in her hair, but it was probably just the breeze. She bent over his palm, held close to his stomach. It opened to reveal a small carving no longer than her thumb.

"It's for your mother," Arcas said. "Go on, hold it."

Rhia picked up the piece of wood and lifted it near her face. An otter stood on its hind feet, paws curled to its chest and an expression of intelligent wonder on its tiny face.

"How beautiful. It looks like it's begging me to romp in the river." She turned it over in her palm. "But it doesn't look like one of Jano's."

"That's because it's not." His gaze flitted to hers before returning to the ground in front of him. "It's mine."

Rhia gasped. "You made this?"

Arcas scratched the back of his neck and stared at his feet, which shifted on the damp brown grass. "I thought if your mother needed a new one—or a spare one, just in case. She did so much to ease Grandmother's pain when she was dying."

It was a lovely gesture. Otter people usually had to content themselves with a carving to represent their Guardian Spirit, for it was unjust to kill such a rare animal solely for the sake of a fetish. From any other boy, Rhia thought, such a token would be an attempt to curry favor with his intended's parents. But Arcas's heart was generous, as expansive as the rest of him, and she wondered if it would ever be hers alone.

She replaced the otter in his palm, looked at his hands, so

huge compared to hers, and marveled at how they had created something so delicate. "Have you shown anyone else?"

He shook his head. "Why would I? It's just a silly thing I do to pass the time while watching the sheep."

"Maybe you're a Spider, too."

"No. Bear. Father's never wrong about these things." His jaw set, and she almost decided not to press the matter. But if he were a Spider, he could *make* weapons, not wield them, and then he would be safe and someday grow gray and wrinkled long before she ever had to hear those wings descend upon his—*stop it!* Rhia gave herself a mental smack across the face. It was no use pondering such things, and she wanted more than anything to be of use.

"You should tell your father about your talents," she said. "He may change his prediction."

"Have you finished your chores?" Arcas cast a sly glance at the house, then at Rhia. "Because I think I left something behind the stables the last time I was here."

He took her hand before she could reply. Two chestnut ponies raised their heads to watch them hurry down the hill, then resumed their placid grazing.

With her back against the stable and her ankles covered in sweet-smelling straw, Rhia pulled Arcas to stand a few inches away. His lips brushed her forehead and the corners of her eyes, and she breathed in the warm, musky scent of his neck.

"Isn't this better than talking about a war that doesn't exist?" he asked her.

"It exists in here." She touched her temple. "So many troubles do, all begging me to listen."

Arcas lifted her chin with one finger. "Then let me quiet them."

He kissed her softly, and she trembled even more than she had the first time—not only from the kiss itself, but from what lay beyond it, what it made her want. Her hands tangled in his hair as she brought his mouth harder against hers. If only they weren't so young....

Girls and boys their age had few chances to be alone together. Becoming a parent would evolve their powers to the second phase, and for that event to occur before understanding the first phase powers—or worse, before these had even been Bestowed—would be like learning to fly before learning to crawl. Rhia thought it unfair that the ways of the Spirits lagged so far behind the needs of young bodies, a particularly brawny one of which was pressed against her now.

A distant voice called her name. With a sigh, she broke away from Arcas's lips. "It's my father," she said.

His arms tightened around her waist. "His voice does carry, doesn't it?"

Rhia laughed and escaped his embrace to dash up the hill. Her legs tired within several steps. She turned to walk backward so she could watch Arcas follow with his slow, deliberate lumber, a Bear in a man's body for certain.

Her heel caught the hem of her long skirt, and she slipped in the mud. The ground was eager to break her fall. Arcas bent double with laughter, which seemed to weaken his legs so they could no longer climb the hill. Rhia scraped herself off the ground and tried to brush the dirt off her backside with all the dignity she could summon. Her muddy hands smeared the spot on her light green skirt into a broad splash of brown. Whatever creature embodied clumsiness would surely be her Guardian Spirit.

"There you are."

Mayra stood behind her, flanked by Galen and Tereus. The three watched Rhia with an unusual intensity.

"Galen would like to speak with you." Tereus extended his hand to his daughter. "Come inside."

"Stay here," the Council leader told his son.

The four of them entered the house and sat around the wooden table. No one spoke for several moments, and Rhia's feet began to fidget. The toes of her right foot pulled the heel of her left shoe on and off several times, then her left foot repeated the action.

Finally her mother cleared her throat. "Galen has some good news." The men shot her quizzical looks. "That is, he has news," Mayra said. "It might be good."

Galen sighed and turned to Rhia. "I need your help."

Rhia's mouth popped open, and she shut it quickly. She'd never seen Galen look for assistance from an adult, much less a girl her age.

"What should I—er, what could I do? For you. What can I do for you?" she managed to stammer.

Galen's dark blue eyes crinkled with anguish. "As you know, my brother Dorius is very ill. Your mother says she can do no more for him."

Rhia nodded. "I'm sorry."

"You could—" His jaw quivered. "At least I would know. Know what's to come, and when."

Rhia looked at her parents, then at Galen. "I don't understand."

"You have the power," he blurted. "You know when death comes."

Her stomach tightened as an icy grip took hold of it.

"The animals," Galen said. "It started with your dog. I've heard stories. Besides—" His back straightened, and he looked like his usual powerful self again. "Discerning others' gifts is one of mine. One of my gifts. Tell me, when you see a sick animal, how do you know if it will live or die?"

She looked away. "It's just a feeling."

"Describe it."

Rhia took a deep breath and focused on the words instead of the urge to run. "I look at them, into their eyes, and I hear a bird. It sounds crazy, but if the bird is flying away, the creature will live, and if it's landing, the poor thing will die. And if it flies, I know how it'll come back."

"How what will come back?" Galen asked.

She didn't answer, just stared at the knot in the table's wooden surface. She wanted to stick her finger in it and follow the swirls to its dark center, but thought it would look childish under the circumstances.

"Answer him, Rhia," her mother said gently.

"Crow," she whispered. "Crow comes and takes them to the Other Side. And I watch them go." She added in an even softer whisper, "I hate it."

No one heard her last sentence, or if they did, it went unacknowledged. Galen scraped his chair on the floor and stood.

"Will you help me, Rhia?" he asked. "Will you come see my brother?"

She gazed up at him and shivered. "You want me to do this with a person?"

"It's your gift," he said. "You have the Aspect of Crow."

Twilight was falling by the time they neared the house of Dorius, Galen's older brother. Tereus had stayed at home to look after a mare who was close to foaling, but Rhia's mother walked with her now, holding her hand so tightly that she twice had to remind her mother not to crush it. Galen strode ahead of them while Arcas lagged behind. Rhia's legs ached, but if she complained, Mayra's fretting would make it worse. She looked for a sight to distract her mind.

The village of Asermos was settling into quiet, though a few dozen people still hurried down the wide main thoroughfare that ran next to the sleepy river. Ponies and donkeys dragged rattling carts filled with bags of wool, grain or early spring vegetables. The animals lumbered down the sandy street to where boats lazed in the harbor. Small bands of revelers made their way from one tavern to the next, a few of them joking in dialects Rhia rarely heard. Now that the river had thawed enough to assure passage, a winter's pent-up demand for goods and conviviality was bringing the village to life.

Near the doorway of the Hound's Tooth Tavern, a tall, broad-shouldered man leaned against the stone and stucco building, smoking a pipe. A sharp, woodsy odor made Rhia's nose wrinkle as they passed. She spared him an extra backward glance. His smooth blond hair was pulled into a short knot at the back of his neck, and his eyes glittered in the lantern light as they studied the town with disdain. A tailored waistcoat of brocaded red velvet and the long, graceful sword at his hip put him out of place not only in Asermos, but in the entire region. Her people's sturdy, simple clothes suited their pastoral ways, and no one would think to tote a weapon as casually as a handkerchief. Further-more, the stranger wore no fetish that Rhia could see; she frowned at this lack of courtesy.

The elders often spoke of men from the distant south—Descendants, they were called—who lacked magical powers and worshiped human gods. The memory of the man's imposing presence remained with her until they reached the narrow street where Dorius lived.

She hadn't seen Dorius in several months. He had suffered from muscle tremors and weakness for over a year before taking to his bed last fall. When she was a child and came with Arcas to play with his cousins, Dorius and his wife, Perra, always made sure the boys included Rhia in their games.

Her steps slowed as they neared the door of the pale green stucco house. What if she saw Dorius's death? How could she look into the eyes of this kind man, old before his time, and tell him there was no hope? She said a wordless prayer to Crow to spare his life and her own sanity.

Galen knocked on the dark wooden door, which opened in an instant. Perra nodded to each of them without speaking, wide gray eyes full of sorrow. Her face seemed to struggle to remain impassive as she looked at Rhia.

The bed lay against the far wall on a carved wooden frame. A thin figure lumped the blankets. Galen led Rhia to the bed and laid his hand on his brother's shoulder.

Dorius woke with a snort and peered around him. His glazed brown eyes focused on Rhia, and she released the breath she'd been holding since they'd entered. The sound of wings was unmistakable but faint; the man's death was far from imminent or certain.

"We'll wait outside," Galen whispered.

After they had left, Rhia dragged a chair next to the bed and sat down. Dorius watched her movements without a word. His sallow skin and shadowed eyes made him look as fragile as his Butterfly Guardian Spirit. Now that his son Jano had married and had a child of his own, Dorius's powers of transformation should have entered the third and final stage, to the point where he could renew his own damaged body. Yet the illness had made him too weak to work his magic, for himself or anyone else.

"I asked Galen to bring you." Dorius's voice was barely a whisper, as if it had already preceded him to the Other Side and left behind a mere ghost of itself. "I'm sorry if it frightens you."

Rhia shook her head but realized the transparency of her lie.

He put a limp hand over hers. It held a trace of warmth, like hour-old bathwater. "My brother said you would know."

Did she? A cloud enveloped her awareness. "What do you think will happen to you?" she asked him.

He laid his head back. Gray and brown hair spread over the pillow, grazing his shoulders. "I'll never be what I was," he said to the ceiling.

Rhia's heartbeat quickened. The beasts she visited never voiced dismay over growing old or sick. They feared only pain, not death. During her own illness, she had fought for life with ferocity. Every successful breath would fill her with an uneasy gratitude. Here was a man losing the will to live, not because of his suffering, but because of his pride.

"Of course not!" She softened the sharp edges of her voice, but the words flowed like ice water. "We are never what we once were. We're born. We live, and if we're lucky, we grow old. Then we die." Someone else seemed to speak through her.

He stared at her in shock, but she continued:

"Don't you see? Every time we change, it's like dying, even if our bodies remain strong. Sometimes we have to leave behind the person we used to be." She squeezed his cool fingers. "Dorius, you of all people should understand that. We can't be caterpillars forever."

He frowned. "I know I'm not a young man anymore. I'm not asking to be young. I just don't want to be…"

"Useless?"

His eyes flashed at her with recognition. "I'm a burden to Perra. I can't tend the sheep, I can't even lift my own grandson. And my magic is gone."

"But you're not."

"What do you mean?"

"All those things—a husband, grandfather, shepherd, worker of magic—they're like—like the curves of a riverbank."

"I don't understand," Dorius said.

"They shape the river and guide its course. But the water itself is the same no matter which way the river flows, no matter what it passes and leaves behind. Underneath everything you put on and take off, one thing will never change—your soul." She touched his arm. "A Butterfly's soul."

Rhia sat back in the chair and wondered at the source of these words. She had pondered the ideas for years, especially during her illness, but she had never uttered them until now.

Finally Dorius spoke, "It's up to me, then, isn't it?"

"Yes." Rhia stood on trembling legs. "Now get up."

He looked at her, aghast. "I can't."

"Do it." Her voice quavered. She wasn't used to giving orders to adults, but it was the only way he could live.

He gestured to his legs. "I haven't walked in months."

"Then crawl."

Dorius started to pull back the covers, then hesitated. "How long do I have?"

Rhia improvised to hide her uncertainty. "If you stay in bed, a few days at the most. If you get up now, I don't know. I can't see that path yet, because you haven't done as I asked." She winced inside at her own audacity but kept her chin high. "I'll help you if you need it."

He waved her off, then with a grunt shoved his legs, gaunt from months of disuse, over the edge of the bed. Rhia pushed the chair within his reach. He laid his arm, already glistening with sweat, along the length of the chair's seat. She wrapped his other arm over her shoulder and ignored his pleas of pride.

He sat still for a moment; then with one great effort, Dorius heaved to his feet. As they wavered in an unsteady balance, Rhia drew in her breath.

The Crow had flown.

She let out a cry of joy. The door flew open, and the others rushed in. Perra took Rhia's place while Galen caught his brother's other arm.

"Get him outside," Rhia said.

They edged toward the door. Rhia moved ahead of them to open it wider. She turned to see Dorius gazing at her with gratitude, and her heart swelled. He would live, he would heal, he would—

Spirits, no. He would die.

She covered her mouth, unable to hide her horror at the vision in her mind.

Dorius writhed on the ground in a pile of golden leaves that were stained red with blood, blood that soaked his shirt and pulsed between his fingers as they tried to staunch it. He cried out his wife's name with his last rattling breath.

He died alone.

Rhia barely heard her own scream above the din of battle. Someone wrenched her through the doorway, out of Dorius's sight.

The vision vanished as the world went dark.

Rhia woke with a shudder, the floor hard beneath her back. Her mother pulled something bitter-smelling away from her nose.

"She's awake," Mayra said.

Arcas's face appeared above Rhia, forehead furrowed in concern. Firelight shone against his hair and skin.

A coarse blanket lay over her, itching her chin. Rhia pushed it away and felt the evening's chill. "Where am I?"

"At my aunt and uncle's house," Arcas said.

She sat up at once, and her head seemed to pound against the air itself. "Dorius?"

"He's fine." Her mother leaned against Rhia's shoulder to support her. "He's outside with Perra, enjoying the night air."

"When is it? How long was I—"

"Not long, maybe an hour." Mayra put her hand to Rhia's sweaty forehead. "How do you feel?"

"It doesn't matter. Dorius—I saw—"

"No!"

Galen loomed behind her mother, a silhouette against the firelight. "Never speak what you know of someone's death, unless it's imminent. Do you understand?"

"But there was—"

"Never!"

She clamped her mouth shut.

Arcas knelt beside her and looked up at his father. "You should have told her that before we came in."

Galen's eyes flared at his son's impertinence. Then he blinked hard and sighed. "It was a mistake. I thought Dorius had no hope, and that's all she would see."

"It's a good thing she's the Crow, then, and not you." Rhia saw Arcas blanch as he realized he'd gone too far.

Galen gave him a cold look. "Wait outside for me."

After a last glance at Rhia, Arcas obeyed. The door banged shut.

Galen sat cross-legged on the floor next to them. "I'm sorry," he said to Rhia. "I'm sorry you have to endure this, that you had to witness my brother's eventual death. Yours is one of the more difficult powers to live with."

Rhia bit back a reply to this understatement.

"The time has come," Galen continued, "for you to take possession of your gift before it overwhelms you."

Rhia swallowed hard. "I have to go into the forest?"

"Not only that." He lifted his head to speak to Mayra. "Rhia needs to study with someone who has Crow magic. I sent a message to a woman named Coranna, who lives in Kalindos, a few days' walk past the place of Bestowing." He spoke to Rhia again. "She will train you in the ways of Crow."

Rhia tightened the rough brown blanket around her to stop the shivering. "How long will I stay?"

"It's a complicated magic, and no one here in Asermos has experience with it."

"How long?" Rhia repeated.

"Perhaps a year or more, for your first phase. Later in life, as your powers develop, Coranna will teach you more."

Mayra clutched the edge of Rhia's blanket with shaky hands. "Isn't she too young?" she asked Galen. "You only said you wanted to test her. You didn't say she had to leave now."

"Others have been younger." Galen touched Mayra's shoulder. "Asermos needs her. Think how her powers could aid your healing work."

Rhia's mother looked away, then turned a few inches to move out of his reach. "You speak the truth, as usual." Her mouth twitched as if it wanted to say more.

The thought of witnessing a person's death again,

imminent or not, made Rhia's heart feel like it was coiling into a knot inside her chest.

"Two generations have passed," Galen said to her, "since anyone here has presided over the dying process. It's difficult for one so near the beginning of life to devote herself to its end, but won't you consider making the journey to learn more?"

Through the front door Rhia heard Perra sobbing, either from the joy at having her husband back or the sadness at the reminder that his life, like all others, would end one day. "When must I leave?" she asked Galen.

He uncrossed his legs and stood. "We can begin our preparations as soon as you're ready."

Rhia imagined the heart of the dark forest, remembered the eyes of the dying animals and the vision of Dorius's bleeding body twisting in the leaves. She steeled her jaw and looked up at Galen.

"I'm not ready."

Two and a half years later, Rhia still wasn't ready. After her vision of Dorius's death, she had resolved to shut down her death-awareness. Throughout Asermos whispers persisted, words of hushed recrimination for her cowardice. On her sixteenth and seventeenth birthdays, Galen had tried again to convince her to begin training in Kalindos, and she had continued to refuse. Even her brothers had added her reluctance to their litany of things to tease her about.

Secretly she hoped that if she denied Crow, perhaps another Spirit would take His place, one who would inspire acceptance rather than fear in herself and in those around her. But no Spirit came or spoke to her; in fact, they all seemed to drift farther away. All except Crow, who flew within the gray space between waking and sleeping, His wings offering a warm, soft promise, His eyes understanding and accepting the darkest corners of her soul.

Each fall, as the oak leaves turned gold and fell to the earth, Rhia would haunt Dorius and examine his surroundings for anything or anyone that could give him the wounds she had seen in her vision. The most casual allusion to tensions between Asermos and one of its trading partners would steal her sleep for weeks.

It was late summer now, and the leaves waved green and succulent on the trees adjoining the meadow where Rhia and Arcas sat close together. His family's small flock of sheep grazed a short distance away. A few of them wandered to drink from the wide, lazy stream that curled in front of the meadow before joining the river near the heart of Asermos. Even the smallest trading ship could not navigate this shallow portion of water, so Rhia and Arcas were blissfully, blessedly alone.

Bits of grass stuck to their outstretched feet, damp from wading. She wiggled her toes and let the sun warm her upturned face, reveling in this rare afternoon away from the farm. Her brother Lycas had taken her chores for a few hours, and she tried not to imagine what favor he might ask in return. That worry was for tomorrow or tonight. Today was here and good.

A white cloth full of ripe raspberries, which she had collected on her way to meet Arcas, sat in her lap. He made a show of pawing through them, brushing the skin beneath her thin skirt before selecting each one, in a brazen attempt to make her blush as red as the berries themselves.

"I can't decide," he said, "if I want to eat these or mash them up in your hair."

"My hair's not red enough for you?" As usual, the summer sun had burnished her sable locks with ruddy overtones.

"Your hair is perfect, but it would be fun to hear you squeal."

Rhia picked up a handful of berries and crushed them in her palm. "Marvelous idea." She smeared his hair from scalp to ends.

His yelp echoed from the stream's opposite bank. He seized her wrist and squeezed until her hand opened to reveal the red ooze, which he wiped across the front of her dress, leaving a small, blurry handprint. "There. Explain that to your mother."

"I won't have to explain anything to her today," Rhia said.

"What do you mean?"

She looked at his puzzled face for a long moment before losing her nerve. "Never mind." She searched for a topic that would deter his curiosity. "Your Bestowing last month. What was it like?"

His dark blue eyes grew distant and guarded. The distraction had worked. "You know I'm not allowed to tell."

"Can you tell me if you were afraid?"

Arcas grimaced. "I thought I was going to die." He glanced at her stricken face. "But no one ever does."

"No one? Can you be sure?"

"My father told me so. He prepares you for everything you need to know."

"But not for the fear. He doesn't prepare you for that, does he?"

Arcas gave an exasperated sigh. "Anyone who dwells on their fear as much as you do will be more than prepared."

She tried to turn her face away from him, but he caught it with the tips of his fingers and gently returned her gaze to meet his.

"Rhia, love, you must go. It's well past your time."

She shook her head. "I'd have to leave you."

"For a while. Then you'll return with your gift."

She thought of the war that would slay Dorius. "But what if while I'm gone—?"

"Shh." He kissed her, and she pulled away.

"You don't understand," she said. "You didn't see what I saw."

"I understand that you're troubled, and that the only way to ease your mind is to learn how to face your powers." His hand moved to her waist, and he nuzzled the bare spot where her shoulder met the curve of her neck. She closed her eyes for a moment to savor his lips against her skin, then gathered her nerve and returned to the subject she had avoided before.

"I have a secret," she said.

He raised his head, his eyelashes flickering with intrigue, but said nothing.

"My mother's noticed how close we are, you and I," Rhia continued, "and so she sent me to Silina."

"Silina? The Turtle woman? I thought she helped women have babies." He drew back to stare at her belly. "Are you—"

"Of course not. Silina does help women have babies. Or not have them."

Arcas cocked his head. "How? How not have babies?"

She grinned at his innocence and incoherence. "With herbs, of course." She pointed to the lacy white flowers waving their heads throughout the meadow. "Wild carrot. I've harvested the seeds at summer's end for my mother ever since I was a little girl. She called them a woman's 'freedom flowers' but would never explain."

"Until now."

"Until now. Also, the—our being together—it has to be during the right, er, phase of the moon."

His gaze scampered over the blue sky until it found the moon's waxing crescent. "Is that a good moon?"

"For me, it's good." She took his hand and kissed the velvet skin inside his wrist, one of the few places on his body not tanned and toughened by his shepherd's work. "For us, it's very good."

Without another word they undressed each other, trembling more than usual, then stretched out on the soft, lush grass. They had lain like this before, exploring and enjoying each other's bodies, yet this time would end not in longing but fulfillment.

Rhia's fingers followed a trickle of sweat traveling over Arcas's broad chest and shoulders. A sudden hesitation seized her. Once they had joined together, how could she ever leave him? Now she understood why they should wait until they had both taken on their Aspects. She was incomplete.

Arcas's expression darkened. "What's wrong?"

"When I go away, will you wait for me?"

"I will." His thumb traced her lower lip in a motion she found both seductive and soothing. "And what about you?"

Rhia tried to answer, tried to put into words the love that would live in her heart until the day it stopped beating. She failed.

Instead she kissed him, long and deep, and pressed her body forward to let his heat burn away the doubt and fear in her mind. Arcas groaned, and his arms snaked down her back to wrap around her waist, eventually parting her legs to accept his searching fingers. A familiar warmth spread through her, infused with an even more familiar need.

He rolled her on top of him, and together, fumbling, laughing at their own clumsiness, they guided him inside her.

Ready as she was to receive him, Rhia had not expected so much pain. It radiated to the core of her body and outward again. The sharpness of her cry made Arcas freeze, his eyes wide.

"I'm sorry," he said. "Oh, love, I'm so sorry." He stroked the hair at her temple. "Should we stop?"

She wanted to say yes, to retreat back into her clothes and maybe even the cool river, anything to soothe the ache. Instead she took a long breath and shook her head.

He moved more slowly inside her after that, and when her eyes were open she saw him studying her face for the signs of pain she tried to hide. Finally he lay still and placed his palms on the ground beside him.

"You," he said.

Rhia paused to wonder if she could do it, if she could bring such hurt upon herself. She closed her eyes and said a prayer for strength to whatever Spirit might be listening.

Her hips moved against his, gingerly, until she felt herself begin to expand around him. Gradually the pain subsided, to be replaced with a sensation that recalled those he had given her with his hands and mouth. Yet this feeling, she knew before long, would carry her miles beyond.

The heat between them became oppressive, and she raised her upper body to cool it. In doing so, she drove Arcas deeper inside her. They both cried out at the shock. His back arched, muscles taut, and his gaze pleaded, "Let me…"

"Yes," she said, and he released himself.

His hands moved over her as if trying to touch her everywhere at once. She cradled his head to her breast, and he pulled her nipples into his mouth as his hips surged beneath her. Never had she felt so powerful, nor so helpless. The cry that escaped her throat was that of a woman she had yet to meet.

The last thing she saw before collapsing onto Arcas's chest was the radiant blue sky reflected in his astonished eyes.

They lay together in silence, their breath slowing. Arcas combed Rhia's hair with his fingers, which slid carefully through the tangles. "I'm sorry I hurt you."

"It will be better next time."

"I can't imagine better."

Rhia smiled, then turned on her back, wincing at the soreness. She felt a sudden need to bathe, and sat up, extracting herself from his arms. She congratulated herself on her rare display of bravery, then stood on unsteady legs and walked to the stream. A rustle of grass told her Arcas was following.

Minnows scattered, silver fins flashing, as her feet swished through the warm shallows. In a dozen steps the stream reached her waist. She scooped the water with cupped hands and held her arms straight before her. As it dripped through her fingers, she murmured, "Bless the Turtle who gives life."

At her side, Arcas answered, "And bless the wild carrot seed that prevents it."

She grinned at him, then bent over to splash water on her face. He tipped her over with a gentle shove. She flailed for an instant before he caught her arm in time to save her from going under.

"Hey!" She smacked his chest with her free hand. "After

what just happened, you might stop seeing me as a little girl to torment."

"Grown women don't smear berries on people." He leaned to rinse the goo from his hair. "Besides, I enjoy tormenting you. Would you rob me of that—" He straightened suddenly, whipping his gaze toward the shore. "Someone's coming."

"I don't hear anything."

"They're far away." He listened another moment, Bear senses tuned. "But coming fast."

They splashed through the water back to the meadow and sprinted up the hill to the place of flattened grass where they had left their clothes. Arcas helped refasten her dress, then yanked on his own trousers and shirt. Rhia heard the rumble of approaching hooves.

Arcas faced the distant edge of the meadow, shading his eyes. Two dots moved closer, one white, one chestnut red.

"Is that your brother, on the gray mare?" Arcas asked her. "He's driving her awfully hard."

"They always do that." Rhia sat on the grass to put on her shoes. "Especially Lycas. He can't go to the market for milk without acting like he's being chased by wildfire." She chuckled to herself, even as her heart fluttered with an inchoate fear.

"It is him. And—my cousin Gorin?" He turned to her. "They don't even like each other. Why would they—"

Rhia held up her hand to silence him. She saw her brother, bent low over the neck of his white horse. His hair, shiny and black like their mother's, streamed behind him in the wind. She began to run.

They met quickly. The rear hooves of Lycas's pony skidded

as he brought her to a halt. His face was wet with what Rhia hoped was only sweat, and his dark eyes burned into her.

"It's Mother," he said. "I think she's dying."

Rhia clung to her brother's waist and tried to ignore the pain that seemed to skewer her body. The pony's gait was swift but not smooth—the impact of each galloping stride threatened to split her in half.

Yet it mattered little. Mother was dying. Rhia had had no time to ask Lycas questions before Arcas had scooped her up behind her brother and they had taken off for her home. Now her voice would be carried away by the wind that whipped Lycas's hair into her face—not to mention the pounding of the mare's hooves and the heave of her breath. The poor thing was exhausted but valiant.

Rhia turned her head, straining to hear the hoofbeats of the pony Arcas rode, the pony brought by Gorin, who had stayed behind to watch the flock. But the wind swallowed all sound, and even this slight movement threatened to unbalance her.

Maybe she should focus on the pain, she thought; better

that than the scene that lay ahead. What would she see when she entered her home? Would the heavy wings alight or rush away? She had never confronted a human whose death was imminent. Now she wished she had, so that her first should not be the person Rhia loved above all others, the one who had given her life over and over, not just at birth but every year since then.

Lycas veered the pony suddenly to the right to avoid a small gray boulder jutting among the long meadow grasses. They turned uphill, yet their pace did not slow, not until they entered the woods, where even Lycas was not so reckless as to plunge headlong. The pony slowed to a walk, shaking her head and splattering froth on the leaves around them. When Rhia had caught her breath, she puffed out the words she'd been wanting—and not wanting—to say, "What happened?"

"She collapsed." Lycas's voice was clear, his breath barely quickened from their hard ride. "Said her heart hurt."

Rhia's own heart seemed to constrict. She waited for him to continue.

"When I left—" his shoulders shuddered "—when I left to get you, she could hardly breathe." He cursed to himself. "Spirits take these brambles." He reached down and pushed a thick rope of wild raspberries away from his pony's chest. Blood seeped from tiny cuts in his arm, but he didn't wince.

"Did someone fetch a healer?"

"Silina was drying herbs with her when it happened. She couldn't do much except keep Mother comfortable. Nilo went to find Galen, in case…"

"In case?"

"In case she dies. Someone has to prepare her spirit." He spoke through gritted teeth. "Since we don't have a Crow."

Rhia's face burned. Her voice caught as she tried to reply. But then the clearing lay ahead of them, and Lycas dug his heels into the pony's ribs. The horse surged forward again, her strength restored, and Rhia had to clutch her brother's shirt to keep from falling.

The sunlight blinded as they broke into the clearing. Her home appeared across the hill. No human puttered in the paddock or in the dogs' pens. At the sound of their approach, three hounds came out of the kennel, stretched, bowed and wagged their tails at them behind the fence.

When Lycas finally brought the gasping pony to a halt in front of the house, the door opened. Their brother Nilo stepped forward to grab the reins.

"It's all right," he told them. "She's resting."

He put his hands on Rhia's waist and lifted her off the pony. Her body seemed to creak as she slid over the dusty, sweaty hide. Though he lowered her gently, when her feet hit the ground, it felt as if two sharp fenceposts had been driven into her hips.

"You two go in," Nilo said. "I'll cool her down." He pulled the reins over the mare's head and led her away at a brisk walk. Rhia glanced back at him, grateful that his gaze had not pierced her with accusation as his twin's had. Though they looked alike and sometimes even spoke in unison, Nilo's thoughts and feelings seemed to travel inward instead of sparking out to burn those around him.

A warmth enveloped her hand, and she looked down to

see Lycas's long, strong fingers wrap around hers. Their grip steeled her courage enough for her to enter the house.

Her father approached them, but she looked past him to her own small bed, where her mother lay. Tereus spoke Rhia's name, and his lips continued to move, but the rest of his words were lost.

Lost in a roar of wings.

The sound crescendoed until she could only feel and not hear the wail ripping her throat. Her knees buckled, and she tried to sink to the floor—*through* the floor, even—but Lycas's grip tightened, and he yanked her to her feet. She tore free and covered her ears, squeezing her eyes shut as if the feeling, the certainty, came from the outer world and she could blot it out, turn away from it. But there was nowhere to turn. Crow was here to stay.

Rhia backed against the door and fumbled for the latch. A harsh voice hissed in her ear.

"What are you doing?" Lycas shook her shoulders. "She can hear you, stupid."

She sucked a breath, choking on her own cries of anguish. Her lips pressed together so hard, her teeth bruised them. When she opened her eyes, she saw her father step in front of Lycas. He pulled her tight to him.

"Papa, I'm sorry," she whispered against his chest.

He stroked her hair. "I know. I knew even before you arrived that we could do nothing. But still I hoped—" Tereus cut himself off and moved to look at her. He smoothed back the strands of hair that tears had adhered to her cheek. "I wish you didn't have to see it so clearly."

"I don't just see it, Papa. I feel it." Her soul seemed as

heavy as a sack of wet grain, and she wanted to collapse, to succumb to the weight of her mother's impending death.

The large bird she felt on her shoulder was not real. She couldn't see it with her eyes or touch it with her hands. But it touched her, its claws piercing her skin, and at that moment it was the most real thing in the room.

"Go to her," Tereus said. "And Lycas is right, you must be strong. Dry your eyes."

Rhia breathed in deeply, every muscle straining to maintain control. Her exhale was less shaky. She wiped her cheeks and the hollows under her eyes.

Her legs moved of their own accord as they carried her across the room, and she was grateful to them. For the first time, she noticed Galen sitting on the floor at Mayra's feet. He watched her with an inscrutable gaze as she passed.

The weight on her shoulder and on her spirit grew heavier with each step. It was a relief to sink onto the bed next to her mother. She reached for Mayra's hand, then hesitated. Mayra's eyes were closed, her face slack, skin wan, dark hair carefully arranged on the pillow. She looked peaceful—and completely unfamiliar.

Who was this stranger? A future corpse. Not her mother. It was safe after all.

She touched Mayra's hand, and her mother's eyes opened. In an instant the distance between them vanished. Rhia felt light again, like only a daughter. She held back tears but knew her eyes shone as they looked upon the dying woman.

Mayra's thumb twitched on Rhia's wrist, as if she were trying to squeeze her hand. She parted her dry lips to speak. Her throat strained with no result.

"Shh," Rhia whispered. "We can speak later, after you've rested."

Mayra narrowed her eyes in disbelief. She tilted her chin to beckon Rhia closer. Rhia leaned forward until their faces were a hand's width apart.

"Yes?" was all her mother said. Rhia looked into her eyes and nodded slowly. A tear fell from her lashes onto Mayra's lips.

"I'm sorry, Mother. I wish…" She gave Mayra a pleading look, expecting her to provide comfort or reassurance, as she always did when Rhia was distressed.

Instead Mayra only stared at the ceiling, eyes wide and fixed. Her hand grew cold.

"Mother?" In a near-panic, she shook Mayra's shoulder. "Mama?"

Mayra blinked and took a slow breath that seemed to pain her. Without looking at Rhia, she whispered, "I'm frightened." Another long breath. "I'm frightened, Rhia. Help me."

Rhia's glance jerked toward Galen. He kept his eyes on Mayra and sighed.

The door opened behind her. The hulking figure of Arcas stood next to Nilo's muscular frame. The two men were silhouetted against the sunshine outside so she couldn't see their faces. A whispered conference with Lycas passed along the grim news.

Rhia turned to her mother and felt on her back every gaze in the house, which was becoming crowded, stifling.

Mayra's lips moved to form one word. "When?"

Rhia looked at Galen. "You can know," he said.

She turned back to her mother. "Wait a moment."

Rhia closed her eyes and clutched Mayra's cold hand. She

turned her mind to Crow, whose presence hovered, shimmering black and violet, near her shoulder. His spirit merged with hers, His knowledge and certainty spreading over and enveloping her consciousness like a pair of dark wings.

Her mother had strength. Not enough to survive, but enough to say goodbye.

"A day or two," Rhia said at last. "I wish it were more, but—" She couldn't finish the sentence: *you don't have enough life*.

Mayra relaxed, her hand going limp in Rhia's. "I can sleep."

"Yes. Good." She realized her mother had feared she would never wake up. "Do you need another blanket?"

Mayra tilted her head from side to side, almost imperceptibly. Her eyes closed in the next instant, and her face went slack. Rhia stared at it, trying to etch every detail into her memory.

A hand lay on her shoulder. "Let us speak in private," Galen said.

Rhia reluctantly let go of her mother's hand and followed him toward the door. As she and Galen stepped out into the sunshine, Rhia looked back to see her father sit by Mayra, his head bowed.

The bright day mocked her mood and the darkness that would always dwell within her now. The air was so clear and sharp she could even see the distant brown face of Mount Beros to the northeast, unshrouded by summer haze.

"I should have gone long ago," she said to Galen.

"There's no sense in regrets."

"Isn't that what you wanted to tell me, that I should have gone when you asked? You were right."

"What matters is that you find peace, peace in yourself that you can give your mother in her final hours."

"Where do I find it?" She gestured to their surroundings. "Under which stone, in which tree?" She kicked a small branch that had blown into the yard during the previous night's storm. "Peace isn't inside me, and feels like it never will be now."

Galen pulled his large leather pouch to the front of his waist. He loosened the ties and withdrew a black feather the length of his hand. He held it out to her on a leather cord.

"It's time for you to have this."

She wanted to reach for it, but didn't. "I haven't even been for my Bestowing yet."

"You will," he said, "after you mourn. In the meantime, this will help you focus on your powers. Your mother needs them."

She took the feather from him and stroked its smooth barbs. "What do I do?"

"You'll know."

Rhia withheld a frustrated sigh at his vagueness.

"How long will she live?" he asked her.

"She'll see another sunrise, but no more, I think. I want to—I want to stay with her all night. Help her, though I don't know how."

"Crow will show you, as much as He can. I will return early tomorrow morning. She needs her family now." He turned toward the house.

"Wait," she said. "What will you do for her? Can you help her pass over? Make her not so afraid?"

"I can help ease her mind with regard to her life. The rest is up to her. And you, of course." He laid his hand on her shoulder again. "I'm sorry, Rhia. It shouldn't have to be like this."

As he walked away, she wondered if he meant to comfort or rebuke her. Probably both: Galen's words never meant only one thing.

In a few moments, Arcas came out of the house alone. With no hesitation, he wrapped his arms around Rhia's small frame and held her while she cried. What she couldn't tell him was that she wept not only for her mother's death but for the part of herself that had once felt fully alive.

Though Arcas's body seemed far from her, she clung to it, as if it alone would anchor her to this world.

05

The candlelight cast a honey-colored glow over the walls of Rhia's home as darkness crept across the sky. She closed the window's curtain and wondered if it would be the last glimpse of the outdoors her mother would ever have. No, she thought. She'll watch the sunrise even if we have to carry her outside.

She turned back to the table, where her brothers and father sat in silence. It would have been generous to call the meal in front of them half-eaten; the food on the plates was rearranged rather than consumed.

Silina sat with Mayra and monitored her breathing. She had offered to attend to Mayra's bodily needs, so the family could attend to their own grief.

Rhia wondered if Silina's assistance only made it harder for them; they were left with nothing to do but look at one another. They had intended to take turns sitting with Mayra while the others slept, but Rhia suspected only her mother would sleep tonight.

"She's awake." Silina's soft voice cut through the silence as if it were a shouted proclamation rather than a whispered notice.

The three men stood. Lycas and Nilo sat again, a grudging deference to their stepfather's place. Tereus moved to Mayra's side.

Silina approached Rhia at the window. "Tell me how I can help. I could feed the hounds or the horses, fetch some water."

"It's been done," Rhia said. "We've checked the animals several times. There's nothing to do but wait."

Silina glanced over her shoulder at Lycas and Nilo brooding at the table. "I think a family could do other things besides wait." She picked up a lantern and slipped outside.

Rhia considered the advice. Over a year had passed since she had spent an evening with her brothers. She sat at the table next to Nilo.

"Tell me a story," she asked them.

They looked at each other, eyebrows pinched. Lycas said, "We don't know any stories that would be, er—"

"Appropriate," Nilo finished.

"I don't care about appropriate. Tell me one of your stories about hunting with Rhaskos."

Nilo's lips threatened to curve into a grin. "Now?"

"They make you giggle," Lycas said to Rhia.

"I know."

He glanced in their mother's direction. "Do you really think—?"

"I think she'd love to hear her children laughing together again."

"If we must." Nilo leaned forward, then took a dramatic pause. "As you may remember, Rhaskos the Goat has slightly less intelligence than the average hound."

"Slightly?" Lycas said. "You insult our hounds."

"Shame on you." Rhia faked a stern look. "For such an affront you must clean their pens twice tomorrow."

Nilo held up his hands. "Slightly less intelligence than the average hound's left dewclaw. Better?"

"You are forgiven." Rhia glanced at her mother. The candlelight played distorting effects about her face, but she thought she saw Mayra smile.

"In any case," Nilo continued, "one morning we went hunting after Rhaskos had a bit too much ale the night before."

"It wasn't that he was hung over," Lycas added. "He was still drunk. See, he had the impression that no matter how much you drink, as long as you sleep, even for an hour, you should wake up sober."

Nilo chuckled. "He thought if it's a new day, you're a new person. His body had different ideas, though."

As they continued the story, with Rhia prompting them as they forgot details, the three of them picked at the cold bread in front of them, then the meat, until most of the food was consumed.

Finally Tereus rose and approached the table. He looked at the twins. "She wants to speak with you, Lycas first."

It made sense; Lycas was older by a few hours and had always been treated as the elder twin. It meant Rhia would be last. She stared hard at the floor and prayed to Crow to let her mother remain awake long enough to speak with her.

Tereus's body dropped heavily into the chair next to Rhia.

"Papa, why don't you sleep?" she said. "We can wake you if—when she's—"

He touched his daughter's cheek. "No. I'll stay up. I can't imagine losing any of these moments to sleep."

"But it could be days."

"Soon enough I'll wake up without her. I don't want to start quite yet."

A choked sob came from Mayra's corner. They looked over to see Lycas bent over their mother's frame. Tereus dropped Rhia's hand and scrambled over to them.

"It's all right." Lycas stood and wiped his face with a stroke of his arm. "Your turn, Nilo."

Nilo took his brother's place at Mayra's side. Lycas returned to the table and sat, his elbows on the table, face in his hands. Rhia felt the barely controlled fury pour off him, and understood for the first time how dangerous he could be. Even with his first-phase powers, he could kill a man in little more than an instant with no weapon at all. The veins on the back of his hands bulged as he clenched his fists in his long black hair. She shifted away from him a few inches.

When he surfaced from his well of rage, Lycas gave Rhia a glare that withered her soul. In that moment, she knew, her brother hated her. The meal in her stomach soured.

"I'll see if Silina needs help with—whatever she's doing." Her chair nearly crashed to the floor when she stood.

She had to smack the latch several times before it gave way and the door opened. Once it closed behind her, she leaned against the house and gulped the stagnant, humid air that had slunk in a few hours ago. Crickets and katydids sang in an uneasy chorus, so the night had not progressed far. No glow lingered near the western horizon, however. The haze of late summer hid all but the brightest of stars, and the setting half-moon gave off a muted glow behind the trees to her west.

A lantern bobbed into view near the barn. Silina called her name, and Rhia gave a weak wave in response.

The Turtle woman held a basket against her ample hips as she approached. "I found some dried chamomile in your mother's herb shed. It will help her relax." The lantern light glowed against the gray hairs that had overwhelmed the brown on her head. "I wish I could do more."

"So do I. Me, that is. I wish I could do more."

Silina put her basket down and hugged her. Between the healer's warmth and the scent of the chamomile, Rhia felt momentarily soothed.

The door opened, and Nilo's impenetrable face looked past her. "It's your turn."

She withdrew from Silina's embrace. "Thank you," she told him as they passed in the doorway. He did not respond.

Sitting next to Mayra, Rhia felt Crow's weight upon her again, but she shoved the awareness to the back of her mind.

"Were you with Arcas today?" her mother asked in a rasping voice.

"Yes."

"And?" The corners of her mother's lips twitched upward.

Rhia's face warmed. It felt like weeks, not hours, since she had made love to Arcas in the sunny meadow. With a sickening feeling, she realized they had probably been intimate at the instant her mother had fallen from the attack.

Mayra squeezed Rhia's hand. "Don't have that look. It's not your fault this happened."

"I should have been here."

"It wouldn't have made a difference. I can't be saved. It's my time. So was it how you thought it would be, with Arcas?"

Rhia looked at the wall above Mayra's head. "It was better. And worse." To change the subject slightly, she added, "I'll miss him when I go away."

Mayra frowned. "I'm sorry, Rhia. I should have made you go into the forest when Galen first asked. I was afraid."

"It was my choice. I was afraid, too."

"I should have pushed you out of the nest, baby bird. If I had—"

"I could help you now. As I am, I can't. I'll never forgive myself."

"I forgive you," Mayra said.

The tears that had swollen Rhia's eyes spilled out onto her cheeks. She wiped them away with the back of her hand.

"I'm sorry," she said. "I should be strong for you."

"You have no idea how strong you are. Someday you'll know. Someday soon, I think." With a great effort, Mayra reached forward and touched the end of one of Rhia's auburn curls. "I hate to think of all this hair gone."

"Mother, don't—"

"I must speak of my death, and all it means." She let her hand fall and gazed at Rhia's hair. "It'll be curlier, like when you were a little girl. Your brothers will look strange to you."

Rhia wanted to ask what Mayra had told the twins, why

their anger had suddenly resurged, but she didn't want to distress her mother. No doubt they would soon tell her themselves.

"When you go to Kalindos…" Her mother's voice trailed off as her breath ran out sooner than expected. She drew another shallow inhale. "When you go to—oh!"

A gasp burst from Mayra's throat, and she began to pant. Her eyes rolled white with pain and fear.

"Mama?" Rhia heard her voice turn into a child's. "Mama, no—not now! Mama!"

Mayra's hands flailed over the blanket covering her, as if reaching for the breath that wouldn't come. An inarticulate plea bubbled from her throat.

Tereus lunged to his wife's side. Rhia drew back, stepping away from the body before her, a body that was fighting the journey from life with every shred of energy.

She shut her eyes but still heard her mother's desperate struggle for the air her lungs refused to grant. A sound like a great wind arose then, swirling past Rhia, moving up, up, and she looked to see if the door had opened to a storm.

She wished she had kept her eyes closed. Though no wind blew through the room, it was anything but calm. Tereus was trying to hold Mayra in his arms, but she pushed him away.

"It's all right, it's all right," he murmured. "Let go. Just let go." His voice, which had started in a whisper, grew louder. He seemed to bite back the words even as he uttered them. As Mayra's struggles became more feeble, he was able to embrace her. He held her trembling body in his arms and rocked her, while Rhia and the twins stared in horror at their mother's futile battle.

At last Mayra fell silent and still. Tereus eased her onto the bed and closed her eyes, praying to himself as he did so. Whispers to Rhia's left and right told her that Silina and Nilo were beseeching Crow to guide Mayra's spirit home.

She looked at Lycas. He stared straight ahead, his face frozen in grief. After a long moment, his gaze shifted to pierce Rhia, though his head did not move. This is what it would feel like to meet him in battle, she thought.

When the others had finished praying, Lycas hissed, "You said she would live the night."

Tereus turned from Mayra. "Leave her alone."

"He's right, Papa." Rhia's lip trembled. "I was wrong. I'm sorry."

"She wasn't ready." Lycas spit his words like venom. "Galen wasn't coming back until morning to prepare her. Because of you." He pointed to Mayra's corner. "She shouldn't have had to die like that!"

"That's enough." Tereus's voice resounded like a thunder clap. "I said leave her alone."

Lycas ignored him and focused his wrath on Rhia. "You couldn't get the time right, you couldn't even comfort her, all because you wouldn't go for your Bestowing."

Nilo put a restraining hand on his brother's arm. "Maybe we should—"

"So now your own mother dies in agony and fear." Lycas tore out of Nilo's grip and advanced on Rhia. "Are you happy now, you little coward?"

Rhia's sorrow turned to rage. She shrieked and flew at her brother.

Tereus stepped between them, moving faster than she'd

ever seen him. His arms stretched out to hold Rhia and Lycas at the tips of his fingers.

"Not one more word."

His voice was quiet, little more than a whisper, but it held more strength than Rhia's scream or Lycas's shouts of recrimination.

Silina moved toward Mayra, heaving the sigh of the habitually practical. "Preparations must be done. Rhia, help me, please."

Rhia turned and took several halting steps toward what had once been her mother. Her feet felt shackled. Behind her, Lycas wept great, racking sobs. The sound muffled, and Rhia guessed that Nilo had drawn his brother close against his shoulder.

Her imagination of the scene would have to suffice, for she would not look at her brothers again tonight.

Rhia knelt while Galen sharpened the knife.

Her scalp smarted from the leather band that pulled her hair into one long mass at the back of her head. Beside her, Lycas, Nilo and Tereus waited their turns.

What seemed like half the village stood outside for their most beloved healer's funeral to begin. Mayra would be buried here on the farm where she had raised her family for over twenty years, nestled in a bower of oak trees. Rhia tried to envision the place of peace that her mother's soul would know forever. But all she saw and heard was the knife, its blade glinting in the light that trickled in from the window, its *shing-shing-shing* against the sharpening stone.

The house was silent. This private part of the ceremony involved no chants, no songs, no celebration of Mayra's life. The Shearing was somber, matter-of-fact.

In theory, Rhia appreciated the custom of cutting one's

hair after the loss of a close relative—a parent, sibling, child or spouse. Not only did it provide an outward expression of grief, it allowed others to treat the mourners with the proper deference and sympathy. Such a wound should not be concealed.

But as Galen came toward her with the knife, she had to fight to keep from lurching away, from leaping to her feet and shrinking into the corner. She told herself it wasn't vanity, that it was the pain of carrying a constant reminder of loss. But she thought of Arcas and wondered how he would view her without her long chestnut tresses, which she knew held most of her beauty.

Galen twisted his hand into the rope of hair to maintain a better hold. She leaned forward to pull the hair taut and tried not to wince. Only children needed Galen's apprentice to hold their heads. She would be brave. She would—

The blade sliced the air with a *whoosh*. There was a slight tug at the back of her head, then the remains of her hair swung forward to caress her ears. She resisted the urge to touch it.

Galen's hand appeared before her, holding a lock of her hair in his palm. It looked longer and redder than she had expected. She took it from him reluctantly, as if it belonged to an unsavory stranger.

From the corner of her left eye, she saw Lycas kneel straight as a fence post, gaze sharp and focused straight ahead, neck muscles tight. The blade sang, and Lycas's body tilted forward from the release of tension. Black hair swept his chin.

Rhia rolled the lock of hair between her thumb and first two fingers. Numbness was setting in at last.

* * *

Later that morning, Rhia and her family gathered at the edge of the bower near the foot of Mayra's grave. The other villagers, numbering in the hundreds, stood around the perimeter of the shady burial area. The sun, only halfway up the sky, filtered through the leaves to dapple the gravesite and promise an unusually warm day.

Galen stepped forward through the crowd, followed by his apprentice, the young Hawk woman Berilla. They both wore ceremonial white robes with hawk feathers sewn into them, but while Berilla's garment bore only a few small brown and black wing feathers, Galen's held glorious red-tipped tail feathers that covered half his body. When he reached the head of the grave, he raised his arms to the side to signal silence. The feathers gave him the splendor of a hawk with wings outstretched.

Rhia knelt with her father and brothers on the green woolen blanket laid out for them. The rest of the villagers remained standing and would continue to do so throughout the ceremony, even if it reached past sunset.

When all was quiet, Galen began a low, mournful chant, a simple tune to calm and focus the minds of those gathered. The crow feather hung heavy around Rhia's neck, and she longed to conceal it. Everyone knew that if she had gone for her Bestowing years ago, she might be taking part in the ceremony right now. She might have helped her mother.

The chant finished, and Mayra was brought forth. Eight of the village's older males carried her body, which was wrapped in a white shroud from head to feet. Rhia had spent hours the night before helping Silina apply thyme and bergamot oils to her mother's skin and wrapping her body in strips of scented cloth.

On top of Mayra's chest and stomach lay dozens of blossoms—blue coneflower and chicory, lacy white wild carrot—and over her throat, the otter fetish that Arcas had carved for her years before. Many of the flowers fell as the men moved her, leaving a colorful trail. The otter remained in place. The men laid Mayra's body next to the grave and stepped back into the crowd.

Galen began to sing her spirit home. Berilla drummed the rhythm while an elderly man played the haunting melody on a wooden flute. The voices of the villagers—everyone but Rhia, Tereus and the twins—rose together to lift Mayra's spirit into the winds, high enough that Crow would find it and carry it home. They would sing until a crow came into sight nearby, called, then flew away.

Without one of its People to do the beckoning, however, the bird's appearance could take hours. Crows could not be summoned and directed like sheepdogs. Rhia hoped the Spirit would have mercy on them all and send one of His minions quickly.

The drummer thumped and the voices sang, never flagging. The sun rose in the sky until its rays angled through the opening in the trees, tingling Rhia's newly exposed neck, which would no doubt be red by the ceremony's end. A drop of sweat trickled from her temple past her ear, and her knees throbbed beneath her. She chided herself for noticing physical complaints when her mother was forever beyond the pains and pleasures of the body. But it was easier to concentrate on the ache in her legs than the hurt in her heart and the stinging behind her eyes that made them full and hot.

No one met her gaze except Arcas. His face held a mixture of sadness and shame. He must have figured out, as she had, what the two of them had been doing when Mayra began to die. She wanted to dash across the funeral ground into his arms. It would ease his pain, if not hers, and she needed to make someone feel better rather than worse. Such would be her role—turning death, the most inescapable reality, into an acceptable part of life.

But how could she move people to accept death when she herself wanted to rail and rave against it, to beat her fists and forehead against the earth in futile defense of the person it had just consumed?

Though she was not supposed to join in, Rhia closed her eyes and sang the chant in her mind, reaching out to the Crow Spirit and begging Him to send one of His kind to end this torture of her neighbors and friends.

A half minute later, a crow called overhead, from the topmost branch of a hickory tree. The chant faded, and the relief, while not expressed aloud, was palpable as everyone looked up to confirm the source of the sound.

The bird cawed a few more times, its head and chest bobbing with each throaty utterance. An unseen crow, probably its mate, returned the call from down the hill. As the crow took off, the branch shook, and a single dead leaf floated to the ground. Autumn was on its way.

The bird passed the bower, wings thumping the air, at once the softest and harshest sound Rhia had ever heard.

A choked cry from her left signaled Tereus's final surrender to grief. She wrapped her arms around her father's neck, and they sobbed into each other's shoulders as Mayra's body was gently lowered into the grave.

Her father's pain rolled off him in waves. Tereus had claimed many times that he would never remarry if he outlived Mayra. Rhia believed it now, and wept for his emptiness.

A feast was held on the hillside after the ceremony. Villagers made a long line for the water and ale, their throats no doubt raw from singing.

Tereus and Rhia sat on their front step, on display—or so it felt to her. The funeral attendees filed past to greet them, but as soon as her father took one of them to the paddock to see the new yearling, the parade dwindled. Her brothers had retreated to a far corner of the farmyard, clearly preferring solitude.

Arcas soon joined Rhia.

"Are you sure you want to be seen with me?" she asked.

"I'm sure I want to be with you."

She gestured to the villagers, who had banded together in groups of eight or twelve to eat. "No one will even look at me, much less share my company. My own brothers haven't spoken to me since she died."

Arcas studied the frayed hem of his sleeve. "They're grieving. Don't expect them to make sense."

"But something doesn't fit. We were getting along last night. I thought they'd forgiven me for not having the power to help her. Then she told them something that set them off."

"Why don't you ask them?"

Rhia looked across the field at the twins. They sat alone,

with no food or drink, Lycas scowling and Nilo directing his stony gaze at the ground in front of him. The village tailor and her husband the horse healer approached the twins to offer condolences. The villagers received polite nods but no words, so they hurried back to the feast as soon as courtesy would allow.

Rhia turned back to Arcas, who made a conciliatory gesture. "They do seem less than receptive right now," he said.

"Arcas, may I speak with Rhia alone?"

She looked up to see Galen, still in his ceremonial white robe. Arcas slid away after giving Rhia's hand a surreptitious squeeze.

The older man eased himself to sit beside her. "I'm sorry. I should have stayed last night. I wanted to give your family some time alone, but—"

"But you shouldn't have trusted my judgment."

His voice held a heavy weight. "Our powers can become cloudy when we turn them on those we love."

"Must I never love anyone, then, so that I won't fail them when they die?"

Galen shook his head. "You can learn to separate your feelings from your magic. But it will always be harder with some. Not impossible, just hard."

Rhia looked to the east, where the pale green valley met the Great Forest. "I wanted Mother to see another sunrise. It was her favorite time of day."

"They say that the Other Side is more beautiful than a thousand sunrises, though that's no consolation." When she didn't reply, he asked quietly, "Are you ready, then? To travel to Kalindos and train with Coranna?"

Ready? She would never feel ready to live among the wild Kalindons, to learn to wield her powers by watching people die.

Nonetheless…

"When do I leave?"

"At spring thaw. By the time your mourning period is over, it will be well into winter, when it's best not to travel. I'll take you into the forest myself."

Rhia knew she should be grateful that the Council Leader had taken a special interest in her, though she suspected it was more for her value as a Crow than for any belief in her ability.

"But first," he said, "I must train you in ways of the Spirits. How to journey within, visit their dwelling places in the Spirit World."

Rhia touched the ends of her shorn hair for the first time. The training would let her escape, give her somewhere to put the pain where it couldn't prick her heart.

Now she was truly ready.

Throughout the next month, Galen taught Rhia the rituals and observances known to the adults of Asermos. She learned chants and prayers to achieve tranquility, without which she might misinterpret or even ignore the Spirits' messages.

Galen also took her into the forest to teach her survival skills, for she would remain alone there for three days and nights before her Bestowing. He demonstrated how to gather wood and start a fire, and how to purify stream water to rid it of animal wastes. He showed her the path to Kalindos, which made her frown—it appeared to be uphill all the way.

Other practical knowledge included handling encounters with large forest dwellers such as wolves, cougars and bears. Of these she feared wolves most, though she knew they posed the smallest threat.

Her favorite lessons, however, focused on spiritual rather than physical challenges. With Galen's guidance, she embarked on trance-induced journeys to the Spirit World. A lifetime of worship rituals, observed without question or deviation, had made the Spirits feel distant and indifferent, especially as she grew out of childhood. Now They came alive within her, each with unique qualities, until They seemed like old friends. She had missed much by postponing her journey into adulthood, and she struggled not to brood over the lost years.

After one particularly arduous but rewarding session at Galen's house, Rhia stepped outside and squinted into the harsh afternoon sun. Dizzy from the glare, she fumbled to shut the door behind her.

A rustle of grass came from her left. "There you are."

Rhia turned slowly toward the voice, contemplating the statement. *Here I am. But where is here? Who am I?*

Arcas touched her arm. "I've been waiting for you."

She gazed at him. He looked *new*, sharp, as if someone had traced the outline of his body with a fine-pointed piece of charcoal.

"Communing with Spirits, I see." He brushed back a curl from her forehead. "Your eyes shine."

She blinked. His outline was fading now, and his edges began to flow into the background of the house and trees.

"Forgive me," she said, "I'm a bit…" She flapped her hand in a circle near her head to indicate her state of mind.

Arcas laughed. "You'll get used to it. Do you have time to take a walk?"

"Your father said I should contemplate what I learned today. I imagine he meant alone."

"I won't keep you long. Promise."

Rhia hesitated. She wanted to hear nothing inside her head but her own thoughts, to dwell within her new experience. But she also wanted to share the encounters with someone who had recently made the same journey.

Besides, she missed Arcas. They had spent little time together in the month since Mayra's funeral. When she wasn't training with Galen, Rhia stayed close to home, both to help with the farm and household duties and to share comfort with her father in their mourning.

"A short walk." She glanced back at Galen's house to make sure he didn't see her disobedience.

They followed a path leading down the hill toward the sheep pen. A long-haired black-and-tan dog squeezed under the fence and bounded over to greet them.

"Fili!" Arcas scolded. With a series of hand gestures, he instructed the dog to return to the flock. Fili snapped to attention and obeyed.

"That's amazing," Rhia said. "She does it just because you said so. Our hounds have to have a good reason. They do things because they want to."

"Fili's a sheepdog, a lot smarter than a hound. She wants what I want."

"Hmm." All in all, Rhia preferred the hounds' independence, and thought that the ability to take orders was a poor measure of intelligence for human or beast.

She shook the remaining clouds from her mind. "Was it like this for you? Journeying?"

"Like what?"

"Everything's different. I look around, and this world seems less substantial. Less real."

"That's because you know there's another world we can't see with our eyes."

"But I already knew. I've been taught about the Spirits' dwelling place since I was a child. I believed in it."

"Believing is not the same as experiencing." He slipped his hand around hers. It, too, felt insubstantial against her skin. "Enough talk about the Spirit World."

But that was all she wanted to talk about, think about. She sighed, which he mistook for an utterance of desire.

"I've missed you." He pulled her close and pressed his mouth against hers. She returned the kiss, but for the first time her mind was not consumed with wanting him. Part of it remained elsewhere.

Arcas didn't notice her distance, or if he did he sought to overcome it by crushing her tighter against him. His hard, pent-up passion demanded release.

He whispered against her neck with breath so warm it made her shiver. "I know a place we can go." He drew his hand over her hip.

She pulled away before his fingers could wake her desire. "Arcas, it's not right. I'm still in mourning."

He let go of her and wiped his face hard, as if to erase his embarrassment. "I'm sorry, Rhia. I forgot."

"You forgot my mother died?"

"Of course not. But I miss you. Even when I see you, it's like you're not really here." He reached for her hand cautiously, as if it might burn him. "Do you still love me?"

"I do, but you can't be the most important thing in my life right now. When you prepared for your Bestowing, I barely saw you for months."

"I didn't change the way you're changing now."

"Then you don't understand."

"Help me, then. Help me understand." He drew her close again, this time with tenderness instead of urgency. She pressed her cheek against his broad chest and wished she could grant his request. But even she didn't comprehend the transformation that had begun. She only knew that becoming a Crow woman—witnessing, sharing and communing with the exit from life—would require her old self to die, either little by little or all at once. What would be born on the other side of this death might be a woman Arcas could never love.

The clothes-laden cart threatened to roll over Rhia's heels as she dragged it downhill toward the stream. When the entire family had lived under one roof, it had taken a pony to bear the burden of five people's laundry, but now even Rhia's strength sufficed.

The sycamore trees ahead had lost all but a few amber leaves, revealing twisted, ghostly trunks. Rhia preferred their bare, tortured beauty over the demure loveliness of the surrounding pines. The oaks had already dropped their golden foliage, which relieved her. Another year had passed without Dorius's brutal demise.

As Rhia neared the riverbank, the sound of laughter broke her reverie. She saw with dismay two of the young village women. Tall and thin, Mali the Wasp was nineteen, more than a year older than Rhia. She was training to be one of Asermos's few female warriors. Torynna, a blond, full-figured Sparrow woman whose song could quicken the blood and raise the spirits of the weary, had just returned from her Bestowing at sixteen years of age. Rumors claimed Torynna was trying against all advice to bear a child so she could progress to her second phase. Then her song could befuddle any who heard it, causing a brief paralysis of will or even complete obedience.

The two women drew a cart between them and shared a piece of red fruit. They gave her halfhearted waves, then Mali said something to Torynna that Rhia couldn't hear. They burst into cackles that made her skin crawl. Her hand froze in greeting and dropped back to the cart pole.

"Good morning, Woman of the Crow," Mali said with the barest hint of a sneer. "Beautiful day, don't you think?"

"A bit cold." Rhia carried the clothes, washboard and soap bar to her favorite washing spot, where a long flat rock jutted into the stream. Its location had less mud and put distance between her and the other women.

"True," Mali said. "This may be the last washing day before the river freezes. But it's pretty, no?"

Rhia sensed Mali was only being cordial out of deference to her mourning. Usually the Wasp tried to devise ever snider comments on Rhia's lack of stature and coordination.

She nodded to Mali and dipped the first garment, one of her father's gray work shirts, into the cold water.

"Rhia, I like your hair short," Torynna said.

"I don't," she replied to the insincere compliment.

"What does Arcas think of it?"

"You'll have to ask him."

"I will."

The washboard nearly slipped out of Rhia's hands. Knowing

the Sparrow girl's reputation, she didn't want her anywhere near Arcas. Torynna turned away with a flashing smile.

The other women unloaded their wash and took seats on the edge of the bank, their skirts tucked up to keep them dry. Torynna began to hum a melody Rhia didn't know. It sounded seductive, even to her ears.

"Guess what I've heard about the Kalindons?" Mali said to her companion. "I hear they live in trees."

Torynna stopped humming. "In trees? Like squirrels?"

"They have houses, silly, in the branches, and some of them don't come down for years. My brother and his friends call them 'termites.'"

"If they live in trees, then where do they piss?"

"Off the edge, of course."

The women's high titters felt like pins against Rhia's spine.

Torynna told Mali, "I heard they eat nothing but break-fast so they can get drunk faster at night."

"I believe it," Mali said. "But what I want to know is, how do they make love with those seven-inch fingernails?"

The bar of soap scooted from Rhia's palm and plopped into the stream. She lunged for it, soaking her sleeve. Mali and Torynna erupted in laughter. After several desperate grabs, Rhia found the bar among the pebbles at the stream bottom. She drew it out of the water, her forearm covered in cold green slime.

"I guess some of us could use longer nails," Torynna said, "then we wouldn't be so clumsy."

Rhia turned to them. She let her eyes focus on a point far beyond Torynna and kept her face impassive.

The Sparrow's smile faded. She glanced over her shoulder. "What are you looking at?"

Rhia said nothing. After a few moments, she shifted her gaze past Mali, whose eyes grew angry.

"What are you doing?" she asked Rhia in a sharp voice.

"Seeing…"

"Seeing what?"

Rhia blinked slowly, then shook her head as if to clear a vision. "Hmm…"

"What?" Mali stood as if facing off in battle. "'Hmm' what?"

"Nothing." She turned back to the clothes. "I wouldn't eat that apple if I were you, Mali."

"Why?"

"And Torynna, you should probably stay away from water from now on."

"What water?" Torynna's voice trembled. "You mean the river?"

Rhia raised her head and stared at the opposite shore as if the answer lay there. "Yes, I think the river. Puddles are probably safe." She went back to her washing.

The two women exchanged hasty whispers tinged with horror, of which Rhia only caught pieces:

"Can she really—"

"—hasn't been for her Bestowing."

"—heard she has visions."

Feeling a pang of mercy, Rhia gave them a broad smile.

Mali planted her hands on her hips. "You're joking."

"Perhaps."

"You are. You don't really see our, our—"

"Deaths? Probably not."

She picked up another shirt and promised herself that this would be the first and last time she would use her identity as death-seer to intimidate others. That vow, she felt, made up for her lack of shame in this instance.

"I told you," Mali said to Torynna in a low voice. "I knew the little runt was lying."

"She was so spooky, though."

"She's always been spooky." A pause. "You want the rest of my apple?"

Torynna giggled. "What were we talking about?"

"Kalindons." Mali's voice took on an edge. "We have a source right here who we can ask."

Rhia ignored them and scrubbed her father's shirt harder to release a muddy spot on the sleeve.

"You mean her?" Torynna said. "She hasn't been there yet."

"She doesn't have to go there to meet Kalindon men. She spent most of her life with two of them."

Rhia stopped scrubbing and stared at Mali.

"Oh, look, she doesn't know." Mali flipped her hand at Torynna. "Just as I thought."

"Doesn't know what?" Rhia tried to keep her voice steady.

"Lycas and Nilo's father. He didn't die like your mama told you. He went back to Kalindos."

Rhia's fists clenched the soggy shirt. "You're lying."

"Ask your brothers. They were the last to find out, the night your mother died." She smiled at Rhia with mock sympathy. "Last, that is, except for you."

08

The door to her brothers' hut opened a few inches. One of Nilo's black eyes peered out through the crack.

"Yes?"

"It's me," Rhia said.

"I know."

"May I come in?"

Nilo slammed the door shut. Rhia turned the latch and entered anyway.

"I won't leave until you explain why you're mad at me, so if you want me gone, you'll have to start talking."

Nilo's mouth set into a grim line. He motioned her to sit on the bearskin rug next to the stove.

It only took Rhia two steps to reach the rug. Their hovel was less than half the size of her father's house and had fallen into a disarray beyond even what one might expect from a place where two young men lived without maternal supervision. The only clean area was a section of wall that held her brothers' collection of daggers. The weapons, with which they had trained for nearly ten years, featured blades that varied in size from a handspan to the length of her forearm. The straight ones were for stabbing, the curved for slicing, but all were sharp, deadly, and spotless.

To sit, she had to move a half-loaf of bread so stale it could have been used as a weapon itself. A tankard held traces of ale in the form of a gooey brown residue that smelled like the inside of a horse's mouth.

"It could be cleaner," Nilo mumbled. Suppressing a gag, Rhia handed him the tankard with the tips of her thumb and forefinger. He set it next to the stove. "Other things have been on our mind besides washing."

"Like the fact that your father's a Kalindon?"

Her brother whirled on her so fast she thought she had blacked out for a moment.

"Quiet!"

She steeled herself. "It's nothing to be ashamed of."

"We're not ashamed, we're embarrassed. To be the last to know."

"You weren't last. I was."

He scowled at her. "Mother thought you knew."

"No one told me, unless it was while I was ill. I don't remember much about that part of my life." *Other than the wings in my head.* "I only found out a few hours ago, I swear to you." She rose and put her hand on his arm. "I would have told you if I'd known. Please believe me."

"Then tell me how you heard." She hesitated. "The truth," he said.

"I was washing clothes today when Torynna and—and Mali came by."

Nilo's head jerked. "Mali?"

"She told me." Rhia put up her hands. "I provoked her. Although they provoked me first."

"What did she say?" His fierce voice, barely above a whisper, was impossible to disobey.

"They were discussing the things they'd heard about Kalindons, and Mali said—"

"Good things?"

Rhia shrugged, in a failing attempt at casualness. "It's hard to say good or bad."

"I've heard nothing good about Kalindons, so unless Torynna and Mali have come into some secret knowledge—"

"Secret knowledge about what?" said a voice behind them.

Lycas stood at the door. Rhia stepped back, astonished that his burgeoning powers of stealth had allowed him to unlatch the door and slip in without her awareness.

Nilo, on the other hand, appeared unsurprised. "She says Mali told her about our father," he said to Lycas. "Today."

"Mali?" Lycas tossed a leather bag onto the table with a loud thunk. A rabbit's stiff brown foot emerged from a tear in the seam. "I trust she spoke well of our kind?"

"Tell him," Nilo said to Rhia. "Tell us what she said."

"I don't want to know." Lycas picked through the flasks near the stove until he found one with contents to his liking. He took a long gulp, then wiped his mouth. "I just came in for a drink, now I need to clean these rabbits. Got three." He reached for the bundle on the table.

"You should listen," Nilo said.

"You want me to do it in here? This place is too clean for you, needs some fur and guts on the floor?"

Nilo moved the bag of dead rabbits out of Lycas's reach. "Rhia, start."

She told them everything. The three had always shared a brutal honesty, which was probably why her brothers were so hurt to think she had kept the secret about their father.

For once, Lycas's face was impassive. When she was finished, he grabbed the rabbit-bag and left the house.

Nilo turned back to Rhia. "I always said Mali was no good for him. They're too alike." He tried to smile, then gave up, since it was an unnatural contortion for his face. "If they married, they'd kill each other, and then Asermos would lose two warriors before the battles even began."

"Battles?" Rhia's pulse jumped. "What have you heard?"

"Nothing certain. Always rumors about the Descendants."

She tried to hold back a shudder and only succeeded in twinging a neck muscle. "I've seen more of them in town lately. Why do they need to come this far north to trade?"

"They don't. I don't think they're really traders. They're spies, seeing if our lands and towns are worth their time and weapons and lives."

Rhia had trouble believing that the strange men she had seen dawdling around the docks and taverns had been related to her people at one time. From their provocative dress that contained so many useless accents to the way they walked upon the earth, as if they owned the soil under their feet, they were different. Perhaps it was the ease of the southern clime they had migrated to after breaking from her people generations ago, or the great cities they had built to hold their pride. Whatever "it" was about them, the Descendants always made her feel, for a moment, ashamed to be human.

"You think they want to invade us?" she asked.

"They want what we have, and they don't understand our ways. Perfect combination for an invasion."

"Something should be done."

Nilo scoffed. "The Wolverines, we've all been telling Torin we should capture a few of these 'traders' and interrogate them." Torin, the third-phase Bear man to whom Arcas was apprenticed, served as the Asermon military leader. He was also Torynna's father, but Rhia didn't hold that against him.

"What did he say?"

"He said it wasn't 'strategic.'" Nilo half grinned. "Lycas told him that waking up one day to find ourselves dead wasn't exactly strategic, either."

Rhia's mind wanted to turn away from the thoughts of war, yet her powers would be indispensable in that event. "How could they defeat us? They don't even have magic."

"When their army is ten times the size of ours, they don't need magic."

"But if they had magic, they wouldn't need those big armies, would they?"

He smirked at her. "Your logic alone is worth a brigade or two."

She laughed, relieved in an odd way that a danger like war could put their sibling feud into perspective. Yet one problem needed to be addressed. She cleared her throat.

"I'm sorry for the way Mother died, so hard and frightened. She deserved better."

"She did." He returned to the stove. "But you're going to Kalindos, to be a Crow woman."

"Too late."

"For Mother, but not for the rest of us."

Rhia wanted to bind Nilo's wrists to the house so that he could never walk onto a battlefield. But he was created to fight, called to be a warrior. Unlike Rhia, her brothers embraced their Guardian Spirit. So instead she told him, "I can't think about losing you, too."

He waved his hand in dismissal. "Anyway, if it's not obvious, I forgive you. *We* forgive you."

"Thank you, but Lycas's forgiveness is not yours to offer."

"True." Nilo scowled at the dirty dishes, then swept a disgusted glance over the rest of the room. "He'd be more likely to give it if you helped us clean the house."

"I'll take my chances. Give me the bread, though."

Nilo picked up the loaf and knocked his fist against it, making a sound like a gourd-drum. "You'll break a tooth."

"It's not for me."

"The dogs'll break a tooth."

"Not for them, either. For ones who have no teeth."

"Ah." He handed it to her. "There you go, birdie girl." As her hand touched the latch, Nilo made one last try: "If you help us clean, we'll give you one of those rabbits."

"I think I'll get one anyway."

Lycas sat on a rock next to a maple tree, amidst its fallen scarlet leaves. Rhia stood within speaking distance of him but said nothing as she crumpled the stale bread in her hands to scatter the crumbs on the dirt.

From the corner of her eye she watched Lycas hang a

rabbit by its heels from the tree and start to clean it. He stabbed into it with a fury, as if the creature had insulted him. His cuts went too deep and gouged the flesh.

Under her breath she offered prayers of thanksgiving to the bird Spirits whose kind would feast on the crumbs: Crow, Jay and—after a moment's hesitation—even Sparrow, Torynna's Guardian Spirit. One could not hold a grudge against the Spirits themselves for the pettiness of their human protégés. Besides, Rhia had returned Torynna's meanness threefold by pretending to envision her death. The least she could do was give her rival's little winged counterparts some crumbs.

Would Torynna take her place in Arcas's affections? Others had left home for their Bestowing and training for only a few months, yet returned to find their beloved in another's arms. Rhia might spend a year or more in Kalindos.

"I was going to eat that," Lycas said.

Rhia tossed the last piece of bread—a chunk too large for anything but a crow—on the ground and brushed her hands together. "Better hurry up, then."

He beckoned her over with the wave of a bloody, short-bladed knife. She stood across from him and waited. Without taking his eyes off the rabbit, he spoke at last,

"Remember the batch of tanglefoot Nilo and I distilled when we were sixteen? The one that almost set the woods on fire?"

"Yes."

"You never told Mother and Tereus."

"Of course not."

"You're good at keeping secrets, Rhia."

"*For* you, not *from* you."

He examined her, then tilted his head in admission. "We shouldn't have acted like you were our enemy. I'm sorry."

"I forgive you."

"Lately the whole world feels like our enemy."

"It's not." She stepped closer to him. "If you're ever going to fight for Asermos, you have to believe you're one of us. Has anyone ever treated you differently?"

He considered for a moment, then shook his head.

"They all knew," she said, "but they didn't care."

His mouth formed a tight line. "Mali cares. Apparently I'm just a 'termite' to her."

"Mali's frightened."

"How dare you?" Lycas's glare nearly set her on her heels. "She's as brave a warrior as I am."

"And you're scared, too. You'd be crazy if you weren't. But being brave isn't about cramming your fear deeper inside you. It's about bringing it into the light."

His eyebrows rose. "You're one to talk about facing fears."

"I know. I made mistakes in the past because I was afraid. I won't do that again."

Lycas laughed and turned back to his work. "Bravery's a habit, little sister, and you're definitely not in the habit." He glanced at her crestfallen face but didn't retract his statement. "Sorry, but it's true. I have faith in you, though. You'll find a way."

A warmth enveloped Rhia. "Thank you."

He shrugged. "Mother told me to be nice to you or she would find a way to nag me from the Other Side."

"Good." Rhia's foot nudged the paw of the biggest, fleshiest rabbit. "This one's rather scrawny."

Lycas rolled his eyes at her. "Take it."

He even let her have the bag. As she turned to walk home, Nilo appeared in the doorway of their hut. She held up the bag and waved. Her grin broadened at the sight of his scowl.

09

The landscape was swollen with winter's first snow the day Arcas visited Rhia.

Nearly a month had passed since she had last seen him, during a chance meeting in town. They had each brought animals to market—she a pair of young hound bitches and he a ram and a ewe—and had been too distracted by business to speak more than a few words. She sensed that a few words would not suffice to discuss the distance that had grown between them since her mother's death.

When she lay alone in bed at night, her thoughts no longer turned by reflex to his face, his arms, his body, except to imagine them lifeless on a battlefield. Gone were the memories of summer heat between their skins.

More often she meditated on Galen's lessons, pondering the mysteries of life and death. She drifted to sleep amidst images garnered from the Spirit World, where pain subsided and anguish disappeared. She welcomed the numbing cold of winter and saw the season's first snowstorm as an excuse to remain at home, inside, cozy and safe.

Now Arcas appeared on her doorstep, and he looked anything but cozy and safe. The hood of his fur parka gave his head a bestial appearance, and the chill air had flushed his face a wild, meaty red. He looked past her.

"Is your father home?"

"No, he's gone to see if Silina's family needs any help after the storm. Their roof leaks sometimes, and her husband is too sick to fix it." She smoothed her hair, wondering if she looked as unkempt as she felt. "Did you come to see him?"

"No, I just wanted to know if we were alone."

She opened the door all the way. Arcas stomped the snow from his boots before stepping into the house. He laid his outerwear near the fire to dry, then without further ceremony, pulled her close to him. She tensed.

"What's wrong?" he said. "Are my hands cold?"

"No. But now is not a good time."

"Not the right moon? I thought—"

"Can we just sit and talk? It's been so long."

"Of course." Arcas moved toward the bed in the corner, still holding her hand. She pulled out of his grip and sat at the table. Instead of joining her, he reclined on the bed and gave her a steady, seductive gaze.

Something inside her stirred, and she felt drawn to him, not with a lover's attraction, but with the compulsion of one under a predator's spell. She turned away to pour herself a cup of cold water. A mass of melting snow floated at the bottom of the pitcher.

"Would you like some?" she asked Arcas without looking at him.

"Please."

She slid the pitcher down the table. After a few moments, he got up and sat across from her.

"I'm sorry if I'm pushing you," he said.

"You're not."

"What I mean to do is pull you. Back into life, that is."

"Life is not my calling."

"It's everyone's calling, even you. Life is the one thing we all have."

How profound, she thought with a sarcasm that shocked her.

"How is your training going?" she asked him.

Arcas studied the bottom of his cup as he spoke. "Torin has me playing a lot of strategy games, to sharpen my skills. I'm the worst player he's ever seen."

"I'm sure you'll do better with practice."

"Not only have I no talent, but no love for the games, either. Planning ahead several moves, getting inside the opponent's mind, sorting through all the possibilities to find the best tactics—not my idea of a pleasant afternoon."

"No one promised your Aspect would be fun. Mine isn't."

"I don't need to have fun, I just need to be inspired." He brightened, then fumbled under the table for a moment before withdrawing a fist. "Put out your hand."

Rhia lifted her palm up. Arcas covered it with his own, then revealed a small white stone that fit perfectly in the center of her hand. Its surface was as smooth as milk and marbled in black. The silhouette of a crow, painted black, was carved into one side of it.

"It'll fit in your pocket," he said, "and whenever you're afraid or nervous, you can run your thumb over the crow and feel your Spirit's presence."

Rhia's words—or more precisely, collections of incoherent noises—stuck in her throat as her lips moved without sound. Finally a sentence formed.

"You made this for me?"

"No, I made it for all the other Crow women in town, but none of them wanted it, so it's yours."

A truth that had gnawed at her for years now sat in her palm, no longer ignorable.

"Arcas, may I ask you something, and you promise to tell the truth?"

His teasing demeanor faded. "If you promise never to speak of it again."

She held out the stone with her fingertips. "What are you?"

Arcas opened his mouth to speak. He pushed back the chair and began to pace the floor.

His movements struck her as odd. It took several pacings before Rhia discovered that his lumbering gait had been replaced with a step so smooth and quick she wouldn't have recognized him had his face been turned away.

"When I went into the forest for my Bestowing," he said, "I expected to see Bear. Look at me—I've got the physique, the strength, the walk—"

"You've lost the walk."

"Because I'm alone with you. I can let my guard down, I hope." She nodded, and he continued. "It was my destiny to lead warriors, to defend my people. I was so sure, my whole life. My father was so sure."

"He saw what he wanted to see."

"That night in the forest—" He tried several times to finish his sentence. Rhia took pity on him.

"Spider came to you."

Arcas stopped and let out a sigh, as if releasing a burden after a long trek. "I wanted to tell Her to leave, to step aside for Bear, but—"

"Bear wasn't coming."

"And it felt so right, inside me." He gave Rhia a look of near-delight. "I can make beauty."

"You can." She fingered the stone in her hand. "But remember the day Lycas rode to find me, when my mother took sick? You heard him coming long before I did. Wasn't that your Bear senses?"

"Not that kind of sense, like hearing or seeing. It's feeling danger or trouble from a long way off, the way a spider senses a tremor in the farthest reaches of its web." He swept the air as if viewing a huge mural. "And I see patterns in things, connections that others don't. Not so different from a Bear's strategic thinking."

"So you've been faking it."

She regretted her choice of words immediately. His face went dark, and his hands dropped to his sides.

"I'm sorry," she said. "What I meant—"

"No, you're right. I've been pretending to be Bear."

"Why?"

"It's easier to be what others believe me to be."

"Your father doesn't know?"

"What happens in the forest is between a person and their Spirit." Arcas spread his long fingers and gazed at them as if they held the memories of his Bestowing. "I never lied to my father. I just never told him the truth."

Rhia looked at the bed where Mayra had died. "Galen told me it's hard to see the truth about those you love. I wanted to believe Mother had more life in her than she did. My desire hindered my magic, he said." She gasped. "He knows about you."

Arcas mirrored her alarm. "What makes you think so?"

"It must be why he told me that. Because he knew from experience. He seemed sad when he said it, as if he were disappointed in himself."

"For being wrong about me."

"No." She got up and went to him. "For trying to guide you down the wrong path, for guiding you at all. He should have let you become who you are on your own. He knows that now, at least part of him does."

"He just wants what's best for our people. We all do."

She thought about the implications of this statement, that Asermos needed men and women to fight a war that might be far on the horizon.

The war.

"Arcas—if you're a Spider, then you won't be a warrior. You can live a long life." *With me.*

He bristled. "I am a warrior. Not by birth—by choice."

"Your Spirit called you for a reason. Maybe our people need your Spider gifts."

Arcas gave a bitter chuckle and tapped the stone in her hand. "Our people don't need more trinkets."

"Trinkets?" She drew back her hand, pulling the stone out of his reach. "Is that what you think this is? Is that why you made it for me, for decoration? I can't draw strength from a trinket." She lowered her voice to a whisper. "You said it yourself, you can make beauty. Beauty has meaning."

He touched her cheek with a tenderness that made her want to weep. "I know it does."

He kissed her then, so softly her lips ached as if he were bruising them with force instead of caressing them with a profound sense of the moment's fragility. His mouth moved to her neck and his hands to her breasts, not demanding, only inquiring. When she tensed, he dropped them to her waist again. Rhia leaned against his chest.

"I want to be with you," she whispered. "But not here. Not where it happened."

"I understand." He rested his chin on her head. "Do you think the hayloft would be too cold?"

She slipped the white stone into her pocket. "I don't think anyplace with us would be too cold."

"Then let's go."

"Wait." She grabbed his hand to stop him. "You need to know that I love you no matter what you are."

His face turned serious again. "Even if I'm a Bear?"

She dropped his hand. "If you're a Bear, you're a fake."

He staggered back as if she had struck him. "A fake? *I'm* a fake? You spent two years pretending you weren't a Crow."

"Yes, I denied what I am, and others suffered for it. I don't want you to have that regret."

"This isn't about protecting me from my own mistakes, is it, Rhia?" He pointed at her. "You want me not to be Bear because you're afraid I'll die, because you're too selfish to share me with the world."

"Is that so wrong? Is it wrong to want a husband who might live to meet his grandchildren? And what about that, Arcas? When you become a father and move to the second phase of your powers, what happens when instead of becoming a stronger fighter, you start predicting the weather and walking on ceilings? How will you hide it then?"

"I don't know how, but I do know this—it won't be your concern."

Rhia's breath turned cold in her throat, and a dull pain filled the space between her ribs. "What does that mean?"

"It means that you and I…" He shook his head and went to the door.

"You and I?" She grasped his arm as he jammed his feet into his boots. "What are you saying?"

"Things have changed, ever since your mother died. You're so harsh with yourself, and now you're doing it to me." He flung his wet parka over his shoulders, splashing melted snow over Rhia's cheek. "This confusion inside me, it's hard enough without your judgment."

"I'm sorry."

He studied her face for a moment, then opened the door. "You're sorry you hurt me, but not sorry for the way you feel."

She steeled herself against the cold air and the allure of her own desperation, the feeling that begged her to say anything to make him stay. "No," she whispered. "I'm not sorry for that."

As she watched Arcas trudge through the snow, the stone in her pocket seemed to grow heavier, until finally she slid down onto the doorstep, shivering through her tears.

* * *

The winter would be a long one.

Snow fell knee-deep, and the hounds frisked like puppies, shoving their muzzles under the white drifts. Some days shone warm enough for the snow to soften, but the ensuing nights gave it a hard crust that made each step a struggle for forward movement. Rhia had to apply beeswax and lanolin to the dogs' paws before wolf hunts to protect the pads from the sharp ice layered within the snow.

In the middle of the winter, the wind roared nonstop for three days and nights, and Rhia and Tereus took turns every hour clearing snow from the door. Drifts piled against windows and turned day to twilight inside their home. When Rhia was forced outside to tend the animals, the wind burned her eyes and made her nose run and nostrils freeze.

The sun shone boldly on those blustery days, making the snow cavort and sparkle like the magic powders Mayra once used in her healing work. Rhia watched the dancing glitter and let the wind dry her tears.

During the brief thaws, she hurried to Galen's house for training. Arcas was never home when she came. She dreamed of him often in the first two months of winter and woke most mornings with a wet pillow, but by the approach of spring his face blurred in her memory, until their love seemed like a beautiful but unreachable childhood dream. She kept taking the wild carrot seed, however, for the herb was plentiful and eased her monthly cramps and headaches.

Tereus had begun to sleep downstairs after Mayra's death, allowing Rhia to have the larger bed in the loft, where it was warmer and more private. She knew he could no longer sleep alone in the bed he once shared with his wife. Sometimes in the dark she heard him weep.

The night before she was to leave for Kalindos, she lay awake worrying more than usual.

"Father?" she said, loudly enough for him to hear only if he weren't asleep.

"Yes, Rhia?"

"How will you manage while I'm gone?"

He sighed. "As I told you the nineteen other times you asked, your brothers will help with the animals, and the neighbors will help with anything else. I can cook just fine."

She withheld comment. His preparations barely deserved the name "cooking," but they would prevent his starvation.

"What if you get sick?" she said.

"I'll take care of myself until I'm well."

"What if you can't take care of yourself?"

"Then I'll lie here and expire. My last thoughts will be ones of deep resentment against you for growing up."

She chuckled. "Stop."

"You asked."

It was as good a time as any to say, "I think you should marry again."

His voice quieted. "I can't."

"Won't you be lonely?"

"There are worse things than loneliness."

Rhia couldn't imagine. "Like what?"

"I'll be fine."

"You should have more children. What if something happens to me and you're never a grandfather?"

"Nothing will happen to you."

"But what if—"

"Nothing will happen to you," he said with a forcefulness that told her more than wishful thinking was involved.

"Father, is this something you've divined?"

He turned over in bed with a small grunt. "I'll be a grandfather. Go to sleep."

She lay in the dark with her hand over her belly and wondered how it would feel round and full of life.

"It's odd to have only one child, though," she said.

Her father's sigh held more exasperation this time. "Galen never remarried after Arcas's mother died in childbirth."

"But he doesn't have a farm. Lycas and Nilo won't stay around forever to help you. They're not made for this life."

"Rhia, do you honestly want to come home in a year to find another woman in your mother's place?"

With that image in her mind, she tried to squeak out the lie of "Yes," but couldn't. "It's not about what I want. It's about what you need." When he didn't answer, she pressed on, "You're not even forty. Please say you'll consider it."

A long silence passed, filled with his choppy breaths.

"No."

From the tone of his voice, she knew it was the final word. "I love you," she said.

"I love you, too. Good night."

Rhia pulled the blanket to her chin and waited for a slumber that refused to come.

10

The next morning, Rhia entered the hounds' pen to feed them for the final time. As they finished eating, they approached her one by one for hugs. Her bonds with the current pack's six members were not as close as the one she had shared with Boreas, but she could identify each of them with her eyes shut, by their barks or even the unique rhythms of their paws.

"Will you miss them more than me?" her father asked.

She looked up, startled, then shook her head, unable to speak.

He entered the pen and scratched the closest hound behind the ears. "The dogs will be fine without you."

"Don't let Lycas tease them."

"I won't." He squatted next to her. "Are you ready?"

"There's nothing to pack. Galen won't let me bring any of my own belongings."

"He'll bring everything you need. When I asked if you were ready, I meant, are you *ready?*"

Her thoughts flitted to Mayra's death. "I'm long past ready, Father."

"Good." He stood with a brisk movement, knees popping. "Because they're coming right now to see you off."

"They?"

"Galen, your brothers, other villagers."

"Oh." She twisted her hand in her long skirt.

"Arcas is with them."

"Oh!" Rhia scrambled to her feet and hugged her father. With a final pat for each of the hounds, she scampered out of the pen to the top of the hill.

A crowd trudged up to meet her, nearly half the size of the multitude attending her mother's funeral. Some carried baskets of food and flasks of drinks—they must have planned a celebration feast in her honor (and absence) after her departure. Tradition called for such, but Rhia had not expected such attention, given the tardiness of her Bestowing. She wondered how much of the food would fit in her pockets.

Upon seeing her, Lycas and Nilo broke from the pack and dashed up the hill. Nilo scooped her up in his arms as if she were a child.

"What are you doing?" she yelled through her laughter.

Lycas grabbed her heels, and the twins carried her toward the woods, her body hanging between them like a dead deer.

"We thought you wouldn't go unless we dragged you," Nilo said.

"Please put me down." A little-sister whine had come into her throat. She cleared it and deepened her voice. "I demand you release me."

"Release you?" Lycas said. The twins' eyes met with a mischievous spark. "Interesting thought."

"Oh, no." She jerked her legs. "If you drop me in the mud, I swear I'll—"

"Ah, you're no fun anymore." Lycas slowly lowered her feet to the ground. Nilo lifted her shoulders until she was standing, then he dusted absolutely nothing off the back of her coat. She turned to him.

"I won't miss you," she said, and hugged him hard.

"My life will be paradise without you, too, little bird."

When Nilo released her, she faced Lycas. "I really won't miss you."

He embraced her, lifting her up. "I'll miss having you for target practice."

When her feet hit the ground again, she smoothed her hair and looked at the approaching crowd, which had crested the hill. Arcas strode next to Galen, his gaze on Rhia, his mood inscrutable from this distance.

Lycas whispered over her shoulder. "If that boy hurts your feelings, he won't be feeling much for long."

"Please stay out of this," she said with enough gravity that her brothers stepped back.

Everyone bowed in greeting. Galen carried a large pack on his back but did not appear to labor under its weight. Rhia spent a moment hoping it contained many varieties of food before turning her attention to Arcas. He smiled at her, though not in the way he used to, and beckoned her aside.

She looked at Galen, who nodded his approval before moving to greet Tereus.

Arcas and Rhia entered the bower of bare-branched oaks, where they stood near Mayra's grave. Her palms grew clammy with sweat, and she drew her hands up into the sleeves of her coat.

"Are you cold?" Arcas asked.

"Why did you come?"

He opened his mouth but no sound came out.

"I've no time to discuss the weather, Arcas."

"I came because I wanted you to know two things."

She held her breath.

"I love you," he said.

A smile spread over her face, then dissipated. "What's the other thing?"

"I think we should be free while you're away."

"Free for what?"

"To figure out if what we have is real. When you come back, you'll be Crow, and I'll be—maybe I'll have accepted what I am. Until then, I don't think we should hold each other to any promises. If you meet someone—" he looked away "—or if I meet someone—"

Torynna's face flashed in Rhia's mind, along with those of a dozen other girls. "Have you?"

He shook his head, a little too quickly. "You know I love only you."

"How would I know that? When I come to your home, you're never there. How can I know anything about what you feel or who you are anymore, when all winter you pretend you don't exist?"

"I'm still me. You know me."

"Not anymore."

"Then I was right to say we should be free."

Rhia felt patronized. "I'm not arguing with you."

"I didn't think you would."

"How could I, when you wait until I leave on the most important journey of my life? Did you expect me to set aside all other cares today and beg you to bind yourself to me?"

"I'm sorry. I've been a coward—about you, about being a Spider." Arcas paused, and she hoped he wasn't waiting for her to contradict him. "I wish things were simpler, Rhia."

She felt none of the cold dread that had permeated her during their last fight. Now only resignation remained. In her mind, their love had been mortally wounded when he walked out of her house months before. Its demise now brought her a mixture of grief and relief.

"What happened to us?" she said.

"I don't know." He stepped forward to touch her cheek. "But something tells me this is not the end."

"I don't want it to be." She wrapped her arms around his waist. He kissed the top of her head and returned her embrace.

Rhia pulled away first. "I'm taking this with me." She showed him the white stone he had given her.

"You'll need it." He ruffled her hair, whose curls now brushed the tops of her shoulders. "Take care of yourself."

"Crow will take care of me."

"Or else He'll have me to reckon with."

When they left the bower, Rhia's brothers regarded them with narrow eyes, probably judging her level of pain to determine whether they needed to inflict some upon Arcas. She gave them a smile she hoped would lull them into at least a temporary peace.

Galen gestured for Rhia to join him. She stood behind him and waited while the crowd processed, Tereus at its head, her brothers following, and the rest of the villagers in a mass behind them. Galen and Rhia brought up the rear as they moved toward the forest.

Rhia took one last long look at the pastures of her family's farm. She could almost see her mother's figure bending to collect the herbs and flowers to soothe and heal her patients.

When they reached the place where their farm met the dark woods, the crowd parted to let Galen and Rhia move through its middle. As she passed them, the villagers reached to touch her garments. She held her composure, trying not to shrink from the mass of hands seeking contact with that which would soon be holy. A child grabbed her skirt and halted Rhia's movement until his mother pried open his fist to let her go.

She was permitted one final goodbye to each of her family members. Nilo and Lycas hugged her together.

"Don't tease the dogs," she reminded Lycas.

"But it makes them feisty," he said.

She ignored him and planted a quick kiss on each of their cheeks. Finally she turned to her father. "Remember what we talked about."

"Boiling water kills the yeast and makes bad bread. I won't forget."

She rolled her eyes and decided to forego further admonitions, especially since her throat was growing tight. Tereus embraced her quickly, then let go, as if his arms wouldn't unlock if he held her for more than a moment.

"Without further ceremony—" Galen raised his hand "—we shall depart."

It truly was without further ceremony, as he turned on his heel and strode into the woods. She had to hurry to keep sight of him, and only had time for a brief wave goodbye to the others. Off to the side, Arcas watched her go.

She and Galen walked without speaking on a well-worn path covered by dry, ash-colored leaves. Sunlight streamed across the forest floor, for the trees had yet to bud. Though she had begun the hike in shivers, the exertion warmed her, and she unfastened her coat.

"Is the pace too quick for you?" Galen asked, long after it would have made a difference.

"No." Rhia tried to hide her panting. "When would you like to stop to eat?"

"Not now."

She fell back into silence and tried to think of something other than food. To the left of the path, a squirrel scratched at the dirt under a thin pile of leaves to extract a buried acorn. Chattering in triumph, the creature scurried up a nearby tree to find a comfortable spot in which to munch and gloat in Rhia's direction.

The path curved uphill, and soon the trees began to change from hickory and oak to pine and spruce. Cones mixed with leaves on the forest floor, which grew more shrouded from the late morning sun. Rhia peered warily at the shadows. They had never ventured this far during her training.

Finally Galen stopped in what seemed to be a predetermined spot, yet to Rhia the area appeared no different than any other place they had passed. But her tired legs and empty belly forbade her to question his timing. Galen sat on a fallen tree and opened the top of his pack.

"We'll eat the fresh meat first. After today it will be dried venison only."

She took the hunk of meat and loaf of bread he offered, trying not to appear too eager. Her mouth refused to cooperate, however, and gobbled down the first half of the food before she even tasted it.

"You certainly have the appetite of a Crow," Galen said. "I've no doubt now, He is your Guardian Spirit."

Rhia forced herself to finish chewing before she asked, "You had doubts before?"

"These things are never certain until the Bestowing." His speech slowed, as if he were choosing his words with care. "Sometimes when one does not honor one's Spirit, another will take Its place."

Rhia's stomach tightened around her meal. "I tried to reject Crow after that day with Dorius, I tried to pretend—"

"Nevertheless, Crow has chosen you. I am certain."

She wondered why he was so certain about her when he had been wrong about his own son.

Galen touched the tip of the brown and red feather hanging from his neck. "A Hawk's sight is only as strong as his willingness to see. My blindness made me fail before, and I prayed I would not fail you." He looked at her. "I have not, and I will not."

"Failure is final," she said, "and so long as Arcas lives, you have not failed yet. He'll find his way, if you help him."

Galen molded the soft part of the bread between his

fingers, flattening it into a thin brown wafer. "I regret that my son's confusion has brought strife between you."

"If he pretends to be something he's not, what future can we have?"

"He is a coward."

Rhia was taken aback at Galen's harsh words, though she didn't disagree with his judgment. She had ascribed the same word to herself for denying her own Spirit.

"A coward, for not defying his father's wishes?" she said. "Have you made it easy?"

"It doesn't have to be easy. It just has to be done."

"Then let him."

"He's a man, not a boy. I do not 'let' him do anything anymore."

"You're his father. He craves your approval and always will, because he respects and loves you. Tell him you know he's Spider and that you accept him for it. Only then will he accept himself."

Galen's patient expression eased her concern. "I know what I must do, Rhia. Give me time to be human."

She silenced herself with the rest of her meal, chastened but not regretting her words. Whether she and Arcas ever renewed their love, she wanted him to be happy. She recalled her last glimpse of him through the trees, how empty and lost he had looked.

"What did you think I would be," she asked Galen, "if not Crow?"

A brief smile flickered over his lips, as if he were embarrassed to share his theory. "Crow is wise in the ways of death, has a strong understanding of right and wrong and an enormous ability to solve problems." His voice stooped to a whisper. "But Raven is wise in all things. She moves and sees through time and space."

The back of Rhia's neck tingled. Raven, not simply another Spirit, but the Spirit Above All Others. Mother of Creation. "But Raven never—"

"Never lends Her Aspect to a human, not since anyone can remember. The Aspect of Raven would make one more powerful than everyone else and upset the balance among humans. We live in harmony because we are different but equally essential to the whole. But some say that in extraordinary times, when the survival of our people is at stake, Raven will bestow her Aspect upon one young woman or man, who will be able to go anywhere, inhabit any time, to save us all."

The forest seemed to grow colder. "And you thought—" she almost didn't dare say it "—you thought it could be me?"

"The way you speak sometimes, as if you possess many times the wisdom for someone your age. It made me wonder."

"Hawks are also wise beyond their years." Rhia hoped she didn't sound obsequious. "Why didn't you think I could be Hawk?"

"Your gifts were obvious when as a child you foretold the deaths of animals. They say that Crow often chooses those who confront and conquer death early in life. Like you."

"I did hear Crow for the first time when I was ill."

"Perhaps at the same time, Raven also brushed you with Her wings before giving you to Her favorite son."

Rhia sat stunned. So many questions burned inside her, each competing for the chance to be the first one asked.

"Before we begin our journey again…" Galen reached in his pack and handed her a small pouch.

She tugged on the pouch's strings to open it, and her mouth watered. An assortment of dried fruit—pears, apples and grapes—spilled like jewels into her hand. She shone a grin of gratitude upon the Hawk. If his offering was a tactic to get her to stop talking, it worked.

As she chewed, she reflected on what Galen had said about Raven. Only a few minutes before, she had had the presumption to tell him how to handle his own son. Now she understood how much experience and wisdom Galen held within his mind, and recalled the awe she had felt for him in her younger years. His forbearance in the face of Rhia's onslaught of opinions showed a patience and control that she needed to learn. Someday she would undoubtedly face grieving family members who would question her ability to serve their loved ones. Even her mother had encountered those who thought they knew more about healing the sick than she did.

When Rhia finished eating, Galen rose without a word, heaved the pack to his shoulders, and continued up the path, deeper into the forest. Rhia scrambled to her feet and hurried to catch up. She did not want to think about being left alone in a place that was becoming stranger by the step.

The afternoon darkened early, due both to the increasing tree cover and the clouds that had blown in from the south. Rhia's feet ached less now, as the path had grown softer from the presence of fallen pine and spruce needles. It looked soft enough to lie down on and sleep until dinnertime. Her mind dulled from exhaustion, and she had seen nothing but the path beneath her feet for what felt like hours.

Suddenly Galen pulled up short, and Rhia walked into his back with an *oomph!* of surprise.

"Sorry," she said. "What is it?"

He pointed to a pine tree about ten paces from the path. Four claw marks gouged its trunk, higher than Rhia could reach even on tiptoe. Strips of fresh bark dangled from them, red as clay, standing out against the gray-brown of the trunk.

"Bear." Galen went to the tree and reached for the claw marks. The bear's paw dwarfed his hand. Rhia imagined the power such a paw would wield in an angry strike.

"A big one," he noted with typical understatement. "Probably groggy from its winter rest. We should make plenty of noise. If it hears us coming, it will move away."

He walked up the path and began singing a favorite Asermon tune, a lively harvest song meant to strengthen field workers through their hard labors. Rhia joined him. Her voice was strong but by no means melodic. The Hawk switched to a harmony that would accompany her limited vocal range.

When the sky's gray was more black than white, they stopped for the night. Galen chose a spot off the path where a clearing would make a safe place for a fire. In the center of the clearing sat a large boulder the height of Rhia's head. It widened at the top, providing a sort of roof, which would shelter them if the rain that the skies promised came to pass.

Rhia cleared needles from a section of the forest floor and built a campfire. She stayed by its side, for it was the only familiar thing in this place, and instinct told her the fire would hold danger at bay. She imagined brandishing a burning stick to ward off a furry, fanged creature.

For dinner, they skewered pieces of rabbit and root vegetables on sticks and roasted them over the fire. Though the meal lacked herbs and oils she would have added at home, she savored it like a harvest feast. It would be the last fresh meat she would eat for days, maybe longer.

"How much farther to the place of Bestowing?" she asked Galen midway through the meal.

"You'll know when you're there."

"How?"

"By the fact that I'm gone."

"Oh," she said in a small voice. "Will that be soon?"

Galen crunched a blackened potato peel and pretended he hadn't heard her.

That night Rhia lay with her back to the boulder, a section of blanket tucked behind her to prevent the stone's cold from seeping into her body. She stared at the fire and waited to hear Galen abandon her. The slightest movement from where he slept at her feet, or even a change in the rhythm of his breath, roused her to terror.

On the other side of the campfire, a bundle hung from a branch, swaying in the gathering wind. The bundle contained their food, which Galen had suspended high enough to keep out bears, raccoons, cougars and even starving little Crow women.

When the wind died down, signaling the sky's temporary withholding of rain, the forest became quieter and louder at the same time. The sounds the wind had muffled now came sharply to Rhia's ears.

A small creature scurried through the nearby underbrush. An owl dove with a soft roar of wings. A scrambling of twigs and a peep cut short told her the nameless animal had just turned into prey. She appreciated for the first time how well the walls of her home muted the night's tiny battles.

A distant shriek sliced the darkness, and Rhia yelped. Galen turned over with a grunt.

"What was that?" she whispered. He snored in response. She resisted the urge to kick the Hawk in the head to wake him. A few deep, calming breaths later, she considered the animals who might make such a sound: screech owl, bobcat? Both too small to eat her.

Just to be sure, she crawled to the dying fire and stoked it until the flames jumped as high as her face. As she warmed her hands, she became aware of her exposed back. Rhia looked over both shoulders and saw nothing but the uninterrupted blackness of the boulder. Galen's figure was invisible, as he had wrapped himself from head to foot in a dark woolen blanket.

Rhia reached for her own blanket and shifted it around her body as she sat before the fire. Crows were bold, fearless of anything that didn't pose a genuine threat. How much more powerful she would be when she shirked her silly fears.

The creature shrieked again, closer. Rhia stifled a cry and scooted back into the sanctuary of the boulder. She lay down and forced herself to close her eyes. The dancing flames cast lurid images on the backs of her lids. She recited a childhood prayer to Swan, her father's Spirit, to cradle her in a dreamless sleep. Exhaustion nibbled at her consciousness, and she began to slip away just as a wolf howled in the distance, long, low and unanswered.

11

Rhia woke into a world of silver.

Frozen rain had covered the trees while she slept, and now each needle bore its own tiny icicle glistening in the faint morning sunlight. The millions of mirrors sparkled reflections against each other to create a dazzling mural. Not a single surface lay untouched by ice. Even the tree trunks held a slick glaze.

Dry except for the edge of her blanket, which had frozen to the ground, Rhia stared at the sight from her place under the overhanging rock. Her muscles ached from the cold and the vigilant posture she had held all night. Even the slightest stretch made them cramp. So she remained motionless, half-asleep, in awe of the beauty that surrounded her. Perfect ice storms such as this had occurred perhaps half a dozen times in her life. The rising sun would soon return the frigid, fragile magnificence to its watery origins.

Quick, light footsteps crunched on the other side of the rock. Rhia raised her head.

"Galen, is that you?"

No reply.

"Galen?"

Against the protest of her muscles, Rhia sat up.

"Galen, did you hear—"

He was gone.

Not just him, but his blanket, his pack, the bundle of food that had hung from the tree—all gone.

Rhia scrambled to her feet, calling his name again and again. The campfire was nothing but a wisp of steam now, doused by the ice. She turned her stiff neck in every direction, hoping to see Galen in the distance, maybe collecting wood or praying in solitude.

A small pack lay in the space where he had slept. She pulled it open to see two clean pairs of trousers and two blouses, all her size. Beneath the clothes lay an extra blanket, a waterskin, a flint, a small shovel for digging latrines and a package of dried venison.

The food, she realized, was to break her fast.

In three days.

And so it begins. She examined her surroundings, which did not appear sacred or extraordinary. The only remarkable feature was the boulder, which was situated in the exact center of the clearing, as if someone used it to hold court.

The footsteps crunched behind her again. She whirled, her hands flying up to defend herself, and saw…nothing, not even a mouse creeping along the thin crust of snow.

The sound came again, this time to her right. Icicles scattered across the ground. She realized with a sigh that they had made the eerie noise, the one that sounded like a dozen tiny someones creeping up on her.

A breeze blew, and the forest around her erupted in chiming, skittering clashes of ice and snow. She backed against the rock and looked up to make sure no branches overhung the place where she stood, for some of the icicles were as large as her forearm. The nearest tree was at least twenty paces away.

Rhia set down the pack, pulled out the extra blanket, a pale brown woolen one, and climbed atop the flat rock. She spread out the blanket and sat cross-legged upon it, keeping her original blanket wrapped tight around her. Though the morning sun was already warming the dark surface of the boulder, the constant ringing of ice against snow made her shiver.

There was nothing to do but wait. Wait, and pray. She closed her eyes.

Spirits, grant my body and soul the strength to last these three days. Send all who can teach me what I need to know, and let me understand your wisdom in my limited mortal way.

You know I'm afraid. Take my fear away, or at least give me the courage to swallow it, however bitter it may taste.

She stopped and opened her eyes. Was she making sense? Her thoughts were as shattered and scattered as the icicles on the ground around her. She cleared her throat and stared up at the clear sky.

"Maybe if I speak out loud, I can make you understand."

Her voice sounded halting and weak, and she was unsure how to put the moment into words. Her pleas were unutterable, her emotions inscrutable even to herself. So she decided to simply wait. Wait, and try to make her mind as empty as her belly.

Rhia lay back on the blanket, face warming to the sun. The icicles' cacophonous plummets echoed the chaos in her own mind.

She had taken her first step into the unknown. It was hesitant and unsteady, but there was no turning back.

The day slouched forward more slowly than any day in Rhia's memory. It was not cut into bits by chores or rituals or conversations—it just *was*. By the time the sun had reached its peak, all of the icicles had fallen. Since the trees no longer bore implements of death or dismemberment, she decided to gather wood for that night's fire. She set off toward the east, never losing sight of the boulder.

Her feet kicked icicles out of her path, creating a spirited music as they clinked against one another on the bare ground. Due to the storm, branches of all sizes were scattered across the forest floor. In just a few minutes she had collected enough firewood to last three days. She arranged it into piles according to size, stepped back to examine her work, then felt suddenly foolish.

Her time was a gift, not something to be occupied. These three days would come once in her life. She should be honored.

Why, then, did she feel little more than nervousness? The sky would darken soon, and she would be sleeping alone for the first time in her life. But sleep was forbidden during the Bestowing, she reminded herself, along with food and water.

Water. Her tongue went dry just thinking about it. She paced around the boulder, trying to take the edge off her agitation. *Special, special, special,* her mind recited with each step. *Honor, honor, honor.*

Water, water, water, her body replied, in the moments between the steps.

Rhia ignored the petitions of her mouth and stomach, determined to concentrate on more important things. Things like prayer and meditation and journeying and communing with Spirits, who were bound to show up any moment.

Whenever her pacing brought her near the sack, it seemed to beckon her. Her fingers and tongue could almost feel the strips of dried venison within, rough and crumbly around the edges but chewy and smoky at the center.

Perhaps she could eat now, then begin her three-day fast again tomorrow. Galen shouldn't have left her by surprise. She needed today just to get used to being alone in the woods. Tonight she could pray for tomorrow's strength, so that tomorrow she'd be stronger, more prepared. No one would know.

Except the Spirits. But were they even here?

Rhia went still, holding her breath. The forest rustled with noises of birds, animals, and wind. On the branches above her head, needle slid against needle as the breeze passed over them. She waited for several minutes, empty, for the Spirits to approach her. Perhaps when she opened her eyes, they would surround her, animals in their iconic forms ready to impart wisdom to their newest seeker.

But they weren't. All that met her squinting eyes were the same trees and rocks that had been there before. Her senses detected nothing extraordinary.

"They're here," she said.

* * *

Though the day had stretched long, night hurried to drape itself over the forest. Rhia could barely see the flint in her hands as she tried to start the evening's fire. Her surroundings were so black, the spark that leaped from the stone onto the pile of dry leaves seared an image onto her eyes that lasted for several blinks.

Soon the fire burned brightly, and Rhia huddled near it, both blankets wrapped tight around her, as if warmth alone could protect her from whatever lurked in the forest. She missed food even more now that she was cold, missed the heat it would help her body produce. She missed the chamomile tea her mother would make for her on the nights she couldn't sleep.

She missed her mother. She wanted her mother.

Pride held in her tears, even here, until they could be contained no more.

"Mama..." She sobbed like a child, shoulders heaving and throat aching. If only she could see her mother one last time, feel Mayra's arms enclose her.

Suddenly she felt a presence in the dark. Every inch of her skin prickled. She dared move nothing but her eyes to peer around. But the firelight scorched her vision, making it impossible to see into the forest.

Had she called Mayra's spirit from the Other Side? The presence felt anything but maternal. Was she angry at being disturbed?

"I'm sorry," she whispered. "I'm so sorry. Please, no."

Rhia's breath came so shallow now, she thought she would faint from lack of air. She should pray for strength and courage, but even if she found the words, her lips were too paralyzed to form them, her throat too tight to utter them.

She strained for any unfamiliar sound, but none came, only the wind whispering through the branches. Her skin bristled every time two twigs scratched together. A tree on the other side of the campfire had lost most of a branch during the ice storm; what remained hung by a few fibers, creaking during the stronger breezes.

Whatever lurked out there was watching her. Testing her. Judging her.

It held her in its gaze as the nearly full moon rose into the sky, silvering the forest floor. It observed her as the moon crossed the sky into high clouds that muted and softened the light to a pale glow.

She didn't know how to pass its test, other than to survive, to fail to die from terror. Right now even that modest goal was a struggle to achieve.

It kept watch over her, silent and unmoving, until the eastern sky lightened with the first blush of dawn. It drew away then, slowly, uttering a single, unbreakable promise.

Until tonight.

Rhia burst into uncontrollable shudders. She hugged her knees until her arms ached, fearing that her body would break apart and crumble into a pile of bones.

When the sun peeked over the horizon, her eyes devoured the orange light as if it were sustenance itself, while part of her wondered if it would be the last sunrise she would ever see.

12

"Why are you here?" the snake asked in an unfamiliar language that Rhia nonetheless understood. He rested languorously on the other end of the boulder, green scales luminous in the sun.

"For my Bestowing," she replied. A day ago it would have felt odd to speak with a snake as if it were a new friend.

"I do not understand this word, Bestowing."

"It's when a person receives their Aspect from their Guardian Spirit Animal."

"Like a snake?"

"It could be a snake." She hesitated. "Are you my Guardian Spirit? Galen said it would be the last animal to come to me, not the first."

"I've no interest in being anyone's anything." The snake stretched and let his tail dangle over the edge of the boulder. "So why are you here?"

"I told you."

"You told me why they sent you. I don't care what's expected of you. Tell me… Why. You. Are. Here."

She thought for a long time. Each answer contained another answer within it. She wanted to help her people, but why? To be of use, but why? As she meditated on the question, her eyelids became heavy from the sun. Halfway to sleep, the deepest answer entered her.

"To become," she told the snake.

"Become what?"

"A part of the whole."

"The whole what? The whole village? The whole people?"

"The whole." She gestured to the world. "Everything."

"I see." The snake was quiet for a few moments, and Rhia sat back, relieved that she had given a correct answer. Then he turned his unblinking eyes on her again.

"Are you not already part of the whole?"

"I—yes. Everything is, of course."

"Then why are you here?"

She sighed and looked around, as if the answer would pop out of the forest floor. "Are you enjoying this interrogation?"

"I ask the questions."

"Why?"

"Because."

"Then how will I learn?"

"Before you add, you must subtract."

"What does that mean?"

If a snake had shoulders, this one would have shrugged. His head turned away from Rhia and rested on the stone, as if their conversation had been a distraction from sunbathing.

Before you add, you must subtract. Did she have two days and nights of riddles to look forward to, or would other Spirits be gentler? Compared to the thing that had approached her the night before, though, the snake was mild enough.

Must she subtract from her knowledge, unlearn everything she knew?

"Hello," said the snake, who had turned his head back to her.

"Hello," Rhia replied.

"So why are you here?"

She shook her head. "I don't know."

"Exactly." The snake disappeared.

Rhia blinked. She leaned over one edge of the boulder, then the other to see if the snake had slithered off. His green body was not among the pine needles and rough stones on either side. When she straightened up again, a shriek darted from her throat.

A monster towered over the boulder.

Its legs alone reached higher than the stone, which extended to the top of Rhia's head. Its fur was a pale tan, patterned with intersecting, irregular patches of dark brown. A long tail swished its flank in the manner of a horse. In fact, the beast resembled a horse that had been stretched and distorted. An impossibly long neck, longer even than its legs, ended in a deerlike head that held two straight nubs of horns, like those of a baby goat.

She looked at the creature's face and a second scream died in her throat, for dark, kind eyes gazed back. It seemed to be smiling at her.

"Wh-what are you?" Rhia said.

"I am proof." The feminine voice spoke in a lilting language in which the end of each word trembled.

"Proof of what?"

"Of the glory of Creation."

Rhia couldn't argue with that statement. "I've never seen anything like you."

"And you never will. My kind dwells in a land farther than your people will ever travel. It would seem to you as far as the end of the earth, and yet there are places even farther and creatures who would appear even stranger to your eyes."

"I would like to see them, too."

"In time, perhaps. They will appear in your dreams as you need them. Right now they are needed by others, people who live in our lands."

Rhia felt honored that this creature would travel so far to appear to her, though time and distance meant little in the Spirit World. She stood and bowed. "Thank you for helping me."

"It is my pleasure."

Rhia waited for the tall creature to begin testing her as the snake had. But she only said, "Speak."

"Pardon?" Rhia asked.

"You must have questions."

Rhia recovered from her surprise. "What are you called?"

"The people where I live call me 'twiga.' Those who lived here long ago called me 'giraffe,' but I prefer my native name."

Her mind roiled in confusion. "Wait. The people who lived here long ago, how did they know you, if you live far away?"

"They traveled around the world, and brought some of my creatures here to keep for themselves."

"To eat? To ride?"

"To possess." The twiga/giraffe gave a modest tilt of her head. "And to admire."

Rhia understood the impulse, but it seemed beyond her people's capability. Then again…

There were those who believed in the Reawakening, the moment in the distant past when the Spirits chose her people to share their magic. Before the Reawakening, humans had dwelled in disharmony with the world and its creatures, placing themselves in the role of gods, as the Descendants now did. The natural world turned against them, and it was only by the grace of the Spirits that her people had survived.

Few Asermons believed this myth. But why would the twiga tell a false story? Though Spirits didn't lie outright, some offered incomplete truths unless asked the right questions.

"Your land, what is it like?" Rhia said.

The animal swung its head in a sweeping arc. "It is much drier than your forest, with grass as tall as my knees. There are few trees, except at the watering holes, where we all gather. Even our enemies drink with us, those who would eat us, for water is the most precious thing in our lives."

Rhia couldn't imagine what would be large enough to eat this creature. "Who are your enemies?"

"Cats, nearly twice the size of your cougars, who live in groups instead of alone. They hunt our babies." The twiga tasted a pine branch with a long black tongue, but declined to take a bite. "Would you like to ask about your own journey, or did you want to talk about me all day?"

A shadow of last night's fear hovered over Rhia. "What lurks in the dark, here in the forest?"

"Oh, all sorts of things, I imagine. Owls, bats, mice—"

"What came to me last night? What will come again tonight?"

"Oh." The twiga's ears flicked back and forth. "I cannot tell you. Another question, please. I would so like to help."

"Will I—will I survive this ordeal?"

The creature blinked her huge brown eyes. "Of course."

"Will I see you again?"

She bowed her head close to Rhia's and breathed warm upon her forehead. "If you need me, come and get me."

The twiga disappeared so quickly that Rhia put her hand into the space where she had stood, in case she were merely invisible. She wished she had been less self-concerned and asked more questions about the Reawakening.

A low buzzing came to her ear. She turned to see a golden dragonfly the size of her finger hovering over the side of the boulder. It darted to and fro, then alighted in the center of the stone and lowered its iridescent wings to the side.

"What do you see?" Its voice, neither masculine nor feminine, sounded out of breath.

Now Rhia was the questionee again. She squatted to peer at the insect.

"I see—" She hesitated to utter the obvious: *a dragonfly*. Perhaps the insect was referring to her surroundings, asking her to describe the forest.

"What do you see," it repeated, green eyes bulging, "when you look at me?"

Unable to devise a better answer, she said, "A dragonfly?"

A wave of heat burst over her as the insect suddenly stretched and swelled, growing up and out until it was the size of a bear. Rhia was too terrified to scream. She fell back on the rock and moved toward the edge, unable to look away.

Its four rear legs fused into one heavy pair upon which the beast now stood. Smaller front legs clawed and grasped as it loomed over her. Its huge green eyes slid apart and shrank to pierce her with their gaze. Its tail slashed the air, glinting gold in the sunlight.

It spoke again, in a language she didn't understand, a language that was guttural and fluid at the same time. It continued its diatribe without pausing, speaking while exhaling and inhaling. She knew then that it was not from any part of this world.

"What are you?" she whispered.

Smoke poured from its nostrils as it seemed to struggle against its own will. Then its voice rolled out again in a rasping, gasping effort, as if its tongue resisted forming words she could understand.

"Dragon," it said. "Fear not."

Rhia nodded, her eyes wide, afraid to blink.

"Fear not." The dragon shook its black-and-gold wings. "It is a command, not a suggestion."

She shuddered at the threat inherent in the words, but sat up and looked into the beast's leering face.

"Are you trying to scare me into not being afraid of you?"

The dragon's eyes narrowed, then relaxed into an almost approving regard. "You are clever, little one."

"Sometimes."

Before the word was out of her mouth, the tip of the thorny tail whipped past her head. The dragon glowered at her. "It will be your undoing."

She dropped her gaze. "I'm sorry."

"For what?"

For catching on to your game, she thought.

"I heard that!" The tail hissed in her ear again. The dragon crouched on the stone, but its lowered posture only made it look more imposing. It growled an incoherent oath. "You learn faster than you understand."

"What do you mean?"

"Know one thing."

She cocked her head and waited for enlightenment. When the dragon only sat, quietly puffing, Rhia grew impatient.

"Know what one thing?"

It gazed at her without reaction, as if it hadn't heard her question. Rhia wished the twiga would return, or even the snake. But the Spirits sent those who could teach her best. So why did she feel like she knew less now than when she woke this morning?

The more she asked, the less she understood. It reminded her of the carved wooden puzzles she'd played with as a child, each piece interlocking to create a whole. But this puzzle only grew more incomplete with each addition, as if adding more pieces resulted in a larger picture. She would never figure out what she came to learn. Her Bestowing would be a failure.

Tears of frustration stung her eyes. She wiped at them in shame.

The dragon frowned at the sight. "Your despair is premature. You will face much greater hardships than your own ignorance."

"I'm not ignorant. I just don't know the one thing."

"But you know all the other things, correct?"

"No, of course not."

"What are the things you know?"

"I know that…" She searched her mind for one truth that hadn't yet been demolished. Hunger, thirst and exhaustion had stolen her ability to think in a straight line. Doubt and fear swarmed inside her.

"Tell me," the dragon rasped, "what do you know?"

"I don't—" Her hands twisted in the folds of her coat. "I can't—"

"You can't tell me? Is it a secret?" The dragon rubbed its claws together in mock anticipation. "Tell me what firm ground you stand upon. Share your knowledge, your certainty. I'd be so pleased to hear it."

Her thoughts scrambled back and forth in time but couldn't land on any one fact, one certainty that didn't slither out of her mind's grasp.

"Rhia." The monster inhaled her name slowly, until she felt as if her very self were being subsumed into its throat. "Tell me what you know."

"Nothing!" She held her empty hands palm up. "Nothing makes sense anymore. No one is what they seem, including me. I don't know why I'm here, what I'm supposed to learn, what I'm supposed to do." She stared at the dragon, hoping it would forgive her honest but insufficient answer. "I know nothing."

The creature gave Rhia a broad smile, then shimmered into oblivion.

The night had swallowed her whole.

She lay gasping—on the ground or on the flat boulder, she

no longer recalled. Something was tearing her apart, rending her from the inside.

The night was squeezing her out of herself.

She had few thoughts to spare for why it was happening or who or what it might be. Every scrap of her mind concentrated on holding herself together, clinging to anything she remembered. Her family, friends, Arcas.

Arcas…was this what he meant when he thought the Bestowing would kill him? Rhia was dying, she was sure, but not a death of the body, like her mother. This was worse. She dreaded the thing that was on the other side of this nothingness, the thing she would become.

The presence in the woods, a living void, had come at sunset, before she even built a fire. It mattered little, for she would not be able to attend the fire, and whatever devoured her kept her…not exactly warm, but not cold.

Not heavy, not light. Not happy or sad, parched or soaked, hungry or sated.

Not anything at all.

She was turning into nothing.

The night had swallowed her whole.

The sky above Rhia was a deep periwinkle, but she didn't see it, only saw through it. She no longer even saw her eyelids when she blinked, if she blinked. She was too busy watching the end of the world.

In a vast vista before her, a river of fire ran next to a river of clouds. They flowed forth toward a distant mountain range, cutting two gouges into the earth, bearing close to each other but neither meeting nor mingling until they converged at the foot of the mountains. At this place, every element fused into one, in the end as at the beginning.

The world was dying and being born over and over before her eyes. She felt as though she could watch forever, that she was seeing the world's Forever inside her own Forever, a Forever doomed to be interrupted soon.

The sky shone a bright blue. Her awareness now included the forest around her, though it felt less real than the visions that had filled her sight every moment she could remember. Her life before the last two days felt like a myth, a dimly recalled bedtime story.

we

are

came a whisper. Something swished in the corner of her eye—a feather, or perhaps a furry tail.

We

Are

it came again, louder. The movement repeated itself, so quickly that Rhia could not even describe the color of the object that passed through her vision.

WE

ARE

She sat up, the ground solid and cold beneath her. "You are?"

NO

WE

ARE

The voices came from everywhere at once, pressing on her head. She stood and turned in a circle.

WE

ARE

Rhia resisted the urge to cover her ears. In the presence of these voices, seeing nothing was almost worse than seeing monsters.

Then the chorus melted together to make one clear voice.

WE

  ARE

Out of the empty space between two pine trees, from the air itself, a tiny brown rabbit appeared—a baby, ears round and legs stubby. Rhia almost smiled at the little creature, until she noticed its feet were not touching the forest floor. No dry leaves rustled at its passing as it moved toward her.

The baby rabbit was about ten paces away when it sat back, fluttered its forelegs and turned into a hawk. The hawk flapped its wings and lifted into a nearby branch. Its wings made no noise, and the branch did not dip and bend under its weight. It grew in length, head and tail fading to white, then uttered the scream of an eagle. The eagle stretched its wings forward as if to grasp the branch it sat upon, and morphed into a squirrel, which chattered and shook its fluffy tail at Rhia.

On and on it went, from squirrel to dove to bobcat to bear to bee and trout, on and on as the day progressed, one blurring into another, some as unfamiliar as the giraffe, until she no longer remembered *any* of the animals, much less all of them.

Finally, as the shadows lengthened, there coalesced before her a furry, feathered, scaly creature nearly half the height of the trees. It consisted of every animal she had ever seen, and many she didn't recognize. Horns, paws, tails, ears poked out in all directions. It hovered like a soap bubble over the forest floor.

Her jaw slackened at the sight. It was beautiful rather than grotesque, this melding of all life. It was like viewing the whole world in one place.

WE ARE, it uttered, and she knew it was right. All one. To separate and divide was to corrupt this truth. She ached with awe at the simplicity and complexity of life, and with regret at the mistakes she had made during her short existence.

The every-animal body swelled and twisted in the fading sunlight. As the last rays slipped over the hill, the creature began to tremble, faintly at first around the edges, then violently from within, as if a great force were trying to hatch out of it.

The sun set, and the body burst. Out of the center flew a giant raven, luminous, iridescent—each feather containing every color as it had at the moment of the world's birth.

Rhia fell to her knees, then her stomach. She had never expected to be in the presence of Raven. The twiga, the dragon, the void-creature, the every-animal—none had provoked the terror she felt now, faced with the Creator of the World, the Bringer of Light, the Spirit Above All Others. She had dared look upon Her for a moment that stretched to an eternity. What punishment could pay for her brashness?

Raven flew overhead, the rush of Her enormous wings creating a melody that pierced Rhia's heart. The Spirit circled around to alight in front of the trembling Rhia.

"Rise and behold."

Raven's voice belonged to another world. It was the sound of the stars flickering in the sky, the pulse of the sun's rays, the wind that shifted the sands of the moon.

Rhia rose on unsteady legs and gaped at Raven. Looking at Her, she felt alive, calm. Complete.

"You are not complete," Raven said. "Not yet."

It was time, then.

"Are you—are you my—"

"I am no one's. My duty, my love, is to all who walk this earth. I appear at every Bestowing to introduce each person to their Spirit."

Rhia dropped her gaze, ashamed at her presumption.

"You are ready." Raven folded Her wings to the side. She darkened until all Her feathers turned a deep violet-black. Her beak became pointier and the ruff under Her neck smoothed. Her body shrank until She was no taller than Rhia.

Until it was not Her at all anymore.

It was Him.

Crow.

Rhia stared at the bird-shaped place where the night had become blacker than itself.

"Good evening," He said with a gallant half-bow. His voice sounded more affable and human than the other Spirits.

Rhia bowed in response. "Good evening."

"You are not afraid."

It was true. Her uncertainty, her hesitancy, her fear, had all dropped away. Whatever she did or said in the presence of this Spirit, He would accept her.

"I've lived with you for many years," she said. "To see you at last is almost a comfort."

Crow seemed to smile, if a beak could conjure such an expression. "Follow me. Bring your belongings. We won't return."

They moved out of the clearing into darker forest, and though Rhia was conscious of walking, her feet, like those of the Spirit, no longer rustled the fallen leaves.

"A comfort, you said." Crow chuckled. "You'd be surprised, or perhaps not, how seldom I hear those words. People are rarely happy to see my face."

"That's why you need me, isn't it? So that they're not afraid of you?"

"Yes, to make a person's crossing a time of peace. I do not relish yanking someone out of their life, struggling like a fish in a bear's paw."

Like my mother.

"Yes, like your mother," Crow said. "You have acknowledged your part in the nature of her death and learned from it. But let guilt burden you no more, or it will stunt your powers."

"But why did—" Rhia cut herself off, anticipating Crow's interruption, which never came.

After a few moments, Crow asked patiently, "Yes?"

"Why did you tell me she would live another day?"

He sighed. "I would never lie to you, Rhia. Because we had not given ourselves to each other yet, our communication was unclear. It was like trying to speak to you underwater. You only caught part of the truth."

"And filled in the rest with what I wanted to believe."

"Yes."

"But once I'd made a pronouncement, couldn't you have waited?"

"Changed the speed of my flight to prove you correct?"

It did sound audacious, now that she thought about it. "I suppose death keeps you busy."

"Even if your mother had been the only person in the world to die that night, I would not have changed the time

I took her." He clicked His tongue against the roof of His beak. "The Spirits do what they will."

"Then what's the use of prayer?"

"If you define 'prayer' as trying to change a Spirit's mind, then it's not much use at all. Sorry. But prayers focus your intentions and define what's important, which may change your own actions. Besides, it pleases us to hear from humans."

"Why?"

"Because we love you."

Rhia stopped, dumbstruck. Crow turned to face her.

"Is that such a surprise?" He said.

"No. I always felt it." She took a step toward him. The trembling began again, this time only on the inside. "Especially your love for me."

"Yet you resisted it." His midnight-blue eyes glittered in the moonlight.

"I did."

"Understandable." Crow shifted his wings. "I'm not popular among most humans. Then again, you're not 'most humans.' To be honest, your rejection stung a bit."

Rhia's face crumpled. "Please forgive me," she whispered.

"You are forgiven. If that was the last time."

"It was."

His gaze was both wise and sad. "Perhaps. Let us continue."

They journeyed onward. The trees grew closer together until their canopy nearly blocked the light of the rising full moon. Judging by the moon's position, Rhia knew they were in the real world, yet Crow's presence gave the forest an otherworldly feel. As the surroundings grew more obscure, she edged closer to the Spirit, her former trepidation returning.

"Where are we going?" she asked, expecting the kind of impatient, you'll-see-when-we-get-there answer she had come to expect from humans and Spirits alike.

"To the place of your Bestowing." He saw Rhia look back over her shoulder. "You will not be lost. It is a place well-known to all who have been Bestowed. The location is the same, though it appears different for each person at the sacred moment. When we are finished, you will wait nearby until someone comes to take you to your new home."

"How long will I have to wait?"

"In human terms, I don't know. Spirits measure time differently."

"How far from Kalindos are we?"

"In human terms, I don't know. Spirits measure space differently."

"Who will find me?"

"In human terms—" Crow winked at her "—someone good."

Rhia's curiosity roused, and she felt buoyed by Crow's jesting. "Someone good only in human terms?"

"Good in any terms one can imagine."

She was about to ask Crow more about her future escort, but was silenced by the sudden view.

The forest parted to reveal an open glade, bathed in light too bright to be explained even by the full moon. As they drew closer, she saw the source of the light: In the center of the glade lay a pale blue luminescent pool. Faint trails of steam rose from the water, which was surrounded by long reeds that looked like dark glass. The reeds swayed and chimed against each other, creating a sound so soothing that she wanted to sink into the pool and envelop herself in the ethereal music.

Crow paused on the outskirts of the glade and faced Rhia so she could see both of His eyes.

"Do you trust me?" He said.

She began to answer a hasty "yes," then considered her response. The Spirit had pursued her throughout life, sparing her as a child so that she could serve Him one day and by doing so, serve her people in one of its most dreadful and honorable duties. When she resisted, He had waited until she could no longer ignore the call.

"Yes," she said finally. "I trust you."

"Then let us enter."

They stepped into the glade.

The wind died, as if the glade were sealed from the forest's bitter weather. She had not noticed until that moment how cold she had felt for the past few days. She removed her coat and looked for a spot to put such a profane item in this sacred place.

"Here." Crow's beak pointed to the grass, which was as green and soft as the rest of the glade, unlike the rough brown vegetation outside. "You can put it all here."

"All?"

"Your clothes."

"Why?"

"Before the Bestowing, you must cleanse yourself."

She turned to the pool and let out a sigh of anticipation. How soft and warm the water would feel against her skin. She began to lift the heavy blouse over her head, then hesitated.

Rhia turned to Crow, who watched her without expression. "Er…"

"First of all," Crow said, "I'm a Spirit. I am everywhere, and I see people in every indignity. Death is rarely comely. Second, I'm a bird. The human body neither allures nor disgusts me. Third…" He drew himself up to full height and fluffed out His feathers. "I'm naked, too."

Rhia suppressed a grin, then removed the rest of her clothes, hiding her reluctance. Regardless of His Spiritness, bird-ness and nakedness (under his feathers, she would add), Crow spoke with a man's voice, which made her feel awkward.

She dropped her undergarments on the pile without a glance at the Spirit's face, then stepped quickly into the pool.

The water greeted her skin with a shock of pleasure so intense it held her in place for several moments. She waded farther into the pool until the water reached her hips, then sat down to let it cover her body.

It was warm, so warm, and caressed her with millions of tiny bubbles that seemed alive, scrubbing her clean without the aid of soap or brush. She bent her head back to soak her hair, and the water crept over her face and scalp with what felt like a thousand gentle fingers, like the way her mother used to wash her hair.

The surrounding reeds provided a screen that made her feel as if she were in her own world. They swayed with a tinkling sound, singing sweetly and slightly off-rhythm, like a chorus of little girls. A heady, unfamiliar scent drifted from the reeds' bowing heads, smoothing the last wrinkle of anxiety from Rhia's consciousness.

She submerged her head, eyes open, to search for the source of the blue light. The water murmured its own language against her ears as she looked to either side. Not only did the light appear to come from every direction, but neither it nor the pool itself had a discernible beginning or end. Perhaps she could swim underwater for miles and never reach the edge.

She surfaced and cupped the liquid in her hands, where it continued to glow. What was this place? *Where* was it? On the edge of the Spirit World for certain, created to cleanse more than bodies. She let go of the need to understand and allowed it to nourish her from the outside in.

After several minutes, when the water began to cool and feel like mere water, she knew it was time to leave the pool. Reluctantly she squeezed the drops from her hair and stepped back to the bank.

Crow waited for her in silence. For a moment she resented the ostensibly male presence in a place so female. But His gaze was as passionless as one would expect from a bird looking upon a human body.

"We shall begin," Crow said.

"May I dress first?"

"If you must. But if you are to learn the deepest secrets about yourself and your future, it is best to have nothing to hide behind. Besides, summer is a long way off. How long before you have another chance to be naked?"

She considered it, then turned away from the pile of clothes, resisting the instinct to check for lecherous gazes in the forest around them.

She stood beside him. "I'm ready."

Crow closed His eyes.

On the other side of the pool an even brighter light shone from above. Growing from the lush green grass were two trees, roughly twice Rhia's height.

The branches of the tree on the left were draped with leaves, which reflected the light with a lustrous green hue. Flowers and fruit of every size and color dotted the tips of even the tiniest twigs. Birds chased each other from branch to branch, chirping and twittering. Butterflies alighted on the flowers to drink the nectar within.

The tree on the right resembled its twin in size alone. Its twisted black branches bore no leaves, fruit, or flowers. They clattered in a wind she couldn't feel, scraping against each other like bones. Scars gouged its trunk in long, irregular gashes that oozed a crusty white sap. No creatures played or fed within this tree. In fact, it seemed as though it would extinguish any life that dared approach it.

Rhia took a step toward this second tree. A sharp sigh from Crow made her stop.

"It is as I feared," He said.

She turned to Him. "What does it mean?"

His beak pointed to the left. "The healthy tree is your wisdom, your strength and resilience, but most importantly your love of life. I give these gifts to you."

She looked at the barren tree again, compelled to touch it, even climb it. "What about the other?"

"That tree is what you will become if you allow death to take over your spirit. If you surrender to the illusion that death makes life bitter instead of sweet."

Rhia frowned. It would be hard to resist such a notion

when surrounded by death, especially if a war came to take her loved ones.

Crow continued, "I promise that joy will always dwell inside you. You must promise me to always find it even when everything has failed."

"Failed?"

"All things fail. Everything dies, but all is reborn as well. Never forget that."

"I don't understand."

"You will."

"I'm not sure I want to."

Crow's head bowed. "Yours is a difficult and treacherous path. Yet few paths are easy in the coming times."

Rhia turned back to the barren tree. "Can nothing be done to help it, to make it bear fruit again?"

"Its fruit would taste as bitter as its bark."

"Can it be cut down?"

"No more than evil can be driven from the earth once and for all." Crow spoke over her shoulder. "Know that tree, accept it, even pity it if you must, but ultimately choose the other if you and your people are to be saved."

"My people? Is Asermos in danger?"

"Your people include more than the Asermons."

"But are they in danger?"

"There are those from a distance who think the turning of the earth means leaving behind the ways of the Spirits. They would force everyone to believe as they do—believe or die."

Rhia should have been filled with dread, as she had whenever stirrings of war rustled within Asermos over the past years. Yet inside all she felt was a hard, cold resolve.

"I won't allow it," she said.

Crow examined her. "You may find the price for this power too high."

"I will pay it."

He faced her fully. "Then you must make that promise I asked of you."

Rhia scoured her memory until she found the most important thing He had said since they arrived.

"I promise," she said. "I promise to find within myself the joy and strength and love of life you give me, even—" her voice halted a moment, then regained its power "—even in the face of despair."

He stared at her with eyes that held the pride of a father. His wings opened to embrace Rhia, pulling her close to His dark bosom.

His body was warm and pulsed with something stronger than a mere heartbeat. She buried her hands in the soft feathers.

Crow let out a low, throaty call, and Rhia was filled with a sensation of power and peace, as if a bright light had entered each drop of her blood and was transported through her body by her own breath.

Her vision stretched out over the future years of her life, imparting not images but feelings.

She would enter death and return again. She would carry souls to the Other Side and leave them to dwell with the Spirits until the end of time. She would sit in judgment in matters of right and wrong, and people would hail her wisdom.

She would be of use.

The light darkened then, but lost none of its power.

Joining the peace within her was a remorse so ravenous it threatened to swallow all memory, all sensation. She would look back in sorrow and anger and let this bitterness corrode those she loved. No one would escape its touch.

Rhia's body tensed as a dark thrill passed through it. She would make someone pay for her pain. Her power could drag others into her despair, and she would never be alone in her grief.

"You will not relent forever." Crow's voice came from within her own head. "I give you this, to be certain."

All at once Rhia was enveloped in a warm, protective love that seeped into her pores and filled every void inside her, including those she didn't know she had. She wept, even as each tear dried the moment it reached her cheek.

"Don't leave me," she said.

"I'll always be within you," Crow replied. "I'll perch on the edge of your mind, and we shall speak in your dreams and visions. But we shall never be together like this again until the end of your life."

She gulped back a plea to let her die this moment.

"You have all you need," Crow whispered. "Go now, and give yourself to the world in my name."

She tried to speak but failed and could only give a weak nod against his soft feathers.

"Goodbye, Rhia."

"No!"

But Crow was gone. So was the pool, the two trees and all the creatures that had dwelled there. The glade itself had turned into nothing more than a modest clearing. Around her the forest was cold again, the wind bitter.

She hurried to dress, and for a moment she doubted the entire incident.

"I'll always be within you." Crow's voice came from somewhere other than mere memory.

She knew then, it had been real, the most real thing ever likely to happen in her life.

"I know," she replied, and collapsed.

When Rhia awoke, she wasn't sure if dusk or dawn appeared through the slits of her eyelids. The sky spread a bruise-colored purple above the trees. She lay there long enough to discern a slight darkening.

She sat up quickly. Wood for a fire. Without it, she would freeze tonight or at least be miserable.

As she struggled to her feet, a void gnawed at her stomach for the first time since the initial day of her Bestowing. She was truly back in the physical world, with all its inconvenient demands.

With a start she remembered the dried venison at the bottom of her pack. Her fingers, numb from the cold, fumbled with the tie for a maddening interval before loosening the knot. She shoved aside the clothes and blankets until her hands found the small pack of food.

It wasn't much, but it would ease the cravings until Coranna's escort arrived. Besides, it was all she had. Perhaps in the morning she could forage for some edible roots, if any could be found this time of year.

A low whine came from her left. She leaped up and away from the sound, one foot stumbling over the other.

A wolf stood at the edge of the clearing.

Rhia froze like a rabbit. She had endured the Bestowing only to be torn apart by the thing she feared most.

The wolf took a step toward her, and Rhia suddenly doubted her dread. The creature's fur was matted and pale with age. Its eyes were sunken, and its skin hung loose on a skeletal frame. Instead of meeting her gaze in a challenge, it glanced at her hands, then looked away.

Rhia's throat tightened as she recalled the last years of her dog Boreas. He had tottered about on fragile limbs, trying to retain his pride as he begged for food the other hounds denied him.

The wolf pack must have rejected this one for his weakness, she thought. *He looks so sad and lonely.*

And hungry. Rhia took a slow step backward and glanced around for a branch to use as a weapon. If the wolf tried to attack her in its condition, she could probably fight it off enough to discourage it.

Rather than advance, the wolf sank to its stomach and whined. It glanced sideways at her hands again. Only then did Rhia remember what she held.

The food that would break her fast. The food she craved, the food her body needed to keep itself warm.

"Oh, no," she whispered sharply. "I can't give you this. I won't. It's mine."

The wolf inched toward her on its belly, then laid its head on outstretched paws as if to await her decision in a more comfortable pose.

"You don't understand." Rhia clutched the venison strips. "I haven't eaten in days. I need this. I can't hunt like you."

But the wolf appeared no more capable of capturing and

killing prey than she was herself. Still, beneath the patchy fur lay a well-muscled body, however gaunt. If she fed the wolf, it might regain enough strength to fend for itself.

"I don't know when they'll come for me," she told it. "It could be days before I eat again. This is all I have."

The wolf's white ears and eyebrows twitched with the rise and fall of her voice, but the creature otherwise remained motionless. It let out a deep, clear sigh.

Rhia took one step forward, then another—only to examine the wolf more closely, she told herself. As she approached, its gaze grew apprehensive, until it sat up and retreated several unsteady steps into the forest. It turned and looked at her again, this time at her face. Their eyes met.

Rhia forgot her arguments for keeping the food. She forgot the hunger that chewed at her stomach and sapped strength from her limbs. She forgot the fear that no one would come for days, or perhaps at all, and that she would be lost in the forest until she starved. She forgot everything but the need in the wolf's eyes. She tossed the food on the ground.

The wolf leaped so fast it made Rhia jump, and she cut short a squeak. It gulped the first three strips of deer meat, grabbed the rest and darted off into the forest. Within moments it was gone.

She looked around with dread. It was dark. Very dark. A thick cover of clouds hid what should have been a full moon. Now she would never find enough firewood to last the night.

Rhia groped around beneath the trees until she located a few twigs and branches. She started a small fire that provided more light than warmth, but at least it would help her find a safe resting place. As she searched, she took small sips of water from the skin Galen had left her.

A cluster of short spruces stood about twenty paces from the fire. Their lowest branches created a sort of roof a few feet from the ground. It was not as secure a shelter as the boulder where she had spent the last few days, but she'd never find her way back there. Besides, Crow had instructed her to wait for Coranna's envoy. She had to trust the Spirit even with her life. Especially with her life.

Rhia laid one of her wool blankets on the soft bed of needles, then crawled under the branches and wrapped the other blanket tight around her, covering her head. She breathed through the fabric of her mittens to warm her hands.

The two sleepless nights of her Bestowing weighed upon her body; not even fear could keep her awake. Shivering, she watched the pitiful fire diminish into a pile of embers, until all went dark.

Eyes were upon her.

Something moved through the forest, closer and closer to where Rhia lay.

Her muscles felt frozen. She listened hard in the dark for any sound that would tell her the direction of the—whatever it was. It seemed to lurk behind, then far in front of her. She sat up and stared into the clearing, which was now and then soaked in moonlight as the clouds dissipated and traveled across the sky.

Needles on the clearing's floor seemed to compress on their own, though nothing had disturbed them.

It moved toward her. Her breath—surely the last of its kind—caught in her throat.

"Who—?"

The branches behind her shifted. Something furry seized her, pinning her arms. A hand covered her mouth and a voice growled,

"Please don't scream."

14

Rhia tried to struggle, to lash out at the unseen foe, but she was held tighter than a fly in a spiderweb. She shrieked an incoherent rant against the palm clamped across her face.

"Easy, little Crow," a teasing voice said. "You've been waiting for me."

She stopped struggling. *"Mmmph mhphmm?"*

"Whatever you said, yes. I come from Coranna. My name is Marek." The man let her go.

Rhia twisted to face—nothing. Only the cold wind surrounded her. She flailed and hit something soft.

"Ow," it said.

"Who are you?"

"I told you, I'm Marek. Coranna sent me." The voice was soft and smooth. "I hope you're Rhia."

Without answering him, she said, "Where are you?"

"I'm as right here as you are." He touched her arm, and she flinched. "Sorry. I'm invisible."

"I can see that. Or rather, not see it. Can you stop? Can you show yourself?"

"I don't have a good grasp on my Wolf powers yet."

Rhia recoiled. "Wolf?"

"Stealth at night. A nice trick, except I can't control it. You are Rhia, right?"

She stared at the place where his voice came from. "Why should I trust you?"

"If you're Rhia, you'd probably like some of this."

A bag dropped out of nowhere into her lap. She opened it cautiously and pulled out—*glorious Spirits, food!*

The rabbit meat smelled fresh and warm, as if it had been cooked that night. A pair of red apples tumbled out of the bag.

She moaned and shoved the meat toward her mouth. Marek grabbed her wrist.

"Slowly," he said, "or you'll get sick."

She remembered her manners. "Thank you. For the food. For meeting me here."

"You're welcome. Now eat."

She did, marveling at the tenderness of the meat. Whoever had prepared it bore an uncommon talent. The fruit was crisp and juicy, cooling her parched throat.

After the first life-giving bites, she glanced around. "Where are you now?"

"Where I was before," he said with a chuckle.

"You really can't be seen at night, even if you try?"

"Sometimes, if I concentrate hard, I can produce a shimmer. Wait a moment." He paused. "Is that better?"

"You mean, can I see you?"

"Yes."

"No."

"Damn." He let out a gust of air. "I've been trying."

"I believe you." She looked at the remnants of her meal and felt a pang of shame. "Would you like some of this?"

"I already ate, but thank you."

"You're wel—"

A cold shiver ran down Rhia's spine. Had they already met? "You said you were Wolf, right?"

"Right."

"Not *a* wolf."

"I don't understand," he said.

"I saw a wolf earlier. It was old and hungry. Alone."

"What did you do?"

Rhia said nothing, feeling foolish to have thought he could turn into a wolf. Shapeshifting was a third-phase power for some Animals—Foxes, for instance—and Marek's voice sounded too young to be a grandfather. Besides, she'd never met a Wolf, for there were none in Asermos, and she wasn't sure if they could shapeshift at all.

"You gave it the rest of your food, didn't you?" he said. "That's why you were so hungry."

She shrugged. "I knew you were coming."

"But you didn't know when," he said. "The wolf may have been a test of your compassion, sent by the Spirits. It'll return the favor someday, you'll see."

Marek's voice felt like a warm breath against Rhia's neck, even though he was a few feet away. She shivered.

"Are you cold?" he asked her. "You can have my coat. I don't need it."

"I've got a coat."

"I noticed." His voice took on a disapproving note. "Wolf skin."

Her face grew warm. "Sorry."

"I'm joking. I've got one, too. Feel."

A furry arm brushed her cheek, and she jerked back.

"I won't hurt you," he said.

"I know." After all, Crow had declared her escort to be "very good." With Marek she felt safe, but not in the helpless way of a child with a parent. She felt safe and strong. "You startled me, that's all."

"I do that sometimes."

"Why is your coat invisible, too?"

"If I touch most of something, it disappears, like me. But not if I only touch a bit. Watch that apple closely." A shadow in the shape of a fingertip obscured part of the apple's peel. "But if I hold it in my hand…"

The shadow enveloped the apple, whereupon it vanished. Rhia grabbed the air for the missing fruit.

"You are a hungry one, aren't you?" he said. "Just like a Crow." He took her hand and placed the smooth apple in her palm. When he pulled away, the fruit reappeared.

"Coranna's the same way," he said. "Never get between her and her next meal—the most valuable advice I can give you in your entire training."

Rhia turned the apple over in her hands, marveling at its reappearance. "Are you Coranna's son?"

"In a way," Marek said. "When my parents died, about ten

years ago, I went to live with her, helped with her duties. I was only ten, not ready to live on my own. We needed each other, so we made our own family."

"That's wonderful. And unusual."

"Not in Kalindos. We don't put so much stake in blood relations. Everyone takes care of everyone else. We have to, or we'd never survive."

"I'm sorry about your parents. I lost my mother last summer."

"I wondered who had died, seeing your short hair."

Rhia twisted the ends of her curls self-consciously. They were only now reaching her shoulders. "Kalindons cut their hair in mourning, too?"

"We share a lot of the same customs. I think you'll find we're not so strange after all."

She looked toward him with an odd sense of shyness. "You're the first Kalindon I've met, and I can't even see you. That's a bit strange."

"You can see me."

"How?"

"Two choices—wait for daylight, when the sun will show me in all my nonexistent glory, or try this." He took her hand and tugged off her mitten.

"What are you doing?"

"Letting you see me."

He drew her hand, palm open, toward himself. Warm skin met hers, a cheek with a light coating of stubble, long enough to be soft instead of harsh. Her fingers curved under his chin. She stared hard at the shape they created as they traced his jaw.

"You'll see me better if you close your eyes."

Rhia hesitated, then followed his suggestion. He was right. The chin was strong but not pointed. She put her other hand under his jaw to steady his head while she explored the area around his eyes. His brows were thin with a slight arch, and what felt like a thick set of lashes grazed his skin. Her fingers continued down the bridge of his nose, which tilted up slightly at its tip. Then she stopped.

"Go on," he whispered.

She was suddenly conscious of the closeness of their bodies, and feared to touch his mouth. Instead she pinched his nose shut.

"Hey!" Marek laughed and tried to pull away, but she kept hold until he grabbed her wrist and squeezed it to make her let go. "That hurt."

"Sorry."

"No, you're not." She heard him rub his nose with his other hand. "What did I do to deserve that?"

"Nothing yet. Are you going to let go of me now?"

"Not until you're finished. For all you know, I'm bald with a harelip."

"Then hold still."

She reached forward gingerly, making sure to avoid poking him in the eyes. The first thing her hand contacted was his mouth.

Her mind ordered her fingers to move on, but they disobeyed, tracing the outline of his lips, which parted slightly at her touch. A reckless desire to slip her fingertips inside overcame her, to feel the warm moistness within. She thought she heard his breath quicken.

Without removing her right hand from his lips, she ran her left hand over his hair, then gasped.

It was short. Very short, the length barely two spans of her fingers.

"You've lost someone," she whispered.

He hesitated. "Yes."

"Who?"

With a gentle but firm motion, he removed her hands from his head. "That's enough. You must be tired." When he let go of her, she felt cold and alone. A blanket was pulled from Marek's pack. "Sleep on the inside," he said, "next to the trunk. You'll be warmer there, and safer."

Rhia considered protesting that she didn't need any coddling, but the rigor of the last few days had taken its toll. She longed to sleep soundly and let someone else take charge of worrying for one night.

She lay facing away from Marek and heard him settle and draw the blanket around himself.

"It's a few days' walk to Kalindos," he said, "but tomorrow we'll get as far as the river where we can catch some fish."

"Sounds lovely."

Her stomach, though nearly full, growled a hearty agreement. Marek chuckled.

She peeked over her shoulder. His blanket was gone, having absorbed his invisibility. She wanted to tug it off of him, slowly, to see when it would slip into sight again.

Instead she turned back to the tree and pulled her own blanket over her head, hoping that her breath would generate enough warmth in the enclosed space. Her teeth chattered now that the ground was soaking up her body's heat. If the temperature dropped further, sleep could become dangerous.

"If you're cold—" Marek started to say, but before he finished the sentence, Rhia had scooted over to press her back against his. The night was too cold to fret over improprieties. She held her hand before her face. Still visible. The gesture reminded her of something.

"When you first got here," she said, "why did you grab me?"

"I thought it would scare you less than having a disembodied voice speak your name."

"I just had my Bestowing. Disembodied voices have become a regular occurrence. But why tell me not to scream?"

"Oh. That was for me. I have sensitive ears."

Rhia thought about his ears, how they had felt between her fingers, just before he had pulled away. She realized, with a mixture of wonder and shame, that she probably knew the contours of Marek's face better than Arcas's. Already her former lover was fading from her mind, which was what he claimed to want. Still, the white stone he had given her pressed her thigh through the trouser pocket where it lay, and she wondered if he slept alone tonight.

"You don't like wolves, do you?" Marek said.

"I'd never met one up close until tonight. Person or animal."

"Odd that Asermos has no Wolf people. Kalindos has plenty."

Rhia tried to think of a good reason. "Wolves kill sheep."

"How many sheep? In a year, for instance."

"Last year there was one, a lamb."

"And how many lambs froze to death during a blizzard or starved after their mothers abandoned them?"

Rhia didn't reply, since the answer was far more than one.

"I would never hurt you." Marek's voice was mild now. "A real wolf would never hurt you, either."

"I've heard stories. A baby was stolen—"

"I've heard that story, too. It was during a harsh winter. But you have to wonder why anyone would leave an infant alone near the forest unless they wanted it to be taken by wolves."

"That's horrible!"

"Like I said, it was a harsh winter."

"It can't be true."

"Truer than a wolf sneaking into a house to steal a human child. Trust me, wolves fear you more than you fear them."

Chastened, she returned to teasing. "Do you fear me?"

Marek's laughter rang through the forest. After it died to a low rumble, he said, "Probably someday."

15

Rhia woke later that night, her muscles stiff from the cold air and hard ground. It was becoming a familiar feeling—other than the few glorious minutes in the warm pool, the last five days had given her nothing but discomfort. Now her body felt heavy as well as rigid.

A thick curl of her hair had fallen across her face, tickling her nose. She untwisted one of her hands from the blanket and reached to push back the rogue strand.

Fingers bumped her forehead hard. She opened her eyes wider.

Her hand was gone.

With a mixture of horror and fascination, Rhia brought her indiscernible hand to her face again. The mitten's fabric felt cold against her warm cheek. She removed it but saw nothing. *The moonlight is playing tricks with my vision,* she thought, blinking hard.

She remembered Marek then, and tried to turn over to alert him to her invisible state. But she was pinned by something heavy across her waist and against her back. Had a branch fallen on her? Wouldn't she have noticed, even in her sleep, if she had almost been struck dead by a piece of tree?

Nothing lay on top of the blanket, so she felt underneath. Her hand brushed against fur. She yelped.

The weight lifted immediately, taking the blankets with it.

"What is it?" Marek said. "Something out there?" He sounded as groggy as she felt.

"Something crawled under my blanket." She sat up and felt the ground for the creature, who by now must have skittered off into the forest. As she did so, her hand reappeared. She held her arm in front of her face, grateful to see it again.

"There's no animal." He sniffed the air. "I would hear it or at least smell it."

"I felt it." Her hands flailed, and brushed the same furry object. This time she seized it. "There it is again."

"That's my arm."

"Oh." She held on to it a moment longer, then realized what had happened. "Oh." She let go.

"You were shivering in your sleep. I was cold, too, so I rolled over to warm us a little."

"You turned me invisible."

"To warm us a lot, then. Sorry if it made you uncomfortable."

"It didn't—not physically, at least."

"Good."

They sat in silence for a few moments. Rhia already felt cold from exposure to the air. She wished she hadn't cried out.

"I guess we should go back to sleep," Marek said. Her blanket appeared. "Here, I took this when I sat up."

She lay down on her back and heard him settle into his original place a few feet away. She tried to relax into sleep, but the cold kept her muscles tight. Her skin seemed to cry out for him—for his warmth, she told herself, though she knew it wasn't the complete truth.

Her teeth chattered again. She tried to clamp her mouth shut, but it made her jaw ache, and she worried she would bite her tongue. She curled up on her side facing Marek, holding in her own heat as much as possible. It didn't work.

"Please come back," she said, not knowing how to ask him in any way but a plain request.

He hesitated. "Are you sure?"

"Very."

He shifted close again. His blanket appeared and covered hers, then he crawled underneath to join her cocoon. She laughed—with relief at the warmth, and with more than a bit of nervousness.

"Much better." Rhia nestled against him, her head tucked under his chin, and placed her cold hands against his chest, which she barely felt through his thick coat. Marek wrapped his arms around her back and pulled her closer. She sighed, a little too loudly.

"Is this all right?" he asked.

She nodded against his collarbone, trying to ignore how well their bodies fit together. "It should feel strange," she thought out loud.

"But it doesn't." He tugged the blankets over their heads

to create a cave of warmth, so dark it didn't matter anymore that they were invisible.

"Good night again," she said, half hoping it wouldn't be.

Marek didn't reply. His hands were tight with tension on her back, and she wondered if he were going to push her away. Did she smell bad? If he smelled animals from a distance, how would her scent invade his nose, without so much as a handspan between them? And what about her emotions? The hounds at home could smell fear; wolves must have twice their ability.

But fear was the least of her feelings. Knowing that she merely had to tilt her chin to bring their lips together, that with a few slight maneuvers her fingers could slip inside his coat— such thoughts fueled the heat building beneath her skin.

"I get stiff lying on my right side," she lied. "I need to turn over. Sorry to disturb you."

Marek lifted the blanket so Rhia could roll onto her left side, then looped his arm across her waist and pressed against her again.

This new configuration was not an improvement. If anything, it was more maddening, for now his hand was splayed on her stomach, only a few fingers' width in either direction from places that begged for his touch.

They lay perfectly still for what felt like an eternity, the only sound coming from their shallow, guarded breaths. Finally her legs grew tired of their tautness, and she stretched them with a sigh. The motion pushed her hips against his groin. He let out a gust of air.

"Rhia…" Marek's voice at her ear was heavy, as if from drunkenness, and she knew for certain that he smelled her desire for him. The spell that let them pretend they clung together for mere warmth had broken. In the dark, with Marek's body the only source of heat, with her new power from the Bestowing ready to burst free, Rhia could not discern a reason to refuse the gnawing passion within.

"Yes," she whispered, and arched her back against him. He groaned and seized her so hard she lost her breath.

Rhia unfastened her coat to let his hands explore beneath it. They roamed her body as if trying to possess every inch. He raked his teeth over the back of her neck, and she gave a violent shudder.

She didn't know this man. Or did she? Or did it even matter? It felt crazy. She had never seen his face, but the smell of his skin, the feel of his hands and sound of his breath sharpened her pangs of lust. A brief flash of Arcas came to her mind, of their serene lovemaking in the sunny meadow, a manifestation of the affection they had shared since childhood. For a moment she mourned what was lost. Then she gave herself over to this pure, vicious need that obliterated all memory and identity.

Beneath the blankets they rushed to remove the fewest clothes necessary. His warm, bare hips slid behind hers, and his hardness pressed against her back. Marek's knee slipped between her thighs to part them.

He entered her with one long, slow thrust. They paused their frenetic grasping to marvel at the sensation. In the stillness, Marek passed his hand lightly over Rhia's breasts, then down her stomach to the place between her legs where they joined. He inhaled as if to speak, but his fingers whispered sufficiently of his awe.

Rhia moaned when he moved inside her, louder as the moments passed and blurred into one long perfect present. Suddenly she remembered his sensitive hearing. She bit her lip to hold back the sounds, so hard she tasted blood.

Marek's body seized, and he clutched her tighter. Her own waves escalated, and the effort to remain quiet verged on agony.

"Rhia…" Marek was barely able to speak the syllables. "You can scream now."

She did.

16

Her cries finally faded, replaced by shaky, uneven gasps. Marek's forehead pressed against the back of her shoulder as he shuddered with the last spasms of passion. Their lovemaking—could she even call it that?—had been brief but fierce, and she felt spent of stamina yet full of power.

Marek gently turned Rhia onto her back. She started to speak before a single finger on her lips silenced her. The same hand cupped her chin and turned it to the side.

He kissed her then, soft and sweet. Their first kiss, and it was as chaste as if they had spent the last ten minutes picking wildflowers instead of rutting like wild animals on the forest floor.

His fingertip traced her jawline. She tittered.

"What's so funny?" he said.

"I just remembered, someone once told me that Kalindons had seven-inch fingernails."

"That's one I haven't heard." His hand left her face and, after a moment of blanket rustling, slid against her waist. "Aren't you happy it's not true?"

"Extremely."

It seemed as if one or both of them should express regret or at least sheepishness for their rash act. It wouldn't be Rhia, for she wasn't sorry. She wanted to see Marek's face, read his feelings, to know if he wished it hadn't happened. But judging by the lazy patterns his fingers were tracing over her belly, his sentiments ranged far from dismay.

"What else have you heard about Kalindons?" he said with what sounded like a smile.

"That you live in trees?"

"True. Our houses rest among the branches. It keeps us safe from bears and cougars."

"Can't cougars climb trees?"

"Yes, but they don't hunt in them. We place our homes in such a way to make it hard for a cougar to get inside. It's less trouble for them just to find a rabbit or deer."

"What about wolves?"

"Cougars don't hunt wolves."

"You know what I mean. How do you stay safe from wolves?"

"We don't." He gave her another kiss, deeper than the first, then descended beneath the blanket. "How many times will I tell you," his voice came muted against her stomach. "Wolves. Are. Harmless."

Rhia smiled as she stroked his hair and lifted her hips to meet his mouth. She doubted he believed his own words. Spirits knew she didn't believe them.

More important, she didn't care, at least not at that moment.

* * *

Morning light pried open Rhia's eyes. Her face was buried in a brown wool blanket that covered something warm.

Marek.

Memories of the previous night spun through her head in an instant before she sat up to see, finally, what he looked like.

He lay sprawled half-covered by the blanket, limbs slack and face serene, like a tired, well-fed dog. A lock of his short, dust-colored hair fell across his pale forehead. As she had discovered from touching it last night, his nose was straight but for a slight tilt up at the end. What she couldn't feel, of course, was the spattering of freckles across its bridge. His cheekbones were high but not prominent enough to give him a gaunt appearance.

Marek parted his long brown lashes and shifted his head to look up at her. His eyes were the same blue-gray as the early morning sky. They held a wary, haunted look.

Then he smiled at her, and something melted inside Rhia, something that had lain frozen for months.

"Like what you see?" he said.

"Before the sun ever rose, I knew you were beautiful."

"Liar." He grinned and scratched his head. "You only knew I wasn't bald with a harelip."

She hesitated to kiss him. What if last night had disappointed him, or what if he only meant to be with her once? Perhaps Kalindons were more casual about these things.

Marek answered her unspoken question by grabbing her around the waist and pulling her forward. She tumbled over his body and landed on her left side facing him.

"It's good to see you again," he said.

"It's good to see you at all."

"I apologize for my transparency. They say I'll learn to control it. It bothers most people, but you seemed unfazed."

"I've seen—or not seen—much stranger things in the last few days."

"But I'm no Spirit."

"True. You certainly have more, what is the word—" she slid her hand inside his coat "—substance."

He tugged the blanket over their bodies and pulled her closer. "Want to see my substance?"

Amid no further discussion, they opened layer after layer of clothes. The rising sun had taken the edge off the night's freeze, and besides, they would allow the cold air no room to come between them. Marek's skin against hers felt warm and smooth and alive. Her own body was reviving slowly, like a verdant field after a long winter, a field left fallow too long.

He passed his hand over the top of her stomach, and she jolted. "It tickles."

"You weren't ticklish last night," he said.

"And now I am."

"I can teach you not to be ticklish ever."

"How?"

"It's all in the mind."

"No, it's in my stomach. And my feet and sometimes under my arms."

"Just relax. Now lie back and hold still." His hand inched across her belly. She forced her arms to stay at her side, rather than shove him away or punch him. "Don't forget to breathe," he said.

She breathed through her nose, afraid to open her mouth lest a shriek of giggles burst forth. Marek's hand stopped.

"Shh." He kept his gaze on her face, mesmerizing her into a state of calm. Though she lay passive under his touch, it felt less like he was controlling her than he was giving her the power to control herself.

"Try again," she said.

He moved his hand again, this time down over the curve of her stomach, below her navel. She closed her eyes and felt the warmth of his palm undo the knots in her muscles and calm the tremors inside her.

"Breathe," he whispered, his voice a balm on her scalded spirit.

A heavy sigh entered and left her, taking with it the fears and concerns that had layered themselves over her mind.

Suddenly his hand jerked away, and he swore under his breath. She opened her eyes to see him grimace as if in pain.

"I don't believe this," he said.

"What is it? What's wrong?"

He sank down beside her on his back and looked at the branches above them with anguished eyes.

"How could I be so stupid?"

"About what?" She shook his arm. "Marek, what are you talking about?"

He glanced toward her stomach. "You could get pregnant. I didn't do anything—"

"No, I can't."

"—to stop it." He blinked, then turned to her. "Wait. Did you say you can't?"

"I've been taking wild carrot seed for months. We don't have to worry."

"Are you sure?"

"Positive."

"Normally the man takes care of these things. The baby-prevention things."

Rhia gave him a skeptical look. "Not where I come from. It's not wise to rely on a man's ability to remember anything."

"I resent that."

"But you're a perfect case. Last night you forgot."

Marek's expression darkened, like the sun under a passing cloud. "You're right. I can't be trusted." He threw back the blanket and rolled to his knees. "We should eat breakfast." He grabbed his shirt and coat and left their shelter.

Rhia had no idea how to penetrate his sudden, self-imposed silence, so she refastened her blouse and put her coat back on, shivering in the morning air. More than anything, she was hungry.

When she scrambled out from under the trees, Marek was untying the bundle of food from the branch over which it hung, safe from wild animals. It plummeted into his hands, the rope singing through the air.

They sat together on a fallen tree to eat the remnants of the previous night's meal. Rhia considered probing for the source of his dourness, but decided against it. She knew enough moody people, including herself, to understand their need for silence. If she asked what was wrong, he would undoubtedly answer with a denial or a noncommittal grunt. Besides, conflict and angst ranked among the two worst seasonings for a good meal.

"I thought Crows talked a lot," Marek said finally.

After a long chew, Rhia swallowed her last piece of fruit. "I know when not to."

Marek contemplated this for a moment, then nodded. "Let's be off, then." He slung his pack over one shoulder, and a hunting bow and quiver of arrows over the other.

She followed him down a narrow trail. The sun yellowed as it climbed the sky, though the tree cover was too dense to allow any direct light to penetrate. When she wasn't making sure not to trip on roots and rocks, Rhia glanced ahead at Marek's striding figure.

He was only half a head taller than she was, which made him shorter than the average Asermon man. His sinewy physique and fluid animal grace made up for any lack of stature, however. In fact, the closeness of their heights pleased her—if they kissed standing up, her neck would not grow stiff.

If they ever kissed again, she thought, then pushed the thought out of her mind, dismayed at how much it bothered her. They had no claim on each other. Their encounter the previous night was due to her newfound joy at being alive and powerful in her body, and to his—well, to his being a human male near a young woman in such a state. It need be nothing more.

A smaller path led off the trail. Marek took the detour, which sloped downhill. He slowed his pace to walk beside her, then took her hand with an almost shy motion. If it was only to steady her over the rocks and roots that stepped the slope, he didn't say so. She smiled and squeezed his hand, looking forward to nothing more than the day ahead of them.

Soon they reached the river, which was frozen several feet out from its bank. The center of it flowed around the remaining ice, devouring it chunk by chunk.

Marek picked up a large fallen branch and stabbed at the ice near the bank until it shifted and broke apart.

"This shouldn't take long. Cold water makes them slow."

He cut a thin piece of rope the length of his body and tied one end to an arrow and the other around his wrist. He loaded his bow, aimed at the hole in the water, and waited.

The silence stretched on for minutes. Only his eyes moved; the taut muscles of his arms and back didn't even tremble from the stress of the bowstring.

A loud snap, whistle and splash combined in one moment. Before Rhia blinked again, Marek reeled in the rope. A speared fish flopped at the end of the arrow. He grabbed it by the tail, yanked it free, then slapped it hard against the rock, where it lay motionless. She felt like applauding, but instead joined him in a hushed prayer of honor to the Fish Spirit. He repeated the process with two more catches.

While the first fish cooked over a small fire, Rhia and Marek sat side by side to soak up the sun on a flat part of the riverbank covered in brown grass. The sensation of lingering warmth was a gift after the winter's chill.

Finally Marek cleared his throat. "I feel like I should say something."

And so it ends, Rhia thought, before it even begins.

17

After a long hesitation, Marek said, "I haven't been with a woman…"

She gaped at him. "You haven't?"

"…in a very long time."

"Oh." She had no other response to this statement, though he seemed to expect one.

"Does that surprise you?" he said.

Rhia almost laughed. He had attacked her with such ferocity, such a naked need, she hardly thought it a routine occurrence for him. She composed a more diplomatic response. "I don't even know you. How could you possibly surprise me?"

He looked at her with astonishment. "Not know me? After last night, of course you know me."

"I know a little." Rhia drew her knees close to her chest. "I know you're a passionate, generous man who's hiding something. That's all."

"That's enough for now."

"Is it? Maybe." She rested her cheek on her knees and examined him. "Remember, I couldn't even see you."

"You can see me now."

"Not really."

His frown told her he understood her meaning. "You will."

"I know. When you're ready." She let herself smile. "Until then…"

He hooked his little finger inside the bend of her thumb, not meeting her gaze. "Until then?"

She met his mouth with a kiss, not caring what it led to or even if it was their last. He returned it with more than a hint of the desire that had joined them the previous night. Then he broke off abruptly and turned away.

"I don't blame you." He got up and went to the fire. "But this is wrong."

She quenched a spark of shame that flickered inside her. "I'm not in the habit of making love to every man who stumbles across me in the woods. In fact, before you I had only one lover." She watched him poke at the fire, his back to her. "But I don't think what we've done is wrong. Maybe by Kalindon standards—"

"Kalindon standards?" He barked a caustic laugh. "What few there are have nothing to do with it. It's me. You can't begin to understand, so like I said, I don't blame you."

"I do understand. You don't want to make a child and move into the second phase until you've mastered your first-phase powers. Neither do I."

He looked at her coldly for the first time. "You really don't understand. Invisibility isn't a first-phase power."

A slow horror crept up Rhia's spine. It should have been obvious, a power so strong in one so young. "You're—you're married?" she finally managed to say.

Marek shook his head as he unwrapped the fish.

"But—" She forced the words out. "You have a child."

"I did," he said quietly without looking at her. "We can eat this. It's a little dry but not burned."

"When?" she whispered.

"Now, before it gets cold."

"That's not what I meant."

He put the fish down and stared across the river. "Two years ago. He went to the Other Side just before he was born."

"Marek, I'm so sorry. You must have—"

"He took his mother with him."

Words abandoned Rhia's throat, and she could only utter a pitiful mew of sympathy. A claw of guilt tugged at her, for her relief that he was no longer married.

She studied him, his body bent over the remains of the fire, and realized what gnawed at her.

"Did you lose someone else recently? A brother or sister?"

"No," he said.

And his parents had died when he was ten. That meant he had been cutting his hair over and over for two years, rather than only once. Such a practice was unknown in Asermos; perhaps Kalindons were different. Regardless, it would mean that he mourned his wife and son as if they had just died.

Someday she would have the wisdom to help a person in Marek's place, help them understand that death was only another step in one's existence. Until then, she could only provide normal human comfort.

She moved to sit beside him, wrapping the blanket around both their shoulders. He pulled apart the fish and gave her the larger piece. She traded it with him for the smaller and pushed his hand toward his mouth.

"No," he said. "Coranna told me to feed you well."

"And you are. Now eat."

"I'm not hungry."

"I don't care."

"I killed her." Marek stared at the fish, as if he agonized over that death, too. "If we'd been more careful, she wouldn't have had the baby, and she'd still be alive."

"Maybe. Or maybe she would have died anyway." The truth felt cruel but necessary. "Crow takes us in His time, not ours."

"Crow knows nothing of human feelings."

"I think He knows everything. I think He suffers with us when someone dies."

"Then why does He keep taking people? Why not just put an end to death and then no one suffers, least of all Crow?" He shook his head. "I know, it's stupid. People have to die, or there'd be no room for those being born. Death is part of life. I know all the arguments. But it's not fair."

"Of course it's not fair."

"And every night I'm reminded. Every night when I can't see my hand in front of my face even by the light of the full moon, I remember why."

Of course. She should have made the connection sooner. He hadn't been ready to become a father when his mate became pregnant; Wolf had punished Marek by perverting his second-phase powers. Rhia had seen similar consequences visited upon young Asermons in the same situation, but never for as long as two years. Once a person accepted the responsibility of raising a child, his or her powers eventually returned to normal. But Crow had robbed Marek of that chance.

She waited a long moment to ask the obvious question: "Why, then, did you make love to me last night? When you're so afraid of—"

"I don't know. Part of me never wants to look at you again, wants to forget I have these feelings. The other part wants to know everything about you, so I can figure out why."

"Why what?"

"Why I needed you—" his teeth gritted "—so much."

Rhia slid her arms around his shoulders and pulled him close. His hands grasped the blanket, then moved to clutch at her back.

They held each other without speaking until Rhia's stomach interrupted them with an indignant growl.

Marek let her go with a chuckle. "Priorities."

Once again, his cooking impressed her. She wondered if she would continue to enjoy the privilege after their journey ended.

"Will I live with Coranna in Kalindos?" she asked Marek once she could breathe between bites.

"I believe so."

"Do you still live with her?"

"No. I have my own home. It's in the next tree, so if you ever want to visit…" He gave her a grin that did a poor job of faking coyness.

"I think I will." She scraped the remains of the fish off the leaves in which it had been wrapped. "Will Coranna mind that you and I..." She didn't yet know how to describe what existed between her and Marek.

"No. In fact, I think she'll be relieved I've—" He broke off his sentence, brow furrowed.

"That you've found someone?" she offered.

"Yes." The phrase seemed to please him. "I've found someone." He brightened. "I want to show you something I think you'll like."

They doused the fire and packed the remaining two fish in ice. Soon they were on their way, keeping to the riverbank when the growth of shrubs and reeds would allow them, otherwise heading uphill to continue through the wooded area, always keeping the rushing water within earshot—Marek's, if not hers.

"We're getting close," he said when the water quieted to the point where she barely heard it. "A calm part breaks off from the main flow. It creates a sort of pool."

"It's too cold to swim."

"For humans, yes. Let's be quiet, so we don't disturb them."

She wanted to ask "Disturb what?" but realized that would involve not being quiet. Marek pointed at his own feet, and she watched the way he walked to maintain silence, flexing his knees and first placing weight on the outside edge of his feet before rolling his arches in. She imitated his stride as best as she could, rustling a few leaves here and there, but on the whole much stealthier than before.

Rhia concentrated so hard on avoiding noise that she didn't notice the sight in front of her until she bumped into Marek.

A large pool of water lay before them, surrounded on three sides by trees and on the fourth side by the influx of river water. A steep muddy bank dove into the pool from the left, its surface slick with water, which Rhia thought odd, since there were no other signs of recent rain.

A quiet splash caught her attention. A face blurped out of the water and examined them with sharp black eyes. Long whiskers twitched. The creature chirped and disappeared under the water again.

Suddenly a lithe brown animal shot out of the water, followed by three smaller ones and a larger one bringing up the rear. Their bodies bobbed and slinked like inchworms as they climbed the bank.

Rhia put a hand to her mouth. "Oh…"

"What's wrong?" Marek whispered.

"My mother. My mother was Otter."

He hissed in a breath. "Rhia, I'm sorry. We can leave if you want."

"No." She blinked hard. "I haven't seen one since I was a child."

One by one the otters descended the slick muddy bank into the water. Two of the kits collided on their way down and rolled over each other the rest of the trip, chattering and scrabbling.

"That was my family." Rhia chuckled. "She made us play games, especially when we were fighting."

"Teach me some," he said.

"Later, I will."

For now she wanted only to watch the otters and remember.

"Now this next one's rather silly."

Marek let out another great laugh that echoed through the

forest. "Oh, *this* one will be silly. Because the last one was deadly serious."

They sat next to the campfire in the evening's waning light as the other two fish fried in a small pan. Rhia's stomach and cheeks ached from laughter. She had demonstrated several of her favorite childhood games, all of which Marek lost with dignity.

"Shh," she told him. "For this one you need to concentrate."

"Wait." He held up a finger. "The sun's setting."

The last few rays disappeared past the hill behind her. Rhia turned back to him to ask what was the matter.

Marek faded from view.

"No!" She grabbed his arm.

"That won't help," he said with a wistful smile that vanished with the rest of him.

She slid next to him so that their shoulders touched, then laced her fingers with his, both hands.

"Now how will we eat?" He loosened one hand and put his arm around her. "I'm here, even if you can't see me."

"This may sound crazy, after having spent three days alone in the forest, but I don't like the dark."

"A Crow afraid of the dark?"

"Not afraid," she said. "Just not preferring it."

"Ah." He placed a quick kiss on her temple. "Now I see what I'm meant to teach you."

"Besides how to not be ticklish?"

"That could take months. But this I think we can do in one night."

"Do what, exactly?"

"First, eat." A levitating stick poked the fish from the fire, and an unseen hand unwrapped them. "Careful—hot."

Though she had learned to live with hunger during her fast, the smell of fresh food made her stomach yearn. She broke up the fish's flesh to cool it, but still burned her mouth in her impatience to eat.

"Why are you afraid of the dark?" Marek corrected himself. "Sorry, why do you not, er, prefer the dark? Was that the word you used?"

"I *am* afraid. It's stupid."

"It's not stupid. It's instinct. Humans are made to live in the day—our eyes only work well with lots of light. If your Guardian Spirit were a night animal, like mine, it'd be easier for you. Or if it were a day creature who never needed the dark to do her magic. Crow dwells in a different kind of darkness. But to work there, you need to stop fearing the darkness of this world." He stopped, and Rhia heard chewing sounds. "Am I making any sense at all?"

She sighed. "I understand what I need to do. I just don't know how to get there."

"What's so dangerous in the dark, in your mind?"

"Anything."

"Specifically. When you close your eyes and feel the fear, what do you imagine? Is it something real, like a wild animal, or is it some unnameable force?"

"Both." She hesitated. "When it comes to beasts, I imagine wolves."

"I thought so."

"But after meeting that old wolf in the forest—"

"And after meeting me."

"And you. You're not what I expected, either of you."

"We're not crazed, bloodthirsty killers. We hunt to take care of our family, to do our part. That's the role of Wolves in Kalindos, to provide meat for our people."

Relief flooded her. "You're not a warrior, then?"

He laughed. "No. If an enemy bothered to invade Kalindos, we Wolves would act as scouts. During the actual battles, though, we'd stay in the village as a last line of protection. It suits me fine. I've no craving for glory." More chewing sounds. "Hmm, somehow we started talking about me. Clever Crow. What else are you afraid of in the dark? Besides us fierce, slobbering wolves."

"You said, 'us.' Are there many Wolves in Kalindos?"

"Several. End of discussion again. What are you afraid of in the dark?"

Rhia sat back and tried to focus on her fears. "The unnameable. How can I explain? It's a not-thing. A void with no presence of its own. I feel like it will suck me into itself and turn me into nothing."

Marek spoke softly. "You could never be nothing, Rhia."

She didn't respond, instead choosing to finish the last portion of her fish.

"Maybe what you fear isn't losing yourself," he said, "but losing your old ways."

"No, I welcome my transformation, my entrance into— into a new way of seeing the world, of relating to others and to the Spirits. I embrace my new way of being."

"Who taught you to recite that?"

Rhia was glad the darkness hid her blush. "My mentor. It's not a recitation, just something he said would happen."

"And it will. Close your eyes."

She cast a skeptical look in his direction, but hearing no response, she obliged. "Now what?"

"Now you stay that way."

"How long?"

"Until I tell you to open them."

"When will that be?"

He sighed. "When I think you're ready."

"I think I'm ready now."

He let go of her and stood up. "I need to hang up the rest of the food before it gets too dark for me to see."

"Wait!" She reached out for him. "Don't leave me."

"I'll be right here, but you won't be able to hear me unless I speak. I can't stop the stealth at night, remember."

Rhia bit her lip. She wanted to open her eyes to scan the campsite for signs of Marek—the rising pack of food, the shifting of the campfire logs. But she knew he was watching.

"And I am watching," he said, "so no peeking."

She crossed her arms over her chest, ostensibly to keep warm but more to reassure herself that she was still there.

The forest lay mute around her. It was too early in the season for bullfrogs, swallows, and spring peepers to fill the twilight with their cacophonous chorus.

There was nothing outside of her.

Rhia's heart thumped against her breastbone, and her breath quickened, shallowed. She felt her hands grow cold and damp. Thoughts raced, too fast for her conscious mind to register. A whimper formed in her throat, but she didn't let it escape.

Just breathe.

Her body finally obeyed.

Her thoughts quieted, and she heard nothing but her own breath, which slowed and steadied as she listened. Her heartbeat joined the rhythm inside her ear and lulled her into a near-trance.

With nothing to see and little to hear, her sense of touch magnified. Her skin prickled, and the darkness pressed in—not smothering or oppressive, but with a caress that both soothed her wariness and demanded her attention.

Three nights ago, the darkness and something within it had chewed up her soul and spit it out again. Even fear had abandoned her by then, leaving only the raw instinct of self-preservation, fighting to prevent the dark thing from annihilating her. Yet the Spirit could not fill her if she had not first become hollow.

The air near her shifted, and without opening her eyes she turned her head to welcome Marek back to her side. He knelt on the ground behind her, then took her hands and opened her arms wide, lining them up with his own so that they were like two birds with wings outstretched.

"What do you feel?" he whispered.

She grew warm with desire, and turned her head to nuzzle him. "I feel you."

"Beyond that. Stretch out with your mind, with your spirit. Reach for everything beyond me."

Rhia faced forward again. Within a few moments, she felt a trickle of energy swim through her, with hesitant, unsteady strokes at first, then with more power and assurance, as if she had given it an unconscious signal to pass.

"Let it flow," he whispered. "Let everything within you uncoil. Feel it course through you."

"What is it?"

He didn't reply, and she sensed that the thing had no name. The stream became a river, the energy of the world flowing through their bodies. It was beyond them, and yet not outside them—it was within them, of them, between them. It had existed before the First People, even the First Animals, and it would flow long after they all went to the Other Side.

It moved beyond the earth, to the stars and moon and sun—past them even, to the darkest regions of the Upper World.

The night cradled her, and she understood with a strange certainty that most of existence was shrouded in darkness and mystery. To move within it and help others do the same, she had to embrace it as it had embraced her.

But Crow had said not to let the darkness absorb her.

"Marek?" she whispered.

"Yes?"

"Promise me something?"

He tensed, almost imperceptibly. "What is it?"

"No matter what happens between us—don't let me lose myself."

"I understand." He intertwined his fingers with hers. "Whatever we become to each other, I promise to keep you in this world."

"Even if I don't want to stay."

"Especially if you don't want to stay."

She turned her head to kiss him. The river of energy ran through their lips as it had their hands and soon found other conduits.

As she floated toward sleep hours later with Marek in her arms, Rhia felt connected to everything that had ever lived and ever would live. She knew the moment and the feeling were fragile, and held on to it with the gentlest of grips, lest it crumble or slip away.

Ahead of her, Kalindos held uncertainty, trials and further transformation. Behind her, Asermos held security, but also pain and grief. Here in the forest, on the path between her past and future, lay a dark place of peace. She would dwell within it a little longer.

18

Rhia couldn't move.

At first she thought Marek's body was wrapped around hers, but she saw him across the clearing, building a small fire for breakfast. Nothing was holding her down.

Nothing, that is, but her own weakness.

Marek glanced over. "Awake at last. Hope possum's all right with you. I was too slow and tired to catch a rabbit this morning." He made no effort to hide his grin. "Your fault, of course."

She pushed back the blanket, muscles protesting. That was all she could do.

"I'm not going to feed you like a baby bird." Marek stoked the fire. "If you help me cook it, it'll taste better."

"I can't get up," she croaked.

He turned to her, startled. "What's wrong?"

"I don't know. I haven't felt this way since…"

Since she was ill as a child. She began to tremble.

Marek came to her. He brushed the hair out of her eyes, then put a hand to her forehead.

"You have a fever. Not too high." He sat back on his haunches and contemplated her. "It's no wonder. You spent three days and four nights without food, then another two nights and a day of walking and—other exhausting things. You need rest."

"Marek, you don't understand. When I was a child, I was sick. It wasted away my muscles until I couldn't walk, could barely breathe. I nearly died."

A flicker of fear crossed his face, then he shook his head. "Why would Crow bring you through the Bestowing just to take you to the Other Side?"

"I told you, He does things in His time, not ours."

"But He needs you too much, to do His work in this world."

Rhia had never considered that idea before, that the Spirit might continue to spare her life for His own purposes. She would have to ask Coranna if Crow people ever died young.

"You'll recover," Marek said, "but you have to rest and let me take care of you." He pulled the blanket back over her, then folded up his own blanket and placed it under her head for a pillow. "We'll stay until tomorrow. Kalindos isn't going anywhere."

With trembling fingers, Rhia tucked the blanket under her chin. She closed her eyes as Marek gently massaged her back, releasing and relieving the familiar pain within.

"My mother used to do this for me," she said.

Marek's hands halted for a moment, then continued their soothing pattern. "Sorry I don't have her healing skills."

"This feels just as good. But different." She stretched, causing the large muscle in her lower back to seize up. She flinched and tried to smile at him. "Considering you helped put me in this state, the least you can do is nurse me out of it."

He chuckled. "I didn't know casting blame was a fever reducer. One of those little-known healing secrets, I suppose."

She hated for him to see her like this, hated that she was weak and always would be. Part of her had hoped the Bestowing would grant physical strength as well as spiritual, but it had sapped her reserves instead.

Marek said something about breakfast, but sleep stole her consciousness before she could respond.

When Rhia woke again, the sun's light had changed little, so she assumed she had merely dozed. She raised herself up on her elbow. The light shone from the opposite direction.

"I slept all day?" she murmured.

Marek's voice came over her shoulder. "You missed the excitement."

"What happened?"

"I made some new arrows." He held up a long thin stick with the bark peeled off and sighted it at her, one eye squinting down the length of the shaft. "More or less." He put down the stick. "Not that exciting, actually. How do you feel?"

She rubbed her face, trying to remove the mist from her mind. "Not sure yet."

"How about some sassafras tea?"

Rhia blinked at him. Tea. Did she like tea? A voice at the corner of her brain said, "That would be lovely." She relayed the message to Marek.

"We'll have to drink from the pot," he said, "since there's no mugs." He put his finger in the pot, which was sitting off to the side of the smoldering campfire. "It's cool enough." He reached to pick it up.

"No," she said, "I'll come over there."

"Are you sure?"

"I need to move."

"Let me help you."

"No." She got to her knees and stayed there for a moment, panting. Marek walked over, placed a small but sturdy branch in her hands, then returned to the fire. She appreciated his confidence in her, even if it was partly feigned.

When she had gathered enough energy, she used the walking stick to bear her weight as her legs slowly straightened. No pain coursed through her, only a bone-deep weariness that would pass with rest and food. She hobbled over to the fire and eased herself to the ground next to Marek.

"Welcome back to the world." He handed her the pot. She accepted it with a barely audible thanks, then as soon as her hands stopped trembling, raised it to her lips.

"How much farther to—phleh!" Rhia spit out the tea. The drops sizzled and popped in the fire.

"Too strong?" he said.

The coughing and hacking prevented her from uttering a word. She struggled to uncontort her face. "What is in that—that concoction?" Her eyes watered from the lingering sour taste.

"It's not entirely sassafras tea, I admit. You've never had meloxa?"

"What's meloxa?"

"Fermented crabapples."

She spit out what was left in her mouth. "What made your people create such an abomination?"

"We have no other cheap way to get drunk."

"You don't have ale?"

Marek looked like he would spit, too, at the thought. "Ale is for babies." He gestured to the pot. "Try it again. It grows on you."

Rhia wiped her mouth. "I'd rather stay sober—and thirsty."

Marek shrugged and took the pot from her. After quaffing a long gulp, he reached in his pack and brought out an empty horseskin flask, which he filled with the contents of the pot.

"I'll make some meloxa-free tea." From a larger flask he poured fresh water into the pot. "Help yourself to food."

Rhia didn't have to be asked twice. She marveled that his foraging skills equaled his proficiency at hunting. Lying next to the meat were at least a dozen roots, cleaned and cooked to a tender crispness.

Marek accidentally sloshed some of the water onto the fire as he replaced the pot to boil. He sighed and cursed.

She looked at his lopsided grin. "Have you been drinking meloxa all day?"

"No, I told you, I was making arrows."

Rhia glanced at the small pile of crooked, flimsy sticks that were likely never to touch a bowstring.

"And drinking meloxa," he added. "You were asleep. I was bored."

"Do Kalindons drink a lot?"

He thought for a moment. "Define 'a lot.'"

"Why so much?" she said.

"You mean me, or Kalindons in general? Because those 'why's' aren't the same."

"Kalindons. Your 'why' is obvious."

"Is it?" He adjusted the pot, steadying it for longer than necessary before letting it go. "The reason why a Kalindon does anything is to be close to the Spirits."

"Hunting? Eating? Making love?"

"Everything. We believe that really living in *this* world is the best way to touch the Spirit World. Not that we walk around in a trance, murmuring 'Bless you, name-of-Spirit, for that fantastic piss I just took.' To watch us, you wouldn't think we were particularly spiritual. To watch us, you'd think us a bunch of shameless sots who bear too much resemblance to the animals who Guard us." He grabbed a root from the pile in her hand. "You'll fit in quite well." He held up a finger. "I meant that as a compliment."

"You must have traveled a lot," she said, "to understand Kalindons from an outsider's point of view."

"Coranna doesn't travel, so I collect her supplies. I've been to all the villages of our people—Asermos, Tiros on the western plains, and even down south to Velekos."

"I've been there." It was the only place outside of Asermos she'd visited. "For the midsummer Fiddlers Festival."

He brightened. "What year? Maybe we were there at the same time."

"I was sixteen, so it would have been two years ago."

Marek's eyes shifted away. "Oh. I wasn't there then."

His wife and child. Of course. Rhia changed the subject before his mood grayed. "Have you ever been to the land of the Descendants?"

"Never that far south. Doubt I'd like it. One of our Bears, a friend of mine, delivered a message there once from the Kalindon Council. He said there were buildings made of white stone as far as he could see. At one point, in the center of the city, he couldn't see a single tree." Marek took on a faraway expression. "The really strange thing is, he couldn't feel the Spirits."

"Not feel them? But they're everywhere."

He looked at the trees, the rocks, the fallen branches.

Rhia whispered, "You think where there's no—" she gestured around her "—*this,* there are no Spirits?"

"Those people don't believe. They have human gods. They worship what they've created, and it's not of the earth. It's of them."

"And that's why they have no magic. The Spirits have abandoned them."

"Or…" Marek hesitated.

"Or what?"

"Or maybe the Spirits only thrive where people believe in them."

Rhia stared at him. "That can't be right. That would mean—"

"That they need us as much as we need them."

"But if every human died, the Spirits would live on."

"And if the Spirits died—"

"They can't die," she said.

Everything dies. Crow's words came back to her. *But all is reborn as well.*

"I think they did once already," Marek said. "Before the Reawakening."

"You believe in the Reawakening?" She remembered her conversation with the giraffe.

"The Descendants are proof. If people can fall away from the Spirits once, they can do it again. Which means they could have done it before. Our ancestors were chosen to survive at the Reawakening because we agreed to honor the Spirits, to keep within our limits."

"In Asermos we're taught that's a myth. We're taught that humans have always lived in harmony with the Spirits. We're not the exception, the Descendants are. They're a warning." She looked at the pot, which was starting to quiver from the water boiling inside. "But after my Bestowing, I'm not so sure."

Marek sat back and took another swig of meloxa. "It makes sense, I suppose, for Asermons to believe that."

"Why?"

"You don't want to think it could happen to you."

"Why would it?"

"Look at your roads, your ships, your farms. Like the Descendants, you're turning the world into a place for humans."

"Our roads and ships and farms are for survival."

His loud guffaw was not unkind, though it did make him cough. "Kalindos will teach you a few things about survival. The Descendants aren't just a warning, Rhia, they're a history lesson. For your village, it should be the same thing."

Rhia's weariness weighed too much to argue further. The implications of his words troubled her, but she saw no solution, no way for Asermos to undo its way of life and remain strong enough to defend itself.

"On second thought," she said, "give me some meloxa."

19

The next day, signs of black bears rousing from winter torpor made Rhia and Marek take precautions to avoid a confrontation. She overcame her embarrassment at her lack of singing ability after hearing him belt out a few tunes of his own. Rhia didn't suppose any bear would approach their caterwauling unless it wanted to become permanently deafened.

They were repeating the same verse for the tenth time when Marek suddenly stopped singing. He grabbed her arm and put a finger to his mouth. She silenced.

Something whistled, then thudded, just above their heads. When Rhia's eyes refocused, she saw an arrow jutting from a tree a few steps away. Her knees turned to water.

"Marek—"

He held up his hand, then went to examine the feathers that fletched the arrow.

"Crazy bitch," he muttered.

"I heard you!" A female voice rang from their left, uphill, or perhaps from one of the boulders nearby.

Marek's gaze swept the surrounding forest. "Alanka, you missed."

"No, I didn't." The voice came closer, its source still obscured. "I was aiming for the centipede."

He turned back to the tree. "What centi—"

From nowhere a young woman appeared, leaping onto Marek's back and crooking her arm around his neck. Her momentum pushed them forward, and she pressed her finger against the trunk, where the arrow had pierced it.

"Right there," she said. It was true: Dozens of pairs of brown-yellow legs stuck out from behind the arrow's head.

Alanka yanked out the arrow. "Welcome home." She made a slurping sound against Marek's cheek, a cross between a kiss and a lick. "About time."

She slid off him, whereupon he turned and swept her into an embrace so hearty that Rhia took a step back, feeling as invisible as he had been these last few nights. The girl's long black braid bounced against the quiver of arrows strapped around her shoulders as Marek rocked her from side to side.

Clearly they were close.

Marek let go of her. "Alanka, this is Rhia. Rhia, Alanka."

The woman's dark eyes appraised her, beginning with her feet and moving upward. When their gazes met, a smile broke across her face. "Hi!" She hugged Rhia, who tried to reciprocate, but Alanka had already let go. "Don't worry, I won't lick you. Unless you—"

Alanka cut herself off. She sniffed the air above Rhia's shoulder, then did the same to Marek. "Ah, good." Her eyes sparkled at both of them, and she ruffled his head. "So you'll finally stop cutting your hair, then?"

He blushed and took Rhia's hand. "Maybe." He tried to draw Rhia near to him, but she resisted. His curious look turned to one of comprehension.

"Alanka's Wolf, too," he told her.

Rhia let out a sigh of relief. If custom were the same here as in Asermos, Marek would as soon take Alanka to bed as he would his own sister. Sharing a Guardian Spirit made two people far too alike in all the important ways for attraction to take root. It was a blessing of the Spirits that such an effective taboo existed, for it allowed co-Animals to work, hunt or fight together without distraction.

"Rhia is Coranna's new apprentice," Marek said.

Alanka's eyes lit up, but in the next moment her smile faded. Her gaze turned almost sympathetic. She cleared her throat. "It's good to have you." Alanka slipped her hand into the crook of Rhia's other arm.

The three of them continued down the path, the Wolves chatting about a herd of elk that had wandered into the foothills after a late snowfall. Rhia studied Alanka from the corner of her eye. She wanted to dislike her, to feel intimidated by her superior strength, self-possession, beauty and height as she would a similar woman in Asermos. But something familiar about Alanka's face made Rhia feel…at home?

A feeling that vanished when she saw Kalindos.

She didn't come upon it all at once. Rather, it came upon her. By the time she knew she had arrived, the village had surrounded her.

Ladders hung all around, some made of wood and rope, fastened to a stake in the ground, and others entirely of wood. At least one person was descending each ladder, scrambling down with the ease of squirrels. Rhia, Alanka and Marek stopped near one of the larger trees. Rhia lifted her gaze and gasped.

A network of wooden homes lay above, stretching among the branches, some extending from one tree to another. Dampness darkened the wood on both the trees and houses. Pine needles dripped with dew, though it was late morning, and moss grew on nearly every surface, absorbing and softening all sound, including Marek's next words.

"We're here."

Half a dozen people stood before her, with more coming from a distance, neither hurrying nor dallying.

"Which one is Coranna?" she whispered to Marek from the side of her mouth.

"None of them. That's why they haven't greeted you yet. They're waiting to give her the honor."

Meeting me is an honor? Rhia thought. *Because I'm a visitor or because I'm Crow?* Galen had told her little about what to expect in Kalindos, and she suspected his reticence had less to do with ignorance than his desire for her to deal with the situation without bias or prejudice.

Or maybe he just didn't want to scare her away.

She tried not to fidget under the gaze of so many strangers. They examined her with the cool politeness reserved for those just passing through. Mixed with their astonishingly mild curiosity was…pity? Perhaps they had heard about her mother, or noticed her shorter hair.

Marek squeezed her hand, and when she looked at him he tilted his chin to their left.

The crowd packed several people deep in that direction, everyone craning necks to peer behind them. The group parted, and a woman stepped forward.

Silver hair fell in waves to her waist and glistened in the shafts of sunlight she passed through. Her face held not a single wrinkle that Rhia could see, and her feet moved in silence, gracing the ground with their soundless presence. Like the other Kalindons, she dressed in the muted colors of the pine forest, but seemed to glow with a light that came from beyond the world.

She moved like death itself—deliberate, fluid and unstoppable.

Rhia wanted to step forward and shrink away at the same time. Was this a dying person's last sight? Would she herself someday become as ethereal and imposing? She couldn't imagine possessing such power, such splendor.

The woman stopped in front of Rhia, who finally remembered to bow. She returned the gesture, then extended her hand, palm down.

"Rhia, welcome. I am Coranna."

Rhia took Coranna's hand and unstuck her own throat. "Yes, you are. Rather, I thought you were. I guessed you might be." She clamped her lips shut before more insipid words seeped out.

A serene smile spread over Coranna's face. She laid her other hand against Rhia's cheek. Rhia fought the urge to lean against the long, strong fingers, like a dog eager to be petted.

"It has been several years since I've had an apprentice,"

Coranna said. "I greet you—we all greet you—" she took in the crowd with a wave of the hand "—with the utmost joy."

Rhia saw nothing close to joy on the faces of the Kalindons. They bore smiles, but wistful ones, as though they were resigned to her presence. Had she disappointed them already? Or did they dread the sight of another harbinger of death? Perhaps their reticent manner was Kalindon nature, though if that were the case, Marek wouldn't fit in. He was anything but reticent.

She looked at him. His bewildered expression said he didn't understand the subdued reception, either.

Rather than bowing as Asermons would, the Kalindons came forward one by one and embraced Rhia, though none with the force and enthusiasm of Alanka. She struggled to keep the names and Guardian Spirits straight, since they didn't wear fetishes. In such a small village, she realized, everyone would know their neighbors and had no need to announce their powers.

On the whole, they appeared shorter and lighter than Asermons. Rhia wondered if their slight builds were due to their famously spare diets. At least it held an advantage for their surroundings—any excess weight would make climbing in and out of dwellings that much more exhausting.

The last person to introduce himself was a taller-than-average man with black hair and eyes.

"Finally." Alanka squeezed Rhia's elbow. "This is my father, Razvin."

The man took Rhia's hand and bowed deeply, as if he were going to kiss it. "It's an honor," he said in a voice as smooth as butter, "for an old Fox like me to meet a beautiful young Crow."

Rhia's shoulder twitched, as if it would jerk back her hand. Mayra had told her never to trust a Fox.

Alanka made a low groan. "Father, please. You're not old."

"But she is beautiful," he said without taking his eyes off Rhia, who sensed Marek stepping closer to her side. "Have we met before?" Razvin asked her.

Laughing, Alanka took her father's arm. "Of course not. Let's go home before you embarrass yourself."

"I believe it is too late." Razvin nodded goodbye to Rhia and let his daughter lead him away. Rhia stared after him.

"Ignore him," Marek said. "He thinks he's charming."

She squeezed his hand. "Thank you for everything."

He pulled her closer and kissed her temple.

"Oh, dear."

Rhia turned to see Coranna looking at the two of them with dismay. In the next moment she covered it with a tight smile and beckoned Rhia to follow her.

Marek mirrored Rhia's confusion. He released her hand. "Go on. I'll see you soon." He looked past her at Coranna's retreating figure. "I hope."

"You can do it. Just don't look down."

Coranna was peering over the wooden railing of her porch at Rhia, who clung, white-knuckled and shaking, to the tree ladder. She had climbed three-quarters of the way up with no trepidation, until her foot had trouble finding the rung and she had made the mistake of looking down to locate it.

The forest floor shrank and swelled, and the movements of the people below became erratic and hasty. Rhia stared at the ground, afraid to blink, frightened at the thought of even momentary darkness at such a height.

"Look at me, Rhia." Coranna's soothing voice teetered on the edge of impatience. "Just do what you've been doing. Climb."

"I—c-can't," Rhia said between chattering teeth. Fear obliterated shame.

"Well, I've got things to do, so I'll see you when you get up here."

Rhia heard Coranna open and close the door of the house over her head. Relief trickled through her veins. One fewer person would watch her fall to her death.

No. Stupid.

She closed her eyes and leaned her forehead against the rung in front of her. A good start, not looking down anymore. The world's gyrations slowed, then stopped. She began to take full but wobbly breaths again.

Fine. She was fine where she was, content to hang on to the ladder for the rest of her life. She would not fall if she never moved again. A certainty. Fine.

Equally stupid.

She would move. Up. Up was closer, and up was where she wanted to go. Right? Yes, up. She would move.

But which to move first, hand or foot? She thought about it for several moments. It had felt natural all the way up, moving hands and feet at the same time, but now such acrobatics seemed impossible.

She loosened the grip of her left hand, then in a panic, tightened it more. A foot, then. She would move a foot.

A toe twitched, then froze. Not a foot, then.

Rhia wished she'd never come to Kalindos. What had made her and Galen think she was worthy to confront death itself, when she couldn't even climb a tree?

Death itself.

Crow.

Please help me, she prayed to her Guardian Spirit. *I can't serve you without the strength to overcome my fears. Grant me courage for the little moments like this, and I vow I'll find it myself for the big ones.*

Without waiting for a reply, Rhia heaved herself to the next rung. She cried out in fear and relief, then did it again, and again, her voice softening with each upward movement, until at last she was moving hand over hand, foot past foot, without stopping. Her breath came hard but steady, and when she reached Coranna's porch, she did not collapse, clutching the floor, as she imagined she would. Instead Rhia stood, straightened her coat and opened the door, as if she had entered such an abode every day of her life.

Coranna half-turned from the stove. "Ah, good. Set your pack down on the clean bed and come eat with me."

Rhia let out a shaky breath and looked around. The tree house was smaller than her home in Asermos. To the left of the door was a kitchen with a stove and low table. To the right sat two beds, one in each corner. The farther one held rumpled blankets; the other, beside her, was neatly made. Rhia ducked under a large branch that grew in through the wall and out through the ceiling, then took the pack from her back and dropped it onto the bed.

The room was clean but cluttered. Clay pots sat strewn across wooden shelves on the near wall. Two piles of clothing—one large, one small—sat against the far wall next to Coranna's bed. Several bright colors and many white items peeked out of the larger pile.

"We never wear black, you and I." Coranna gestured to the lumps of clothing as she carried two steaming plates to the table. "Nothing against Crow and His feathered finery, but there's no sense accentuating the macabre. Death is grim enough without us traipsing around like bits of midnight. Besides, black dye costs too much."

Led by the scent of food, Rhia joined her at the small, low table, which sat a few feet from the stove. Soft cushions covered with rough-textured cloth took the place of chairs. A large brown woven rug warmed the floor and gave the kitchen area a cozy feel, as if it were its own space separate from the rest of the house.

They settled into the modest meal and ate without speaking. Rhia burned with questions—about Kalindos, Marek, Razvin and Coranna herself—but didn't know how or even whether she should speak first.

Finally, Coranna pushed her plate aside and sighed with contentment.

"So what do you think of our village?"

Rhia wasn't sure what she thought yet, and could only compose one certain observation: "It's quiet."

"For now. Winter still has a hold on Kalindos. Spring has been teasing us, flirting with us, but never staying more than half a day. Once spring hangs up its coat and takes its shoes off, this village will transform into something quite different." She appeared to restrain a grin. "Also, the Kalindons are busy preparing your welcome celebration."

Rhia swallowed. "But they seem so underwhelmed to see me."

"You'll be one of us once you begin your training."

"When will that be?"

"In a few days, depending on the weather. Until then, you must rest, obtain your bearings." She swept her hand to encompass the house. "Get used to living in trees."

A jangling sound came from the door. Rhia looked over to see a small clay bell. A thin rope, now taut, rose from the bell into a tiny hole in the door. Coranna got to her feet with surprising agility and opened the door.

Marek stood on the porch. He waved to Rhia. "Hello."

Coranna looked between the two of them. "Marek, we need to discuss something. Alone." She glided back to the table. "Give me a minute to clean from lunch."

"I'll do it," Rhia said.

"Ah, one of the benefits to having an apprentice." Coranna picked up her cloak. "After you've cleaned up, take a rest. You'll need your strength in the days ahead."

She gestured for Marek to precede her down the ladder, which he did after a worried glance at Rhia. Rhia marveled at their nimbleness at climbing and wondered if she'd ever zip down the ladder as if it were as natural as walking—if, in fact, she'd ever be able to descend the ladder at all. More than anything, though, she wanted to know what they were discussing. Herself, no doubt.

It took only a few minutes to wash and dry the plates and mugs. She found an ice chest in which to store the extra food and wondered if most homes in Kalindos had as many amenities as Coranna's. Certainly her Crow gifts were indispensable.

A few small doors sat in the wall at eye level. She opened the closest one to a rush of cold air and a wall of solid green.

It was a window, sealed tight against the elements when closed, but opened to provide a clear view of the ground near the tree. Rhia peered out, fighting the vertigo.

Marek and Coranna stood about twenty paces from the tree's trunk, he with his arms crossed, shaking his head. Coranna gestured toward her home—toward Rhia—with calm restraint. Marek turned away as if to leave. Coranna put a hand on his arm, and he moved to brush it off. Rhia strained to hear their words, but the wind in the pine needles drowned their voices to mere murmurs.

Marek looked up at Rhia then. His eyes seemed to plead for her to run. Coranna did not follow Marek's gaze, but spoke to him urgently, squeezing his forearm.

The wind faded. Marek turned on Coranna, and Rhia heard him shout, "What if you can't?"

Coranna bowed her head and said something Rhia couldn't hear. The Crow woman reached for him, and he did not resist her embrace. His arms folded tight against his chest, as if clutching something precious, protecting it from Coranna's grasp. When she let go, he stalked away without another word.

Rhia shut the window and latched it with a trembling hand. Her curiosity drained, she ignored the once-fascinating contents of the house and crossed to sit on the edge of her bed. She pulled her pack into her lap and stroked it like an anxious puppy.

No dogs would live here, since they couldn't climb trees and would probably eat more meat than they were worth. Who would comfort her, then, in her uncertainty? She missed her hounds, with their wiry fur and calm assurance. Here they would be miserable, with no wide patches of sunlight in which to stretch and laze the day away. The afternoon was already fading, the sun having descended behind the nearby mountains. Kalindos was a place of darkness.

Minutes passed, and Coranna did not return. Rhia's wary

gaze alit on the piles of clothing across the room. The garments were crushed together and sure to be rumpled. Her hands twitched at the thought of a useful task.

She knelt before the smaller pile and shook out the articles of clothing one by one. They were clean, and the wrinkles could be steamed out over the stove.

Not a single dress or even a skirt lay among the clothes. Had these been boys' garments, perhaps belonging to one of Coranna's grandsons? No, the cut of the fabrics allowed for a woman's figure—certainly not a buxom one, but Rhia had no concerns in that regard.

She almost laughed as the answer came to her. When scaling trees all day, it wouldn't do to wear a skirt to display oneself to the world.

The door opened with a bang.

"Sorry," Coranna said, "it sticks when the weather is humid." She closed the door and perused her house with a satisfied sigh. "It feels more like a home here already. Good, you found the clothes. They're a mess. I'm not much for chores, I'm afraid. Are they the right size?"

"Yes, thank you. I wasn't expecting such generosity."

"What were you expecting?"

Rhia didn't know how to answer without sounding naïve or insulting.

Coranna waved it off and came over to help sort the clothes. "Alanka invited us to have dinner with her and her father tonight. I hope it's all right I accepted."

"That would be—" She stopped, remembering the familiarity of Razvin's face. "Coranna?"

"Yes?"

Again Rhia struggled for the right words and could only come up with directness. "He's my brothers' father, isn't he?"

Coranna stopped folding the blouse in her hands and fixed Rhia with a kind expression. "I've known Razvin my entire life. When he left your mother he was a troubled young man, full of bitterness." She sat on her bed. "Until Alanka came along. He's changed, but I don't blame you for bearing him ill will."

"Should I tell him I know?"

"Yes, when the moment is right." Coranna nudged the pile of clothes with her foot. "I suppose you figured out why women here don't wear skirts."

"I killed it myself." Alanka grinned at Rhia over the steaming pot. "My first hunting trip without Marek. Usually Wolves hunt in pairs or groups, where one hunter drives the prey toward the other, or flushes a bird to shoot. Alone it's harder, but not impossible." She gestured to the bubbling stew. "Obviously."

The home Alanka shared with her father had a similar layout to Coranna's, with the addition of a curtain between the two beds and a larger table, at which the two elders now sat, shelling nuts to accompany the grouse stew.

"Speaking of Marek," Alanka said, "I invited him to come to dinner tonight. Even though we wouldn't be able to see him."

"He said no?"

"Said he was tired. He didn't look tired."

Rhia sighed. "He's avoiding me, I think because of Coranna, but I don't understand why."

Alanka glanced over her shoulder at the others and

lowered her voice to a whisper. "Marek's not unhappy with you. He's a loyal person, and for a few days those loyalties will be divided."

"Why?"

She scrunched up her face with the pain of keeping a secret. "Coranna will tell you, when she thinks it's time. Until then, just have faith." She put a mug of meloxa tea in Rhia's hand. "And enjoy yourself."

"Is dinner ready yet?" Razvin called from across the room. Rhia had scarcely looked him in the eye since arriving. To think that the man who had caused her mother so much pain could inspire adoration in Alanka—but perhaps he had changed over the years. Her brothers were twenty-three now. Surely in two decades a man—even a Fox—could learn devotion.

They sat around the table like a family—the young women on one side, Razvin and Coranna on the other, father facing daughter across the table. Rhia was relieved to sit as far from Razvin as possible.

The food was delicious and helped take her mind off the tension growing inside her. She took a tentative sip of the meloxa tea. To her surprise, it was much more palatable than the brew Marek had proffered in the forest. Which wasn't saying much, only that she didn't feel compelled to spit it on the floor. Alanka must have sweetened it to counteract the sour apple flavor.

Razvin was telling a joke. She understood why her mother would find him attractive. His animated way of speaking, the mischievous glimmer in his gaze, even the way he tilted his head when he told the punch line—all could easily enchant someone who didn't know better.

The table erupted in laughter, which Rhia did not join.

Alanka nudged her elbow. "Let me explain. See, the Mouse thinks that the Hawk is offering him a gift, but actually—"

"Don't ruin it by explaining, Alanka," Razvin said. "Rhia's just tired from her journey with Marek. Doubt they got much sleep." He and his daughter shared a chuckle.

Rhia's words blurted out. "Actually I was distracted by thoughts of my dead mother."

The other three fell silent. Razvin lowered his gaze to his plate and seemed to stare through it to the floor below. Coranna's face held no expression; she looked content to watch the drama play out.

"Oh, Rhia," Alanka said. "I could tell you lost someone by your hair, but your mother— I know how that is. Mine died when I was eight. It was awful. I can't imagine losing Father."

"I'm sorry, too," Razvin whispered under his daughter's chattering. "Mayra was a good woman."

"Who's Mayra?" Alanka split a quizzical look between them. "Father, did you know her?"

"If she was a good woman," Rhia said to Razvin, "then why did you leave her?"

"I didn't—"

"She had twin boys, did you know that? My brothers."

"Wait…" Alanka said.

"For what it's worth," Razvin said, "I didn't abandon her. Not by choice. I was chased out of Asermos, rejected because I was Kalindon, not good enough for one of their women." His upper lip almost curled into a snarl before he regained control of it. "I left willingly because I didn't want to cause your mother more pain and shame."

"What could cause more pain and shame than being abandoned with two children?" The meloxa had loosened her tongue, and she was grateful to it. "Why didn't you take her with you?"

"She wouldn't have come."

"Did you ask her?"

He waited a long moment before saying, "No. I didn't believe—and I still don't believe—that Kalindons and Asermons can even live as mates, much less as husband and wife."

Rhia flushed as she thought of Marek.

Coranna's scoff broke her silence. "Nonsense. More likely it's Foxes and Otters who don't work."

"So do I have it right?" Alanka said, her thick brows knit. "My father is also your father?"

"No, sweet," Razvin said, "Rhia's mother Mayra is the mother of my sons. They're your half brothers, because you have different mothers, and her half brothers, because they have different fathers."

"In my lifetime alone, I've known," Coranna counted on her fingers, "six Kalindon-Asermon marriages. Don't listen to him, Rhia."

Rhia grew more confused. Did Coranna now support her relationship with Marek?

Alanka looked at Rhia. "So what does that make us?"

"Nothing." Rhia caught herself when she saw Alanka's dismay. "Nothing but friends, that is."

A smile crinkled the corners of the girl's eyes. "I always wanted a sister."

Rhia took her hand. "Me, too."

Razvin pushed his plate away and folded his hands under his chin. "Not a day passes when I don't think of the woman and the sons I left behind. I cannot say that I regret it entirely, for if I had stayed in Asermos, Alanka never would have been born, and she is the greatest joy any father, any person could ask for."

"It's true, I am." Alanka snickered, then flushed as she realized the moment had been wrong for a joke.

"The day I left your mother," Razvin continued, "I felt as if my heart had withered within me. When I heard she had married—" he blinked as he tried to recall the name "—your father, I rejoiced even in my pain, for I knew him to be a good man. A stable man. One who would never squeeze a single tear from her beautiful eyes." He took a deep breath. "Please accept my apologies to your family. I can't expect you or them to ever love me, but I'd work every day to dispel your hatred."

Rhia gave a slight nod, trying to convey that she had heard and understood him, but that she had not yet accepted him as a potential friend. As she nodded, her mind felt sloshy, and her eyelids grew heavy.

"We'd best be getting to bed." Coranna rose from the table and thanked them for their hospitality.

Alanka hugged Rhia at the door. "I have to hunt tomorrow morning, but in the afternoon I can show you around." She whispered, "Places the older folks don't know about."

"I'd like that." Rhia looked at Razvin. "Tereus."

"Pardon?"

"My father's name. The one who married her."

He tilted his chin. "Of course."

"And your sons—" she looked at Alanka "—your brothers, are Lycas and Nilo."

A wistful smile curved the girl's lips. "I have brothers. Can we visit them someday, Father?"

"Perhaps." His face said it would never happen.

On the walk home, Rhia whispered to Coranna, "I'm sorry if I acted ungraciously, but I don't trust him."

"No reason why you should, given your family's history."

"Do you trust him?"

Coranna chuckled. "Never trust a Fox."

21

In her dream, Rhia stood alone on a flat plain. No undulations broke the monotony of the ground, which was covered in patches of bleached fuzz that couldn't earn the name of grass. The gray of earth and sky blended, as on a foggy day, yet no moisture permeated the air or restored the barren ground.

The horizon darkened, as if something beyond the sky were casting a shadow. The dark area spread like a stain. A low murmur reached her ears and quickly sharpened into a raging, rioting blast.

Before she could decide whether to block out the sight or the sound of the approaching menace, she realized the cloud was made of crows—hundreds, perhaps thousands.

Crows flying straight for her.

She should welcome them—these were her brothers and sisters—and yet she knew they were coming to take her to the Other Side. No human stood to greet or guide her, and the birds had no souls she could detect.

Rhia turned to run, not to escape, for that was impossible, but rather to stretch her life even for a few terrifying moments. Anything was better than nothing.

By the third step, the crows were in front of her, coming from the other direction. She turned to the side, and they flew there, too. Every way she faced, the flock roared closer.

They were near enough now that she saw each thumping wing, pure black in the dull light. Their beaks split opened in continuous caws, revealing angry red throats that would swallow her whole.

With a surge of certainty, she raised her palm toward the looming flock.

"No."

Her eyes opened onto darkness. The wind whispering in the trees replaced the shrieks of the crows. Out of newborn habit, she reached for Marek before the creak of wooden walls reminded her where she slept. Behind her, Coranna snored softly.

The tree was all around, cradling her, crooning her back to sleep, but she fought to stay awake and decipher her dream.

Was it her own death she envisioned, or that of others? Perhaps each crow represented a separate death—a war? Had her command stopped the onslaught? Could she hold back death?

She wished her father were here to interpret the dream. But she was on her own now and couldn't run to Papa every time something puzzled or frightened her.

Rhia turned over and listened to the faint creaking of the branches in the breeze. When she was up and about, she hadn't noticed how the tree house swayed, but lying in bed she felt the gentle rocking and understood why Kalindons chose to live within the trees rather than below them. It was impossible to forget that one was a part of the forest, as dependent on it for survival as on air itself.

Lulled into a drowse, Rhia let go her quest for immediate understanding. *The meaning will show itself in time,* she thought, and slid back through the curtain of sleep.

She began the morning refreshed, surprised that the meloxa had not left her crusty-minded the way a few mugs of Asermon ale would. Perhaps a substance in the tea counteracted the brew's toxic effects.

Coranna woke slowly and grumpily, muttering her distaste for "larks," which Rhia took to mean "early risers." The older woman's mood brightened when she tasted the breakfast, whereupon she proclaimed that Rhia could add cooking to her other honors.

After breakfast they gathered roots for Coranna's powders. As they meandered through the damp forest, Coranna discussed the practical aspects of being a Crow person:

"Obviously people don't die every day, even in Kalindos, so I perform other duties. I serve on the village Council, as elected, and I act as a judge, an arbitrator of disputes. This is common for Crows, who have a natural tendency for dispassionate objectivity."

Rhia added this to the qualities she needed to develop. More than one person had accused her of being judgmental, which was a trait rarely found among good judges.

"Also," Coranna continued, "we need never worry about obtaining our own food. The other villagers take care of us, in return for our services. I'll eat anything, but if you have any special likes or dislikes, let Marek know."

Rhia almost said, "Marek knows what I like," but refrained. She couldn't yet determine Coranna's attitude toward her relationship with him.

"But then again," Coranna continued, "he probably knows you better than any of us at this point."

Rhia gave a noncommittal grunt and pretended to search beneath a rotting log. "Will we see him today?" she asked in what she hoped was a casual tone.

Coranna hesitated. "I asked him to stay away."

Rhia dropped the log, which rolled on her foot. "Ow. Why?"

"Marek will assist me with the first part of your training. To do that, he needs to forget his own sentiments."

Rhia extracted her foot from under the log. "I don't understand."

"You will. Your training starts tomorrow." She gestured toward the west. "The Spider Woman says the weather will be right."

"What kind of weather do we need?"

"Cold."

Coranna moved on abruptly, as if to signal the end of the conversation. Rhia followed, already feeling in her bones the coming chill.

"Tell me all about my brothers."

"They're…" Rhia searched the forest around her for a flattering word to describe Lycas and Nilo, and finally gave up. "Infuriating."

Alanka's dark eyes gleamed when she looked up from the wild turkey she was plucking. "I wish I knew them. Do they look like me? Without the breasts, of course."

"Very much. My mother thought Lycas would be Wolf—his name means wolf. But they're both Wolverines."

Alanka threw her head back in a howling laugh. "You grew up with twin Wolverines? You're tougher than you look."

Rhia smiled to herself. No one had ever called her "tough."

She scooped the liberated feathers into two sacks—the vane feathers would fletch arrows and adorn ceremonial costumes, and the soft, small down feathers would stuff mattresses, pillows, and the linings of coats.

A dark feather reminded her of the crow nightmare. "Can you interpret dreams?" she asked Alanka.

"No, but I can pretend. Was Marek waving a snake at you? I know what that's about."

Rhia laughed, then told the details of the dream to Alanka, whose face turned as grave as Rhia had ever seen it, allowing for the fact that she had only known the girl one day. "What do you think it means?"

Alanka shook her head and returned to the nearly naked bird. "I'm a hunter. I stalk, I kill, I offer thanks to the Spirits. That's all, and I'm glad. Your path is complicated."

Rhia stroked the feather, flattening the barbs against its stiff vane. "My training begins tomorrow."

Alanka started, then covered her alarm with a shaky grin. "That's wonderful. I can't wait for the feast." Her foot nudged the bird. "Brother Turkey will be there, too." She coughed, then swallowed audibly.

"What's wrong? What's so spooky about my training?"

"Nothing, nothing."

"Is that why no one in Kalindos will look at me?"

This time Alanka met her gaze with regret in her eyes. "Rhia, please don't ask me anymore. I hate keeping secrets from you, but you'll have to find out for yourself." Her demeanor lightened. "What I do know is that when I met you on the path yesterday, I hadn't seen Marek so happy since his mate died."

Rhia warmed inside but kept her voice solemn. "It's terrible, what happened to her."

"I wish it were less common. Elora's our Otter healer, but when a birth is complicated, that's when we could really use a Turtle." Alanka flipped her braid over her shoulder away from the turkey. "After Marek's mate and baby died, Elora sent two women to Asermos early in their pregnancies, so they could give birth with the help of your Turtle woman. She knew they'd need extra care."

"Did they survive?"

Alanka nodded. "The mothers and babies, all fine and happy. I wish I could say the same for Marek."

"It's odd that he can't control his powers after all this time. Wolf must be a hard Spirit to serve."

"I think Wolf would be happy to stop punishing Marek if he would stop punishing himself."

Rhia decided to change the subject. "Do you have a mate?"

"Thought you'd never ask." Alanka counted on her fingers. "There was Adrek, a Cougar, he was the first. After that came Morran, a Bobcat, then Endrus, another Cougar." Alanka sighed. "Learned my lesson finally. Thrice bitten, once shy, right? Cats don't stay around. Now there's Pirrik, Etar's son. He's Otter, so maybe it'll last."

"My mother was Otter. You can't find anyone more loving."

"I know, he is. And playful. Together we've come up with some amazing games—not the kind for children, either. And if I ever get sick, Pirrik could take care of me, but—"

"But you like Cats."

Alanka blushed. "Love Cats."

"What are you going to do?"

"I figure, when I'm ready to have a child, I will, even if my mate can't or won't marry me. I'll worry about finding a dependable husband later."

"Is that the way it's done here?"

"If necessary." Alanka sighed. "In Kalindos, marriage isn't about having children. It's about finding the person to share your spirit with forever." She gestured between them. "People like us, Wolves, Crows, Swans, Otters and others, we want it to be both—to have a family with our soul mates. But it doesn't always happen that way." She stared wistfully into the village. "Too many Cats."

Rhia thought about why the Spirits would call different Animals to the two villages. Stability meant everything for a farming community like Asermos, so most Guardian Spirits there had animal counterparts that took only one mate at a time, making a personal commitment like marriage easier. Here in Kalindos, where life was more precarious, people would feel compelled to have children often and early. Just not too early, she thought, remembering Marek and his involuntary invisibility.

Thinking of how she couldn't see Marek at night reminded her that she couldn't see him today, either, and why.

"Do you remember your first day of training?" she asked Alanka.

The girl beamed. "It was only half a year ago, right after my Bestowing. I went hunting with Marek and Kerza, the third-phase Wolf. She can become invisible whenever she wants, day or night. Anyway, I'd always been good with a bow and arrow, but after my Bestowing, it was like they were part of my own body—I only had to look at something to hit it. It was magic." Alanka inhaled deeply. "And the smells and the sounds—the whole forest came alive. I felt like I'd been blind before that day."

"But your training wasn't frightening?"

"Not at all."

"And you didn't do any special ritual."

Alanka shrugged. "A prayer or two to start off, and of course the usual thanksgiving to the Spirit of the hunted."

"And the feast afterward—what kind of food did they serve?"

"There was no feast, we just—" Alanka shut her mouth tight. "Never mind."

Rhia let it go. She had enough pieces of the puzzle to demand the entire picture.

When Rhia arrived home early that evening, Coranna was packing a large sack.

"Where are we going tomorrow?" Rhia asked.

"You'll see."

"When do we leave?"

"Early."

"What's going to happen?"

"You'll see."

"I don't want to see." Her palms grew damp within her clenched fists. "I want to know."

Coranna stopped packing and looked up. Rhia wouldn't let herself break the astonished stare, even when the woman rose to her full length, more than a head taller than Rhia. "You don't want to know."

"Until it's too late to change my mind, you mean."

"Change your mind?" Coranna's laughter clanged like a bell. "The day Crow chose you, it was already too late to change your mind."

"Then why not tell me?"

Coranna pursed her lips and nodded. "But eat first." She glided to the stove and spooned out two bowls of stew.

Foreboding knotted Rhia's gut, but she emptied most of the bowl. She pushed it away and looked expectantly across the table at her mentor.

"Do you fear death?" Coranna asked her.

Rhia knew any equivocation would lead the conversation nowhere. "Yes. Everyone does."

"Because death is the ultimate unknown. Few people speak to us from the Other Side, and even fewer return. That's why everyone fights it, and why everyone fears it." Coranna leaned forward, candlelight dancing over her face. "But you're not everyone. If people look in your eyes at their last moment and see a reflection of their own terror, their crossing will be a time of struggle rather than peace."

"I understand. I must learn not to be afraid. But how?"

Coranna hesitated only an instant. "By facing your own death."

"I need to be put in danger? From what?" She imagined a slavering beast hungry for her flesh. "Will I be safe?"

"You'll be perfectly safe. I'll be with you. Marek will be with you."

"Oh." Rhia sat back, relieved. A simple exercise in bravery. Nothing could devour her soul more than the not-thing in the forest the night before the Bestowing. At least this time she wouldn't be alone.

"You will die," Coranna said.

Rhia looked up at her, dazed. "W-what did—what did you say?"

"We will journey up Mount Beros to a sacred place. I will take your coat and begin the ritual. The wind will do its part and take the heat from your body until life has slipped away. Then I'll bring you back."

Rhia's mind refused to understand. "Bring me back from…"

"From death."

Someone inside her head was screaming, faintly, as if from a distance.

Rhia laughed out loud, but the sound rang hollow against the wooden walls. "You're joking, aren't you? For a moment I actually believed you." She flitted her hand against her chest.

Coranna blinked slowly. "You have to die."

The shrieks in her head grew louder. Rhia pushed back from the table and stood up. "That's not—" She put her hands out as if searching for an object in a dark room. Something to grasp, something to hold her up before she—

Fell.

Her knees hit the floor at the rug's edge. She barely noticed the bruising impact, for her head felt full of air and water and scream. She gasped for breaths that came too hard and quick. Her hands went cold, as if she had already started dying.

Coranna sat beside her and stroked her back. "I know it's frightening."

Frightening? Rhia thought. *A rustle in the dark is frightening. A spider crawling across a bare foot is frightening.* She clutched the edge of the rug.

Coranna spoke again, softly. "Would it help to know that it could be much worse? Freezing is relatively painless, I'm told. You're fortunate—it was summer when I began my training." Her hand stilled on Rhia's back. "I had to drown."

Rhia gaped at her and finally forced out a few words. "This ritual—it's grotesque."

"It works. Nothing overcomes the fear of death better than facing and conquering it yourself." She cupped Rhia's chin in her hand. "It's the only way to become a true Crow."

Rhia remembered what Marek had shouted to Coranna yesterday. She pulled away. "What if you can't?"

"Can't what?"

"Can't bring me back."

"You don't trust me?"

"Why should I?"

Coranna seemed to grow impatient with the argument. "Because you have no choice."

Rhia sucked in her breath. It was not her choice to die,

to be born again, to have these troubling powers, to be Crow. She had resisted it as long as she could, but she would have protested forever had she known.

"Perhaps I shouldn't have made you eat first." Coranna crossed the room and opened the window. "Come, get some fresh air. If you feel sick, use the bucket, not the window. We don't want to surprise anyone down below."

Rhia forced her feet to plant themselves under her and drag her body to the window. The air was biting cold, which heightened her senses but reminded her of the ordeal ahead. She rested her chin and arms on the sill and tried to breathe.

"How long will it take?" she asked in a dull voice.

"It's less than a day's journey up—"

"How long will it take me to die?"

"That's up to you. You'll fight it at first, out of instinct. But once you surrender, it won't be long. An hour, maybe two, depending how cold it is. I'm told it's like going to sleep. You'll wear light clothing from head to foot to protect your skin from frostbite."

Rhia winced. "It's not fair," she whispered, though she knew it was an absurd argument.

"I know." Coranna's voice softened. "Being Crow is a great burden and a great honor. We must have faith that He only chooses those few who are able to withstand hardship, loneliness and the pain of mortality."

Could Crow un-choose her? Rhia wondered. If she could just get away, maybe they could renegotiate their pact.

In any case, she would not win this argument with Coranna, not in a straightforward manner. Her shoulders sagged.

"All right," Rhia said. "I'll go."

Coranna sighed. "Thank you." She touched Rhia's face and kissed the top of her head. "I promise it will all happen according to plan."

Yes, it will, Rhia thought, *but not your plan.*

Rhia took a last long look at Coranna's sleeping face before shutting the door behind her.

Her hastily prepared pack left her off balance as she tiptoed across the rope bridge connecting Coranna's and Marek's homes. She may not have even packed sufficient supplies, but it didn't matter. If Marek said yes, he would make up any deficiency. If he said no, she'd be on her way back to Coranna.

Back to death.

A wooden slat beneath her feet creaked. She held her breath and glanced back at Coranna's home before moving on to Marek's door.

It opened before she could knock on it. She stared into darkness.

"You shouldn't have come." Marek's voice cracked on the last word. An invisible hand grasped her shoulder and pulled her into the house.

"I couldn't— I can't—"

"Shh." Marek folded her into his arms. She clung to him and sobbed without tears.

"Coranna wants to kill me."

"I know. I know." He caressed her back in long, soothing strokes.

"There must be another way. I can study her methods, learn by watching—"

"You can't just grasp it with your mind." He held her at arm's length. "Your soul has to learn it, too, that death is nothing to fear."

She wished she could see his face. "What if it doesn't work? What if she can't bring me back?"

Marek fell silent. Even his breath stilled.

"I heard you ask her yesterday," Rhia said. "You said, 'What if you can't?' Marek, could she make a mistake and leave me on the Other Side?"

"With the right conditions, Coranna can bring anyone back. She's done it before for other Crows." He brushed the hair out of her eyes. "But when you come back, part of you might stay over there. And the part that is here might wish it wasn't."

Her spine went cold. "Why?"

"Death seduces. It brings peace, they say, and contentment and so many other things we spend our lives trying to find."

"So they say." She gave an impatient sigh. "But if death is some kind of paradise, then why do we all fight so hard to avoid it?"

"Good question." He touched her pack. "What's in here?"

"Everything I have."

His voice turned cautious. "Are you moving in?"

"No, I'm leaving Kalindos."

"Why?"

"*Why?* Because Coranna's going to kill me." She struggled to keep the panic from her voice.

"You can't run off on your own."

"I know. Take me away."

Marek's breath caught, then he let it out in a huff. "Where would we go?"

"Anywhere. Just don't let me go to the Other Side." She grasped his shirt. "I want to stay here. With you."

He pulled her close again, the intensity of his embrace no doubt reflecting the turmoil inside. She hated herself for asking him to betray Coranna, but she had to live.

"Save me," she whispered. "Please."

He let go of her abruptly, almost pushing her away. "Help me pack."

They scrambled for as many necessities as they could gather in a few minutes. Marek slung the pack in front of his chest, where it disappeared into him, followed by his bow and arrows.

"You'll have to climb on my back to take on my stealth. Scouts always patrol at night."

He squatted so she could wrap herself around him. After she had disappeared, he stood and opened the door.

"This ought to be fun," he said dryly, at the top of the ladder. He gripped the rungs hard as he descended, while his labored breath slid between his teeth.

When they reached the ground, he trotted north through the village. His footsteps glided over the soil, disturbing not so much as a pine needle. Rhia pitied his prey, who would be hard-pressed to detect his approach.

The same could not be said for his fellow Wolves. Two patrolled the outskirts of the village. Marek stopped when he saw them, then changed course so that he and Rhia would travel downwind of the sentries.

He was so occupied with avoiding humans that he ran into the path of a prowling cougar. Marek leaped to the side, startled. Rhia lost her grip and fell backward onto the ground. The cougar spied her, shook off its own surprise, and gathered itself to pounce.

Rhia's arm shot up to protect her face, though she knew it was useless. Marek shrieked her name.

A sharp twang, accompanied by a muffled crack, came from the right. A heavy weight thudded in front of her.

Rhia lowered her arm to see the cougar lying in the dirt not two paces away. Its gaze fixed on her, then dimmed as it gave a last tremor.

She sat up. An arrow, still quivering, protruded from the back of the cougar's neck. It had severed the spine in an instant, the same way the creature would have killed her.

"What are you waiting for? Run!"

Rhia looked up to see Alanka lying on top of a large flat rock, the bow vibrating in her hand.

"Thank me later," Alanka said. "If I see you again."

A hand grabbed Rhia's shoulder. She scrambled to her feet and climbed on Marek's back.

"Now we're even," he said in Alanka's direction. Then he began to run. Behind them rose a plaintive song for the cougar's spirit, a hunter's tune that mixed triumph and mourning. Alanka's vibrant voice faded as they ran, and Rhia wished she had had the presence of mind to tell her goodbye.

Over the crest of a steep hill and down the other side they flew, silent as snow, until Kalindos lay miles behind them. Her arms and legs ached from gripping his body.

Finally Marek halted behind a thicket of brush and waited. If he had been a real wolf, his ears would be twitching back and forth, listening for the faintest noise.

"We're safe for now." He let her slide off his back, then collapsed, panting, on the forest floor.

"Do you think Alanka will tell Coranna?"

"If Alanka wanted to keep us in Kalindos," he said, "she would have escorted us back."

"You told her you were even. Did you save her life?"

"Once or twice. We all make mistakes in our early hunting days. Alanka's, er, bolder than most." He chuckled with the little breath he had. The pack appeared, and two blankets were drawn from it. "We'll rest here for a bit. Keep warm."

They shifted together, drawing the blankets around their huddled forms.

"Where are we going?" she asked him.

"A trapper's shelter, about a hour's walk from here. Near the river, way upstream. Depending how frozen it is, maybe we can escape by water."

She took his hand. "Marek, I made you betray Coranna. I'm sorry."

"You didn't make me do anything. And you're not sorry." He drew her close. "Neither am I."

They sat together a while longer, gathering warmth and strength, then set out again more slowly, side by side into the waiting darkness.

Every time she shivered, Rhia remembered the fate that would have awaited her in the mountains. A death without pain, perhaps, but not without suffering. She remembered a lamb in Dorius's flock that had frozen in a late frost. It was stiff and gray and hard, like a stone sculpture of itself. She imagined her body's heat leaving her—the chill would start at her hands and feet, then move up her limbs until it reached her heart, which now pounded in protest at the thought.

Yet her people needed her. If dying was the only way...

She tried to calm her mind, to reach out to her Guardian Spirit for answers, wondering if even Crow himself could convince her to undergo the ritual. But no Spirit's voice rose above the storm of fear inside. Instinct drove her onward.

But what drove Marek to help her? Why did he place his allegiance with a woman he'd known only five days, rather than the one who had given him both a home and a purpose?

"If Coranna can bring people back to life," she asked him as they walked through the dark forest, "why doesn't she do it more often?"

"It has to be special circumstances. She obviously can't bring everyone back."

"But how does she decide?"

Marek uttered a sour laugh. "If I knew that I'd be Crow." He lowered his voice as if talking to himself. "Maybe not even then."

Rhia sensed that they were dancing around a place of pain. A picture of the situation was forming in her mind, and she began to grasp the complexity of Marek's devotion to Coranna. She had been either unable or unwilling to revive his mate and child.

"You would have liked Coranna," he said, "if you'd come to know her. She seems aloof, but it's only because the life has made her that way."

"Life as a Crow woman?"

"A Crow woman in a place where death is everyone's neighbor. In Asermos you would have found it easier."

She thought of her home, of her family and of Arcas. Already they felt far away and less familiar than this forest and this man. Could she ever return to her village? What kind of life would she lead without the full use of her powers? Her heart grew leaden in her chest.

Marek squeezed her hand. "It's not far now."

A soft gurgle of water floated beneath the hiss of wind in the pines. The tree cover thinned enough for Rhia to see clouds loom high in the sky, illuminated by the sinking gibbous moon.

A battered hut sat on a flat piece of land about twenty paces from the river. Part of one wall had caved in so that from a certain angle the hut looked more like a lean-to. A rickety canoe lay on its side on the icy bank.

"Winter hasn't been kind to this place," Marek said, "but at least it has a roof."

They crept inside and huddled together against one of the sturdier walls. Now that the wind was no longer stripping away their body heat, Rhia could imagine becoming warm.

Marek's pack appeared, and he withdrew some dried venison. "Tomorrow I'll catch fish."

"Thank you."

She felt his shoulders move in a shrug. "It's what I do," he said.

"No, I meant thank you for bringing me."

"Couldn't let you go off wandering alone in the forest."

She wondered if he really believed she would have left Kalindos without him. If he had refused, she would have gone back to Coranna. At least the ritual offered a chance to return to life. A night this cold could kill forever.

"Here's the plan." Marek bit a piece of venison and chewed for a moment. "We'll take the canoe down the river to Velekos. Coranna's last apprentice lives there. Maybe he can train you."

Another Crow! Perhaps she could yet fulfill her duties. "What phase is he?"

"He might be second phase by now."

"Oh." Rhia bit her lips, dry and chapped from wind and fear. She wouldn't have to die. But could this Crow man teach her everything she needed to know?

"Then again," Marek said, "if he had entered the second phase, he would have returned to train again with Coranna." He took another bite. "But he may be able to help you anyway."

Rhia didn't respond. The meat felt dry as dust in her mouth.

"I can find work on one of the Velekon fishing vessels." He put an arm around her shoulders. "We'll be fine."

She nodded without conviction. In Velekos she would be alive, but what else would she be? Could her Crow powers soothe the dying if her own heart still harbored a fear of death? How could she assure them that beauty and peace lay on the Other Side if she had never journeyed there herself?

They would see through her lies. They would die afraid.

And someday, so would she.

Marek turned her chin toward him. She sensed the intensity of his gaze, as though he were searching her face for something he feared.

"What's wrong?" she asked him.

His breath rasped in the silence as he whispered her name. Suddenly he kissed her, hard, with a hunger that bruised her lips and obliterated her dread. Past and future faded as she gave herself over to the moment and the feel of his hands on her body. Whether it was wrong or right, it was life— something she craved without shame.

They clutched each other in an embrace that was more than a pure, naked craving, more than an ethereal joining of spirits. Rhia wanted to call it love, but that was impossible. Love was kind and content, always giving more than it took. What lay between her and Marek burned whatever it touched, and she wondered what it would leave in its wake.

Despite the cold, or maybe because of it, they shed all their clothing. Rhia needed to feel every inch of his skin against hers. They lay facing each other on his spread-out cloak. She traced the outline of Marek's face and nearly wept with the desire to see his eyes.

Suddenly he appeared, gazing at her with a mixture of trepidation and the thing-she-wouldn't-call-love.

She gasped, and he shimmered into invisibility again.

"I saw you," she said.

"It worked?"

She nodded.

"Because of you," he said.

He touched every part of her, fingertips filled with fascination, as if memorizing each detail of her body. The warmth of his mouth and hands marked a map on her skin in the bitter air, each kiss or caress leaving a trace of itself behind.

Rhia ached for release, which came the moment he entered her. She felt his gaze on her face as she cried out.

They clung together afterward, limbs shaking with cold

and exhaustion, finally parting to dress quickly and wrap themselves in every blanket they'd brought.

"I can't make you leave your home forever," she whispered. "I can't do that to you."

He placed a finger across her lips. "Listen to me. I feel more alive, more of a man with you than I've ever been. You can't take me from my home, Rhia. You *are* my home."

With no words to reply, she drew him close, craving his heat, for it seemed the sole source of life in this harsh world.

As her consciousness tumbled into slumber, a thought rattled within her mind, that Marek had made love to her as if it were the last time.

A crow yanked Rhia out of sleep. She jerked to a half-sitting position, nearly knocking her head on a jutting plank.

The bird called again. Through wooden slats Rhia saw nothing but white, and her disorientation grew. Was she dead already? Was the Other Side on the other side of these walls?

Something stirred beside her.

"It's late," murmured a familiar voice.

She turned to see a sleepy-eyed Marek, and reality flooded back in an instant. They were running from her destiny.

Without answering, she crawled over him and pushed open the door. Fresh snow covered the riverbank, and the bright morning sun stabbed her eyes from all directions. Her stomach felt heavy and sour.

She shaded her eyes and stumbled outside. The startled crow hopped away, flapping its wings to hasten its escape. At the edge of the icy river, it threw her a cautious glance, then ignored her to continue its search for breakfast.

No other birds had ventured out into the brittle morning. Rhia recalled the stifling summer afternoons when crows alone would ignore the heat, refusing to let any weather interfere with their plans. Blustery days made them cavort and dance in the winds, not cower in their nests for shelter.

They waddled the world as if nothing could harm them.

Marek appeared in the doorway. He rubbed his eyes and said, "We should take a look at that canoe."

"I can't."

Rhia found herself sitting on the snowy ground as if she had melted there.

"I can't run away, Marek." She covered her eyes. "But I can't go back. I'm so scared."

"I know. I'm scared, too." He knelt beside her. "I can't lose you."

The mirror of his fear suddenly made Rhia feel like a child. If she left now, she would always remain as she was, alive but incomplete, untrusting in her Spirit and in her own powers. Like Marek.

The path she now trod was her own, not Crow's. Only she had the power to merge them into one.

She drew what felt like the deepest breath of her life. "Take me back."

Marek stared at her for a moment that seemed to stretch into the afternoon. His hesitation unnerved her. Would he refuse? Without him she could never find her way back to Kalindos, much less to Mount Beros.

His eyes grew wet. He looked down at her hands and grasped them tight in his own. "Let's go."

* * *

Breakfast was cold, and the air colder. Rhia and Marek ate as they walked. Her stiff legs pained her but loosened after about an hour of steady movement.

Movement that slowed as they climbed higher. The slope of the hill confused her.

"Aren't we going back to Kalindos?" she asked him.

His face was stone. "We're going to the mountain."

"How will Coranna know to meet us there?"

"She already knows." His jaw tightened. "She knew you would run, and she knew you would change your mind. Hoped, at least." He looked at her. "She trusted you to return, and she trusted me to bring you."

He didn't need to add, "I almost didn't."

Rhia understood his reluctance, for she shared it. Her Bestowing had taken her to the end of her spiritual and physical endurance, and she had survived, surely stronger. But the Bestowing was not death. Her lungs ached as if already straining for a last breath.

Her mind fought to distract itself. It observed the way the trees grew shorter and sparser here, and how the snow was drier, curling in wisps through the air, which held a sharp, bitter taste.

These observations numbed her thoughts until she and Marek began to climb the steepest ridge yet. They clambered up using roots and rocks as toeholds and had to remove mittens to maintain their grasps.

Finally the ridge leveled out onto a meadow, which seemed to cower in the shadow of a mountain whose distant profile Rhia had known her whole life.

The silver-white peak of Mount Beros pierced the sky, jagged and unforgiving. A fresh sheen of snow blanketed the meadow, thin and soft, like flour on a kneading board. Tiny purple flowers poked their heads through the snow, but rather than adding cheer, they only served to accentuate the starkness of the landscape.

Rhia looked across the meadow at the foot of the mountain. A woman sat on a shaggy red-and-white pony, the reins slack so the horse could graze. Blond hair fell straight past her shoulders. The woman stared at Rhia for a moment, then turned her head as if to speak to someone behind her.

Another figure appeared then, leading her own small, sturdy pony, a bay with two front white-stockinged feet. The person's long silver hair shimmered to her waist.

Coranna.

It was too late to turn back.

23

Rhia's legs felt like they had lost their bones. She wobbled, and Marek steadied her as they crossed the meadow.

Coranna's eyes did not condemn her. In fact, the Crow woman acted as if all had gone according to plan—which it had, from her point of view.

"Welcome, Rhia." She gestured to the other woman. "This is Elora, an Otter healer of Kalindos. She will help you recover after the ritual."

After I'm dead. Rhia nodded, unable to utter a greeting. As instructed, she sat in front of Coranna on the bay pony. Elora followed, and Marek trailed behind on foot. No one spoke.

They entered a path shadowed by more trees, and Rhia missed the sunshine immediately. Her heartbeat quickened, every instinct straining in protest against this journey. The world tilted suddenly, and she clutched the pony's black mane to keep from falling off.

Faced with the inexorable climb to the end of her life, her thoughts began to scramble for a way out.

I'll fight this, she told herself. *I'll live as long as it takes for them to give up. Then I'll—*

What? Go back to Asermos as a failure? Tell her people, "Sorry, I could have helped you in your journeys to the Other Side, brought peace to your lives and deaths in a time of turmoil, but I was afraid of a little cold weather"?

An idea occurred to her: Perhaps this ritual was a test of her faith in Coranna and Crow. If she displayed obedience to the will of the Spirit, maybe He would spare her, not make her cross over.

She clung to that scrap of belief as they journeyed up the mountain. Soon they were above the tree line, where only knee-high scrub broke the monotony of rock and snow. The air bit at her face.

A power pulsed ahead, dark and seductive. She wanted to shrink from it, but Coranna sat behind her, arms encircling her to hold the reins.

They rounded a bend and came upon a cave hewn into the gray rock, big enough for two or three people. Outside the cave was a flat area the size of a small horse paddock. It jutted out from the mountain to create a platform.

Coranna halted the pony, dismounted and beckoned for her to do the same. Rhia imagined grabbing the reins and galloping away, knocking over whoever might stand in their path. She and the horse would run until they reached— where? Someplace warm.

She slid off the pony's back. He was shorter than the horses at home, and her feet slammed into the ground sooner than expected. She didn't bother uttering an oath of discomfort. Whatever pleased or pained her body was irrelevant now. Her hands shook as she looped the reins over the pony's head to tether him to a sturdy piece of scrub.

Elora dismounted and opened the pack attached to her own pony's blanket. She unfolded a plain white garment and handed it to Rhia.

"This will cover you and protect you from frostbite." Her gaze was sympathetic. "It won't keep you warm."

Rhia took the garment and examined it. It was like a stocking for an entire body. It even had a small hood and veil that would cover her ears and most of her face.

"Thank you," she said, her voice wooden.

Coranna instructed Rhia to change into the strange white garment. As she did so in the cave—out of Marek's sight—she realized she was donning her own funeral garb. There was no sense anymore in pushing away such morbid thoughts. From this day onward, death would surround her, infuse her dreams, become a sacred but unremarkable occasion. She would learn to view the end of life as a mere passage to another form of existence, however final it appeared to others.

If she survived.

Elora was right. The garment, though it covered nearly every inch of her, right down to her fingertips, was light and porous and seemed to draw heat away from her body. Even in the cave, the wind cut through the thin material.

She began to shiver.

In the clearing, Coranna set up a rattle and a small drum. From a pouch she withdrew some herbs, separating and measuring them into several pots. Her face was a mask of concentration. Rhia wondered if she herself could ever watch someone die with such distance. Unless she learned to do so, the sorrow would cripple her.

She ventured halfway out of the cave. In the middle of the clearing, Marek was building a tiny fire, the size for burning herbs, not for keeping humans warm. The fire sat off-center within a wide circle of stones.

His expression was somber and shadowed. Did he mourn her upcoming death or that of his long-ago mate? Even he probably didn't know. She drew the white veil tighter around her face.

Elora watched her with concern. "How do you feel?"

"Fine," she heard herself lie.

A spark leaped from Marek's flint onto the twigs and leaves he'd laid out. The blaze was small but would serve its purpose. Coranna entered the circle and perched the pot over the fire. In a few moments a pungent odor Rhia didn't recognize filled the air. Marek bowed to Coranna and withdrew from the circle. She returned the gesture and faced Rhia.

"It is time."

"May Crow envelop you in his wings, set you on his back, and carry you home."

Coranna anointed Rhia's eyelids and lips with warm, thick oil scented with the strange substance. Despite her fear, Rhia felt a ripple of peace flow through her at the Crow's touch.

Peace that disappeared with the next gust of wind. She gritted her teeth to keep from moaning in pain. Her body wanted to curl up in defense against the onslaught of cold, but she steeled her muscles into holding the kneel as long as Coranna wanted. Even this hardship was probably part of the test.

It's not a test, said a voice inside her. *You're really going to die.*

She closed her eyes and heard, in the farthest distance, the flapping of wings.

I know I am. She shivered.

The sun had started its descent by the time Coranna left the circle. She picked up her rattle and handed the drum to Marek. At her signal, he drummed a slow rhythm, which her feet matched. She walked around the outside of the circle, heel to toe, each step placed with care as if it were the first she had ever taken.

The chant began, low in Coranna's throat. The chill darting down Rhia's spine had no rival in the wind.

The wings grew louder.

Marek looked up then, and Rhia followed his gaze. A single crow perched on the cliff above them. In a moment, another joined it. They bent their heads together as if sharing information or intimacy.

Rhia craned her neck to look behind her, off the edge of the mountain. Below her circled several more crows and their large raven cousins. Were they responding to the ceremony or the prospect of dinner?

She scrambled to her feet. They wouldn't take her. Inside the circle, she began to pace, stomp and rub her arms. If she kept moving, the birds would see that she lived, and maybe they'd leave for a faster, tastier meal.

A whimper escaped her throat, and she stuffed a fist against her mouth. It rattled her teeth as another violent shiver quaked, almost knocking her over. If she kept moving, she'd never be a corpse, tasty or otherwise. Fear filled her with an eternal energy that would burn forever. The people around her would die from old age long before she finished pacing and stomping and blowing on her hands.

Her hands.

She stopped and stared at them, flexing the fingers that no longer felt a part of her. The stiff joints bent long after her mind told them to, and much more slowly. She was losing her hands.

"Move," she whispered to her toes, and tried to wiggle them. They obeyed, once. "Move," she said through gritted teeth.

She raised her hands to blot out the sight of her unresponsive feet. She couldn't do this. It was too much like her childhood illness, when she had woken one morning with tingly feet and palms and a day later couldn't so much as turn her head without help. Everyone had waited, helpless, for the weakness to paralyze her heart. Crow had come, also waited, then left without a word.

He was not here yet, inside this sacred circle. He would not come until she was nearly dead. He would not comfort her until she accepted her fate. Until then she was alone in her battle for survival.

"Bastard." She spit the word toward the sky, suddenly full of spite. "You send your minions to hover over me, think I'll be afraid and give up, give in to your demands. I'm—" A shudder overtook her, interrupting her speech as her jaw locked and vibrated. "I'm not a little girl anymore. Even when I was, you couldn't take me. You won't get me now."

She forced her legs to carry her back and forth, though she barely felt the earth under her feet anymore. Coranna walked a steady pace around the circle, eyes closed and rattle shifting in the offbeats of her steps. She seemed so serene, so removed from this place and time, that rage welled within Rhia.

"Look at me!" she screamed at Coranna. "I'm dying. You're killing me and you don't even care. How do you live? How many others have you killed?"

Marek stared at her.

"What are you looking at?" Her eyes felt full of hot sparks that could leap forth and sear him. "I can't feel my hands and feet anymore. If I were blind I'd think they'd been cut off. Imagine what that's like."

He lowered his gaze and maintained the steady rhythm on the drum. A distant part of her admired his composure, even as the greater part wanted to tear out his eyes with the fingers she could no longer detect.

Coranna passed between them. In her long white coat, she looked *so warm*. Rhia sprang to strike her.

The circle snapped her backward as if it were a solid stone wall.

Rhia tested the edge of the entire circle with her elbows, since she had lost feeling in her lower arms now. Every inch held. She was trapped.

"No…"

The Crow woman passed her again.

"Coranna, please, I'll do anything if you let me go. I'll take all the other tests five times over, memorize every ritual." A strangled laugh erupted from her chest. "I understand now. I don't need to die to understand. I have no fear. Not a bit."

She shook her head as hard as her stiffening neck would allow. Another path occurred to her. She faced Elora.

"What about you? Healers need assistants. I served my mother before I turned into this horrible Crow thing." Her hands pressed together in a plea, though the fingers would not bend to clutch each other. "Do you have children? I can help with children."

Elora gazed at her with more compassion than Rhia could tolerate.

She turned to Marek. "It's not too late to run away. I'll bring you home with me." She pointed to Coranna. "Then you wouldn't have to see her every day and remember what she took from you."

Marek's jaw tightened, but he wouldn't look at Rhia. She noticed that he also avoided the sight of Coranna, to whom she turned again now. Another shiver came and went, then she took perhaps the last step her feet would recognize.

"Coranna…" She wanted to kneel, but knew she'd never get up again. "Coranna, I want to become what I am, not something I want to be."

Her mind reviewed the last sentence. Had it made sense? Had she even said it aloud? How long had she been standing here wondering about the last sentence? How long had she been standing here wondering about how long she had been standing here wondering about the last sentence? Now how long—

The edges of her mind had frozen. She imagined the crystals forming inside her head. Pretty flakes floating, joining, making certain thoughts impossible, impassable, like snow-covered roads. Pretty. Frozen. Pretty.

She blinked and discovered she was still standing, though it felt more like floating. She looked down to see her feet on the ground. Perhaps the right one would move. No. A while later it occurred to her to try the left foot. Before she could attempt it, another shiver rattled through her. How long had it been since she last shivered?

She must keep moving, though she had forgotten why. Maybe she had to reach those people nearby. Did she know them? She should find them. Now.

Something solid smacked her face hard. That should hurt, she thought. Someone shouted a word that sounded like "Rhia!" (What's a "Rhia"?) and the thumping noise, the one that had inhabited the background of her world as long as she could remember, suddenly stopped. Voices spoke, but not to her, and the thumping started again eventually, taking a while to regain its steady rhythm.

When her eyes opened again, she saw a world on its side—on the left a sky, on the right, a mountain, out of which grew rocks and little bushes.

It was better to be on the ground, she told herself as she drew up her legs to curl into a ball. Warmer that way. Like this she could live forever. If she wanted to. Did she?

It was all the same, life and death. She knew that now. It didn't matter whether she lived or died, or if anyone did. It didn't matter if the Descendants conquered Asermos or Kalindos or any of the other villages. The world didn't matter, not the "real" one, or the one where the Spirits dwelled, or the Other Side.

Another shiver, brief. The last one. She was too tired to shiver anymore. Sleep yanked at her, and she gave in for a moment. She needed strength to fight. Sleep would strengthen her.

Darkness.

No.

She opened her eyes wide. The sun had descended behind the mountain, casting a shadow over the clearing where she lay. Was it still the same day? As if from a distance, she heard a woman's low chant, but the drum and rattle had silenced. The sky was a deep blue in the direction she gazed.

The chant cradled her in a soft, dark embrace. It dulled the edges of her thoughts and memories, turning her mind as impenetrable and inanimate as a stone. Her breath and heartbeat slowed, until she thought they couldn't get any farther apart without stopping altogether. Yet they kept coming, each breath lasting an hour, it seemed, each heartbeat a day.

If she held her last breath, could she keep it inside her and live forever? Had anyone ever tried? She would, with the next breath, in case it was the final one.

She waited, but the next breath never came. Not that it mattered.

Crow was here.

24

If black could glow, He did now. His feathers were woven of black light, and Rhia marveled at how the light intermingled with itself as if it were a solid substance like thread or rope. Such a thing was impossible in her world, which she sensed she was about to leave behind.

"You came back for me," she said without speaking.

"I told you I would." His voice smoothed the last strand of her fear. "I always come back."

"You look beautiful."

His feathers fluffed, sending shafts of black-violet light in every direction. "Why, thank you. So do you."

"No, I don't. I probably look dead."

"I'll show you. Are you ready?"

"Show me what?"

"Everything."

"Yes."

His beak reached for her. When it touched her heart, all that was heavy turned light. She was free.

She stood outside the circle and observed the young woman in white slumped on the ground.

"I'm so small," she said to Crow.

"Not anymore."

Her vision shifted then, not away from the scene, but widening so that it encompassed all that lay around her, as if the back of her head were now transparent. Nothing—and everything—was a part of her now.

Coranna stopped chanting and knelt beside the woman's body. She anointed her forehead again, with a different oil than at the ritual's beginning, then turned to look directly at them.

"She can see us?"

"Of course. Wave goodbye."

"How long will I be gone?"

"To them, no more than a few minutes."

Them. Marek stood at the mouth of the cave, face soaked in tears. Coranna gave him a nod of reassurance, an effusive gesture for her, but he turned away, just out of reach of Elora's sympathetic embrace.

Rhia turned away as well. "I can't watch his pain. It feels like my own."

Crow faced the circle. "Wave goodbye to Coranna. It's important."

Rhia had no hand to raise, so she merely thought about waving, about sending a warm farewell to the woman she had hated a short time before. Coranna lifted her own hand

and smiled. Then she drew the white veil over the eyes of the Rhia-that-was.

Crow's feathers, even softer than Rhia remembered, brushed through her.

Peace. Light.

A bright tunnel opened before them, off the side of the mountain, where there should have been a view of the Great Forest and the valleys beyond.

The moment they entered, everything else disappeared. Not only was there no pain, but Rhia wondered if there ever had been such a thing. All she recognized was love.

It was bigger and smaller than the love between mates or siblings or between a parent and a child. It was the love of everything for everything else, all added and multiplied and found in one place. Though it came to greet her now, it had always been within her reach.

If she still had eyes, they would have filled with tears.

"Is this what everyone sees?" she asked Crow.

"This part is common to all people. What you see after the tunnel of light is unique to you."

"What do animals see?"

"Impossible to describe to a human. You wouldn't understand, any more than a dog would understand what you are about to witness."

Rhia looked up and down the tunnel. "I don't understand *this*. How will I understand what comes next?"

She felt Crow smile.

The Other Side.

It came to her as sounds she could see, sights she could

smell, tastes she could touch. All senses took each other's places, then merged into one.

Honey-flavored light bathed her from the inside out and the outside in, until there was no longer any difference between out and in.

She almost laughed when she thought of the name of the place: the Other Side. What was it the Other Side of? Hadn't she always been here? All time shrank into one moment, a Forever Now. She never wanted to leave, and took comfort in the certainty that Never would never come.

The spirits of the dead surrounded her, but dead was too...*dead* a word to describe them. Their lives had always been and always would be, here, nestled in the realm of Crow.

"Why are you black?" she asked him. "You should be every color, like Raven, to match your home."

"Black is only what you see in your world. Look at me now."

She turned to him. He was still black. Perhaps it was a joke. But as she gazed longer into the depths of his darkness, she did see, hear, taste, smell, feel every color. They were not arrayed in a twisting, dancing rainbow—the way Raven had appeared to her before the Bestowing—but rather they each lay behind and pulsed through the others. All colors were one in black, just as all spirits were one in this place.

The oneness was interrupted suddenly, by a figure in the corner of her vision. A little girl.

Rhia.

She whispered her own name as though it belonged to someone else.

"Why am I here already?" she asked Crow.

"You left part of yourself behind when you almost died before."

She watched the girl run and cartwheel among invisible hills, as confident as a colt. "Is that why I've been weak ever since?"

"Perhaps."

"May I take her back?"

"Ask her."

She could not move. Instead she willed the child to approach her, which she did, unafraid. Her long red hair glinted in sunlight too earthly for this place. The Rhia-that-was stared at the Rhia-that-is with somber green eyes.

"I've been waiting," the child said.

"I'm sorry."

The younger Rhia smiled. A front tooth was missing. "I like it here."

"Me, too."

"Can you stay?"

Rhia cast a secretive glance at Crow. Maybe if they asked very politely...

He cocked His head as if hearing a far-off call. "It's time to go. They need you."

"Who?" She didn't know anyone. Or rather, she knew everyone and everything, but no one and nothing in particular.

"Your people."

"I'm needed here."

"Not yet." Crow turned his back. "Please follow me."

"No! I want to stay." The child's presence goaded Rhia's own petulance. "I need to stay."

"You'll be back someday to stay forever. Until then—"

"Please." If she had knees, she would kneel. If she had hands, she would clutch Crow's feathers in supplication. "There must be lost souls who need shepherding, souls who can't find their way to the Other Side. I can help them. I can help you. Here."

Crow turned to her slowly, revealing a look as desperate as she felt.

"I need you to return."

Rhia met His gaze and felt her will relent. "Why?"

His eyes darkened from midnight blue to a piercing black. "Another time of conflict approaches, a time when death will fall from the sky like hail."

Rhia absorbed His words with a calm that surprised her. What Crow spoke of was distant and impossible, like the spooky stories the elders would tell children around the campfire at Harvest Festivals, tales of rage and chaos in the times before the so-called Reawakening. In this place, she could imagine no trouble touching her or anyone she knew.

She looked at the little girl's outstretched hand and felt her flow into her own being.

She had to learn to trust Crow. And herself.

"Bring me back."

Crow bowed. "Until next time." With a great thumping of wings, He took off, leaving her behind.

A heavy weight threw her into darkness. Cold air swiped her face. She struggled for breath, lungs pierced with pain, and realized that the heavy weight was her own body.

A voice called her name from far away.

Marek.

She tried to open her eyes, twitch her fingers, any signal to show she was there.

Help me.

Coranna's chants thrummed the air, as they had before Rhia had died. All of this was her death in reverse—the cold, the chants, Marek calling her name.

Except for the pain. Death hadn't hurt like this.

Panic seized her body as she fought for the first breath. Her heart wanted to beat, was promising to pump life again, but demanded air as ransom. Her lungs seemed to be waiting for her heart to start first. Neither wanted to grant life, for they were each too cold to try.

Come back, she cried to Crow. *I'm trapped in a body that doesn't work. It's too late to live. Let me die.*

No response.

Please. It hurts.

"Rhia." Coranna spoke at her ear. "Welcome back."

No!

"You're going to live," she said. "Your body will wake up soon."

"How soon?" Marek asked.

"Be patient." Elora's voice came from farther away. "If she comes back too fast…"

"Shh." Coranna spoke with a level voice. "She can hear your doubts, which are quite unnecessary. Right now we need to give her spirit time to remember what it's like to live."

I don't want to live. I want to go home.

"What if she doesn't want to live?" he said. "What if she's suffering? If Rhia can hear us, then she's aware, which means she knows she can't breathe. Doesn't that hurt?"

Yes.

"No," Coranna said.

What?

Coranna must know what this is like, Rhia thought. *Maybe she's lying to keep Marek calm. But what about me? Am I not supposed to suffer? Is something wrong?*

"Let me talk to her," Marek said.

There was a sigh, then a shuffling of feet and cloth. Marek's voice came closer.

"Rhia, you may not know it, but I'm holding your hand. Please come back so you can feel it again." He steadied his voice. "All I want is to lie next to you and bring you to life. But I can't yet. Elora says we can't warm you too fast or you'll die again, maybe for good this time. Coranna's never brought anyone back twice.

"Just live. The rest will follow, but you have to want it." He leaned closer. "I won't let you not want it."

Rhia's mind cried out to him, uncertain whether it was to call him closer or push him away. It was like shouting through a mouthful of dust.

He spoke to Coranna. "What's it like, the place where she was?"

After a long pause, she replied, "The details change for each person, but most experience it as a place of light and acceptance."

"She must have loved it. She hates the dark." He spoke to Rhia again. "Remember what I taught you that night, about the energy that flows between you and me and everything? It's here in this world, too."

She felt a pressure against her chest, and didn't know

whether it came from inside or outside her skin. Had her heart beat, or had Marek touched her?

Regardless, it meant she would stay.

Breaths came at last, shallow and slow, and each one brought immeasurable pain, as if the air were filled with tiny daggers. Rhia wanted to cry but had no tears, to scream but had no voice.

She was wrapped tight inside something thick and soft that protected her body from the ground, which no longer stole her heat. The wind did not touch her here, so they must have moved her inside the cave.

She hated breathing, but forced herself to continue. The others waited in silence around her. She wished they would chatter about anything, to distract her from the pain and the laborious struggle for life.

Perhaps they slept. She couldn't wait to sleep. She couldn't wait to move, to eat, to drink. To live.

So she did want to live, after all. Though it wasn't as good as death—nothing ever would be, she knew now—life would surpass this paralysis that evoked the weakness that had depleted her many years before. Her strength had never returned in full, and for that she was bitter even to this moment. If only she were stronger, she would have recovered by now. Instead she was causing these people to sit in a chilly cave overnight waiting for her to get around to living.

Serves them right, she thought.

A giggle bottled up inside her and finally escaped in a tiny burst of noise. Inside Rhia's head it sounded like a hiccup, which made her want to laugh more. A panicky delirium took hold.

Someone drew near and pressed a fingertip to the side of Rhia's neck, calming her. She felt her own pulse greet the person's touch.

"It's stronger now," Elora said. "Steadier."

"So she lives," Marek whispered. "If she hadn't—"

"She does," Coranna said. "She will."

Marek was silent for several moments. "Forgive my lack of faith." His voice held true contrition. "I shouldn't have doubted you."

"You have every right to doubt me," Coranna said softly.

Elora held the back of her hand to Rhia's forehead. "She's still cold. It will be a long night." She tugged the blanket tighter. "Perhaps you two should sleep."

"No," Marek and Coranna said together.

Something inside Rhia thawed and cracked like a river in springtime. The worst pain yet, but it was a relief. If she hurt, she lived.

"Then one of you heat some rocks on that fire," Elora said. "Soon it will be time to add warmth to her body."

"I'll do it." Marek scooted out of the cave. Rhia imagined him ducking to avoid hitting his head on the ceiling. By now he would be invisible, so she did not try to open her eyes.

Scraps of memory flitted through Rhia's mind, the hours before Crow had come to take her away. She remembered pacing, fuming and—

What had she said to them? In desperation she had raged, begged for her life, gone any way but gracefully to her death. The shame flowed through her like the blood that slowly returned to her limbs.

She had been a coward, of course.

A horrible memory, clear as rain now, replayed her last words to Marek, about Coranna: *You wouldn't have to see her every day and remember what she took from you.* She remembered the pain that crossed his face and made him turn his eyes away from both of them.

And Coranna—surely those words had pierced her as well. Rhia curled up inside herself and dreaded her return to life.

But life was coming. When Elora pulled Rhia's arm out of the bundle and checked her wrist for a pulse, she felt the healer's soft hands, though at a distance, as if her own skin were several inches thick.

"Bring the stones," Elora said. "The blood is starting to flow to her limbs. If this happens too fast, the cold, stagnant blood from her arms and legs will flood to the rest of the body and drop her temperature again."

Rhia felt alarm. Could she die again? She had so many questions, but her throat was too cold to speak.

And getting colder. Her heart began to skip beats— thumping fast, then not at all, then fast again. Her breath rattled.

"Hurry!" Elora said. Rhia was turned on her back, her other arm released from the bundle. Warm, hard objects were placed under her armpits and at the base of her neck.

"What's happening?" Marek sat close to Rhia's head. She wanted to reach for him, for the warmth he had given her those cold nights in the forest.

"She's dropping," Elora said in a clipped voice. "I'll need to do a spell."

"Dropping? What's that?"

"Marek, come here." Coranna snapped her fingers. "Give her room. Elora, do you need anything?"

"Only silence."

No, not silence, Rhia thought. She needed to hear voices, needed to grasp something from this world.

Elora laid her hands on either side of Rhia's pelvis, paused for a moment, and began to chant.

The roiling, high-pitched song went straight to Rhia's blood, infusing it with a warmth that traveled up one side of her torso and down the other. Unlike Coranna's low, soothing intonation that called the spirit out of the body, this chant shocked and invigorated. Elora sang of the summer sun, and the yellow-white orb itself seemed to journey through Rhia's body, stopping at the places where her legs joined her hips.

The healer repeated the action at Rhia's shoulders, then at the base of her throat, until her chest and abdomen felt almost normal. Her heartbeat was steady now, without skips and jumps, and her breath came with a reassuring regularity. Warmth leaked slowly into her arms, legs and head, this time without the sensation of cold flowing back to her body.

She opened her eyes.

Marek whispered her name from a few feet away.

"Wait," Elora said. She appeared in Rhia's view, and even in the low glow of the fire, her eyes shone with concern. "Can you speak?"

Rhia blinked and opened her parched mouth. Her tongue felt like a dead leaf.

"Here, some water." Elora held a wet cloth to Rhia's lips and dabbed the inside of her mouth.

"Thank you," Rhia whispered. Her voice sounded hollow. "I almost died, didn't I? Just now?"

Elora raised an eyebrow. "Not on my watch, little woman." She twisted behind her to pick up a flask. "Can you swallow some honey water?"

Rhia tried to nod, but the most she could manage was a twitch. "Yes."

Elora removed the warm rocks from her neck and her right armpit. "Marek, help me turn her on her side for a moment."

Unseen hands took hold of her left shoulder and hip and eased them forward. Her hand hit the ground with a thud as the dead weight of her arm dropped. Elora tilted the flask and let a few drops spill into Rhia's mouth. She swallowed one of the drops, as the rest dribbled out the side of her mouth. After she had consumed two or three swallows of the warm, sweet liquid, they laid her on her back again.

As she spoke, Elora drew the blanket tighter around Rhia and tucked it under her chin. "Sleep now. I'll wake you for more honey water. Your body needs fuel for strength. By morning you'll have your limbs back." She patted Rhia's hand. "Won't that be nice?"

Rhia managed to smile, although to an outsider it may have looked more like a grimace.

Marek cleared his throat. "Elora, may I…"

"It's safe now." The healer's face showed doubt. "But ask her first."

A hand brushed a lock of hair from Rhia's face. "Rhia," Marek said, "would it be all right if I lay next to you? To give you more warmth."

She wanted that more than anything, but feared to admit

it. He would have left behind everything he knew to save her life, if she had only asked. And in return for his devotion, she had assailed him with more fury than she knew she possessed. How could he forgive her so easily?

She turned her head to look at Coranna. The older woman's hair glistened in the firelight as she leaned forward to speak.

"When someone's freezing to death," she said, "they become irrational. They say things they don't mean. I warned Marek ahead of time, so let him help you. Don't be silly."

Rhia looked straight up where she thought Marek's face would be. "Do it."

He nestled beside her and tugged another blanket over their bodies. He pulled her tight against him and drew his leg across hers, surrounding her like fog around a mountain. His warmth seeped into her, carrying blood and life to her most remote and desolate regions.

The Kalindon throng that mobbed Rhia upon her return two days later could not be the same subdued folks she had left behind.

They were wild.

When they reached her, the shouting crowd lifted her off her pony onto their shoulders. She wobbled with a strange sense of weightlessness and looked back at Marek.

"Enjoy!" he said with a wave of the hand.

Singing and laughing, they carried her to a clearing in the woods where a bonfire burned, surrounded by smaller fires which cooked a variety of meats. Her mouth watered at the scents. After two days of honey water and dried fruit, she'd happily eat a porcupine, quills and all, with a side of roasted pine bark. Or maybe just a side of more porcupine.

She noticed that none of the food had been touched. A long table sat off to the right of the fire, filled with dishes of fruits and nuts and berries. Her stomach would have growled if it weren't lurching with the rest of her.

Alanka scurried up holding a bundle of cloth. "Wait, wait, wait, everyone. You can't expect the guest of honor to preside looking like that." She gestured to Rhia's appearance. The villagers groaned with impatience as they set her down. "You've waited three days to eat," Alanka said to them, "you can wait a few more minutes. Now stay here."

She yanked Rhia through the crowd to a dense growth of shrubs. When they were hidden from sight, she tugged at the ties on Rhia's trousers. "Take those off."

"What did you mean, they've waited three days to eat?"

"We've been fasting since you left." At Rhia's surprised gaze, she said, "In solidarity, of course. Plus, it helped us save up extra food. And appetite."

"You all knew." Rhia slowly unfastened her trousers. "You all knew I was going to die."

Alanka cringed. "I'm so sorry. Coranna told us when Marek left to meet you after your Bestowing. I wanted to tell you, but she said it would only make it worse. Will you forgive me?"

Rhia couldn't bear for the moment to turn somber. "That depends on what you're planning to dress me in."

With a flourish and a grin, Alanka held forth a long gown of the darkest, most vibrant violet Rhia had ever seen outside of wildflowers. The velvet material sifted through her fingers like the lushest spring grass. A moan of admiration escaped her lips.

"I'm to wear this?"

Alanka cocked her head. "No, you're to scrub pots with it."

"But I thought women here only wore trousers."

"Then it must be a special occasion." She waggled the dress. "Put it on, we're starving."

Rhia shed her clothes, then sighed as Alanka slid the dress over her head. Her friend tied the strings in the back, and the garment tightened to accentuate Rhia's few curves. A short, flowing cape hung from the back of the gown, making her feel like she bore a set of light, graceful wings. The garment provided just the right amount of warmth for the spring day, as the sleeves extended to her wrists and the neckline to her collarbone.

Alanka let out a low whistle. "I'm not sure I should bring you out there."

"Why? Does it look bad?"

"It does not look bad. But if you go out there, the men may never spare me another glance." She tilted her head. "Ehh, I could use the rest. Let's do your hair."

Rhia sat on a stone while Alanka braided her hair in an elegant looping style. Soon she was ready—at least on the outside.

Coranna's voice came from the other side of the brush pile. "Shall we go?"

Rhia hesitated, so Alanka turned her toward the village and gave her a little shove. As she stepped into sight, Coranna took her hand and led her toward the bonfire. The crowd quieted. They parted to let her pass, heads half-bowed, almost as if they would drop to their knees. Rhia prayed they wouldn't.

The two Crow women approached the long table and stood at its head. Coranna drew herself up to her full, intimidating height and held out her hands to the crowd.

"Thank you for all your efforts, both physical and spiritual, on behalf of my new protégé. It pleases me to tell you that she completed the ritual with courage and serenity."

Rhia kept her face neutral as the crowd whooped and clapped. She didn't want to show pride in the lie or embarrass Coranna by displaying a dubious expression.

When the applause subsided, Coranna said, "Her magic and wisdom will serve all of us, but remember that she is still learning to use her powers, as, in a way, we all are. I present to you Crow's new gift to our people—Rhia of Asermos."

Instead of cheering, they all stared at Rhia with expectation. Was she supposed to perform magic for them? Sing a song about her trip to the Other Side and back?

Coranna leaned over and whispered to the top of Rhia's head. "Speak now."

Her heart went cold, almost as cold as when she died. "I have to give a speech?"

Coranna patted her shoulder. "Make them glad their deaths may be in your hands."

Rhia slowly turned back to the crowd. The glare of the torchlight in her eyes let her see only the closest people, none of whom she recognized. She resisted the urge to twist her hair.

Suddenly she understood: When they looked at her, they didn't see a once-crippled child scared of shadows, but rather a powerful woman who had undergone heroic tests proving her worthiness.

"Thank you," she said. They seemed to like that, so she said it again. "Thank you for accepting me into your midst. I hope to learn much from you and—and be a source of goodwill—of continuing goodwill—between Kalindos and Asermos.

"Though our cultures differ, we are all connected to the Spirits who bless our people with a world of beauty and power, which they share by granting each of us the magic and wisdom of one of their creatures."

She glanced at Coranna, who returned a look of encouragement.

"My Guardian Spirit," she continued, "is Crow, whom many dread and fear worse than any predator, for His embrace is everlasting." *More or less,* she reminded herself. "But know that you will not leave this life alone. And believe me when I tell you that a beautiful world lies beyond."

The faces dropped at the suggestion, and she realized that this line of rhetoric might be morbid for such a gathering. A mug lay on the table near her hand. She raised it and said, "But tonight, let us celebrate life and all its gifts."

The crowd cheered, and everyone who could reach a mug lifted it high and drank with her. It was a testament to her new fortitude that she did not spew out the nearly pure meloxa before or after it trickled down her throat.

The music struck up again, though at a more leisurely pace than before, and the food was brought forth. Rhia sat at the head of the long table with Coranna, the other six members of the village Council—including Alanka's father Razvin—and their mates or spouses. The younger folks who weren't serving food lounged around the bonfire, laughing and jostling for space. She wished she could join them—a wish that disappeared when she realized that her table would start eating first.

Some foods she recognized, others not, but all of it was tasty and served with enthusiasm. She gave a grateful smile to the observant young man who deposited a flask of water next to her plate; he must have noticed she wasn't washing down her meal with meloxa. He returned the smile, which warmed her insides even more than the food and drink.

Her dress tightened as she ate, and she tugged at the unyielding fabric at her waist. The tautness forced her into a straight posture, in contrast to the figures around her slouched over their meals and drinks, leaning to hear each other's words amid the din.

Coranna introduced the man to her right as Etar the Owl, one of the seven Council members. Rhia recognized him as the father of Alanka's mate Pirrik, but decided not to mention it in case Etar wasn't aware of their relationship. Not that one could hide anything from an Owl.

"What do you think of Kalindos, Rhia?" Etar asked.

"It's beautiful. Er—" She glanced at the cavorting around the bonfire. "Startling."

"It's no place for people our age. Right, Coranna?"

"Speak for yourself, old man." Coranna tugged his long gray ponytail. Rhia sensed the two shared more than friendship.

"My bones aren't what they used to be." Etar gave an exaggerated wince as he crushed an acorn against the table with a small rock. "Some days I can't bear the thought of climbing out of my own house. 'Down' is a lot harder on the knees than 'up.'" He picked the meat out of the nut. "Nonetheless, days like today make it all worthwhile."

"Do you have such celebrations often?" Rhia asked.

"We hold feasts when people enter or leave this world," Coranna said.

"You did both in one day." Etar held up his mug in salute. "So the party is twice as big."

Coranna turned to him. "She almost died again after I brought her back."

He regarded Rhia with keen interest. "What was that like?"

Again, she couldn't lie, not to an Owl. "I was terrified the second time, before Elora saved me. But when I died the first time, I was so cold, it was as if my feelings were frozen, too. I didn't care if I lived."

"It's Crow's blessing," Coranna said. "Allowing us to leave our bodies without fear or pain. After the initial struggle, we become numb." She shifted the food on her plate without eating it. "When I drowned, it hurt at first, the water crushing me from the inside. I swore I wouldn't fight it, but I did. I battled for every breath I couldn't get."

The surrounding crowd was raucous, but the three of them sat in a bubble of silence.

"Once I gave in," Coranna continued, "everything began to sparkle. I was so enthralled with the sunlight dancing above me, I didn't notice the darkness creeping in, until suddenly it was all I could see. Then it was over and Crow was there." Her eyes met Rhia's with intimate understanding.

"So tell me." Etar leaned across the table to speak low to them. "How long do you think I have to live?"

Rhia blanched at the impropriety, but Coranna's laugh rang out. "Etar, I've told you, we won't play this game."

"Give Rhia a chance," he said. "Besides, I've drunk so much meloxa, whatever she tells me I won't remember tomorrow."

"But without an illness or injury—" Rhia looked at Coranna "—how can I tell how long he'll live?"

"You can't predict an accident. Those things don't lurk inside people." She leaned back in her chair and gestured to Etar's body. "But sicknesses do, even when people feel well."

"You want me to tell him when he'll die?" It went against everything Galen had taught her.

Coranna eyed her neutrally. "It's up to you. He wants you to see, and I won't stop you."

"But you're both drunk."

"Don't be so stodgy, Rhia." Coranna waved her mug, holding the handle with one finger. She placed Rhia's hand on Etar's arm. "It helps if you touch him."

Rhia gulped. With all her remaining courage, she took her hand off his arm. "No. I won't do it."

"Just as well. I like a little mystery in my life, anyway." Etar rose to his feet with a grunt. "I need to stretch these old bones. Coranna, want to take a walk with me?" A passing server offered him a fresh mug of meloxa, which he accepted with a smile.

"I'd love to." The crone tossed her hair like a young girl as she stood, then leaned in close to Rhia. "You passed an important test just now. You trusted your own wisdom more than my authority." She squeezed Rhia's shoulder. "Just like a Crow."

They left her to wallow in bewilderment. She examined the contents of her mug, then pushed it away. If more "tests" lay ahead tonight, her judgment should remain clear.

The same young man who had just served Etar placed a new mug of meloxa in front of her. He winked a dark brown eye and said, "I heard you like it sweet."

"Thank you." As handsome as he was, she hoped he was referring to the drink.

When the server moved away, she scanned the table for more water. Her eyes met those of Razvin, seated at the opposite end. He studied her in a way that said his glance had not begun only the moment before.

Rhia's old instincts told her to drift away to the safety of those she knew well. Instead she took her mug and strolled to Razvin's end of the table.

He contemplated her approach with surprise, and when she arrived, he barely emitted a "Congratulations, Rhia."

"Thank you." She took a confident swig, suppressed a wince—this meloxa was no sweeter than the previous one—and met his searching stare. "Did you enjoy the food and drink?"

"I should. I helped prepare it."

"Then thank you again." She turned to leave, then stopped. "Your daughter saved my life a few nights ago. I hope I can repay the honor someday."

"I hope you never have to."

She hesitated. "How many Bears and Wolverines have been called in Kalindos recently?"

His gaze grew wary. "A few."

"More than usual?"

"A few *is* more than usual. Kalindos is a place of peace. Unlike your home."

"Asermos has never attacked anyone. Our wars have all been defensive."

"True enough." He turned back to his plate and murmured, "But not all wars are fought with arrows and swords."

She studied his posture to discern if his dejection were genuine. Had the Asermons treated him the way he claimed?

Would they do the same to Marek? She thought of Mali and Torynna's mocking words at the riverside.

Until she made up her mind about Razvin, it would be best to show sympathy. Besides, making enemies on the Kalindon Council would not be the wisest tactic.

"On behalf of my people," she said, "I want to apologize."

Razvin looked up at her with astonishment, his face guileless for the first time since they had met.

Someone tugged Rhia's arm.

"Why do you waste time talking to my father," Alanka said, "when you could be dancing?"

Razvin's composure returned in an instant. He gave Rhia a suave grin. "Go on, you deserve to enjoy yourself tonight, and you certainly won't with a tired old man like me."

"Father, stop fishing for compliments."

Rhia let Alanka drag her toward the bonfire. The musicians were limbering up to play a faster tempo.

"Do you know how to dance?" Alanka asked Rhia.

"Of course. We have parties in Asermos, too." She looked up into the trees, which held men and women in various combinations, striking poses of flirtation and acts far beyond. "But not like this."

"I thought so. Oh!" Alanka twisted to face Rhia, her back to the bonfire. "See the man with the long blond hair? The one in the green shirt? That's Morran, the Bobcat I told you about." She shook her head. "Better off without him. He drinks too much." She pointed her chin to the left. "Endrus the Cougar, with the brown hair. He drinks too much, too."

"What about Marek?"

"He has reason to drink." She shrugged. "But it's never

made him miss a hunt, or even a single shot, which is more than I can say for Morran."

Rhia held up her mug. "How can anyone drink this?"

"They didn't sweeten yours enough, did they? Let's get some more honey."

The fiddler shot into a spirited tune, joined in a few moments by a man on a wooden flute and another strumming a stringed instrument. Young people bounced into the circle as if on cue and began to dance—in small groups, couples, or alone. The elders stood on the outskirts and clapped a rollicking rhythm.

Buoyed by the music, the food, the drink and her brush with death, Rhia put down her mug and joined the dance. For the first time in days, every inch of her felt warm.

Someone grabbed her waist. It was Morran, who laughed when he saw her surprise.

"I won't keep you," he said. "There'll be a line soon."

"A line to dance with you?"

He laughed even louder, his head thrown back and brown eyes squeezed shut. "No, with you."

Morran was a good dancer, despite the quantity of meloxa he had ingested based on the lopsidedness of his smile. Perhaps the drink had lent him its fluidity.

Before the tune had even reached its peak, she was handed off to Endrus, who had thin arms and a wicked grin. He was shorter than Morran, which relieved her neck. The tempo increased, stealing their breath and precluding both the capacity and the need for intimate conversation. They spun faster around the circle, laughing as their steps grew sloppy trying to keep up with the rhythm, which grew in speed and complexity, as if the musicians' only goal was to exhaust and confound the dancers.

Just when she knew her legs or lungs would burst from the strain, the song ended. Without pausing, the troupe slid into a slow, sensuous tune, adding a drummer thrumming on a taut skin.

Rhia stepped back from Endrus, wanting neither to offend nor join him.

"My turn," a familiar voice over her shoulder said. With a glance of mock resentment, Endrus bowed and turned away. He latched on to the first willing girl within reach.

Marek slipped his arm around Rhia's waist and drew her hips tight to his, a look of about-to-be-satiated hunger on his face. They moved as if the music had melded them into one body. If she closed her eyes, she could pretend they were the only two people in the forest again.

"How long do these parties last?" she asked him, wondering when they could slip away together.

"Until the food and drink runs out." He twirled her slowly in his arms, reeling her out and back in again, so that the distance only accentuated their return to closeness. "Note that I say food *and* drink, not food *or* drink. As long as we have one or the other, we'll stay up."

"How long?"

"Three, maybe four days. Or five. We grab sleep every other day or so." Without letting go of her hand, he brushed a stray lock of hair from her cheek. "You may not have seen it yet, but life here is hard. Sometimes in the winter we have nothing to eat. Not just 'nothing but nuts and berries.' Nothing. It's a rare winter when someone doesn't starve."

She gestured to the overflowing tables. "And yet you waste all this food at a feast. Why not save it for hard times?"

"A celebration's never a waste. Besides, all times are hard. Even more reason to sweeten moments like these, right?"

She looked at the exuberant Kalindons. Perhaps there was no better way to praise and thank the Spirits for their gifts than to relish said gifts until one collapsed.

"Has anyone ever died at one of these parties?" she asked Marek.

"Only you would ask a question like that." He chewed his lip as he thought. "Not that I remember. We believe that during these feasts, the Spirits protect us from ourselves."

She chuckled. "They'd better."

Her smile faded when she caught sight of an unfriendly face. The same young man who had waited on her so solicitously not long before was now scowling at her from the side of the dancing area. His thick, dark brows shaded glowering eyes.

She put her chin over Marek's shoulder. "Who's the husky man with the brown hair, the one by the table wishing me dead?"

Marek sighed. "That's Skaris the Bear. We've been friends since we could walk."

"I don't understand. Why is he glaring at me?"

"Skaris is like a brother to me." Marek looked at the Bear, then back at Rhia. "Because he is, in a way. His sister was my mate."

Rhia dropped her defensiveness for a moment in favor of sympathy. "I see. But he was so nice to me a while ago. I think he was even flirting a little."

"That was before he knew you'd taken his sister's place."

She stared at Marek, her shock causing her feet to miss a step, then another. He seemed to have even startled himself with his words.

"I have?" she said.

They stopped dancing.

"Rhia, I know we haven't known each other long, but we've been through so much together, and I—" Marek's face reddened in the bonfire light, and his words stumbled over one another. "When we ran away from here, even though I believed you would change your mind, just like Coranna said, I would have taken you to Velekos if you'd wanted." He shook his head. "It seems crazy now, but it's true. Still, I have no claim on you."

"You don't?"

"No, I—" He looked at her with wide gray eyes. "Do I?"

Her face heated. "Alanka told me that relations between men and women in Kalindos are a little more, er—"

"Informal."

"Yes, more informal than I'm used to. But I don't— I only— I—" She groaned at her own ineptitude, then looked him in the eyes. "I only want you."

Relief infused his face just as the sun sank behind the hills. Marek's outline shimmered, then disappeared along with the rest of him. He uttered a crude curse. "Sorry," he added.

She shook her head in sympathy. "How will I find you later?"

"Follow the floating meloxa mug. Or—" he steered them toward the edge of the circle "—come with me now."

They slunk out of the crowd into the shadows. When the firelight was just a warm glow in the distance, Marek stopped, held her face in his hands and gave her a long, searching kiss. She sighed with relief. In the chaos her life had become, nothing felt as normal as this.

He pulled her close and breathed into her hair, the shuddering kind of breath taken after a fright. "When you died, I felt so numb, like I was as frozen as you. And when you came back, I wanted to warm you, put my hands and mouth all over you until you were the Rhia I remembered."

"Do I feel different?"

"You feel like yourself."

"I feared I'd be hard and clammy, or I'd smell like a grave, or—"

"Shh." His hands slid down her back as he inhaled. "You feel, and smell, as good as ever."

In the distance, a shriek ripped the air.

26

Marek jerked to face the sound. "It's Coranna."

"Don't wait for me. Run."

He was gone. She sprinted toward the scream and joined the villagers heading north of the bonfire along one of the paths.

In the short time she'd known Coranna, she had never heard her raise her voice, much less release such a plaintive cry. Her chest tightened with more than just the physical strain of sprinting through the underbrush.

The crowd stopped beneath a small tree house and parted for Rhia. Perhaps they spoke to her, but she heard nothing under the rush of Crow's wings. She fought the urge to clamp her hands to her ears and scream to cover the sounds.

Coranna knelt beside Etar's supine figure, fighting back tears as she stroked his lifeless arm. The wings in Rhia's head gave a last loud thump, then faded into the background below the crowd's chatter.

"What happened?" a woman behind her whispered.

"He fell," another answered. "I saw it happen."

"Did the ladder break?"

"No, he stopped as he was climbing and clutched at his chest. On the next rung he just dropped."

"Poor man," the first woman said. "I didn't know he was ill."

"He hid it well. If I'd known, I'd have sent him more food this winter."

Was he ill? Rhia wondered, and suddenly wished she had looked inside him when she had the chance.

Pirrik burst through the crowd on the other side, Alanka following.

"Father!"

Pirrik sank to his knees and cradled Etar's head in his lap, oblivious to the blood flowing onto his hands. He released a long, hollow cry. It was echoed in a moment by a woman's wail, which grew louder as it neared. A pregnant girl appeared at the front of the crowd. When she saw Etar's broken body, she swooned.

Alanka leaped to catch the girl before she fell, then rocked her in a tight embrace. From her appearance Rhia guessed she was Pirrik's younger sister, and she realized that Etar had already been a third-phase Owl at the time of his death.

"Poor Thera," one of the women behind Rhia whispered. "I hope the baby doesn't come too soon now."

Coranna caught Rhia's gaze and beckoned her over. She hurried to join her, hoping that no one observed her half-second hesitation. Coranna nodded to Etar's other hand. Rhia grasped both hands so that the three of them formed a circle.

Everyone fell silent. Rhia closed her eyes and heard nothing but Pirrik's and Thera's stifled sobs.

Her world went bright again. Coranna was there in the corner of one eye, and Etar in the other. They both smiled. She mimicked their expressions easily, for they were all surrounded with a pulsating light that emanated love from its core. The experience was a pale reflection of her own death, but it left her brimming with joy.

As Crow approached, Coranna let go of Etar's hand, and Rhia followed suit.

Etar's smile disappeared. His eyes filled with confusion, and he looked as if he were about to shake his head in protest. Then he vanished, enveloped in the wings of Crow.

The bright world faded as well, and she was back in Kalindos. Even before her eyes opened, she felt the damp ground beneath her knees. Yet the awareness of the Other Side lingered like a haze, and for more than a moment she ached to return.

The crowd let out a collective sigh. Coranna placed a gentle hand on Pirrik's shoulder.

"Your father's gone," she said. She stood and squeezed Thera's hand. "I'm so sorry." Her voice wavered, and Rhia sensed that this death hit Coranna harder than most.

An older woman wept as she comforted Thera. Rhia recognized her as Etar's sister Kerza the Wolf. Alanka knelt beside Pirrik. He leaned into her embrace and muffled his sobs against her neck.

Elora appeared then with a blanket and healing bag. One look at the faces of those gathered around Etar's body told her it was too late. Coranna beckoned Elora to join her and Rhia away from where Etar's children grieved.

In a low voice, Elora asked, "What happened?"

In an even lower voice, Coranna replied, "I hoped you could tell me."

"People say he fell."

"Yes, but why? He may be old, but he's far from feeble. Something took hold of him in the moments before he let go." She blinked hard and frowned, as if remembering something, then turned to Rhia. "Find me half a dozen strong men who can carry him to the pyre."

Rhia turned toward the crowd, her mind swimming from the moments on the Other Side. A few men had already stepped forward for the onerous task. Rhia quickly found three more. When she returned, Elora had cleansed the blood from Etar's head and bound it with a swath of bandage. His body was wrapped in the blanket she had brought.

The crowd parted for the solemn procession of the corpse. Faces that had been lit with giddiness less than an hour before were now cast in sorrow. Many muttered to themselves in prayer.

Unsure of her role, Rhia shadowed Coranna all the way to the funeral pyre. The Crow woman seemed to be reining in her own emotions like unruly horses. Rhia wasn't sure if the lump of sadness in her own throat came from the death of the intriguing old man, or from her brief return to that place of bliss and peace. Thinking of it made her feel more homesick than thoughts of Asermos. Her hands and feet tingled as if warming, though she hadn't been cold. The exhaustion from the long ride and the dancing had disappeared.

The pyre consisted of long wooden slats, stacked to create a container that reminded Rhia of a hollow log house that would accommodate the body of one adult. Atop the pyre, overlapping its perimeter, lay a thin stone slab, presumably to shelter the wood and keep it dry. The six men laid Etar's body on the slab. Coranna asked them to find a few guards to take the first shift.

"I'll do it." Marek's voice came from just behind Rhia. "Let me get my bow."

Coranna stood next to the pyre and took a deep breath before turning to face the crowd.

"My fellow Kalindons, Etar—our friend, father and brother—has gone to the Other Side." Though by now word had spread, a cry of anguish rose from the people. The man who had played the drum covered his face with his hands. A gray-haired woman leaned against a tree and quietly keened.

Coranna continued, her voice fighting to remain steady. "Please, return to your homes and pray for his easy passage. At daybreak we will gather to say goodbye. Afterward we will celebrate his life, both the one he lived with us and the one he will live with the Spirits for all eternity."

She turned away from the crowd, who took her signal to disperse, which they did in silence, some weeping and shaking their heads. Rhia joined her on the pyre's platform.

Elora appeared at the other edge and exchanged a glance with Coranna. They uncovered Etar's body. Rhia reminded herself that this death was among the less ugly ones she would likely see.

Welcome to the rest of your life, she thought with a pang of self-sympathy.

Eyes closed, Elora put her hands on either side of Etar's head. Her fingers probed his neck.

"Lift his side just a little toward you," she said. Coranna and Rhia obeyed. The healer slipped her hands under him and felt the length of his spine. She stopped when she reached the midpoint. "He broke his back in the fall."

"But what made him fall?" Coranna asked her.

"Did he drink a lot of meloxa?"

"No more than usual."

Rhia spoke up. "One of the villagers said when Etar was climbing the ladder, he clutched his chest in pain."

Coranna looked at Elora. "Did he ever come to you with symptoms?"

"No," the healer said, "but you know how men are, too proud to admit any illness until it kills them. And sometimes Crow simply strikes with speed and mercy." She smoothed the bandage on Etar's head, tenderly, as if the action could help him. Her face turned thoughtful. "If I were third-phase, I could determine even now if he had been sick."

Coranna put her hand on Elora's. "You're exhausted from our journey. Go, rest and pray now. Rhia and I will keep vigil."

After a last mournful glance at Etar, Elora slipped into the darkness.

Rhia watched Coranna stand, unmoving, at the side of the corpse. "What do we do now?" she asked finally.

"We wait," Coranna said.

"Wait for what?"

"For morning."

Rhia glanced at Etar. Had Coranna's questions for Elora been simple curiosity or did they reflect a deeper suspicion? Rhia wished more than ever that she had done "the wrong thing" and granted Etar's request to tell him when he would die.

"When do we clean and wrap the body?" she asked Coranna.

"No need. It will be burned tomorrow at sunset."

"You don't bury your dead?"

"The soil here is too rocky. Like all Birds, his ashes will hang from the tree where he once lived."

"Oh," was all Rhia could think to say. Kalindons and Asermons differed in so many ways it was getting harder to believe they were the same people. She thought of what Marek had said about the nature and length of Kalindon funerals, and remembered that her own party had been a funeral of sorts.

"Coranna?"

"Yes?"

"If you can return people from the Other Side, the way you did for me—"

"Why don't I do it for everyone?"

"I know you can't undo every death, but how do you decide?"

Coranna didn't respond, and Rhia feared she had blundered by asking such a question.

Finally Coranna said, "To reverse Crow's flight, a bargain must be struck. Life for life."

Rhia grew cold. "For a person to come back to life, someone else has to die?"

"It's not simply one life for another. It's time on earth that I must trade."

"Another life is shortened?"

"Yes. By the same amount of time as the returned has remaining in his or her life."

The forest swayed around Rhia, and not just from the wind. "Then who—for me—?"

"Everyone."

Rhia gripped the edge of the pyre to steady herself. "When you say everyone—"

"All of Kalindos. Except the children, of course. They're not old enough to consent to such a bargain."

"How long—" Rhia felt sick. "How much time did I take from them?"

"It depends how long you live. Spread among the adult villagers, if you live another thirty-five years, to be my age—which I pray you will—that's scarcely more than a month of life each."

A month. She had stolen a month from each Kalindon. One fewer month to hold their children, to raise their faces to the afternoon sun, to sleep in their beloved's arms.

"Why would they?"

"Because a Crow is a rare and valuable thing. A Crow is, frankly, worth five Otters or ten Wolves."

"It's true," Marek's voice came from the darkness, where he stood guard.

"It's not true," Rhia said. "We each have equal gifts to offer our people."

"Equally necessary, perhaps, but not equally common." Coranna wagged a finger at her. "So take care of yourself."

"Take care of myself? When every day I live, someone else lives one day fewer? How can I live, knowing what I've stolen from them?"

"You didn't steal it. They gave it."

Rhia looked toward Marek, then shifted closer to Coranna. "What about him?" she whispered. "When his mate and the baby—"

Coranna held up a hand to silence her. "Marek?" she called into the dark. "Would you please fetch my ceremonial robe? It may need to be steamed before the funeral tomorrow."

Marek replied his assent. After several moments, long enough for him to move out of hearing range, Coranna turned to Rhia, her face pinched.

"He tried. He tried to give his life for the woman and their child. He pleaded with me. But for Crow to trade one life for two, especially when one was just born—it asked too much of the Spirit. Their lives would not have been long, and the bargain would have killed Marek in that moment. I couldn't let him go." Her lower lip trembled once. "So I didn't."

"What about other people here? Couldn't they have given life to save them?"

"It must be done within a few instants of death, the way it was with you. For them, there wasn't time."

Rhia turned away and hid her face in her hands to staunch the tears before they could flow.

Coranna stepped closer. "You will learn to stand at a distance from others' pain."

"I don't want to."

"You must, to give them the strength they need." She took Rhia by the shoulders and turned her. "You can show compassion without becoming…"

Hysterical? Rhia thought. *Deranged?*

"…occupied."

I don't want this, she pleaded to Crow. *How can I ever?*

Coranna's grip tightened. "Remember how happy Etar looked when he crossed to the Other Side?" Rhia nodded, though she recalled how Etar's smile had vanished the moment before Crow's wings shrouded him. "That's our reward," Coranna continued. "And when the villagers look to us tomorrow for solace, and we grant it to them, then their gratitude, their peace, will take away the hurt."

Rhia stared at Etar's corpse, her own body filling with dread. "Would he have lived another month if you hadn't brought me back?"

Coranna's mouth opened in a silent gasp. "There are some questions," she said finally, "that only Crow can answer."

The night's hours crawled by, making Rhia long for summer's generous sunlight. The torches surrounding the pyre played shadows over the forest floor, matching the specters dancing within her own mind. Not since the second night of her Bestowing had she felt so alone and confused. Guilt nagged at her as she wondered what Etar could have done with one more month of life. Now that he was dead, would other Kalindons shoulder an even larger time burden? She tried to believe that her ignorance of the ritual's true cost made her blameless. Failing that, she reminded herself that the deed had been done and there was no use agonizing over it now. But in fact the consequences grew every day she went on living.

One of the torches wavered in the corner of her eye, and she turned to it just as Marek spoke her name.

He tugged her arm. "Come over here for a moment."

She glanced at Coranna, who nodded and returned to whatever prayer or meditation they had interrupted.

Marek led her outside the circle of torches. He whispered in her ear, "My mentor Kerza needs to speak with you. Alone."

"Etar's sister?"

"Tell Coranna you need to visit the outhouse, the one on the north side of the village. Kerza will meet you there. You won't see or hear her until she speaks. She'll know if it's safe to show herself."

Rhia assented and returned to the pyre. After a short while, she excused herself, picked up one of the smaller torches, and made her way to the outhouse.

As she neared it, a woman's whisper beckoned from behind the small wooden building. Rhia followed the sound until a hand gripped her wrist. Though she'd been expecting contact, she nearly yelped in surprise.

"Thank you for coming," Kerza said. "I didn't know who else to turn to."

"I don't understand."

"I should show myself, so you'll believe me. I think it's safe."

A white-haired woman appeared beside her, hazel eyes reflecting more than sorrow. They burned with bitterness.

"Help me," Kerza said. "My brother was murdered."

Rhia was surprised at her own lack of surprise. "I wondered that myself."

"I don't wonder." Kerza's whisper sliced the air. "I know. He was poisoned."

"Who did it?"

"Someone on the Council." She made an impatient gesture with her hands. "Let me explain. My brother and I both sit—I mean, he *sat* on the Council." Her voice shook. "He had been the elected leader for five three-year terms."

"Fifteen years? In Asermos our Council leadership rotates at least every two terms. That way no one person can impose their will for too long."

"Exactly. A few Council members have proposed such term limits. The measure has been defeated again and again, always on a four-to-three vote." Her gaze lowered. "If I'd known this would be the result, I would have changed my vote. But he's my brother—he *was* my brother—and I had to be loyal to him."

Rhia nodded. "You think someone killed Etar because they thought it was the only way to get him out of power."

Kerza pressed her lips together in a tight line, as if holding back a storm of sobs.

Rhia touched her hand. "Why are you telling me this? Why do you think I of all people can help you?"

The Wolf woman drew in a deep, shaky breath through her nose. "The three Council members who tried to pass the measure were Zilus the Hawk, Razvin the Fox..."

Rhia's eyes widened. Could the man who abandoned her mother and brothers still harbor such treachery?

"…and Coranna."

Rhia let go of Kerza's hand and stepped back. "You don't think—"

"I don't know what to think. But I know you spend time with Razvin and Coranna. All I ask is for you to keep your eyes open. Tell Marek what you learn, and he'll tell me." She grasped Rhia's elbow, her fingers like claws. "You owe Coranna your loyalty. But a Crow's greatest duty is to the dead." Kerza suddenly cocked her head to the side. Her nostrils flared. "Someone's coming. I must go."

She disappeared, winking out in a moment rather than shimmering, as Marek did at sunset. The hand released Rhia, who reached out to feel the air around her. Nothing.

Her merely human senses told her no one was approaching, but she crept into the outhouse just the same, as if it were her purpose all along. She locked the door, then sat on the wooden seat, listening, too frightened even to relieve herself.

If Etar's death had been dealt by a purposeful human hand, rather than the whim of Crow's flight, then it could not be Rhia's fault. No one ever spoke of murder as Crow's will—illness, accidents, even wars could be the result of spiritual forces beyond any individual's control. But Crow did not raise the hand of one man to slay another. To believe otherwise would exonerate the murderer as a mere tool of the Spirits.

She gathered her nerve and crept back to the pyre, where Coranna waited, as still as the stone beside her and the body that lay upon it.

* * *

When the eastern horizon began to glow, the village came to life. Waiting at the pyre, Rhia saw distant figures descend ladders from their homes. As they approached, each person, even the children, bent to pick up as many branches and twigs as he or she could carry.

Coranna stood at the head of the pyre, now in the pure white ceremonial robe that Marek had fetched for her. Crow feathers lined the seam that ran from her wrists to her neck. She gestured for Rhia to take a position at the pyre's foot.

The sun rose over the hillside, casting a red-orange glow that outshone the torches' pale brilliance. Coranna softly intoned the chant of the body, while one by one, the Kalindons approached the pyre, mounted the platform and stood for a few moments next to the body. They uttered hushed prayers, then placed the wood they had gathered next to the pyre. Some lay flowers or herbs on Etar's chest.

Last to proceed were Etar's sister and children. They all bore cropped hair and looked as if they had not slept. Kerza avoided Rhia's gaze. The three each placed an owl feather on his breast, tucking them into the blanket so they wouldn't blow away. Then they took their places nearby, standing rather than kneeling, no doubt because of Thera's pregnancy.

Coranna held her arms out to the crowd. "We gather to mourn Etar's death and celebrate his life, for both shall touch us forever. It is on our behalf alone, not his, that we mourn, for Etar himself has journeyed to the Other Side, to a new and glorious existence." She lowered her arms. "He was a man of wisdom, of humor, of justice. His service on the village Council lasted twenty years, most of them as leader, the longest tenure in memory. He found ways to fulfill our people's wishes and still be true to his Spirit. If I may speak for all Council members, we have been blessed and humbled by his service."

The other elders nodded—including Razvin. His piety and grief had a forced quality—at least to Rhia—as if he were trying too hard to mourn. She couldn't identify Zilus the Hawk, and as for Coranna…the thought that she could be a murderer was too terrible.

Other Kalindons came forward to speak of Etar, extolling his wisdom and lamenting the void that he had left behind. His son Pirrik told of Etar's devotion to his late wife, who had preceded him to the Other Side seven years before.

When Pirrik stepped down, pale and unsteady, Coranna returned to the head of the pyre. "We will now sing home his soul."

She began the chant to call Crow, as Galen had at Mayra's funeral. Rhia joined in, tentatively at first, in case the words or inflections differed from those of her home, but this ritual was identical even to the rhythms of the breath. Soon the others lifted their voices to the cold morning air.

Unlike the day they buried her mother, a crow appeared right away calling over and over. Rhia watched it swoop low through the forest, passing through patches of morning sun that glistened violet off its wings.

For a moment she wished she could follow it into the sky. Then she looked at the grateful faces of the Kalindons, the people who had given up a bit of their lives for her, and knew with certainty that her place was in this world.

28

The party—now only a wake—resumed as if it had never stopped, albeit at a muted level of revelry. Rhia helped Coranna and Marek gather more wood for the funeral pyre. Much of it was damp from melted snow and had to be dried by hand using the torches.

She laid an armful of dry wood at the foot of the pyre and examined the raised stone platform on which it stood. It bore the scorch marks of many funerals—she wondered how many bodies had turned to ashes here. Her mind cleared, and she felt the traces of souls who had lingered close to earth after the deaths of their bodies. One remained.

Coranna stepped quietly onto the platform next to her. "We have enough wood for now. Marek is making a reserve pile in case the night is damp."

Rhia kept her gaze on Etar's face. "Why do some of them stay?"

"A few wait because of unfinished business or an over-attachment to this world. It's part of a Crow person's duty to encourage them to cross over completely."

"Why has he stayed?"

Coranna hesitated. "Perhaps he wants to see his grandchild born."

"I hope that's why." Rhia wanted to utter the alternative—he remained because someone had shoved him from this world.

"Etar has not spoken to me from the Other Side," Coranna said. "If he lingers after Thera has her baby, I will contact him to determine his soul's intentions."

Rhia forced herself to ask, "Why not now?"

Coranna gave her a long look. "I need privacy, and special materials. I prefer to perform that ritual at home."

"Tomorrow, then? I'll help with anything you need."

The Crow woman's gaze darkened. "Tomorrow, yes."

Rhia gestured to Etar. "Do they ever stay for good?"

"No. Crow wouldn't allow it." Her head gave a little bow. "Our Spirit's patience and understanding are enormous as it is."

Rhia bowed her head in imitation and restrained her thousand-and-one other questions.

"We're finished for now," Coranna said, loudly enough for Marek to hear. "Go and join the wake, both of you."

Rhia stepped off the platform and turned to Coranna. "Are you coming?"

"I'll be along shortly." Coranna turned back to the pyre, and as she did, the façade of composure fell from her face.

When they were out of her earshot, Rhia told Marek, "I spoke with Kerza last night." She hesitated, not knowing if she could tell Marek she questioned his Wolf mentor's motives. But if she couldn't trust the man who had been willing to give up everything for her, she was truly alone here.

"I don't know who to believe," she said. "Kerza suspects Coranna and Razvin, and someone named Zilus." He nodded. "But why should I believe Kerza?" she asked him.

"What she says is true, about the term limit conflict. Council meetings are public."

"I've asked Coranna to contact Etar." To his surprised look she replied, "He still lingers near this world. Maybe he has something to tell us."

"I hope so. It's a lot of rituals for Coranna to do in such a short time. She brought you back to life, now she's handling the funeral of one of her best friends—"

"Were Coranna and Etar more than friends?"

"Sometimes." They glanced back at Coranna's figure, glowing white in a patch of sunlight. "He's the closest person to her to die since her daughter."

"I didn't know about her daughter." Shame coursed through her, for her indifference and suspicions. "I never asked Coranna about her."

"Them, not her. Coranna had two daughters, but only one survived to have her own children. The younger daughter died before I was born, a fever of some sort. The older one died in the same fire that killed my parents. Coranna had to call her spirit home along with all the others."

Rhia stopped and covered her face. "I never asked you, either, how your mother and father died."

"I didn't expect you to. I didn't ask about your mother's death. Figured you'd tell me when you were ready."

Was she ready? Ready to admit her greatest error, her deepest shame? She looked at Marek's patient face.

"What happened to Coranna's grandchildren?" she asked him.

"Her son-in-law took them to Tiros to live with his family. Said he wouldn't watch his children die in this forsaken place." Marek shook his head. "It broke Coranna's heart. She could have gone with them, but she wouldn't leave Kalindos. This is home, she said, for better or worse."

Rhia looked at the mist-draped forest, at the Kalindons moving as one around the bonfire, and understood.

Bellies full and thirsts quenched, Rhia and Marek sat near the fire while Zilus the Hawk captivated the crowd with stories, most of which featured Etar as a younger and considerably less wise Owl. Zilus's pointed gray beard bobbed as he recreated exaggerated scenes, complete with imitated voices. Before long, everyone was laughing and toasting Etar's memory. Rhia found it hard to believe that Zilus held anything but fondness for his fellow Council member, but perhaps that was the impression he was trying to convey.

As the shadows in the forest lengthened, Zilus grew solemn, and many of the Kalindons leaned forward.

"Is this a special part?" Rhia whispered to Marek.

"He always finishes with the story of the Descendants. Likes to go out with a dramatic flourish."

Rhia knew the story but perked up to hear how the Kalindons told it.

"Once upon a time," Zilus said, "all people in the world were one. Everyone had animal magic the way we do in

Kalindos, the way the people of Asermos do," he gestured to Rhia, "and the people of Tiros and Velekos. We traded in peace and rarely fought, unless it was over a mate." He nudged the elderly woman sitting next to him, who laughed and returned a soft shove.

"But one day," Zilus continued, "a fishing party traveling south from Velekos was beset by a terrible storm that carried them out across the Southern Sea, all the way to the other shore. When the clouds lifted, the men fell on the deck of their boat and blessed the Spirits that had spared their lives. Then they stood."

He paused and looked the children in the eye, one by one. "What do you think they saw?" he asked, drawing out each word.

Rhia knew the answer: a golden shore near the mouth of another river, a land where the weather was always warm, a paradise untouched by humans—though not for long.

"They saw," Zilus said, "a shining city on the golden shore, a city with buildings of white stone that reflected the sun so brightly it hurt to look at it. A city that was empty."

"Wait," Rhia whispered to Marek, "does he mean they saw it in their imagination?"

"No." He squinted at her. "They saw it. It was there."

"They didn't build the city?"

Someone behind her made a shushing noise. She pressed her lips together and leaned forward to hear Zilus tell more.

"The fishermen rowed to the city and stepped within. They walked on roads paved with solid stone and imagined how quickly their carts could roll over such paths. They saw enormous houses and imagined how quickly they could fill them with children and servants. And lastly, they came to the largest building of all. It was so huge, if you stood in the center of it, you couldn't see the outer walls."

The eyes of the youngest children widened at the thought.

"And in that building," Zilus said, "were stone statues of people—men and women who each wielded a different weapon. One man, a spear, one woman, a bow and arrow. One man looked as if he held the lightning itself in his hand. The statues bore no chips, no marks, not so much as a speck of dust. It was as if the former inhabitants had vanished that very day.

"The fishermen fell to their knees, thanking these statues they thought were gods for delivering them from the storm and bringing them to this city."

"Did the gods answer?" asked a little girl to Zilus's left.

He tweaked her nose. "No, silly, they were just statues. But the fishermen believed they were gods. They believed so hard they brought those carvings to life in their own minds."

"They worshiped a bunch of statues?" a boy said with disdain. "What did the Spirits do?"

"Well, that's the sad part. The Spirits of these men felt forsaken. So they took their magic back." Zilus's hand snatched the air. "That's what happens when we don't honor them. The Spirits grant us their Aspects, and they can take them away if we aren't worthy." He folded his hands. "Now you'd probably like to hear what happened to the fishermen."

Everyone nodded, although most knew the end of the story.

"They returned to Velekos and told everyone what they had seen. Word spread, to Asermos, Tiros and even to Kalindos. Many of our people were seduced by the idea of an easier life, one that would depend less on the cycles of the seasons, less on what they considered the whims of the Spirits. They left their villages for this shining white city in the south, and as they departed, so did their magic depart from them.

"And to this day, the Descendants, as we call them, have no magic."

"Will they ever come back?" asked the little girl.

Zilus gave her a wistful half smile. "Not in peace, I'm afraid." He raised his empty meloxa mug. "My throat is dry. I thank you for your attention, and thank you even more for refilling my drink."

The musicians warmed up, and the crowd moved back to clear a space for dancing.

Rhia turned to Marek and drank in the sight of him while it lasted, for the sun was about to disappear. "In Asermos we're taught that the Descendants built the white city on the shore they found. That they created the gods in their own image."

"Interesting." Marek frowned at the bottom of his mug, which he could see due to the absence of meloxa. "Either way, they're there now and bound to be trouble someday."

"But if they didn't build the city, who did?"

"The people before the Reawakening, of course."

The giraffe had told Rhia of such inhabitants. It was hard to doubt a Spirit, but the teachings of her childhood remained rooted inside her. "I don't know what to believe anymore."

"Then if you ever meet a Descendant, you should ask them which is the true story."

"Maybe neither is exactly true."

Marek looked to the west. "Time to light the pyre, at sunset." He took her hand. "Stay with me after I disappear?"

She kissed him, long and sweet, and when she opened her eyes, he had vanished.

Along with most of the villagers, they made their way to the pyre. Etar had been placed inside and the upper stone slab removed. Juniper branches covered and surrounded the body, along with the dry wood they had collected today.

The crowd quieted. Without a word, Coranna lowered a torch to the base of the pyre. Marek and Rhia did the same at their positions. The oil-soaked wood snapped and cracked, and the heat formed a wall that threatened to push Rhia off her feet. She stepped back from the platform and watched through the slats of the pyre as the flames ate their way toward Etar's body.

When the fire reached the edge of his blanket, a great *whoosh* went up. Coranna had doused his garments with meloxa to hasten the flames. Bits of cloth floated upwards before bursting into small showers of ash.

Within moments, Etar's skin cracked and blackened, peeling away from his flesh. Rhia wanted to run from the sight and the stench, which was barely allayed by the fragrant juniper branches. But no one else turned away, and no one showed disgust—only sadness—so she watched with them, honoring Etar during his body's last moments.

The evening wind blew brisk and dry, feeding the flames' frenzy. Eventually the corpse was little more than a charred skeleton. Each time another joint fell apart and the body shifted, Rhia jumped a little at the sudden movement. Her heart slammed against her own ribs, which she was more conscious of than ever. Inside her were the same bones that split and crumbled in the nearby flames.

Slowly the fire dwindled to embers around what little remained of Etar—many small bone fragments amid a scattering of gray ashes. The crowd dispersed, most of them heading back to the clearing to eat and drink in a greatly subdued mood.

Rhia couldn't move, much less eat and drink. Coranna brought forth a clay container that resembled a large vase with a cover. She started to call Rhia, then stopped when she saw her face. Instead she beckoned to Marek.

Rhia forced her feet to unfreeze and took an unsteady step. Her stomach pitched at the movement, but nothing would stop her from fulfilling her duty. She approached the pyre, whose stone platform pulsed hot, and stood next to Coranna.

The Crow woman held up the clay container. "We'll gather a bit of the ashes now, then tomorrow morning, after the stones have cooled, we'll collect whatever hasn't blown away." She reached the vessel toward the pyre. "Hold my sleeve, please."

Rhia pulled Coranna's sleeve taut so it would not burn on the stones of the pyre's platform. Using the rim of the container and a piece of bark, the Crow scooped up a small pile of ashes. She drew her arm back, then held the vessel in both hands while murmuring a short prayer.

Finally Coranna straightened and sighed. "I'm off to have a drink, or possibly several drinks, in Etar's honor." She touched Rhia's cheek. "I suggest you retire for the night."

They bid her good-night, but when she had moved away, Rhia said to Marek, "I can't rest now. We don't know why Etar died."

He took her hand. "Rhia, judging by your face, you're barely able to speak, much less probe a mysterious death."

She had to admit it was true. The activities of the past few days had drained her energy. The aches that had disappeared after Etar's journey were returning even stronger, as if angry at their banishment.

She let Marek lead her back to his house. He kept a slow pace so that Rhia could see the way despite her limited night vision and lingering light-headedness.

When they arrived home, she sank onto the soft pile of skins that made up his bed and felt him stretch out beside her.

His finger traced the edge of her jaw. "You were very brave tonight."

"I wasn't. I almost lost my dinner. It was awful, seeing him disintegrate like that. But you must be used to it."

"I haven't seen that many burnings. The children don't watch. The sight and smell make perfect nightmare fuel."

She touched his chest and felt his heart beat. The steady pulse under her palm reassured her. "Did you see it happen to your parents?"

"No. The fire that killed them—"

"Of course." She cringed at her own insensitivity. "I'm so sorry."

"Don't be. At the time, I was numb. I couldn't believe it. We lost so many people. But all I could think about was how relieved I was, how lucky I was to be spared. When something like that happens, you feel guilty for surviving, but you're secretly happy to be alive, to have the chance to feel anything at all."

They spoke no more, for they did need to feel, at that moment, anything that would separate them from the dead. As they made love, Rhia tried to memorize every stroke, every shiver, every sigh that passed between them, as if her memory could keep them both alive forever.

Later, though her body wanted to drag her into slumber, she stayed awake long after Marek had fallen asleep. Every time she closed her eyes, flames danced on the back of her eyelids, licking and gnawing, their flesh-hunger yet unsated.

So she lay in the dark listening to Marek breathe, marveling at the miracle of each inhale and exhale.

"Never be ashes," she whispered to him.

On the forest floor below, the Kalindons danced and sang, defiantly.

29

The sun rose, and Rhia with it. She tucked the blankets tighter around Marek to replace her warmth, then slipped outside without a sound. In the near distance of the village center, the wake continued.

Coranna stirred when Rhia opened the door to their home. "Did Etar's ashes already," she mumbled. "We have to rebuild the pyre, but that can wait. Go back to sleep. Or at least make no noise, whatever you do."

Rhia shut the door, more loudly than necessary. "You said you would contact Etar today."

She opened one eye to glare at Rhia. "I just went to bed."

"I'll brew some chicory to wake you up." She went to the stove. "I can heat water for a bath, if you like."

Coranna groaned. "I feel half-dead myself."

Without turning from the stove she replied, "Then it shouldn't be that hard to reach him."

After a long moment, Coranna said, "Chicory would be good."

They skipped breakfast and, after dressing in a loose, plain gown, Coranna went to her shelves and retrieved a small box of dark polished wood. She pulled a bundle of brown cloth out of the box and unwrapped it to reveal a thick stick of tightly wound leaves.

"What's that?" Rhia asked.

"Not for apprentices, that's what. It helps me leave this world behind. Would you drum for me? Begin when I finish the chant. Keep silent unless I ask you to speak."

Rhia picked up the drum and sat on the edge of her bed. Coranna knelt on the thick green rug between their beds, then lit the herb stick. The heady aroma seemed to swell the space inside Rhia's head, and she bit her lip to force herself to focus.

Coranna began to chant—a high, keening sound that prickled Rhia's spine. It was a lament as well as a beckoning and contained all the woman's anguish at the loss of her friend. She had told Rhia to maintain a distance from others' pain, yet her own emotions assailed the air like sparks. But perhaps the grief itself called Etar. Despite the wonders of the Other Side, his friend's sadness might tug at him one final time.

The chant faded. As Coranna reclined on the rug, Rhia secured the drum between her knees and began to tap a light rhythm in the tempo Marek had used when she died.

Coranna lay motionless for several minutes, eyes moving behind her closed lids. All at once her back stiffened, and she covered her ears as if to blot out a loud noise, then lowered her hands.

"I've found him," she whispered, then her voice turned to a scold. "Etar, why are you here? Elora says your grandchild will be healthy and strong, just like his mother. You should leave us now."

"I seek justice for my death," said a voice that came from Coranna's mouth but was not quite hers. "I wasn't ill, not that I was aware."

Rhia flinched at the implication. She could have given him the answer if she had looked inside him that night.

"I believe I was poisoned," Etar said. "A young man gave me a mug of meloxa. Skaris the Bear."

Rhia held back a gasp. Marek's friend, his mate's brother.

"Why would Skaris want to kill you?" Coranna said. "He's too young to take your seat on the Council."

Etar hesitated. "Perhaps someone asked him to do it."

Rhia nearly stopped drumming. She knew who helped prepare the food and drink that night. Against her instructions, she spoke. "Razvin had the chance. I think he was watching me while I spoke with you."

Etar was silent for a moment. "I told Razvin I would ask you to estimate my remaining life, and he bet me a month's worth of meloxa you wouldn't do it."

Coranna spoke indignantly. "You wagered on my apprentice's integrity? I expect more reverence from you both."

"No, you don't," Etar said. "Rhia, when Razvin watched you, he may have been wondering if he could collect on the bet."

Rhia bit back an argument. Perhaps she judged the Fox harshly because of what he did to her mother. If she let past grievances cloud her reasoning, she couldn't help Etar's search for justice.

"Begin with Skaris," Etar said.

"We will." Coranna softened her tone. "Please trust us to do what's right, and leave now."

"No." Etar's spirit-voice strained from her throat. "Coranna, don't let me drift away."

Her body tensed. "You must. Fly with Crow, Etar. Find your peace."

"I can barely see you now." His words slowed and elongated. "It's like looking through a fog."

A tear squeezed from the outer corner of Coranna's eye. "Go," she whispered.

With a farewell that Rhia could sense but not hear, Etar faded from the reaches of this world. Coranna rolled onto her side. As tears dripped onto the rug beneath her, she hugged her knees to her chest like a child.

Rhia stopped drumming, hating herself for doubting Coranna's display of emotion.

A scrabbling came from the ladder outside. A moment later, the bell rang. Rhia opened the door to see Alanka.

"Good morning!" the Wolf girl said.

Rhia rubbed her eyes. "Did we have plans?"

"We do now. Thera's having the baby."

Rhia looked at Coranna, who was slowly sitting up, then back at Alanka. "So?"

"So we have to be there." Coranna got to her feet and approached the door. "You're certain the baby is coming?"

Alanka nodded. "I waited to wake you until we were sure. Kerza and Elora are already there." She waved her hand to hurry them. "It's coming fast."

"That's a blessing," Coranna grumbled, then pointed to

Rhia's pile of clothes. "Change out of that dress. It'll get messy."

"I'll tell them you're on your way." Alanka hurried down the ladder.

Rhia shut the door and rushed to change her clothes. "Are Thera and the baby in trouble?"

"I hope not." Coranna pulled on a pair of trousers and shoes. "Crows always greet newborns with prayers and rituals." She crossed the room and stood by her shelves of pots. "Where did I put that lavender?" She uncorked several containers. "Crow brings us into life and takes us away. The nice part is, we get to hold them first."

"Hold who?"

"The babies. It reminds all who are present that every moment of life we have, even the first one, is by the grace of Crow. Ah, here's the lavender. Ready?"

Rhia hurried to follow her down the ladder, concerned about Thera but wondering when and how they would confront Skaris.

After they reached the forest floor, Coranna said, "Also, if something goes wrong with the birth, Spirits forbid, we're there to ease the other sort of transition between two worlds. Have you ever seen a baby born?"

"A few. My mother was an Otter, and sometimes she helped our Turtle woman with the births."

"Good. You can help. I can't cope with all that blood."

Rhia almost tripped over a root. "But what about the people we deliver to Crow?"

"That's different. Dead people don't bleed for long." An ear-shattering shriek pierced the forest just ahead of them.

Coranna pressed a hand to her temple and winced. "That would be Thera. I hope."

A few men were gathered near the healer's low tree house, which featured a short staircase rather than a ladder, to ease the climb for the sick and weak. One young blond paced and cracked his knuckles; Rhia figured him for the father. He flinched with each cry of the laboring mother and looked as if he wanted to run far away.

When they entered, Thera the Hawk was resting between contractions on a low stool and leaning against her aunt Kerza. Alanka paced on her other side and brightened when she saw the Crow women.

"I made you mint tea," she said. She scuttled to the stove and poured two mugs of amber-green brew, appearing relieved to leave the birthing area for a few moments. "I've never seen a baby born," she told Rhia in a hushed voice.

"How is she?"

"Angry, sad, happy, everything. Elora says it's going quickly, especially for a first child. I'll introduce you."

When they met, Thera gave Rhia an exhausted half smile, which vanished as the next contraction came.

"I think this is it!" Elora said. "Alanka, get her other arm."

Coranna was setting up some herbs on a low table nearby, humming quietly to herself. She accepted the tea Rhia offered with a nod. As Thera let out another holler of pain and determination, Coranna gripped the mug with white-knuckled fingers.

"When do we start?" Rhia asked her.

"As soon as my head stops pounding." She gave Rhia a tight smile. "Which should be today." She set down the mug with reluctance, then bunched a handful of lavender flowers and stems in a small, tight bundle the length of her hand.

"I can see the head!" Elora shouted.

Rhia resisted a look over her shoulder and held the bundle so Coranna could tie it. She inhaled and felt the herb soothe the tense muscles of her temples.

"There's no magic here," Coranna said, "except what Raven gave us when She created lavender." She took the bundle and sniffed it, relaxing as she exhaled. "Sometimes the greatest wisdom is knowing when magic is utterly unnecessary."

The notion comforted Rhia, especially since her magic was not an everyday sort.

Coranna lit one end of the bundle and set it in a clay bowl. The scent wafted through the room, carried by the breeze that slid through the two open windows.

Thera's howls softened to whimpers. "Please let it be over," she said.

"We're almost there." Elora's hands were hidden under the swell of Thera's belly. "When you feel the next contraction, I want you to push as hard as you can."

Thera gave a long, defeated moan. Coranna, eyes closed, intoned a low chant, one that repeated a simple line of welcome. As the chant grew in volume, Coranna raised her hands, palms up and out. Alanka and Kerza took the signal to join the song, crooning softly in Thera's ears.

Rhia knelt a few feet away, closed her eyes, and lifted her voice with the others. The chorus of women, together with the scent of lavender, lulled the room into a place of serene, hopeful waiting—at least on the outside. Being with Kerza and Coranna in such a close space pushed the thoughts of Etar's death to the front of Rhia's mind, from which she could not banish them.

"Here's the shoulders." Elora braced her feet. "Give us one more push."

Thera's shriek ripped through the room, and Rhia struggled to maintain the steady chant. Alanka broke off the song to whisper words of encouragement to Thera, who was sobbing through gritted teeth.

The girl let out a last cry of pain and triumph, and Elora exclaimed, "There he is!"

Rhia opened her eyes in time to see a dark mass slip into the Otter woman's hands. Elora rubbed him dry with a rough blanket, and the baby let out a screech that rivaled his mother's. An answering cry of celebration went up from the crowd gathered outside the house. Thera released a hoarse laugh through her fatigue.

A bit of thin rope lay just out of Elora's reach, and Rhia leaned forward to hand it to her. The healer smiled.

"You've done this before, haven't you?" She tied off the umbilical cord, then wrapped him in a clean white blanket. "You may present him to Thera."

Rhia looked at Coranna, who, though still chanting with her eyes closed, nodded her permission.

The baby squalled like a hungry puppy as Rhia took him into her arms. "He's beautiful, Thera. He's—" She looked around. "Am I supposed to say something profound?"

"There are no words." Coranna was at her side. She passed her hand over the boy's dark, damp hair. "Crow has granted him a life. We can add no further blessing to that."

Rhia brought the baby to Thera, who reclined in her aunt's arms on the birthing stool. "Thank you for the honor of presenting your child," she said as she eased him into his mother's embrace.

"Thank you," Thera said in a husky voice. "Oh, you're right. He is beautiful." Everyone laughed. "His name is Etarek, in memory of my father."

Coranna began another song, one that lifted their voices in joy. An echoing verse rose from outside, from a village that had seen too much sorrow.

30

Later that day, Marek and Rhia met to discuss the latest developments regarding Etar's death. At the wake—which was now also a birthday party for Etarek—they found a table toward the distant end of the village center. The table was covered with dirty plates and mugs, abandoned when the music had struck up again.

Rhia began to collect and stack the dishes. "We should take these to be cleaned."

Marek gently took the plates from her. "You're still a guest of honor until this party's over. Just sit and let me get us some food and drink."

Rhia agreed, but after he left, nervous energy drove her to continue organizing the soiled dishes. Noticing a cup and plate beneath the table, she moved the bench and crawled under to retrieve them.

"What's that smell?" said a deep voice.

Rhia sat up, bumping her head on the bottom of the table. Three sets of legs surrounded her, two on one side. She scrambled to her feet away from the voice.

Skaris the Bear loomed over her. Two men she didn't recognize stood on the other side of the table. Skaris's large brown eyes looked bleary, and she could smell the meloxa on his breath as his face hovered close, sniffing.

"Smells like—" he said to the man who had spoken "—smells like dead crow."

Their raucous laughter reminded her of the big black birds themselves.

"What do you want?" she asked, regretting the question as soon as it left her mouth.

"Not much," said the blond, who Rhia thought might be a Wolverine. "Just what you took from us."

She shivered in her understanding. She turned to look around for anyone to help, but most people had retreated to the bonfire, where the loud music would prevent them from hearing her.

"Don't be afraid." While she had been scanning her surroundings, Skaris had twirled a lock of her hair around his finger. He pulled on it, not hard enough to hurt. "You've been to the Other Side. What could possibly scare you now?"

"Not a little drink, I'm sure." The Wolverine pushed a mug of meloxa across the table. "You must be thirsty."

The man who had spoken first, with light brown hair and a scraggly beard, frowned at the mug. "What's that?"

Skaris grabbed the meloxa and held it up in a mock toast. "A second chance."

"No…" Rhia tried to move away, but the Bear seized a handful of her hair.

The bearded man's face crinkled in confusion. "Second chance for what?"

Skaris turned to Rhia, breathing hot on her cheek. The dark humor had left his eyes. "Why don't you crawl back in your grave and give us our month back, hmm?" He pulled her hair to tilt her head. "Drink up."

Rhia cried out in pain and reached up to spill the mug. The Wolverine vaulted over the table to grab her wrists.

"Wait," said the bearded man, "I thought we were just going to scare her a little."

Skaris raised the mug to Rhia's mouth. "It takes a lot to scare a Crow, Adrek."

She recognized the name as one of Alanka's former mates, a Cougar. Her eyes pleaded with him, but he seemed paralyzed. She pressed her lips together to keep out the drink she knew must be poisoned. The Wolverine took both her wrists in one large hand and pinched her nose shut with the other, cutting off her breath. She howled behind her closed mouth, muffling the sound. No one would hear. No one would help. Her legs kicked out, searching for a knee, a groin, anything to make Skaris or the Wolverine let go.

The toe of her boot hit something hard. The Wolverine shrieked and released her. She squirmed in Skaris's grip, which had tightened in his surprise. He struggled to keep the mug right side up.

Rhia watched with confusion as the blond man stumbled away, blood trickling down his calf. A simple kick couldn't make a Wolverine so much as yelp, much less scream and bleed. He lurched out of the shadow, and in the waning afternoon light she saw an arrow fall from his lower leg.

Adrek cursed and fled. Skaris yelled after him to come back, to no avail.

"Let her go." Marek stepped out from behind a distant tree, an arrow nocked and aimed.

Skaris's arm clenched, and for a moment Rhia thought he would use her as a shield. Then he pushed her away and held up his hands.

"Calm down, Marek. We were just having a little fun. Having a few drinks." He lifted the meloxa he had been trying to force down Rhia's throat.

Marek paced forward, his bow unwavering. "Then drink."

Skaris looked at the mug. "What, this one?" He started to turn it over, splashing a few drops on the needle-littered ground.

"Drink it!" Marek was only about twenty paces away now. He lowered the bow slightly. "Or I make sure you never get to the second phase."

Reflexively Skaris covered his groin with his free hand, as if that would stop the arrow's impact. His chin tilted up. "You'd shoot an unarmed man? Where's your honor? You want to fight, let's fight, but no weapons."

Rhia looked at Marek, wanting to tell him no. He could never beat a Bear in hand-to-hand combat. Skaris was bigger, and undoubtedly stronger and faster, even when drunk.

Marek drew the bow even tauter. "Drink that, and we won't need to fight."

"Don't," Rhia told Skaris. "It's poisoned, isn't it?"

He downed the mug in one long swig, then tossed it aside.

"Fooled you." He wiped his mouth and gave a long, triumphant laugh.

Suddenly the Bear's eyes widened. He uttered a short gasp that was almost a hiccup, then pounded his chest with his own fist.

Rhia backed away, horror stealing her screams. Skaris clawed at his throat as if to yank out what was inside, the substance that ate his breath. He fell to his knees, bulging eyes staring at her with recrimination.

"No!" Marek lowered his bow and ran to her side.

"We have to get help," she said. "Maybe Elora has an antidote."

Marek reached for Skaris. The Bear clutched his hand, then in one move, leaped to his feet and punched Marek in the face.

Marek slammed to the ground and gaped at Skaris standing over him, not the least bit poisoned.

"You think I'd try to kill your mate?" He glowered at Marek. "What kind of monster do you take me for?"

Marek raised himself up on an elbow. "Why else would you try to force her to drink?"

"To scare her, to make her sick, to make her miserable."

"Is this about your sister?"

Skaris raised a fist like a weapon. "Don't talk about my sister. She'd be alive if it weren't for you."

Marek flinched as if the Bear had struck him again. "What does this have to do with Rhia? Why do you hate her?"

"Because she stole a month from my life, from everyone's life."

Marek passed a hand over his left cheek, which already held a wide red bruise. "She's a Crow. Our people need Crows."

"Kalindos won't get this Crow. When Rhia finishes her training, she'll take everything she's learned back to Asermos. Why should we pay for someone else's gifts? What did they ever do for us?"

"Plenty," Rhia said. Skaris tilted his head toward her, never taking his eyes off Marek. She continued. "When it's time to enter your second phase, there'll be no advanced Bears here to teach you. You'll have to come to Asermos to train with Torin. And he'll be glad to have you. We all will."

"Liar!" He turned toward her, and Marek pounced. He leaped on the larger man's back and locked an arm around his neck. Skaris roared and backed up hard against a nearby tree. The impact made a cracking noise, which could have been a pine branch or one of Marek's ribs. He groaned but held on.

In the distance, voices shouted, coming closer.

"Help!" she cried. "Over here!"

With a heave of his broad shoulders, Skaris pulled Marek over his head and flipped him onto the ground, then kicked him hard in the side. Marek curled up in pain, but when the next kick came, he grabbed Skaris's foot and pulled him down.

They wrestled and scuffled, neither landing another solid blow, until several Kalindons fell upon them, led by Adrek, who had apparently scampered off not in fear, but to find help.

Four men pulled the fighters apart. Skaris looked unscathed, but Marek's torn clothing revealed a bruised and bleeding torso. The men led them back into the center of the village, toward the bonfire, followed by the excited crowd, none of whom spoke to Rhia.

Coranna met them near the center of the village. Her expression was neutral, that of a judge now. "What happened?"

Marek wiped the grime from his face and said nothing.

Someone cleared his throat. Adrek.

The Cougar stepped forward and told Coranna everything that had happened since their arrival at the table, the truth reluctantly spilling from his mouth as he spared Rhia an occasional glance of resentment. When he reached the part about the injured Wolverine, Marek interrupted. "It's barely a scratch, as I planned. I only wanted to make Drenis let go of her. I thought I was saving her life."

"I don't understand." Zilus stepped forward, supported by a walking stick. "What made you think the meloxa was poisoned?"

Marek looked at Rhia, who in turn looked at Coranna. The Crow woman frowned and nodded. Rhia took a deep breath and let the words—and their consequences—fall where they may.

"I have reason to believe that Skaris poisoned Etar."

A murmur ran through the crowd, punctuated by Skaris's cry of disbelief. "What? I never—why would I want to kill Etar?"

"I don't know," she said. "He didn't know, either, but he was sure of it."

Skaris struggled against the grip of his captors. "What are you talking about? Who was sure of it?"

"Etar," Coranna said. "Rhia speaks the truth. I contacted him this morning to find out why his spirit still lingered. He seeks justice."

Skaris gave her a long, incredulous look, then said, "I want a new judge."

Coranna nodded. "For a crime such as this, no one in Kalindos can be truly objective."

"I'll send a message to Velekos," Zilus said, "directly to their third-phase Hawk, and ask her to send a judge." He looked at Skaris. "And an Owl as well, to question the defendant."

"Good," Skaris said. "Then you'll know it was all a waste of time."

Zilus ignored the Bear. "Now that the river has thawed, they should arrive in less than a month."

"In the meantime," Coranna declared to Skaris, "you shall be held in your home, under guard night and day."

Skaris pressed his lips together, wisely saying nothing more without the aid of an advocate. He spared Rhia one last glare as they took him away.

A hand touched her shoulder. She started, then looked up to see Razvin.

"You'll be safer without him free," he said. "We all will."

She nodded even as her suspicions of the Fox flared.

"The boy who confessed," Razvin said, "was one of Alanka's…friends."

Adrek stood alone, his face etched in bitterness as he watched Skaris be led away.

Razvin's hand grew heavier on Rhia's shoulder. "I'd do anything to protect my daughter. I trust you share my concern."

Rhia wanted to shift away, but Kerza's plea for her to learn more about Razvin forced her to continue the conversation.

"Protect her from what?" she asked him.

"Any threats, within Kalindos or—not."

Did he consider her a threat to Alanka, merely because she was Asermon? If so, his animosity was deeper than she had first appreciated.

"Excuse me." Rhia held back a shudder and approached Adrek just as he turned to leave the area.

"I wanted to thank you," she said. "For getting help, and for telling the truth."

The Cougar scowled at her. "I just didn't want to see anyone get hurt. It doesn't mean I want to be your friend."

She took a step back, speechless for a moment. "I don't deserve this. What did I do to you?"

"Only what you've done to all of us."

"First of all, I didn't know the price for my resurrection. Second, if it's so terrible, why doesn't everyone hate me?"

"Because they're fools? Because you gave them an excuse for a party? How should I know?" He shook his head. "I won't bother you if you don't bother me. Let's leave it at that."

He walked away. Marek approached her, holding his left side where Skaris had kicked him.

"I have to pay Drenis restitution for shooting him."

"What kind of restitution?"

"Provide him with food and water and anything else he needs during his recuperation, starting tomorrow. It's just a flesh wound, but I'm sure he'll drag out the healing just to watch me serve him." He shrugged. "The punishment would have been a lot worse if I hadn't done it in your defense."

"Or what you thought was my defense." Rhia turned his chin to examine his wounds. "Elora should look at these cuts."

"They just need cleaning, and some ice for the bruises. Skaris could have killed me if he wanted. It's not as bad as it looks." The sun disappeared behind the mountains, and Marek faded from view. "Well, now it's worse than it looks, since it doesn't look like anything at all."

They scavenged some food from the wake and returned to his home, using a basket and pulley to hoist their dinner. Marek hung a blue cloth from his porch railing to signal his presence, then changed it to the red Do Not Disturb flag.

Rhia washed the cuts on his face as thoroughly as possible, considering she couldn't see them.

"Do you really think Skaris killed Etar?" he asked her as she wrapped a chunk of ice within a cloth.

"Not on purpose." She reached out gingerly to find his head without poking him in the eye, then held the ice to his swollen cheek. "Maybe someone else put the poison in the drink and had him serve it."

"But how would that person know Etar would get that particular mug unless they told Skaris which one to give him?"

"Good point. Skaris had to have known. But it doesn't make sense. Why would he do it?" She helped Marek remove his shirt, which reappeared as it left his body. "If Kerza was right, and it happened over a Council dispute, the Owl from Velekos will find out who planned it."

"But a second-phase Owl can only detect a direct lie, so they'd have to run through every name in the village, looking for a yes-or-no answer."

Rhia stopped, holding his shirt. "Unless it wasn't one of the Kalindons."

"Then who?"

"What if Etar died for something bigger than Council politics?" She held up a hand in a preemptive plea against his interruption. A thought buzzed around her mind, something that had seemed insignificant at the time. It came to her half-formed. "Didn't you tell me one of your Bear friends went to the Descendant City? The one who couldn't feel the Spirits there."

Marek let out a small gasp. "It was Skaris. He brought them a message from the Council."

"Maybe the Descendants turned him into a spy."

"Skaris? Not likely. He's too boastful to be a good secret-keeper." He took the cloth to cleanse the cuts on his side. "Your village has been living under the shadow of a Descendant invasion for years. You must think any odd event is a sign of war."

"The Descendants have every reason to invade Asermos," she said, "and no reason not to."

"No reason, other than the slaughter of their troops. If your village coordinated its magic, you could stomp any opponent into the ground."

"We'd need time to coordinate our magic. Someone would have to warn us of the enemy's movements weeks in advance." She sat on the edge of the bed. "I'm not making this up. I had a vision years ago. Someone I know will be killed in the battle."

"Have you told them?"

She shook her head. "It's forbidden."

Marek sat next to her and took her hand. A shadow of nothingness obscured her palm. "When I think of all you have to see and hear as a Crow, I don't blame you for wanting to run away."

Rhia's toe nudged the cloth used on Marek's wounds. It

was covered in mud as well as blood. "You got filthy in that fight. Would you like me to heat water for a bath?"

"Oh, that would be—" He caught himself. "No, I'll do it."

"You got this way on my account, so it's the least I can do. Besides, you took care of me for days in the forest." She pushed him gently down on his back. "Rest while it heats."

Rhia collected a bucketful of water from the cistern that sat on the rope bridge between his home and Coranna's. His stove was tiny compared to the Crow's, and by the time the water heated, he was asleep. She wet a cloth and flicked some warm water in the direction of his snores.

"Hey!" He spluttered, and she heard his feet hit the floor.

"Your bath's ready."

"Then help me undress," he said in a tone that invited more than sympathy.

She obliged, resisting the urge to demand more from his body than it could comfortably offer. He sat on the floor, leaning against the bed, while she cleansed him. His murmurs of appreciation made her long to see his body in the warm lantern light.

With the leftover water, he scrubbed and rinsed his hair. As he rubbed it dry with a clean cloth, he said, "Sometimes having short hair comes in handy."

She broached a difficult question. "Will you keep cutting it?"

His hand stopped moving, and he set down the towel. "I knew you were wondering." He put on a fresh shirt from a pile in the corner, then ran the towel over his head again. "It's growing, isn't it?"

"Hair will do that."

He was silent as he finished dressing, each article of

clothing vanishing as he put it on. "I don't know, Rhia. It still hurts. I was there."

"For the birth?"

"Usually fathers wait outside, but some women prefer their mates or husbands to be with them. I wonder if it isn't to make us appreciate how much they suffer to bear children." She heard him sit on the bed with a heavy sigh. "Kalia wanted me there."

It was the first time he had spoken his mate's name to Rhia. Kalia was real now.

"It was bad," he said, "from the beginning. There was so much blood. The baby, he tried to come out feetfirst. He kept ripping her apart from the inside, until finally—she begged Elora to cut her open."

Rhia closed her eyes. Such surgeries were impossible to survive without a third-phase Otter or second-phase Turtle.

Marek's voice went dead. "But it was too late. When they took him out of her, he wasn't breathing. And neither was she."

"I'm sorry," she whispered.

"It was nighttime, so she couldn't even see me before she died. I was already invisible."

She sat next to him on the bed. "She knew you were there. She knew you—" Rhia stumbled over the word "—loved her."

He drew a strand of her hair through his fingers, sliding down to the ends, which came to the shelf of her collarbone when pulled straight. "Can I ask you how your mother died?"

"Her heart, it—gave out."

"Was it quick?" he whispered.

"No." She felt herself shrink inside. "We all had a chance

to say goodbye. But it wasn't enough time, and I—I couldn't help her cross."

His hand drifted to her cheek and caressed it with the backs of his fingertips. "You must have felt terrible."

"I still do."

"And yet, your hair grows long."

"Because I only wear my guilt on the inside."

He sucked in a sharp breath. "You think my mourning is some sort of display?"

"I think it's punishment, and not just for you. How do you think Coranna feels each time you cut your hair?"

"She made a bad choice, and we all have to live with it. Except Kalia and my son. They don't get to live with anything."

Rhia touched his chest. "I don't think Coranna made a bad choice. I'm glad she chose you."

"If you knew Kalia, you wouldn't say that."

Eyes stinging, she drew back her hand.

"I'm sorry," he said. "You must wonder if I compare you."

"Don't you?"

He sighed. "We were so young. We'd loved each other since childhood, but the older we got, the less we understood each other. It's hard to explain."

Rhia thought of Arcas. "You don't have to."

"We fought all the time," Marek said, "about stupid things, things I don't even remember. When we found out she was pregnant—" He shifted his weight on the bed. "We didn't rejoice at the thought of raising a child together when we could barely stand to be within the same walls. We only thought of ourselves, not the baby. So Wolf and Swan turned our new powers from blessings into curses."

"What happened to her Swan magic?"

"In their first phase, Swans can interpret their own dreams, and in the second phase, they can do it for others."

"I know," she said. "My father's a Swan."

"He waits for others to tell him their dreams, right?"

"Of course."

"Imagine your father following everyone around, begging to know what they had dreamed the night before, and then only being able to see what those dreams said about him."

Rhia couldn't imagine. "How awful for Kalia."

"Soon no one wanted to be near her, or they would tell her a false dream to keep their own privacy. She couldn't sleep at night with her head so full of questions and worries. But when she felt the baby move inside her the first time, she understood what it meant, how enormous it was to be a mother. Instead of fear, she felt happiness. And Swan returned her true powers."

Rhia filled in the ensuing silence: *But Wolf didn't return yours.*

Marek lay down, drawing his breath in a wince. "The more I thought about it, the more afraid I became. It was like I was getting younger instead of older, maturing backward. I started staying out all day, sleeping in the forest so no one could see me. It's a wonder they didn't forget what I looked like. When Kalia needed me most, I failed her."

Rhia realized how similar his struggle against his Spirit was to her own, and wished she had trusted him sooner with the truth of her mother's death.

She lay beside him and held his hand between both of hers. "I wish I could say something other than, 'I understand.' It sounds so hollow."

"No, not from you." With an audible effort, he turned on his side to face her and drew a blanket over them. "I know Coranna waited years for you to be ready to become Crow. I remember when we first got word of you."

Rhia thought how differently events would have turned out if she'd come then instead of now. "When Kalia died, were you…"

"Together? Yes and no. I planned to help her raise the child, but our spirits were no longer connected enough to be mates, much less husband and wife. We both expected to find other people to marry someday."

The way Kalindons separated marriage and childbearing made Rhia uneasy. "What if you'd found someone first? Who would help her take care of the child every day?"

"I would. Everyone would. Children are too valuable to be raised by only two people."

She was suddenly glad she had brought several months' worth of wild carrot seed. The thought of having a baby without the security of a husband horrified her. In Asermos, a woman in that situation would depend on the generosity of her family and maybe a few neighbors.

"We should stop making love for a week or two," she said. "It's getting close to my risky time."

"There are things I can use to make it safe for us. A little awkward, maybe, but—"

"Completely safe?"

"There's no such thing as completely safe."

"Then let's not."

He stretched a leg to cover hers. "Will you sleep here, anyway? This bed's too big without you now. Look how happy the blankets are to wrap you up." He flapped the covers and made a tiny cheering noise. "See? They never do that for me."

She chuckled. "So we'll simply lie next to each other, as chaste as geldings?"

"We could just sleep, or…" His hands wandered under the blanket until they found their warm destination. "We could find other means of pleasure." Rhia arched her back, imagining the means. He slid closer and touched his forehead to hers. "Listen," he said, "you're the most beautiful person I've ever known. Never think anything else. Promise me?"

"You don't have to say that."

"Promise me. Promise you'll never feel that you're less than anyone, no matter what."

She guessed that "no matter what" meant, "even if someday you return to Asermos and we never see each other again." But between now and "someday," she would have him and gladly let him have her.

"I promise."

31

Nearly two months passed, and still the judge and examiner did not arrive from Velekos. The southern village's third-phase Hawk had died, so a Kalindon messenger had to deliver the request in person. He returned with a promise that the Eagle and Owl would arrive as soon as their court schedule permitted.

Coranna continued training Rhia in the rituals she could perform in the first phase of her Aspect: the prayer of passage, to ease the dying person's spirit out of this world; the body-chant, sung to complete the separation after death; and the calling of the crows, to carry away the spirit and end the funeral. Someday, when Rhia entered the second phase—after con-ceiving a child—she, too, would be able to speak with departed souls, especially those who lingered close to this world.

Coranna also taught her how to block the terrible visions of a person's eventual death. Not only did the visions bring knowledge too heavy to bear, they could also produce black-outs, like the one Rhia had experienced with Dorius. In a battle situation, where she would help the healers decide which of the wounded could be saved, repeated visions would render her mad and useless.

Rhia spent her nights with Marek, though she couldn't see him after sunset, except for a slight shimmer now and then as a result of intense effort on his part. Every night she would run her fingers through his hair—as casually as possible—to discover it growing long and soft. His bouts of brooding dwindled to the occasional inward gaze of reproach as evening light faded and he with it. He left their bed before sunrise to hunt, then slept most of the day. Though she was glad his nocturnal ways left time for her studies, she doubted he would fit in on a farm, where work lasted sunup to sundown. Yet the thought of returning home without him gave her a dull pain below her ribs, as though she had swallowed a stone.

She no longer dreaded the forest and its darkness, but instead learned to hear its song. Each tree was a unique in-strument, with the winds its players. The steady southwest-erly breeze whispered most of the day, creating a background hum that reminded Rhia of a gentle rain on wheat fields. The north wind swept down from the mountains, usually at night, in a swirling chaos that twisted the branches, leaves, and needles into a riot of sound. Wind from the southeast brought rain—nearly every day for a month—and with it an arrhythmic patter as water dripped from the trees onto the roofs of the houses and the rocky terrain below.

On occasion she would see the old lone wolf from a

distance. His pale yellow eyes watched her, and she learned to grow calm under his gaze. Though it went against her stomach's demands and her principles of separating the wild from the tame, she saved pieces of her dinner for him when he looked gaunt. Sometimes at night she heard his solitary, unanswered cry.

Though Rhia knew a certain faction of Kalindons would always resent her, most of the villagers opened their hearts and homes to their guest, making her feel like one of them. Yet a dissonant note lurked beneath the overarching harmony— Etar's death and its mysterious circumstances. She avoided the home of Skaris, who watched her from his window with what felt like a burgeoning bitterness. Her lingering suspicions of Coranna—who had an opportunity and perhaps a motive to kill Etar—made Rhia's studies difficult, and her qualms concerning Razvin were only slightly tempered by the obvious adoration he shared with his daughter.

One night, several days before the summer solstice, Alanka and Razvin invited Marek, Coranna and Rhia to dinner. Though Rhia found it difficult to be in the same room with Razvin, her appetite insisted she attend. As Marek had warned, most nonfeast days in Kalindos featured a maximum of two unsatisfying meals. When a Kalindon hosted guests, however, the meals were large, to honor all who attended.

"What do you miss most about Asermos?" Razvin asked Rhia as they sat down to eat that evening.

She contemplated her surroundings. All the windows were open, the sun shining through the western one, long before its summer bedtime. A cool breeze wafted through the airy house, and the trees whispered a soothing tune.

"Bread," she said finally.

The others laughed.

Razvin gave her a teasing grin. "Not your family, your friends, your—" he glanced at Marek "—anyone else?"

She hid her discomfort at the diminishing memory of Arcas. "I miss bread. It rounds out a meal, makes it complete. If I could give one Asermon gift to Kalindos, it would be bread."

Razvin's smile disappeared. "We can't have farms here to grow the wheat, and we don't want them. How many trees had to fall so your land could be tilled? How many animals had to be enslaved so you could have your bread?"

"I like bread," Marek said in an even voice. "At the Fiddlers Festival in Velekos, they served slabs of meat between two hunks of bread, all dipped in juices. Messy but delicious."

"Meat from animals bred for slaughter, with no chance for escape, no dignity of the hunt." Razvin kept his eyes on Rhia. "Farming makes you soft."

Her face heated. "You call having everyone live through the winter 'soft'?"

"You only live through the winter if the harvest has been good. If there's a drought, or too many insects, then people starve anyway, and more of them, since there are more to feed."

"In good years we store extra food to keep that from happening." She didn't point out that Kalindons gorged on their extra food at feasts rather than save it.

"If all those fields and stores of food were taken from you, you wouldn't survive a year."

His words gave her a sudden chill. "Why would they be taken from us?"

He shrugged. "A storm, perhaps. A flood."

"An invasion?" she said.

The table went silent. Razvin stared at her with fear-tinged eyes. Then he blinked his gaze back into beguilement. "Who would dare invade the all-powerful Asermos?"

"Anyone who thought they could defeat us. The Descendants, for instance."

He looked at her darkly. "If so, you've brought it on yourselves. When you create a world that others covet, you shouldn't be surprised when someone tries to take it from you. Look at Kalindos. We're safe as long as we have nothing worth stealing. Safe and happy." Razvin lifted his mug to the others. "Here we prefer to live on the edge."

"We don't *prefer* it," Coranna said. "The edge is forced on us by our surroundings. You'll understand when you're my age—Kalindos is my home and I'll never leave it, but these old bones will take any ease they can get." She turned to Rhia. "When you return for second-phase training, bring as much bread as you can carry."

Marek brightened at Coranna's words, then his brow creased and his gaze dropped to his plate. Rhia wondered if he were imagining her return after bearing another man's child. The possibility had receded beyond the grip of her own imagination.

Alanka merely picked at her food and said nothing.

"Well, sweetness?" Razvin asked her. "Don't you have a request for some Asermon treasure? Bread? Cheese? Ale?"

Despite Rhia's fullness from the meat and nuts, her stomach yearned for a meal of nothing more than bread, cheese and ale.

"What about a nice Asermon boy?" he asked. "They grow them bigger there, I hear."

Alanka pushed away her plate. "Father," she said without looking at him, "why do you have to be such a monster?"

Razvin stared at his daughter while a dozen emotions played over his face. He began to speak.

But instead of forming words, his mouth emitted a strangled yelp. He clutched his head and lurched from his chair, which clattered to the floor behind him.

"Father!" Alanka ran to his side. He pushed her away with a growl, then crouched low, hands on the floor. His back arched, and the animal cry that came from his throat curdled Rhia's blood.

Razvin's body twisted in agony as it shrank. Red hair sprouted from his neck and arms, becoming thick as fur.

Rhia gasped. It *was* fur.

Razvin was turning into a fox.

Claws sprang from the knuckles of his fingers and toes, and he shrieked until his face elongated into a red-and-black snout. Then the human noise turned into a snarl. His limbs shortened and lengthened into doglike proportions. Eyeteeth sprang into fangs. Last came the tail, and Rhia averted her eyes to keep down her dinner.

The fox lay panting on the floor for a moment, then rose to flee. Razvin's clothes hung loose on his body, which wheeled in panic upon finding no escape from the room. He tripped on a bunched-up sleeve and smacked his snout on the floor.

"Father?" Alanka approached the fox slowly. "Can you hear me?"

A light flickered in the creature's black eyes, as if he recognized her voice.

"He's come into his full power," Coranna said. "Foxes can shape-shift in the third phase."

Alanka shook her head. "But I'm not pregnant. I haven't been with a man in over a month." She looked away. "Not that it's anyone's business."

Rhia started. "One of my brothers." She put her hand to her mouth. "I'm going to be an aunt."

"Me, too!" Alanka bounded over to hug her. "I don't even know them, but I'm so happy." She muted her enthusiasm and turned back to her father. "But what do we do with him?"

"Let him out," Marek said. "See if foxes can climb trees."

"That's not funny." Alanka glared at him. "He can probably understand us."

The fox uttered a rattling bark, then with a high-pitched cry, flopped onto his side and changed back to human form, much faster than he had become a fox.

No one spoke as Razvin stared at the wall for a long moment. Then he said, "That was incredible."

Alanka knelt at his side. "Are you all right?"

"Incredibly painful, but nonetheless…" He looked up at Alanka. "Does this mean—"

"No." She held up her hands. "It must be one of your sons, going to be a father."

"Oh." He eased himself to a sitting position and rubbed the base of his spine. "Did I have a tail?"

Rhia couldn't forget Razvin's words of foreboding. All along she had felt that Etar's death was somehow connected to the future of Asermos, though she couldn't explain it out loud in a way to make anyone, even Marek, understand. Razvin held the answers, she was sure of it now.

The morning after the Fox's transformation, Rhia waited outside his house, hiding in a clump of brush, while Alanka was out on a hunt with the other Wolves. Razvin appeared and removed the blue flag from his porch, signaling the house's emptiness. He descended the ladder and set off toward the river empty-handed. As he moved, his head swiveled slightly, as if looking for someone—or ensuring that he went unobserved.

She followed, and managed to keep him just on the edge of her sight until they were far away from the village. She walked slowly to maintain her stealth, but as she neared the rushing river, dared to proceed more quickly, counting on the water to mask the sound of her footsteps.

A thicket of sycamore trees appeared. She slid from one mottled white trunk to the next, listening in vain for Razvin's steps. He must have changed course, she thought, disappointed with her first attempt at tracking.

Voices.

She recognized only one, that of Alanka's father. The other man spoke with what she thought was a southern accent, like that of Velekos, but more foreign-sounding. She caught a word or two, but the cascading water muffled their remarks.

A bit of pale gray moved in the corner of her eye, from deep within the forest. She searched the shadows for a clearer glimpse. Was it another stranger, come to meet with Razvin? No more movement occurred, and she decided to press on, keeping an eye behind her lest she become surrounded.

She changed her angle on the riverbank. A ledge concealed a small area right next to the shore. If she dared, she could crawl to the rim and hide in the long grasses growing there. It might be the only way to hear them.

Rhia dropped to her hands and knees and crawled forward, making sure not to rustle the grass closest to the river.

"What about the Wolves?" she heard the strange man say.

"There are no Wolves in Asermos," Razvin replied.

"Are you sure?"

"Besides, my daughter is a Wolf. I'll give you nothing you could use against her."

Rhia inched forward and finally glimpsed the two men. The one speaking with Razvin held what looked like a flat box, on which he made odd markings. His fair skin and hair were smooth, the latter tied in a short gathering at the base of his neck. He couldn't have been more than a few years older than Rhia. Beyond him in the shallows bobbed a canoe bearing strange designs.

"And why should I trust you?" the man asked. "How do I know this isn't a trap?"

Razvin's eyes narrowed. "I assure you, I have no love for the Asermons. When Skaris brought me news of your plans, I felt no sympathy for them. But I must keep Kalindos safe, like you promised. One man had to die already for this bargain, a Council member I suspected of getting close to the truth."

I knew it, thought Rhia. *Etar.*

"Murders mean attention," the stranger scolded. "Does anyone suspect?"

"That's the beautiful part. Our friend Skaris tried to poison an unwanted guest among us. I merely switched the mugs so that the Councilman would die instead of her."

Rhia's throat grew sharp and acrid, as if part of her stomach had risen into it. Skaris had tried to kill her, and Razvin had saved her life, if only for his own purposes. So Etar *had* died because of her.

Razvin continued. "Most people believe the boy did it, though they suspect him of being a tool of someone more powerful." He chuckled. "Which he is, without knowing it. And what he doesn't know can't hurt us, right?"

The stranger harrumphed. "Poison, heh? Clever. You're not as barbaric as I assumed."

Razvin's voice sharpened. "Barbaric?"

"Is it true the Asermons call you Kalindons 'termites'?"

"I wouldn't know." Razvin gripped the stranger's arm. "Listen to me—my daughter stays safe. You promised."

A breeze made a small wave lap on the shore, less than a legspan from where they sat. The foreigner shifted back to avoid getting wet, revealing a long, shiny sword lying at his side.

The sword of a Descendant.

She drew in a sharp breath, then covered her mouth. Razvin tilted his head in her direction. He had heard her, or at least heard something that caught his interest.

Oblivious to the disturbance, the Descendant nudged Razvin and gestured to the markings. "I don't believe some of these Aspects, especially the third-phase ones. Crow people bringing back the dead, Hawks sending messages to each other over hundreds of miles with just their minds. My superiors won't believe it, either, unless you show me some proof."

Razvin held very still. "I didn't tell you about the Aspect of Fox. All three phases enhance our natural cunning, the ability to learn secrets with which to manipulate people and events. The first phase allows us to read emotions from the most minute body language. For instance, I can tell you're afraid of me, even though you carry a sword and I don't."

"No, I'm—"

"The second phase is camouflage. If I remain perfectly motionless, I can blend in with my background to such a degree that I might as well be invisible."

"Show me."

"If I do, I won't have enough energy to display my third-phase powers."

The Descendant gave Razvin a skeptical look. "Which is what? Telling the perfect lie?"

Razvin laughed, long and loud. "No, I was born with that power. I didn't have to wait to become a grandfather, like I did for this."

He stood and took a dramatic pause before removing all of his clothing. Even at his age, he possessed an admirable physique, and Rhia's mind careened away from the image of her mother admiring it, too.

When he was naked, Razvin crouched on his hands and knees. The Descendant remained still while looking like he wanted to run away.

Razvin changed more quickly this time, though the process looked no less agonizing. His shrieks morphed into howls as the fox shape overtook his body.

The Descendant's eyes widened with panic. Uttering a string of curses Rhia had never heard before, he leaped to his feet and tried to back away, but bumped into the embankment where she was hiding. He turned to fumble for his sword, and she saw his face, etched with terror.

Razvin stared up at him, panting, his mouth appearing to form a smug grin. Her hounds gave that look after stealing meat, when they would treat the ensuing chase as a game they would never lose.

With a cry of rage and fear, the Descendant lunged, swinging his sword at Razvin's mocking face. The fox hopped back in time to avoid the blade's arc. Tongue lolling, he turned to run, but the muddy bank gave him little traction. The Descendant lashed out again and sliced the tendon above the fox's left heel. Razvin squealed in pain and slipped again, one leg useless. His claws scrabbled the mud as the soldier closed in. The next blow, a stab to the throat, cut short Razvin's cry and threw him to the ground.

The Descendant swung again and again, hacking at the fox's lifeless body. Fur and flesh rained red on the riverbank.

"Beasts!" The man slashed and chopped with a wild panic, as if Razvin would rise if there were anything left of him. "You're all nothing but beasts!"

Rhia's stomach lurched, and her vision blurred and spun. Crow's wings throbbed inside her head in a rush of rage at the senseless murder and desecration. She pressed the dry grass against her mouth to stifle the cry of anguish, the pain and fear Razvin had experienced at the moment of his death. It was as if he were dragging her to the Other Side with him in his hasty retreat from life. The wing-beats were so loud, she had no idea if she screamed or not.

The Descendant speared what was left of Razvin the Fox

on the tip of his sword and flung him into the river. He lost his grip on the weapon in the process, and it plopped into the muddy shallows several feet from where he stood. He cursed again, then cut himself off as he heard a noise behind him.

No.

He looked straight toward Rhia. He wiped the gore from around his eyes with a bloody sleeve, then stared hard at the place where she hid. He didn't look certain he saw her, but if she moved or even breathed…

The wind gusted then, pushing down the grasses between them. The Descendant gaped at her for a long moment. With his face full of fear, he looked younger than ever.

She leaped to her feet and ran. Though she had taken him off guard, he caught up to her within a few strides. He grabbed for her, his fingers slipping off her back. She sprang forward. If she could just reach the forest…

A hand locked onto her wrist and yanked up and back. Something popped, and she spun as a lightning bolt of pain screamed down her right arm and up into her neck. She shrieked and dropped to her knees.

"What did you hear?" His face, reeking of fresh blood, pressed close to hers. He jerked her arm again, producing shocks of agony that blinded her. "Tell me what you heard, witch."

She didn't know this word, "witch." Maybe she could pretend she understood nothing. She began to babble, spouting gibberish in the hopes he would set her free.

"Don't you dare put a spell on me." He cuffed her across the jaw, sending her sprawling on the ground, where she lay stunned.

"Get up." He jerked her arm again, and though she wanted to resist, the pain forced her to follow to keep from passing out. Tears blurred her vision. She stumbled downhill until her feet hit mud and she realized where they were going: toward his sword.

"No!"

She kicked out, and her foot found the meaty part of his calf, making him cry out. His grip loosened and slid down to her wrist. He grabbed her other arm and held her fast. "I don't want to hurt a woman, but I can't let you get away, and I can't let you work your magic on me."

"I'm a Crow," she sobbed. "My magic can't touch you yet. Please let me go."

"Let you go? So you can warn Asermos of the invasion? I won't let that happen."

"Invasion?"

His face fell as he realized he'd revealed a secret she hadn't been certain of.

He gave an angry tug, and they lurched toward the spot where the sword lay, mud and blood washing away in the shallow water. The Descendant spoke to himself under his breath, perhaps girding up the will to slaughter a woman in cold blood.

When he let go of one arm to reach for the sword, she twisted out of his grip and turned to run. She took only a few steps before he grabbed the neck of her blouse and threw her on her back with a thud. Her shoulder screamed again.

She stared up at him, his fine hair now caked and straggling over his frightened face. Beyond him the sky shone blue. A crow called from a nearby tree, waiting for the dead fox to wash ashore—or to see if another feast awaited it.

They would start with her eyes, she knew. Crow had neither mercy nor cruelty—He just was, and in a few moments she would see Him again.

32

The Descendant gripped the hilt of his sword with both hands and lifted it, preparing to drive the blade through her breast. He hesitated, and she thought he might change his mind. Then his gaze grew hard. He gritted his teeth and drew back for the blow.

A mass of gray flashed over her, and the soldier disappeared with a cry of surprise. She rolled to her knees to see a wolf snapping at the throat of the Descendant, who was trying to beat it off with the hilt of his sword.

It was the old lone wolf, the one whose life she'd saved.

She scrambled to her feet, wanting to help the creature. But the Descendant had a solid hold on his weapon, which was swinging wildly. Teeth and steel flashed, and she knew she could only save herself. One of them would die.

She ran, putting the growls and shouts behind her. Each step jarred her shoulder and sent a hot burst of pain through the right side of her body, but she had to run. Her entire village depended on her escape.

A yelp came from the river. Rhia stopped, listened and heard nothing. Even the birds had quieted. The wolf had given its life to repay a few scraps of venison.

The Descendant would follow soon. She couldn't outrun him. She looked around for a tree with branches low enough to climb. A hemlock grew about fifteen paces to the north. Its thick layers of branches would conceal her if she could just climb.

Shuddering, she explored her right shoulder with her left hand. A hard knob at the front of the joint told her it was dislocated, which meant it could be put back in place. She'd seen her mother do it, including with her brothers.

Could she do it to herself? Even the leather-tough Wolverines had screamed when Mayra reset their shoulders. But relief would follow agony, and in her current state she could barely move, much less climb.

"Where are you, little girl?" the Descendant shouted in the distance.

Rhia dashed to the tree and sat hidden behind the trunk. It was either fix her shoulder or feel the Descendant's sword. She crammed the front of her blouse into her mouth.

She bent her right knee and clasped both hands around it. Her eyes closed, and she calmed herself the way Galen and Coranna had taught her, taking several deep breaths in through her nose, out through her mouth.

Help, she prayed to any Spirit who might be listening.

She extended her neck and leaned back to straighten her arms. A gratifying *pop!* coincided with a wave of pain that sparked her vision red. Though inside her mind she was screaming, she uttered only a soft grunt. It hurt too much to cry out.

In a few moments the pain subsided dramatically. She shifted her right shoulder in a slow, cautious motion. It would be sore for a while, but it was back in place.

She began to climb, favoring her right arm, though it helped steady her as she shifted from branch to branch. The limbs nearly cracked from her weight, which meant they probably wouldn't hold the Descendant if he found her.

"I hear you," a mocking voice called.

She halted her climb and settled into the crook of a large branch.

"Was that one of your friends I killed back there? Razvin didn't tell me Wolves could shape-shift, too, but I figured it out. Was that his daughter I just gutted?"

He thought the gray wolf had been a Kalindon, she realized. So he still knew nothing about Wolves. But he knew many of her people's other secrets, and would soon share them with the rest of the Descendants.

Unless she killed him first.

But with what? She looked around—no branches hung by only a few fibers so that she could tear them off to use as a weapon. It was too far down to risk jumping on him, stealing his sword and stabbing him left-handed, as if that were a realistic scenario to begin with.

If he climbed up after her, maybe he would fall. Or if he found her and decided he couldn't retrieve her from the tree, he might stay at the roots and wait for her to come down. Eventually other Kalindons would come looking for her—maybe Kalindons with bows and arrows.

Or maybe just Coranna. He could kill the unarmed old woman easily, or use her as bait to get Rhia out of the tree and then kill them both. She couldn't take that chance.

If only she could summon Crow to take this man to the Other Side. Her spirit quaked at the thought of wielding such power.

The Descendant came into view between the branches. His shirt was stained with even more blood, some flowing from his own wounds. He bore a pronounced limp, and the trousers of his right leg were torn and bloody.

"Where are you?" His voice was tinged with panic and fury. "If you don't come out, I'll kill everyone in Kalindos. We agreed to leave your village alone if Razvin told us what he knew about Asermos, but since he's dead, I see no reason to hold to that bargain. Unless, of course, you come with me." He leaned against her tree, panting. "I won't kill you, I promise. I'll show you luxuries you can't imagine. You won't have to live like a savage anymore."

He put a hand to his head, drew it away and looked at the fresh blood on it. He wavered, then steadied himself, muttering under his breath.

"You couldn't have run far, not in such a short—"

A twig snapped to Rhia's left, and the Descendant whirled. With what looked like a great effort, he lifted his sword and charged in the direction of the noise. In his haste, he failed to notice the squirrel bounding up a nearby tree—a squirrel that was the likely cause of the sound.

A distant "Aaauurgh!" of frustration reached her ears.

Perhaps he was losing his way in the forest. Served him right if he were eaten by a bear or cougar or stumbled onto a copperhead snake.

When she no longer heard his voice or footsteps, Rhia scrambled down from the tree and ran as fast as she could back to Kalindos.

She saw Alanka on the outskirts of the village, plucking and cleaning a large bird. Rhia stopped, then turned to approach the village from another direction.

Too late. Alanka's sensitive ears heard her before she took another step. She waved at Rhia and beckoned her over. Her usual cheery greeting was cut short when she saw Rhia's face.

"What happened to you?"

Rhia put a hand to her cheek and remembered the sharp blow the Descendant had given her. The pain in her arm had dwarfed it. "It's nothing. Alanka—"

"Who hurt you?"

Rhia stood mute as a mouse. Where to begin?

"Rhia, you're scaring me." Alanka shook Rhia's right arm, making her cry out in pain. "What's wrong? Tell me what happened."

Rhia glanced toward Kalindos. She had to tell the others right away so they could warn Asermos. But Alanka deserved to hear it first.

She gestured to the fallen tree Alanka had been sitting on. They sat together, and Rhia took her hand.

"I just saw your father."

"So?"

"He met with a man. Someone from the city of the De-scendants. A soldier, I think."

Alanka jerked her hand out of Rhia's. "No. He doesn't have any business with them. They don't even trade with us."

"He wasn't trading, at least not for goods. He was—he was telling the Descendant about Asermons and their powers."

Her eyes grew wide. "Why?"

"So they could invade us."

"No!" Alanka leaped to her feet. "He would never do that. He's a good man."

"He made a bargain to protect Kalindos, to protect you."

"No!" She stopped pacing and turned in the direction Rhia had come from. "I'll find him and ask him myself."

"You can't."

She kept walking. "Why not?"

"Alanka, he's dead."

The girl stopped as if she'd taken an arrow to the heart. Slowly she turned to Rhia, her face white. "It must be someone else. You saw someone else. Not Father."

"He shifted his shape, and the Descendant—he lost his mind. He killed your father while he was a fox." She stood and approached Alanka. "I was right there. The Descen-dant saw me."

Alanka backed away. "You're lying. If he murdered Father, why didn't he kill you, too?"

"A wolf saved me. The soldier killed it, but their fight was enough time for me to escape."

The girl stared hard at the ground to Rhia's side, black eyes flickering. She seemed to be searching her mind for any ex-planation other than the one Rhia proffered.

"Where did this happen?"

Rhia described the area.

"I know where that is," Alanka said. "I'll see if you're telling the truth." She grabbed her hunting knife and bow and arrows, and began to run.

"Alanka, no! The Descendant may be out there." Her voice ached from the pain in her jaw. "Why would I lie to you?"

Alanka stopped and turned once more. "You never liked him." Then she bolted deeper into the forest.

Rhia called her name again and again, but it was too late. She turned for the village, hating herself. Had she told Alanka the news too willingly, too harshly? If someone had accused her own father, Tereus, of such treachery, she wouldn't trust them, either.

With her last bit of energy, she ran toward the center of the village. Her weary legs carried her to the base of the trees where Marek and Coranna lived. Coranna's blue flag waved in the slight breeze. Rhia called their names and heard the panic in her own voice.

Coranna poked her head out of one of her windows. "Marek's here. Why are you shouting?" She squinted at Rhia. "Are you hurt?"

They hurried down the ladder, Marek first. He leaped to the ground and gaped at her face, which was no doubt swollen by now.

"Call a Council meeting," she told Coranna. "Razvin's dead, and he's betrayed us all."

Without waiting for further explanation, Coranna hurried off. Marek led Rhia to the small clearing nearby where the

Council met, where a ring of seven flat stones gave each member a permanent seat.

"Can you tell me what happened?" He held her and rubbed her back as if to warm her. The shock of her experience was starting to set in, and she wanted to lie down and pretend it was all a dream.

"Let's wait until the Council arrives. It's hard enough to tell twice." She looked up at him with dread. "I saw Alanka on the way here."

"Where is she?"

"She didn't believe me, so she went to see for herself."

"Is she safe?"

"I hope so. The man who murdered her father is probably gone by now, back to his people. Unless he's looking for me. Besides, I couldn't stop her."

Marek examined the bruise on her face. His expression grew feral. "I'll kill this man for hurting you. Who was he?"

She uttered the hard words. "He was a Descendant."

"A Descendant?" said a voice behind them.

They turned to see Zilus the Hawk striding toward the center of the circle, hurrying himself with the aid of a walking stick. Behind him filed four more council members, two men and two women, Kerza and Coranna. Without Razvin and Etar, they were now only five.

"Tell us what happened," Zilus said, "from the beginning."

She waited until they were seated, then let go of Marek's hand. He meant it to give her strength and support, but she needed to be seen as strong on her own if they were to trust her story. He stood behind her outside the Council circle to listen.

She told them everything, fighting to keep her voice steady and the words in the right order. She wanted to hop on the fastest pony and charge through the forest until she arrived home. The Descendants could be on the verge of an invasion as she spoke.

The Council members shook their heads and wept to hear of Skaris's attempt on her life, then Razvin's betrayal and death. They shuddered at Rhia's account of the Descendant's brutality.

"We have to warn Asermos," she concluded.

"Of course," Zilus said. "I can send a message right now. Does your village have any third-phase Hawks?"

"No. Galen has only one son, and he doesn't yet—" She stopped. Arcas may have found another woman in her absence. "It's possible. Try."

Zilus unfocused his eyes and slipped into a trance state so quickly it startled Rhia. He had done it without drum or rattle or so much as a word of chant. Within a few breaths he lifted his hands as if he were reaching out in the dark to find his way. They searched the air in front of him and finally hovered, both palms facing one direction.

"I feel Galen's mind," Zilus murmured. After a few moments, his hands lowered. "But he cannot hear me. I'm sorry."

Rhia regretted the relief that tinged her disappointment. "I'll go ahead to warn them, if I may borrow a pony. The rest can come later."

"The rest of what?" Zilus asked.

"The rest of the people who are coming. To help them." She wondered at her choice of words. Which village was her home? "To help *us*."

"Help you how?"

"Help us fight, of course." She scanned the Council members' dubious faces. Would they refuse to lend aid? She turned to Marek for support. He wasn't there. She spun in a circle, thinking he had shifted his position, but he was gone.

"Where's Marek?" she asked Coranna.

Everyone looked around but no one remembered seeing him leave.

"Let's get back to the matter at hand," Zilus said to Rhia. "You want us to send our own forces, those who are sworn to protect Kalindos, to fight for your village?"

"Please…" she sputtered, searching her mind for a convincing argument. She had to make them help. She threw a desperate glance at Coranna, who nodded in sympathy.

One of the other male elders spoke up. "Asermos is large and strong. We're not. How much help could we be?"

Rhia found her voice. "We need every man and woman, every bit of magic we can get. It still might not be enough, with their bigger army and knowledge of our powers."

"But if we go to Asermos," Kerza said, "who will defend Kalindos?"

"The Descendants won't come here. It's too far, and you have nothing they want. Besides, that was part of the deal they made with Razvin."

"Razvin's dead," Zilus said bitterly.

"The leaders don't know that," Coranna pointed out, "and I doubt that soldier would admit to murdering their main informant."

Kerza gestured toward the southwest, in the direction of Rhia's home. "If the Descendants invade Asermos, why should they stop there? They'll be here next."

"Only if they win," Rhia said. "If we defeat them they may give up. And if we can't defeat them there, how can you do it here?"

Zilus shook his head. "Even in peace Kalindos needs every person it has."

"If we join you and lose," the first elder said, "the Descendants will enslave us as well. If we stay out of it—"

"If you stay out of it," Rhia retorted, "Asermos will remember how you weakened our friendship."

"If it were the other way around, would your village come to our rescue?" Kerza asked her.

"In a heartbeat."

"You can spare the fighters," Zilus said. "We can't. To defend your people would cost us too much."

"Not to defend us could cost you everything." She wanted to shake him, shake them all. "Why can't you see? They're not my people, they're *our* people. The Spirits brought us together, never to be separated."

"What about the other villages?" he said, "Tiros and Velekos? They're larger than we are. They can help you more."

"They may be too far away to help in time," Coranna said.

"Besides," Rhia added, "a Kalindon betrayed us. The rest of you should pay Razvin's debt."

Now Kerza was angry. "He hurt us, too. He had Etar killed, remember?"

"If you help defend us," Rhia said as softly as she could, "then your brother won't have died in vain."

"I think it's time we take a vote," Zilus said. "We owe you an immediate decision, if nothing else, so that you may depart right away."

As the five Council members murmured procedural matters amongst themselves for a few moments, Rhia scanned the surrounding forest for signs of Marek. Why would he have left when she most needed his support?

The vote was taken quickly: Four to one against sending military aid to Asermos, with Coranna the lone dissenter.

"You may take your pick of horses to ride back to Asermos," Zilus said to a stunned Rhia, "and we will give you supplies for the journey. But you'll go alone."

"No, she won't."

Alanka stood outside the circle of stones. She stepped forward, hunting knife in one hand and something gray and furry in the other—the tail of the wolf who had saved Rhia's life. Alanka stood by her side and faced the Council.

"My father has shamed us all." Her voice caught, then steadied. "We shouldn't compound that shame with our cowardice." She turned to Rhia. "I'll go with you, sister. I'll fight for you and for my brothers, and I will bring honor back to the name of Kalindos." She glared at the Council members and said no more.

Rhia took her hand, and together they left the circle.

33

"First we need to find Marek," Rhia said when she and Alanka were out of earshot of the Council members. "He'll want to come along." At least, she hoped he would.

"Where is he?" Alanka's voice was still leaden.

"He disappeared while I was telling everyone what happened. The sun hasn't set, so he didn't vanish. He left."

"Why?"

Rhia stopped to think. Had he abandoned her, knowing she would ask him to accompany her to Asermos? Had his former cowardice returned? Where was the protectiveness he had shown when Skaris and his friends had tried to make her drink—

"I know where he is." Rhia took off.

Alanka followed her to Skaris's house, which held an eerie quiet for a midafternoon. The blue flag was gone, and so was the guard assigned to keep watch over the prisoner.

Rhia gripped the ladder, which was made completely of wood, more stable than a rope ladder.

Alanka stopped her. "You can't climb with that shoulder."

"I have to see." She went up a few rungs, using her right hand only to steady her, not to pull.

Alanka sighed. "Then I'm right behind you."

Rhia climbed faster than she ever had before, and swallowed hard when she saw spots of dried blood on the highest rungs. When they reached Skaris's porch, the door was slightly ajar. Rhia pushed it open.

Skaris's guard lay sprawled on the floor, moaning from a blow to the back of his head. The table was overturned, and the two chairs lay scattered and broken.

Alanka knelt beside the guard. "What happened?"

"Gone," he whispered. "They're both gone."

Rhia and Alanka packed little, and in less than an hour, they were ready to depart. Rhia wanted to wait for Marek, but knew that every moment could be crucial in Asermos's preparation for war. Another villager reported seeing Skaris running away, with Marek in pursuit, unarmed. Zilus ordered three Cougars to find them and bring them both home alive.

Rhia waited beside the dark bay pony while Elora fit her shoulder with a sling. Coranna approached with a collection of herbs in a jar.

"Be careful not to break it," she told Rhia. "They will prove useful when…" Her voice trailed off.

"When people start to die. Thank you."

Coranna placed the jar in Rhia's pack and leaned close. "I'll keep fighting. Maybe I can change the Council's mind."

"I hope so. I can't do this without you."

"You're ready for whatever comes. Crow chose well when He selected you." She put her hand to Rhia's cheek. "Always have faith in the Spirits. It can't hurt, and sometimes it's the only thing that can save you."

Rhia embraced her for the first time, wishing she had never doubted her mentor. Coranna smelled like a heady mixture of all of her herbs and potions.

She helped Rhia onto the pony's back, then turned to Alanka, who approached with her bow and a full quiver of arrows. "Take care of her," she instructed the girl, "even if she won't let you."

"I promise." Alanka's face looked older and more drawn than before. She mounted behind Rhia, who reached down and grasped Coranna's arm.

"Send Marek as soon as he returns."

Coranna's expression clouded. "Rhia, if he has hurt Skaris, he won't be free to leave Kalindos. And even if he's free, he may not come. He's been…unreliable before."

Rhia shook the doubt from her mind. "He'll come."

"Remember, a Wolf's first duty is to protect his home."

"Exactly," Rhia said. "I'm his home."

She wheeled the pony away, kicked him into a canter and left Kalindos far behind.

They stopped just before nightfall to make camp. Without speaking, Rhia cared for the pony while Alanka built a fire and assembled a dinner from the food brought from Kalindos.

"Wait." Alanka held out her hand as Rhia was about to take the first bite. "I need you to do something." She slipped her hunting knife out of her boot and handed it to Rhia, then pulled her braid taut.

"Cut it very, very short," Alanka said.

Rhia stood and wiped the blade on her trousers, though she knew Alanka kept it spotless. She eased her arm from the sling and carefully straightened it—sore, but well enough for the task. She moved behind Alanka to grasp the thick, soft braid.

"I've never done this before."

"Can't imagine it's very complicated," Alanka said.

As the blade slipped through the rope of black hair, Rhia said, "I'm sorry for your loss." The words sounded empty, though the sentiment could not have been truer.

"I'm sorry you had to see it." Alanka felt her remaining hair, which swept past the tops of her ears. "Cut more."

Rhia obeyed, slicing more and more hair until Alanka let her stop. It was even shorter than Marek's was when she first met him, the length not much more than a finger's width.

Alanka passed a hand over her scalp. "It will be much cooler. I hear summers are hot in Asermos."

"Some days are. The river makes it humid."

"Are there a lot of mosquitoes?"

"Not as many as in Kalindos." She laid the braid on the log next to Alanka and sat down. "Ticks are worse—the little ones are hard to find and can make you sick. One of our hounds died last year from a disease carried by ticks."

"That's terrible."

"Yes. Fleas are bad, too, but garlic helps." Were they really talking about bugs and the weather, after what had happened? "Would you like to eat now?"

"I'm not hungry."

"Me, neither." Rhia contemplated her food. "My whole life, no matter what happened, I've never lost my appetite."

"I saw the blood."

Rhia looked up at Alanka's face, shadowed now by the trees and not her hair. "What blood?"

"By the river, where my father died." Her voice was a monotone. "I saw the blood and bits of red fur and—other things near the wolf's body." She hugged her knees and began to rock herself gently. "I wonder at the last moment, if his thoughts were a fox's—if he felt only the instinct to survive and take care of himself—or if he thought of me."

"He always thought of you." She laid her hand on Alanka's knee. "You were his world."

A single tear rolled down the girl's cheek. "Now whose world am I?"

Rhia let Alanka rest her head against her shoulder. Her sister shuddered with grief, but her eyes released no more tears. Rhia did not dare cry for Marek in front of Alanka, since the two losses could not be compared. Yet the void of fear inside her gaped bigger than any she could remember, and it threatened to swallow her whole.

The next day they made good time. The mare's speed was hardly blinding, but she possessed excellent stamina. Rhia figured that if the weather held, they should reach Asermos late the following day. She hadn't realized until now how close the two villages were; the place of Bestowing must have required a significant detour.

Unaccustomed to riding long distances, Alanka climbed onto the pony's back with stiffness and reluctance on the final morning. Rhia gave her some of the pain-relieving herbs Coranna had packed for her aching shoulder. Even the pony was weary, so for the sake of all, she set a more relaxed pace.

Yet she squirmed with impatience at the thought of the approaching Descendants. Would Razvin's murderer report that she had overheard and escaped? If so, they might attack sooner. If not—if the soldier hid his blunder for fear of punishment—Asermos would have the advantage.

Alanka twisted her body in an attempt to stretch. "I'd be happy never to ride another horse again."

Rhia risked a light laugh, the first since they had left. "It's hard to get around Asermos without one."

"I can probably walk farther than I can ride. And this pain-killer is making me sleepy." She sagged and let her legs dangle loosely around the horse's flanks. "You think our brothers will like me?"

"They'll like tormenting you. The trick is not to let them see you mad." She remembered that one of them would be different when they arrived. "I wonder which is going to be a father, and with what woman?"

"Do they have mates?"

"Nilo, not that I know of. Lycas liked a Wasp woman named Mali when I left."

Alanka grunted. "A Wasp woman? Sounds friendly."

"She's just what you'd expect—sharp and nasty. But she's a warrior, like he is."

They rode in silence for a few moments, then Alanka remarked, "I've never been this far from home."

"You've never been to any of the festivals?"

"I wasn't allowed. Father doesn't—" she corrected herself

with a flinch in her voice "—didn't care for outsiders. Not during my life, anyway. Obviously he spent time in Asermos when he was younger."

"Yes."

After an uncomfortable silence, Alanka said, "It smells different here. Less pine."

"Wait until you smell the livestock. It'll knock you out."

"I can't wait to meet a dog for the first time. Are they like wolves?"

"Not as much as you'd expect. My family raises wolfhounds, which—sorry—hunt wolves, along with deer and rabbits. They're bigger than wolves. Their heads come to my waist."

"How can you afford to feed them?"

"They eat anything. There's always meat not fit for—"

The pony suddenly leaped sideways with a panicky cry. Rhia grabbed her mane to help keep her seat, nearly pitching onto the ground, where a long black snake recoiled with a hiss. Alanka yelped, and a moment later a thud came from behind Rhia.

She steadied the horse and turned to see the girl lying motionless on the trail.

"Alanka!"

The serpent slithered off into the brush, and Rhia recognized it as a harmless rat snake—harmless to the pony it startled, that is, not to the rider thrown. She slid off the horse and looped her reins around a branch, not trusting the skittish creature to stay put.

As she knelt beside Alanka, the girl's shoulders began to quiver. She rolled on her back, and Rhia saw that she was laughing, quaking, gulping great lungfuls of air.

"I need a drink," Alanka said, then burst into another gale of hysterics. Rhia helped her sit up, then rubbed her shaking back until the cackles faded into hiccups. Alanka rested her elbows on her bent knees and put her face in her hands.

"Can you go on?" Rhia asked.

Alanka nodded and wiped her wet eyes. Rhia led her to the pony and gave her a few sips of water.

"I'm sorry," Alanka said. "That'll teach me not to relax on horseback."

The brief spark of humor in her eye reminded Rhia of Razvin. His last moments flashed in her mind, causing her heart to thud with the memory of his anguish and fear. She carefully remounted the pony, hiding her shakiness from Alanka, whom she helped up behind her.

As they neared Asermos, Rhia's anxiety grew. What would she see when she came out of the trees? Fields in bloom or in ruin? She urged the pony into a canter and felt Alanka tighten her grip.

A meadow lay ahead, to the right of the path, and she heard a sheep's low bleat at their approach. When they reached the meadow, a young man with long dark hair stood to greet them. Arcas.

Her heart leaped—with delight or trepidation, she couldn't tell. He shaded his eyes in her direction, then broke into an astonished grin and ran toward her.

"Rhia!"

She slowed the pony and guided her through the scattering sheep. Arcas met her in the center of the field.

"Get your father," she said, cutting off his greeting. "They're coming."

34

Rhia told them everything. Arcas's face paled at the news, but his father listened with typical stoicism.

"I'm not surprised the Descendants are invading." Galen stood to pace the scuffed wooden floor of his home. "The warning signs have been there for years. But that one of our own would betray us…"

Rhia glanced at Alanka, who sat at the table with the three of them, her gaze downcast. "Razvin didn't consider himself one of us. A lot of Kalindons agree with him. Even those who would never act against us won't come to our defense." Rhia sat back in her chair. "I thought they accepted me as one of their own. They gave up pieces of their lives for me, after all."

Galen nodded with a look of regret.

"What do you mean?" Arcas said.

"You knew, didn't you?" Rhia asked Galen. "You knew I'd have to die, and how my life would be paid for."

Arcas gaped at her. "What?"

"You wouldn't have gone if I'd told you," Galen said.

"You don't know that." Rhia shook her head. "You should have told me."

"I'm sorry." Galen's voice held genuine contrition. He put his hand on Rhia's shoulder and gazed down at her. "I did what I thought best at the time, but I may have been too sparing with the truth."

Rhia doubted he would change his actions if given another chance, but perhaps he was right. Even if she had gone to Kalindos knowing it meant her death, she would never have accepted the ransom of others' lives to bring her back.

"What are we going to do about the Descendants?" she asked him.

Galen crossed the room to a small desk in the corner. "I'll notify Torin so he can begin a battle strategy. Tomorrow the Council will hold a public meeting to discuss the news with the village." He opened a drawer and pulled out a parchment map, which he unfolded on the table. "Some Asermons may wish to evacuate to Tiros, or at least send their children. It lies in the opposite direction from the invading forces, so they'll be safe there for now. I'll send a message to the Tiron Council leader asking him to accept our refugees." He pointed to a mark south of Asermos. "Velekos is too close to Descendant territory. They may even be invaded first. We should warn them if we can get a messenger there in time."

"Razvin's soldier didn't mention Velekos," Rhia said.

"But it makes sense." Arcas traced an imaginary line between the Southern Sea and Asermos. "Velekos lies between us and the Descendants. They're a smaller village and don't pose much of a threat. If conquered, they could even be forced to fight against us."

Rhia shuddered at the thought of her people waging war against each other with their magic. Arcas was right, though, and he was thinking like a Bear.

"I must go." Galen took his hawk feather fetish from a peg on the wall and hung it around his neck. As he opened the door, he nodded goodbye to Alanka, then gave Rhia a tight smile. "Welcome home."

As she watched him go, she wondered if she were truly home.

"Alanka and I should leave, too," she said to Arcas.

He frowned and shuffled his feet under the table. "I missed you, Rhia."

Alanka glanced between them, then her eyes widened. "Oh." She pushed her chair from the table. "Where's the outhouse?"

Arcas gave her an apologetic look. "It's outside."

"Of course. I'll be there. Outside." She hurried out, sending Rhia a grimace as she left.

"Sorry," he said when the door had closed again. "I didn't mean to embarass her. But what I said is true. I missed you."

She shook her head. Razvin's slaughter, Marek's disappearance, the impending war—all made it impossible to handle the strange mix of emotions Arcas inspired in her.

"I must see my father." She stood and moved toward the door. "And our brothers. They need to know their father is dead, and that they have another sister."

He followed her. "I'll take you."

"Shouldn't you be meeting with Torin? You're a Bear, right?"

"No, I'm not."

"I know, but—"

"Everyone knows."

Rhia stopped and stared at him.

"After you left," he continued, "I thought about what you said. You were right. Besides, the Bear Spirit never answered when I reached out for Him. And Spider—" He pressed a hand to his temple. "She wouldn't let me go. It's what I am."

He parted the top of his vest to reveal a delicately carved wooden spider hanging from a thin rope around his neck. "This was my third attempt." He fingered the fetish. "The legs broke off the first two."

She took a step toward him. "Does this mean—"

"I'll still fight when the Descendants invade." He held up a hand at the sight of her dismay. "It's what I've trained for, all my life. Asermos needs every warrior. I won't be the best, but I'll be there."

She gazed at his determined face, ruthlessly browned by the sun, and admired Arcas more than ever. Whether she loved him, however, remained to be seen.

"I understand," she said. "I'm proud of you, and grateful for your service to Asermos." The words sounded so formal. All she could think of was the rush of Crow's wings over his body. "I just hope I never have to—"

"Shh." He touched her hand. "There'll be enough death soon. Let's not speak of it now." He lowered his head to kiss her.

"I'm sorry." She stepped away, cheeks burning. "I must find my family."

* * *

Tereus was kneeling beside one of the mares, cleaning her left front hoof, when Rhia and Alanka approached the house on foot. She paused to watch him, to soak in the pastoral serenity that might soon be lost forever.

He sat back on his heels and wiped the sweat from his forehead. Rhia was relieved he hadn't cut his hair again since Mayra's death. He wore it in a short braid that fell a few inches below the shoulders.

He looked up then and squinted, as if he didn't believe what he saw.

"Papa!" She started to run. He dropped the hoof pick and held out his arms, a bewildered look on his face. She hugged him carefully, to avoid hurting her shoulder again.

"Rhia, what are you doing home?" He smiled at Alanka. "Who's your friend?"

She introduced them, and after Tereus bowed he touched Rhia's sling. "What happened to you?"

"Too much to tell twice more today. Are my brothers here?"

He cast a glance at the setting sun. "They should be back with the hounds soon, and hopefully some fresh dinner."

"Then my story can wait until they arrive."

A distant holler came from the other side of the field. Rhia shaded her eyes to see two black-haired men waving their arms.

"Is that them?" Alanka's voice sounded hopeful for the first time in days.

"None other." A smile crept onto Rhia's face.

The dogs reached her first, their long gray legs devouring the uphill climb, tongues lolling with the exhaustion and exhilaration of the hunt.

Alanka yelped in alarm at the approach of the six-hound pack. "You said they were big, but—" Her words were smothered in fur and slobber, and soon she was laughing.

Lycas and Nilo arrived then, each carrying two rabbits, which they dropped on the ground so they could hug Rhia.

"You're early," Nilo said as he let go of her.

"We weren't expecting you until next spring." Lycas grabbed her around the waist and scooped her off her feet as though she were made of feathers. "Who can I complain to about the change in schedule?"

As Lycas put her down, Rhia sensed the difference in him. She touched his skin, which had grown thick and tough. The second phase had strengthened his defenses.

"Please say it's not Mali," she said.

He looked at Tereus. "You told her?"

Her father held up his hands. "I said nothing. They just arrived."

The twins turned to Alanka, who was trying to keep her feet among the milling dogs. Rhia gestured to her.

"Lycas, Nilo, this is—"

"Your sister Alanka." The girl approached them and looked back and forth at her brothers' faces. The three stared at each other for a long moment, then Nilo turned to Lycas.

"She looks like you," he said.

"No," Lycas countered. "Definitely more like you."

Rhia groaned. "You both wish you were half that pretty. Stop gawking and greet her."

Stunned, the men began to bow, then gave up and wrapped Alanka in a hearty hug.

"Ack," she said over Nilo's shoulder, "I can't breathe."

They let her go and examined her face again. Their expressions sobered in the same moment. Lycas touched the side of Alanka's head.

"Why is your hair short?" he asked with trepidation.

Alanka began to cry.

Over dinner, Rhia's father and brothers listened to her tale with grave demeanors.

When she finished, Tereus rose and collected their dishes, moving slowly, as if he had aged a decade while they talked. "My dreams make sense now."

"You've seen this coming?" she asked him.

"The images were too cloudy. Now it's clearer. There are other pieces, though, that don't fit." He turned to them. "I need some time alone to figure out what it all means."

"Go upstairs," Rhia said. "We'll clean up."

The four siblings washed and dried the dishes without speaking. For once, Lycas joined his twin in a stony silence. They had gained a sister, lost a father and learned of a war, all in one evening.

When the house was clean, they gathered their mugs and the jar of ale, and slipped outside. Rhia spread a large blanket on the ground. The sun had dipped below the horizon, sending tendrils of color threading through the wispy clouds.

Alanka stared at the view. "I've never seen a sky so big."

"You should see Tiros." Nilo handed her a mug of ale.

"Flat, dry, boring, but nice sunsets." To Rhia he said, "Would you do something for us?"

"Is it a trick?"

"No. We'd like you to call our father home."

Rhia realized that in the flurry of panic on their exit from Kalindos, no one had remembered to hold a funeral for Razvin. Perhaps Coranna had performed it after they left. Yet the man's children deserved comfort.

"I've never done it alone." She looked at the darkening sky. "I hope it's not too late for crows."

"You can do it." Alanka touched Rhia's elbow. "But if you'd rather not—his death was hard on you, too."

"I'll do it." They knelt in a circle on the blanket and joined hands. Rhia closed her eyes, letting the sound of the wind in the trees clear her mind. She chanted low at first, uncertain as to the quality of her voice. It sounded awkward to her own ears until she got her full breath under it. The tone cleared and resonated at the back of her throat. As the other three joined her, she felt the call float to the sky and spread through the air.

Just as her mouth began to dry, a crow cawed from the top of a nearby pine, then swept across the field where the ponies grazed. The chant faded as the bird flew away.

She opened her eyes. "He's gone." She wished she could feel Razvin's spirit leave, but he had probably crossed over days before. The declaration appeared to soothe her siblings, though. They remained motionless for several moments. She considered asking her brothers if they wanted to shear their hair, but they might assent only to avoid hurting Alanka's feelings, not out of any true sense of loss. No doubt they would cut their hair when Tereus died, though they weren't blood relatives.

Finally Lycas stirred. "You have a way with those birds. Maybe you could call a pheasant for tomorrow's dinner?"

She returned his slight smirk and said nothing.

"Thank you, Rhia." Alanka squeezed her hand, then sipped the ale and stared at the sunset. Her lower lip trembled, and she looked overwhelmed by the foreign sensations. Rhia herself felt out of place here. Earlier she had marveled at the simple act of leaving a building without a ladder. The cord of her crow feather fetish chafed the back of her neck; she hadn't worn it since the day she left home for her Bestowing.

Lycas tousled his new sister's hair, what there was of it. "We're glad you're here."

Alanka's mouth twitched. "So you can torture me?"

"Rhia!" Nilo gave her good arm a light cuff. "You weren't supposed to warn her. Now there'll be no fun at all."

"You're just mad because we outnumber you," Rhia said.

He scrunched up his face. "Two of us, two of you—how do you figure?"

"Two women are twice as formidable as two men."

"No argument here," Lycas said. "If Mali has a daughter, I'm dead." He frowned. "I'm already dead, though, once I tell her that her pregnancy means she'll have to evacuate."

Rhia cringed. "They'll have to drag her to Tiros."

Lycas's face was serious. "It'll destroy her not to fight. I know how she feels. We train for years for a moment like this. We live for it, terrible as that sounds."

"It's not terrible," Alanka said. "You're defending your people, your land."

A dark look passed between the twins, and Rhia knew that it was not the defense of freedom that boiled their blood. They were Wolverines, born to kill. No doubt their hands itched to close around a Descendant's throat.

To break the spell that war had cast upon them, Rhia nudged Alanka's arm. "How do you like the ale?"

"Tastes better than meloxa." Alanka belched, to her brothers' amusement. "But I need twice as much to get half as drunk."

"We have ways of drinking faster," Nilo said, "time-honored methods passed down through the ages from big brothers to little sisters."

They talked and drank until long after the stars appeared. Rhia banished her thoughts of death, danger and betrayal. For one summer night, at least, it was enough to be young and alive and with the family she loved.

35

Galen called a public Council meeting early the following afternoon. When Rhia, Tereus and Alanka arrived at the long
town hall by the riverside, it looked as though the entire village
of three thousand had showed up. Most crowded outside; only
one person from each household could attend the meeting.
This rule ensured that everyone would hear the proceedings
from someone in their home and no one would go uninformed.

"You go in," Tereus told them. "Your parts in this are
bigger than mine."

Alanka agreed, frowning. Rhia worried that Razvin's name
would be spoken with venom in this meeting. She squeezed
her friend's hand and led her through the crowd toward the
center of the stuffy room where a long wooden table sat.

"If they can see you, they might not mention your father."

"I can't blame them for being angry. I know I am."

Alanka's hand swept her forehead. "There's so many people in one place."

"You're not used to it." Neither was she, Rhia realized. After the Kalindon serenity, the bustle of Asermos threatened to suffocate her. But here she would remain, though she felt she had left a piece of herself behind in the forest, a piece held firmly in the jaws of a certain Wolf.

Rhia and Alanka found seats near the table just as Galen and the ten other village Council members filed in and took their seats around it. The Hawk waited several moments for the crowd to quiet, then stood next to his chair at the center of the table. The wave of silence spread from the front to the back of the room.

"By now," he said, "most of you have an idea why I've called a meeting of the entire village. Rumors fly quickly in Asermos."

A man in the front row stood. "Galen, are the Descendants invading or not?"

Galen took a deep breath. "We have reason to believe so."

The hall erupted in dismayed cries and impromptu discussions as the word spread to the folks outside. Galen gave them a chance to assimilate the news, then held up a hand for quiet.

"We have sent extra scouts, Bats and Weasels, both south and west to monitor the progress of Descendant troops. We don't know yet when the invasion will take place. It may be days, weeks or months, but we must prepare. I have asked the village of Tiros to take in any Asermons who wish to evacuate. Those who wish to leave or send their children should prepare to do so immediately."

Galen gestured to a tall, thick-set man standing against the wall to the side of the table. "Torin would like all Bears to assemble immediately after this meeting at his headquarters to review military strategies. Wolverines, Wasps and all archers meet them in Deer Meadow at first light tomorrow to begin maneuvers."

Many audience members appeared to calm at the thought of the Asermon defense forces. Few of them, Rhia included, understood the true power of the village's army. At least, she hoped that there was more to it than met the eye, for there could have been no more than a few hundred Bears and Wolverines, a few dozen archers—Bobcats, mostly—and perhaps a dozen Wasps. Others would help fight, but the total forces available did not approach a thousand.

Silina the Turtle woman raised her hand, and Galen gestured for her to speak. She stood slowly. Rhia had never seen her so somber. Even when Mayra had died, Silina's sorrow had been tempered with tenderness. Now her face held pure dread.

"Galen," she said, "in the last day, since the rumors began, I have had several visits from Asermons who wish to—" she bit down on the word "—hasten toward their second-phase powers in time for the battle."

It took a moment for the implications to set in.

Galen cleared his throat. "I'm not sure I understand. You're saying that some villagers—"

"Want to make babies to gain power," she said. "I can't say it any clearer than that."

Rhia saw her horrified gaze reflected in Alanka's face as the crowd descended into heated mutters.

"You can't do that," Alanka whispered to Rhia. "Look what happened to Marek when he wasn't ready to be a father."

His face etched in silent pondering, Galen sat down to indicate the topic was open for all to discuss.

Silina raised her voice. "Please, I beg everyone to reconsider such an act. The Spirits require us to be truly prepared before passing to the second phase—prepared to be parents, that is."

"I agree." Torin stepped forward. "We've all seen the perversion of powers that results from the rash acts of young people." He cast a scowl over the gathering, and Rhia wondered if his daughter Torynna had gotten pregnant early, as she'd planned. "We can't risk such chaos at a time like this."

One of the other Council members, a Horse woman named Arma, rose to her feet. "But Torin, wouldn't the Spirits want us to protect ourselves? Why else would they give us powers if not to use them in our defense?"

"It's not right," Silina retorted. "What about the children left behind when their fathers are killed in battle?"

"If the fathers are second-phase," Arma said, "they're less likely to die in battle to begin with."

Murmurs of assent ran through the audience. On the opposite side of the room, a Wolverine Rhia didn't know raised his hand, then spoke without waiting to be acknowledged. "Many of us will die whether we're first-, second- or third-phase. The population of Asermos may be decimated. We need all the children we can get."

"Children without parents?" Silina said. "What kind of life will they have if we lose?"

"If we lose," Arma said, stepping forward, "the Descendants will take the spoils of war. Including women."

Rhia put a hand to her chest. Rape was a weapon as old

as war itself. But if some women were already pregnant with Asermon children, at least the Descendants could not wipe out bloodlines with their own seed. The logic chilled her.

"It takes time to get pregnant," Silina pointed out. "New powers might not even be available in time for the battle."

"We don't know that," said the Wolverine. "Galen said the invasion could be weeks or months away."

Rhia looked at the Hawk, as did many of the other villagers. Galen made no move to speak, but merely absorbed the arguments around him. The opinions seemed equally divided between those in favor of the idea and those opposing it.

Rhia understood the temptation to reach for power; it had existed as long as her people possessed Animal magic. But the Spirits forbade such actions. Even those like Marek, who broke the rules accidentally, suffered consequences. For a person—or an entire village—to create children for the sole purpose of gaining power…

But in a desperate situation, their lives, their freedoms, their way of life, might depend on such power. Perhaps the Spirits would forgive them.

The debate raged for several more minutes, and still Galen sat silent. Eventually the number of people waiting for him to speak exceeded the number of people trying to speak themselves, and the crowd quieted.

He stood and seemed to meet the gaze of each person before addressing them. "Thank you for your attention. This idea troubles me, to say the least. You have heard well-intentioned, well-reasoned arguments on either side. If you are waiting for me to tell you what to do, I'm afraid I can't satisfy that wish. The decision to become a mother or father is one that cannot be dictated by Council decree. It is between you, your spouse or mate, and your Guardian Spirits. Search your hearts and ask the Spirits if you have the wisdom to handle both the new powers and the new responsibilities of parenthood. Advancing too quickly can have terrible consequences for the individual and the community alike."

Galen concluded, "We will meet again when the scouts have returned. Until then, the warriors have their orders. Everyone else—" A wisp of sadness brushed his face. "Prepare."

As the crowd filed out, beginning from the back, Rhia caught a glimpse of Dorius, Galen's brother. She remembered her vision of the man's death, his bleeding body writhing under the golden oak tree. Did it mean that the Descendants would not invade until autumn? Perhaps the war would last until then and Dorius would be killed in a later battle or skirmish.

She rubbed her forehead, as if the action would smooth her thoughts. For all she knew, the vision could take place next year or the year after. It hadn't shown a clear enough glimpse of his face to guess his age, and since Butterflies maintained a youthful appearance far longer than others, his death could occur years from now.

Regardless, Galen should know. But he had forbidden her to reveal her visions of others' death.

Alanka laid her hand on Rhia's knee. "You haven't said a word about Marek since we left Kalindos." Though they were not alone, the hall's background noise allowed them privacy. "I wouldn't give up hope. He may yet come. They may all yet come." Alanka's voice took on an edge. "And if they don't, and we lose this battle, may those lofty trees fall on their heads."

Rhia was in the kennel a few afternoons later, showing Alanka how to groom the hounds, when Arcas appeared on foot over the top of the hillside.

Alanka elbowed her in the ribs. "You think he wants to, er, gain power with you?"

Rhia sighed. Even if Marek never came, even if he were dead or had decided to stay to defend Kalindos, she couldn't bear the thought of another man's hands, another man's scent, on her body. Not for Arcas, not even for Asermos. "I can't."

"I know." The Wolf girl assessed him from a distance. "If you don't want him, there must be other women who do."

"Don't remind me."

As Arcas came closer, the hounds leaped against the fence to greet him, wagging their long gray tails.

"I missed you fellows." He ruffled the fur on the closest one's head. "And you ladies, too." He waved to the females who bounced and barked behind their larger companions.

"Hello, Arcas." Alanka started forward, undeterred by the rampaging dogs.

He squinted into the sun at her. "I hear you're deadly with an arrow. We could use someone like you."

"I've never shot a human before." Alanka touched her collarbone where her long braid used to hang. "But I'd be honored to try. I mean, honored to be trained as a warrior."

Arcas bowed his head to her. "Thank you." After an awkward pause, he cleared his throat. "Would you like to go for a ride?" He directed the question to Rhia, but, ever-courteous, included Alanka in his glance.

"Not me," Alanka said. "I still haven't recovered from the trip from Kalindos." She rubbed her backside and gave an exaggerated wince.

Arcas turned to Rhia. "Your father said the two chestnut ponies need more exercise."

Rhia looked away and nodded. She couldn't avoid him forever. "I'll get the bridles."

Once on horseback, Arcas set out toward the southwest. Rhia followed. "Why are we going this way?"

"I have something to show you." He held up a hand. "It's a surprise, so don't ruin it with a hundred questions."

They rode in silence through the sun-speckled woods. Finally Arcas asked her, "What did you miss most about Asermos?"

"Now that I'm back, I realize I missed the clouds. In Kalindos you can't see more than a patch of sky at any time, so the shapes of clouds get lost. I missed deciding what they looked like."

"What else did you miss?"

"Bread. Ale. Cheese."

"And?"

"And dogs."

He sighed. "What do you miss most about Kalindos?" She didn't reply. The trail widened, and he slowed his pony to come beside her. "You met someone there."

"I met many people. They were good, mostly. Even Razvin—he loved his daughter so much he was willing to do anything to protect her. People there, they love fiercely."

"Do they?"

She didn't meet his eye. "Look at Alanka. She traveled all this way to help us, because she's my friend and my sister. She knew she might be greeted with hostility because of what her father did."

"No one would dare treat her badly now that she's fighting for us."

"Wolves usually hunt as a group. She may be able to draw from that for battle tactics."

"Good idea. I'll ask her." His fingers idly combed the end of the pony's red mane that swept the riding blanket. "Are there other examples?"

"Examples of what?"

"Kalindons who love fiercely."

Her heart twisted. "I believe so," she said softly.

"You wait for someone else to come."

"I do."

Arcas fell silent beside her. Framed by the trees, a wide field lay ahead, where stalks of wheat, still early-summer green, undulated in the wind.

He grabbed one of her pony's reins. "Close your eyes."

"Why?"

"It's the surprise. Trust me."

She shut her eyes, clamping the pony tighter with her legs to maintain balance. With no sight, the sounds and smells of the field and trees came stronger. Soft stalks brushed Rhia's legs, releasing a dusty scent. Soon the way was clear; they must have reached a path in the middle of the field.

"It's just a little farther." Arcas led them a bit farther, then halted both ponies. "Open your eyes."

She did, and gasped.

Ringing half the field were a dozen trees in every color of autumn. Leaves of scarlet, orange and gold leaped from the background of green forest.

"Do you like it?" he said. "I made it for you."

She turned to him. "You did this?"

"It's a sunrise." His arm swept the expanse of trees. "Those red and orange maples are the clouds, and the golden oak in the middle is the sun."

The golden oak? Her gaze jerked back to the trees.

"No…"

She kicked the pony into a gallop and dashed across the field to the yellow tree. As she approached its roots, a dizziness overcame her. She halted the pony and slid off onto her feet before she could fall.

Arcas rode up. "What's wrong? Don't you like it?"

"How did you do this?"

"Spider magic. I didn't hurt the trees, I promise. They'll grow back green next year."

"Will the leaves fall early?"

"I don't know," he said.

"You have to know. It's important!"

"Why?"

"I've seen this." She knelt on the ground and put her hand on the thin grass. "Something happens here."

He drew in a breath as he grasped her meaning. "The battle." Arcas looked at the sun. "To get here from the southwest, the Descendants will go around Velekos, which means they'll arrive sooner, and probably stronger." He dismounted and knelt next to Rhia. "Is it me you see?"

"I couldn't tell you if it were." She relented at the sight of his fear. "It's not you." She touched his cheek. "That doesn't mean you won't die."

"I'll be careful."

A golden leaf fell between them.

She sprang back as if it were covered in poison. "Tell your father they're coming. Go now!"

"But the scouts—"

"Don't wait for them. Get your troops ready."

Arcas leaped onto his pony. She grabbed his leg.

"Don't tell Galen how you know."

"I won't." He leaned over and pulled her into a kiss, then let her go before she could protest. "May I see you tonight?"

Rhia knew he was asking more than what he said out loud. "Arcas, I don't think—"

"Just to talk."

She nodded. Their business was unfinished. "Come for dinner."

He gave her a bleak smile. "I love you, Crow woman, more than ever."

His pony took off through the field toward Asermos. Rhia gazed into the woods as two more golden leaves drifted to the ground. They would come through here, with swords and spears and Spirits knew what else.

Death was on its way.

36

The discussion around that night's dinner table was grim.

Arcas revealed the Asermon army's two-tiered strategy to Tereus, Alanka and Rhia. First they would try to defeat the Descendants using only "mundane" magic—the natural fighting abilities granted to warriors by the Spirits, along with certain weapons enhancements such as "spelled" arrows that could penetrate armor. If the invaders were not deterred and Asermos faced a desperate situation, they could call on the Spirits for more extreme measures. This last-resort plan, however, might cost more power than they could use without self-destructing.

"We must plan for either contingency," Arcas said, "because we don't yet know the enemy's strength. Our scouts haven't returned."

"Maybe they've been captured," Alanka said.

Tereus shook his head. "Bats and Weasels are too fast, too

stealthy. Even if one or two were captured, the rest would make it back, on foot if they had to."

They finished the meal in silence, and Rhia wondered if the others were imagining the same scenarios of horror as the one in her mind.

After dinner, Arcas and Rhia went for a walk in the woods, to finally discuss the subject that filled her with almost as much dread as the war itself.

"You used to be afraid of the forest after dark," he said.

She thought of the night Marek had taught her not to fear. "That was before."

"Of course. The Bestowing changes us in many ways, though for some of us the changes take longer to understand."

She touched his arm to reassure him. "I'm proud of you, Arcas, for being who you are. And for fighting as a Bear, though I worry for your safety."

"Why?"

She stopped and turned to him. "You know why."

"I don't think I do. And I'm not being coy."

Would he really make her say it? "Because you're my friend."

His face seemed to pale, even in the moonlight. "A friend? That's all?"

"It's all I can be to you now. Maybe forever."

"Then you do love someone else."

"Yes."

"Someone who isn't here." His voice hardened. "Someone who failed you. Someone who was too much of a coward—"

"He could be dead for all I know, and if he's dead, it's because he's not a coward." She reined in her indignation. "But if he's alive, he'll come."

"How do you know?"

"I don't know. I just believe."

"Rhia, can't we just try?" He took her hands in his. She knew she should pull away, but they were so warm, and she was so afraid. "I'll be going to war soon, and I might not come back." He brushed her hair from her cheek, then followed it over her shoulders with a touch that made her shiver, a touch that recalled distant memories of laughter and pleasure and heat.

"This man you love, if he were coming, he would have arrived by now." Arcas spoke with sympathy, as though his first concern were for her happiness, not his own. He pulled her closer, so slowly it was as if they had grown together. "Would it be so bad to be with me again?"

He kissed her, full and deep, and she knew it was over. She could kiss a thousand men who weren't Marek, and they would all feel fake. Her body now knew it as much as the rest of her.

Rhia shrank back and lowered her head. "I can't."

Arcas let go with a groan, then pressed his fists to his forehead. "I was such a fool. If we'd promised ourselves to each other before you left, you wouldn't have fallen in love with him."

She hesitated only a moment. "Yes, I would have." He stared at her. "I'm not sure it would have made a difference," she said, "whether you and I were together or not. With him, everything felt—feels—so honest."

He held up a hand between them. "There's such a thing as too much honesty."

"I'm sorry."

Arcas wiped his face hard with both hands, as though he could obliterate his own emotions. He let out a long sigh. "All right, then. I'll walk you home."

"Go," she said. "I'll see you tomorrow. Torin wants to discuss how I can help the healers help the troops."

"By figuring out which of us can't be saved?"

She nodded, a gesture he echoed ruefully.

"It's an honorable duty," he said. "I pray you don't get hurt on the battlefield."

"So do I, for you."

His face pinched the way it had when he was a misbehaving child. "I'm sorry I upset you."

"Go," she repeated. "I just want to be alone."

He lingered for another few moments, as if he wanted to say more, then disappeared down the path.

She sat on a nearby rock and watched the trees shift in the faint breeze until tears blurred her vision. Everything was lost to her, or soon would be. The Asermons had little time to prepare for the Descendant troops. Aid from Kalindos would not come. She would feel the slaughter of her people as Crow carried them away, one by one. Sobs racked her ribs, unhindered by pride or shame.

When her breathing slowed and she felt able to face Tereus and Alanka with dry eyes, she dragged herself to her feet to begin the short walk home. The crescent moon hung low in the sky, angling silver rays beneath the tree canopy to shine on the path before her. In her dark mood, the night felt like home.

Rhia came to a clearing on the outskirts of her family's farm. She looked past the horses' paddocks at the small log house, wondering who would live in it if the Descendants overtook Asermos. A sudden movement startled her.

A man was hurrying through the clearing, about a hundred paces away. When he saw her, he stopped.

It's true what they say, she thought. Too much moonlight can drive a person crazy. For the vision before her was both familiar and foreign, like a reflection in a rippling pond.

Marek. In the moonlight.

"Rhia!"

Stunned, she watched him run toward her. She could see him. It was night, and she could see him.

He neared her, and Rhia's shock gave way to joy. She closed the gap between them and threw her arms around his neck, ignoring her shoulder's yelp of pain. He repeated her name as he clutched her back. She closed her eyes to revel in the sound of his voice, but only for a moment. She had to look at him.

Rhia drew away a few inches, pushed back his light brown hair, and gazed at his face. "Marek, I can see you."

"I can see you, too." He kissed her with a hunger that matched her own.

She broke away. "Why? Why are you—"

"Visible? Because I came for you."

"I don't understand."

"The night we set out from Kalindos, three days ago—" his breath came fast "—the sun went down, and there I was. Because I came, because I'd give my life to protect you. I guess Wolf decided I was finally worthy."

She hugged him hard again, then let go suddenly. "What do you mean, 'the night *we* set out'?"

"There's a hundred of us. We disobeyed the Council's orders and came."

"A hundred?" Nearly a third of Kalindos. "Where are they?"

"Meeting with your Hawk right now. Coranna came, of course, and Elora and many of the Cats and first-phase Wolves." His words spilled over one another. "The other second-phase Wolves stayed behind with their families. But all of us hunters can shoot, though most not as well as Alanka. She told me where to find you tonight, by the way, and for me to hurry."

Rhia was still pondering the ramifications of the Kalindon force. "The Descendants know nothing of Wolves—"

"So we're your secret weapon." He gave her a sly grin.

She caressed his cheek, rough with the stubble of a long journey. "Marek, thank you. This could mean everything."

He flinched as her hand came near his left eye. She turned his head toward the bright moon. One side of his face was swollen, and a deep cut slashed the skin above his eyebrow.

She took a step back. "Skaris."

Marek's gaze grew guarded. "I went to his home to—talk to him. Skaris knocked out the guard, overpowered me and took off. I followed, but he was faster."

"Did you find him?"

"The next day—" he hesitated "—at the bottom of a deep gorge near Mount Beros."

She swallowed, afraid of her next question. "Was it suicide?"

He spoke slowly, as if uttering carefully chosen words. "It looked like it."

She decided to probe no further, wanting to hear neither lies nor the truth.

Marek filled his hands with her hair and kissed her again. "Will you forgive me?"

Rhia's breath stopped. "For what?"

"For leaving your side to avenge you. It was stupid. I could have been killed or arrested, when I should have been helping you."

"I understand." She locked her gaze on his. "If anyone hurt you, I'd do the same."

She didn't say, "I'd kill for you, too," words that would acknowledge Skaris's possible fate out loud, but it was what she meant. Inside, she begged Crow not to take Marek in the upcoming battle. If she lost this man to death, it would be the Spirit Himself who would taste her revenge.

When Rhia brought Marek home, Alanka chattered endlessly, telling her Wolf-brother everything she'd learned about Asermos and warfare.

"They have these long bows for battle—" she held her hand high off the floor as they sat around the table "—that shoot really, really far. And the arrows are heavier. It's hard to get used to, but we won't exactly be hunting turkey out there." Her smile flickered off as the concept of killing a person became less abstract.

Tereus entered the house then, home from a late meeting with Galen and the Kalindon arrivals. He welcomed Marek like an old friend. They became acquainted over a pitcher of ale while Rhia and Alanka fed and watered the hounds.

Rhia's father joined her in the stable as she checked the ponies a final time before bed.

"I told Marek he could sleep out here in the stable." He

handed Rhia a soft blanket. "The hayloft is more comfortable than the floor in the house."

She hung the blanket over a rung of the loft's ladder. "Thank you for letting him stay with us." She looped a thin rope through the latch of the gray mare's stall door. The wily pony had a knack for escape.

Tereus sat on a bale of hay. "He told me about his mate and child."

Rhia nodded as she tied a double knot in the rope. The revelation didn't surprise her; people opened up to her father. More than anyone she knew, he listened without judging.

"The well of Marek's devotion runs deep," he said. "You need that."

"Because I'm difficult?" Her teasing grin made him laugh.

"I lived with your brothers for five years before you came along. Compared to them, you're a lamb." His voice turned serious. "But your path is a hard one, and you need someone who will remind you that this world is a good place to be."

She remembered the promise she had made to Crow, that she would hold on to her love of life even in the face of despair. "I do. The Other Side is so beautiful and peaceful. I think about it every day."

His gaze mixed gratitude with sadness, and she knew he was imagining Mayra in that realm, as Rhia often did. "For you it's the Other Side," he said, "and for me it's the dream world. We Birds love our wings so much, sometimes we forget our feet and where they belong."

She sat next to him on the hay bale and watched his face in the lantern light. "I miss her."

"Yes." Tereus seemed unable to say more, so he took her hand and kissed her forehead. "I'll see you in the morning."

"In the—?" She understood suddenly—he did not expect her to return to the house that night.

A short while later, she and Marek climbed into the hayloft. The air was stuffy, so she opened a small window under the eaves.

"It's not a tree house," she said, "but at least we're sleeping up high. Sorry about the horse smell."

He chuckled. "I'll get used to it eventually."

She wondered what he meant by "eventually." Over the course of the night? During his short stay in Asermos while the battle raged? Or longer? She had been so happy to see him alive—to *see* him at all—that it only now occurred to her to wonder how long he would stay, how long she would stay and if they would stay together.

He spread the blanket over a deep cushion of hay and sat cross-legged upon it. She mirrored his position, and he took her hands. After a long silence, he cleared his throat.

"I spoke with your father."

"He told me."

"He did?" Marek's face showed surprise, then indignation. "Why would he do that?"

"Do what?"

"Tell you."

She shook her head. "Tell me what?"

"Oh. He didn't tell you." He chided himself with a slight smile. "I'll start over."

"Please."

He took a deep breath. "I asked him about marrying you."

A glow of joy flared inside Rhia, and she wanted to throw her arms around him and shout, "Yes! Yes!" but she realized he hadn't actually asked her to marry him yet. She kept her face impassive and said, "Why? You wanted his permission?"

Marek blanched at her lack of reaction, then recovered. "No, I wanted his opinion."

"On what?"

"On whether you would say yes."

"And what was his opinion?"

"Tell me your answer," he said, "and I'll tell you his."

"Ask me the question, and I'll tell you my answer."

Marek laughed. "Is there any game you can't win?"

"If that's the question, the answer is definitely 'no.'" She got up as if to leave.

He grabbed her waist and pulled her down into the soft hay beside him. "Hold still so I can ask you to marry me."

"Hurry up, then."

He took her hands. "Rhia, I want to spend every day of my life with you. I want your face to be the last thing I see before I sleep and the first thing I see when I wake. If you can stand to do the same with me, then we should marry."

She simply looked at him.

"Each other," he added.

"I'm still waiting for the question."

He molded her left hand into a fist and pantomimed it shoving a dagger into his heart. Then he sobered, his eyes still glittering. "Will you marry me?"

She gazed at his face and thought that if she lived to be seventy and traveled as far as the Southern Sea, she'd never behold anything as beautiful as Marek in the moonlight.

"Yes."

He sighed, seemingly with relief as much as happiness, then kissed her—softly at first, then with growing passion, which she returned. He eased her down to lie on the hay, taking care not to jostle her sore shoulder.

She placed her palm on his cheek, and he turned his head to kiss it.

"I love you," she said.

His eyes opened to meet hers with alarm. "I haven't said it, have I?"

"Not with words."

"I'm sorry." He spread his body against Rhia's so that every part of him touched a part of her. "I love you."

"I know you do."

"And I'm not just saying that because I want you so much I'm going to burst into flames."

She laughed, then suddenly drew in a breath.

"What is it?" he said.

Her heart pounded at the thought of broaching the topic. "When I left Kalindos, I was in a hurry."

"And?"

"And I forgot my wild carrot seed. I haven't been taking it."

"Oh."

The silence stretched between them. "What should we do?" she asked him.

He lifted her chin and kissed her softly. "How do you feel about having a baby?"

She gave him the only honest answer. "I don't know. Sometimes I feel like a child myself, but after all I've been through, sometimes I feel eighty instead of eighteen."

"I'm glad you're not eighty."

"What about you?"

He hesitated, but when he spoke, his voice didn't tremble. "I know that I want to have a child with you, to watch it grow up as we grow old." He sighed and propped his head on his arm. "The question is when. When becoming a parent isn't scary anymore? When the war is over? When life is perfect?"

She was relieved that he shared her ambivalence. "How does anyone know when they're ready?"

"What about your Aspect? Can you safely move to the next phase?"

"Can I? Yes. I've had these powers for ten years. They've just grown stronger since my Bestowing. But do I want to? That's another question." She hesitated. "If I become a second-phase Crow, I'll need more training. I'll have to go back to Kalindos."

His brow creased in a deep frown. "And you don't want to?"

"Not yet." She gestured to the barn around them. "My family is here. They need me. And I need them."

"More than you need me?"

"Why do you say that?" Her face heated. "Marek, if we get married, wouldn't we live here?"

He rolled onto his back and ran a hand through his hair. "I'd be the only one of my kind in the whole village."

"So would I."

"But you have to get used to that. Crows are rare. Wolves need a pack."

"I'll never get used to being Crow," she said, more sharply than intended. "And you can be part of a new pack—with me and my family. You can hunt with my brothers." *If they survive the battle.*

"It's not the same."

They lay silent for a long moment, staring at the beams of the barn's roof. Finally Rhia spoke, "You knew all along that we would come to this, that someday I'd return to Asermos with everything Coranna taught me. That was the reason I came to Kalindos in the first place."

"I know." His voice hardened with petulance.

"This is my home, Marek. I love your village, I love the forest, but this is where I belong."

He drew a deep, shaky breath, then let it out slowly. "Then it's where I belong."

She turned to him. "You mean it?"

He put his arm around her waist and drew her close. "I do." His eyes were sad. "Just don't expect me never to be homesick."

Before either of them could mention the fact that in a few days, Asermos might cease to exist, she kissed him. Their mouths meshed, warm and soft, and he pulled at the hem of her blouse until she let him tug it over her head.

Her dread of the future dissipated with the spread of his hands over her skin, a sensation as familiar and precious as breath itself. She threaded her fingers through his soft hair and savored the way it filled her hands, thick and long, grown nearly to his shoulders now. She guided his mouth lower until his lips met the curve of her breast. In the distance a chorus of wolves howled, accentuating the silent stillness in the barn. Rhia shivered, but no longer in fear.

Marek's mouth hovered just over her nipple, tendering a warm promise of pleasure. She bit back a plea, which would only make him tease her longer. Every nerve waited, taut as a bowstring.

Finally his tongue flicked, once, and her back arched. He grasped her waist, keeping her exactly where he wanted her.

"Patience," he whispered. "Even if we can't make love, I want to make it last."

Marek drew off the rest of her clothes, sweeping his fingertips and tongue across each new space of bare skin, pausing at her feet to treat each toe as if it were a rare treasure. He made his way back up, and Rhia's muscles melted as his breath warmed the skin between her thighs. An eternity passed while she waited, hands clenched with anticipation.

Then he began.

Slow as honey his mouth flowed against her. It knew where to find what it sought, but it teased and dawdled, until she released her frustration in a laugh that was almost a sob.

As if in reply, his tongue's tip found the center of her bliss and caressed it again and again with a light, firm stroke that carried her up one of the highest peaks she'd ever approached—then left her there, balanced on the edge.

"You wouldn't dare stop," she hissed.

"Not if I want to live."

He slipped one finger inside her, then another, curving them into the heart of her swollen fullness. Her moans pitched higher as his mouth returned to the place where she needed it, the pleasure more intense for its brief interruption. She wished they were alone in the cold forest again, out of the range of others' ears.

Rhia shuddered again and again in a haze of bright, burning ecstasy that flowed into every corner of her body. She almost begged him to stop, but knew it would be futile.

At last he drew away to kiss and caress her legs and hips until she returned to earth.

"Come here," she said.

He obeyed. She sat up and reached to untie his shirt. He restrained her hand for a moment, then relented. She drew the shirt over his head and gasped.

His chest and torso were bruised and bandaged. Even in the dim light she saw more than a hint of Marek's days-old injuries. Skaris couldn't have done such damage during their brief encounter at his home. The truth stared at her: Marek had hunted the Bear, fought him hand to hand, and won.

Her finger traced the largest bandage, over his right side.

"I did it for you," he said.

She struggled to keep the tears from her voice. "I never asked you to kill for me."

"Then I did it for me, so I could sleep knowing that the man who wanted you dead could never hurt you again."

She thought of the Descendant who had come much closer to murdering her than Skaris had. "You can't protect me from every danger."

"And you can't stop me from trying."

Marek should have died; Skaris was stronger, faster and in every other respect a better fighter. She should have lost him.

"If you don't stop staring at my wounds," he said, "I'll make myself invisible."

"No." It was the last thing she could bear. She tugged at his trousers, unfastening them. "Let me see you. I want to see all of you."

He lay back on the hay, never taking his eyes off her, as she finished undressing him. Though she had seen him naked in the daylight many times, she relished the sight of him stretched out, ready for her, in the near-darkness.

When she took him in her mouth, Marek's groan was so sharp it was nearly a snarl. The sound of it quickened her own desire. He swelled and hardened between her lips. His hands grasped her hair—hands that had found their prey and taken its life in a fury born of love and loyalty. Spirits forgive her, but the thought of it made her want him more.

Rhia let go, then crawled over him to stare down at his flustered face.

"You're not stopping," he said.

"Not if I want to live." She lowered her hips and drove him deep inside her.

His eyes flared with surprise, which vanished in the next instant. He clutched her body and turned them over in one motion. He pinned her left arm over her head but left the right one free, even now remembering her injury while reason abandoned him.

Marek gave himself to her with hard, fierce thrusts, plunging her deeper into the cushion of hay. She gloried in his feral power, that it was hers alone and always would be. He muffled a roar against her neck, and when his release came, he sank his teeth into the tender skin above her collarbone. She gasped, and met his orgasm with a sudden, sharp one of her own.

He collapsed upon her but did not withdraw, instead hugging her hips to his as he rolled to the side with an incoherent oath. They lay with limbs entangled, muscles trembling.

"Are we still alive?" she asked finally.

"You would know." His breath came in rough pants as he

kissed her hungrily. "Rhia, I love you so much. There's nothing I wouldn't do for you."

She didn't need to see his eyes to know the truth of his words, but in their blue-gray depths she found the certainty she sought. Marek would anchor her to this world. For him, she would gladly spurn the Other Side and its inhuman peace.

They kissed endlessly as the short summer night drifted on. Eventually he stirred within her, and they made love again, slowly, letting the Spirits work Their will upon them.

37

Rhia woke before first light. As she dressed for chores, she watched Marek sleep, for once visible to her before sunrise. *Visibly exhausted,* she added to herself with a smile. The approaching doom of invasion accentuated her joy in this simple yet profound moment.

Later that morning, Rhia, Alanka and Marek headed to the wheat field to train for the upcoming battle. Rhia and Coranna met with Elora, Pirrik, Silina and the other healers to set up a makeshift hospital. The wounded would be brought to the tent for care and, if necessary, to have their souls called home. A few of the healers would work in the field to help the fallen soldiers, but Crows were deemed too rare to put in harm's way. Rhia fumed at the restriction but couldn't argue with the logic.

When she was finished, she joined Alanka, who enlisted her assistance in arrow-making. She showed Rhia how to cut the feathers and adhere them to the shaft with birch tar.

Alanka had to redo most of Rhia's early efforts, but as the day wore on, Rhia's fingers grew accustomed to the exacting work.

"Adrek came from Kalindos to fight," Alanka mentioned.

"I'm surprised." Rhia had never mended the rift between her and Skaris's Cougar friend. "I thought he didn't like me."

"I'm sure he only came for the adventure. He probably thought there'd be a victory party." She lowered her head. "Pirrik came, too, but he won't talk to me."

Rhia could offer only a sound of sympathy. Alanka's father had killed her mate Pirrik's father, Etar. It was hard to imagine how they would overcome such a barrier.

"Don't look," Alanka said, "but a certain Spider is crawling this way."

Arcas strode toward them, wearing a thick leather battle vest and a matching set of gauntlets on his forearms. A sword swung in a scabbard at his left side. Watching him from a distance, Rhia noticed how much his physique had changed since she left Asermos. Gone was most of the bulk that came so natural to a Bear, replaced with a Spider's grace and wiriness.

Alanka gave a soft whistle at the sight. "If I weren't in mourning…"

Rhia jabbed her in the back with the blunt end of an arrow.

"I'm joking," Alanka whispered. "I have no appetite for your leftovers."

"Good morning, Alanka." Arcas nodded to Rhia. "Rhia." His voice was clipped, and the corner of his left eye twitched. "Alanka, are you ready to begin?"

She thrust a stack of arrows into a quiver, which she strapped across her body. "Ready."

He had set up a target in the wheat field about a hundred paces away.

"Can you hit that scarecrow?" he asked her.

Alanka squinted at the figure. "Where?"

He pointed. "Right there, with the red shirt."

"No, where on its *body* do you want me to hit?"

"Oh." He seemed surprised. "The heart's a good place to aim for a kill shot. We don't know yet what kind of armor they'll—"

Alanka had already let loose an arrow, which was sticking out of the scarecrow's "heart."

Arcas cleared his throat. "That's, er, good. Let's see if you can hit the head."

"The eye?"

His laugh sounded skeptical. "Sure. Try for the eye."

"Which eye?"

"Pick one."

"Left." With a motion that blurred in Rhia's sight, she nocked an arrow and shot it into what would have been the scarecrow's left eye. Arcas just stood.

"Amazing." He rubbed his chin and looked at Alanka. "From how far away can you do that?"

"As far as the bow can shoot."

"Can the other Kalindons shoot like you?"

"Sure," she said, though Rhia knew she was being modest. "Marek taught me. He's not quite as fast as I am, though."

Arcas looked across the narrow end of the field at the gathering of Kalindons. Some marveled over the longbows, others surveyed the lay of the land and still others quaffed mugs of ale.

"Which one's Marek?" he said.

Rhia closed her eyes, awaiting the inevitable.

"Oh." Alanka hesitated. "You haven't met Marek yet?"

"Call him over," Arcas said. "Let's see what he can do."

Alanka mouthed a "sorry" toward Rhia as she set off for the group of Kalindons.

An excruciating silence fell between Rhia and Arcas. He untied and retied his left gauntlet, then the right one. She organized the newly fletched arrows into stacks of twenty, then double- and triple-checked the count. They continued to say nothing.

Alanka crossed the field, followed by Marek.

"Welcome." Arcas bowed to the Wolf. "I can't begin to express my gratitude to you and your people."

Marek returned the greeting. "It's our honor to serve under your command. Just tell me how I can help."

Arcas gestured to Marek's bow, then at the scarecrow. "Alanka's set a tough example to follow, but if you can just hit the target, I'll be impressed."

Marek gave Alanka a competitive glare, then readied himself to shoot. He eyed the target carefully as he set the nock of the arrow against the string.

"See?" Alanka said. "I told you he's not as fast as I am."

A crack sounded at the target. One of Alanka's arrows fell to the ground in pieces, split by Marek's shot.

"Sorry," he said to her. "I'll make you a new one."

"Outstanding." Arcas beamed at the target. "We could actually win this battle." He thumped Marek on the back. "Have you found somewhere to stay? Our house has extra space."

"Thank you." Marek glanced at Rhia. "I've found a place."

Arcas registered the look. "You know each other?"

She stepped to Marek's side. "We met in Kalindos."

Alanka shifted her feet on the grass in obvious embarassment.

Arcas looked at the other three in turn. "Wait—is this—Rhia, this is him?"

"Yes," she said quietly.

He examined Marek with an impassive gaze. "So you decided to come after all. Good." He turned away, and Rhia's throat unclenched.

Before she could blink, Arcas drew his sword with one hand and shoved Marek to the ground with the other. He held the sharp tip to Marek's throat, so close that blood would have flowed if the Wolf had so much as swallowed.

"Arcas!" Rhia started to reach for him, but Alanka held her back—wisely, since any motion might have fatal consequences. Marek's life balanced on the edge of the blade.

"You stole my mate," Arcas hissed.

Marek spoke through gritted teeth. "You want me to be ashamed?"

"I want you to be dead."

"Why? So she can hate you instead of just not love you?"

They had attracted the attention of the nearby Kalindons, who watched with casual interest. Out of hearing distance, they probably assumed the fight was a practice maneuver.

Alanka moved for the bow near her feet.

"Don't," both men ordered in unison.

"Arcas, please…" Rhia whispered. "We need him. I need him."

He started to tremble, but his sword arm remained as rigid as stone.

Then Marek did something unexpected. His right hand reached out and wrapped around the blade.

Arcas gasped and almost jerked back in a reflex.

"Don't move," Marek said in a low voice, "or you'll slice my palm to the bone and I won't be able to draw a bow. What will your commander say when he finds out how I got hurt?"

Arcas stared at him. "What are you doing?"

"Seeing if you'd really kill me. Evidently you wouldn't, if the thought of merely maiming me sends you into a panic."

"Let go."

"No."

Their gazes were locked. "What do you want?" Arcas said.

"Peace. Let this be the first and last time we fight. Rhia has chosen. If you love her, let her live with that choice."

Arcas's eyes narrowed suddenly, and Rhia feared he would thrust the sword forward, but then he nodded.

"Thank you," Marek said. "Now relax your elbow so I can remove this thing from my throat."

After taking a moment to collect his pride, Arcas obeyed, and Marek slowly moved the sword aside, far enough to let him rise. With care his fingers released the blade, and he got to his feet.

Arcas sheathed his sword, avoiding the eyes of the others. "I'm sorry," he said to Marek. A muscle in his jaw twitched. "Please forgive my loss of control."

"Think nothing of it. If I were in your place I'd have done the same thing." As Arcas turned to leave, Marek added, "Except I'd have killed you."

Arcas paused briefly in his departure. "I need to check on the other troops," he said without looking back.

Alanka bounced on her toes. "You were amazing." She pinched Marek's arm. "No one intimidates Kalindons."

Rhia asked Marek, "Did you mean what you said? Would you really kill him if the situation were reversed?"

"Not if you told me not to." He put his arms around her and kissed her nose. "I'll obey you as well as your hounds."

"My hounds aren't the least bit obedient."

"Hmm. Interesting."

Shouts came from the other end of the field, where Arcas's sunrise trees stood. A rider on a dark bay pony burst from the woods, sagging in her saddle.

Rhia turned to the others. "It's one of the scouts!"

They ran with the rest of the soldiers to meet the scout, a Bat woman named Koli. Torin, the Bear commander, was listening to her report, pacing as he pondered her words, which clearly troubled him.

"What are they saying?" Rhia asked her Wolf companions, who shook their heads.

"Too many other people talking," Marek said.

"Someone needs to attend that horse." Rhia pushed her way through the crowd, Marek on her heels. She took the reins from the grateful Koli and began to hot-walk the pony in a wide circle. The huff of his breath and clop of his hooves drowned out much of the conversation, but at least Marek had gotten close enough to hear. From what Rhia gathered, the enemy had moved within striking distance and could invade as soon as tomorrow.

When her path brought her near Torin and Koli again, she overheard an alarming fact.

"There's armor for the horses," Koli said. "They mean to use them in battle."

Rhia pulled the pony to a stop.

Torin clenched his fists. "That will put us at a disadvantage—not only because of their greater height but because they think we won't harm their mounts."

"We will if we have to," Lycas said. "We'll do whatever it takes."

The pony nuzzled Rhia's hand, no doubt searching for a treat. "We can't," she said. Everyone looked at her, and she drew the bay gelding forward with her. "The horses didn't ask to fight. They don't deserve the pain and death of war."

"What would you have us do?" Lycas's voice filled with scorn. "Ask the Descendants very nicely to dismount so we can kill them?"

"He has a point," Arcas said. "On foot we're no match for a cavalry."

"You both speak as if it's easy to kill a horse whether you want to or not." Torin gestured to the woods. "They'll come out of those trees and cut us down so fast, our archers will have time for only one shot, if that. The only solution is to keep them off the battlefield in the first place."

"What about a row of pikes?" Arcas said. "We could conceal it under leaves at the edge of the woods and lift it just as the horses step out of the trees."

A gasp of revulsion permeated the crowd.

"Good idea," Lycas said to Arcas, then raised his voice to Torin and the other people gathered around. "Our lives—

our entire village—might depend on it. We don't have the luxury of coddling enemy weapons, even if they have pretty fur and big brown eyes." He glared at Rhia.

Her anger boiled, but she wouldn't let her brother see it. "Torin's right, but killing the horses isn't the answer. Mother used to make a potion to calm our ponies during a bad thunderstorm. What if we used it to sedate the enemy's mounts, enough that they can't be ridden into battle?"

Elora stepped forward. "Do you have any of this potion left?"

"I'm sure we do. Father said it's been a mild season for storms."

"With a small sample, I could make more," the healer said. "But how do we administer it in time?"

Torin frowned. "Someone would need to sneak into the enemy camp tonight and slip the potion into the water troughs."

The crowd hushed as everyone examined their toes. It was a suicide mission.

"I'll do it."

Rhia stared at Marek, who held up his hand.

Torin approached him. "I don't believe we've met."

"Marek, of Kalindos." He returned the general's bow. "As a second-phase Wolf, I can become invisible at night and move with complete stealth. I'm the only one here who can do that. It makes sense to send me." He held up his bow. "I'll fight when I return."

"*If* you return." Arcas took a step toward Marek. "Why would you risk your life for us?"

Marek simply looked at Rhia. She shook her head and begged him with her eyes not to go.

But it was too late.

Rhia and Marek stood outside her door early that evening. The others—Elora, Tereus and Alanka—stayed inside to give them privacy. Koli waited near the stables on a fresh pony to take Marek as far as it was safe to ride without being discovered.

Rhia placed the long clay bottle of potion in Marek's palm. "My mother used to put five drops in each trough to calm the horses. Elora said twenty should be enough to put them in a lasting stupor but not harm them."

He nodded.

"And the horses can catch your scent," she added, "so be sure to stay downwind."

He nodded again.

She shook a finger at him. "Only do as much as you can safely. Skip a few troughs if you have to."

He nodded a third time. "Rhia?"

"Yes?"

"I'll be fine."

She dropped his hand. "Don't say that like it's a given. You could be killed."

"Or worse—captured and kept from your advice forever." He smiled as if it were a joke, but his eyes remained sober.

Rhia looked toward the setting sun, berry-red on the horizon, a portent of a hot, muggy day to follow. "It's getting late. You should go."

"I should. Summer nights are short—I'll need every moment I can get to complete this mission."

"And then come home."

His lips twitched. "Home? Here?"

"Back to me."

"Same thing."

He put out his hand, and they entwined their fingers, palms meeting, for a long moment.

Then he was gone.

Rhia returned to the house. Alanka, Tereus and Elora watched as she slumped to sit at the table.

"If Marek succeeds," Tereus said, "we may have the advantage. The Descendant riders' weapons and armor are all suited for horseback. On foot, they'll be much less effective." Rhia nodded and picked at the unrecognizable meat her father had prepared. He gently broke the silence again, "We should sleep. Torin's men will be here well before dawn for the horses, and I expect we'll all go with them then."

The Asermon horses would not be used to fight, but to deliver messages, carry supplies and transport the wounded. Nevertheless, they could be hurt or killed, and Tereus was offering an enormous sacrifice by donating most of his herd of ponies to the war effort.

"Yes," Rhia said. "Let's go to sleep."

They all sat, unmoving, for at least another hour.

When the sky was empty of light, she retreated to the stable to sleep in the hayloft. After unrolling the blankets from last night, she made a pillow from a new clump of hay. Yet her head did not long for it.

She sat near the small loft window and stared out at the field where she had first seen Marek the night before, in full control of his power. Pressing the blanket to her face, she inhaled his scent and prayed to Wolf for his safety. The words clunked together in her mind, unable to carry the feelings they wanted to bear to the Spirit. She could only clutch the cloth and whisper Marek's name until she fell into a fitful sleep.

38

Darkness draped over the wheat field. The soldiers hid within the tall, pale green stalks. Somewhere among them lay Rhia's brothers, each armed with several daggers of various sizes and purposes, like the other Wolverines. She had barely recognized them when they arrived. It wasn't their battle dress or the war paint they had slathered on their faces. Their eyes had changed to those of killers. She had become an abstract concept to them, one among thousands they fought to protect.

Protect from what? she wondered as she stared out at the field from the open flap of the hospital tent. If the Descendants won, what then? Would the Asermons be allowed to vacate their lands unhindered, or would they become slaves, forced to burgeon the Descendants' strength and dominance? What would happen to the surrounding villages if Asermos fell?

And the Spirits? The Descendants had driven them from their own city with derision and scorn, if they had been there to begin with. Would the Spirits remain here if no one revered them, or would they take all the magic back to their own realm and lock it away forever? Worse yet, what if Marek were right, and the Spirits themselves would die if no one lived to believe in them?

She curled her arms around her own waist and shivered, despite the warm night that was coming to an end. Her eyes strained to pick out the archers behind a stone wall, downhill to her right. In contrast to her brothers' stony countenances, Alanka's eyes had shown a gut-clenching fear as she approached the battlefield. Rhia knew it lay as much in the dread of killing as in the fear of dying.

Several sharp-eyed Eagles stood within the archers' line. They would call out targets and determine weaknesses in the enemy armor or formations. Now they watched the trees at the other end of the field for any sign of movement.

Even in the darkness the golden oak shone forth, a reminder both of Arcas's love and the death that awaited his uncle Dorius. Though Butterflies weren't considered warriors, Dorius's powers of transformation and rejuvenation meant that he could withstand many blows before being mortally wounded. Besides, in a situation as desperate as this one, the army needed any man strong enough to swing a poleax.

She had considered warning Dorius to avoid the battle, but knew that he would fight regardless. For all she knew, Crow was determined to take the man's soul on this day. To stand in the way of His will felt wrong. But knowing that someone she had cared about since childhood was about to see his last sunrise made her own insides feel dead.

"You should eat."

The arrows sang again, and this time a distant chorus of rage and pain reached Rhia's ears. She shrank back into the shadows.

War had begun.

The sky turned a pale purple, light enough that she could see across the field where the enemy was marching.

Marching. Not riding.

"He did it!" She clapped her hands like a child. "Marek got to the horses before the battle."

"Then where is he?" Pirrik asked.

A great cry rose up from the clearing beyond the wheat field. The enemy charged, straight for the field, swords glittering even in the faint light of dawn. Perhaps they thought the archers were the Asermons' only defense and they were oblivious to what awaited them among the swaying grasses.

Lights bobbed among the charging soldiers. "Why are they carrying torches?" Rhia asked. "It's easier for the archers to see them."

Coranna gasped. "They're going to burn the field."

"No!" Rhia strained to see. "My brothers are in there."

The Descendants had reached the edge of the wheat now. Torches dipped into the grain, and the dry grasses began to burn, just as the Asermons leaped from their hiding places to swarm the oncoming enemy soldiers.

"They'll all be trapped." Rhia heard the panic in her own voice. "Why would they burn the field?"

"To create a smokescreen. They didn't know our soldiers were there," Elora said. "Now they can't get out, either."

Without a word, Pirrik shouldered his healer's kit and dashed toward the fray.

Smoke rose from the far end of the field, along with the

clash of metal on metal. She gaped at the strength of the Wolverine attack—each one battled three Descendants, whirling and jabbing, occasionally hurling a heavy-bladed dagger into the throat or chest of an oncoming opponent. The Wolverines' knives should have been no match for the longer Descendant swords, but they had the training and courage to swoop close enough to the enemy soldier to stab between the plates of his armor and feel his last rattling breath. When their blows struck home, they roared with what could only be described as glee. The longer they fought, the more energy they seemed to possess.

Other warriors were holding their own against the Descendants. The Wasp women, armed with light, whiplike flails, fought with less strength than the Wolverines, but with twice the speed and evasive capability. Several times Rhia thought one of the women would fall under an enemy attack, only to see her roll or leap away at the last moment. Sword-wielding Bears roamed the outskirts of the field, shouting orders and picking off Descendants who tried to escape to the surrounding woods. Then the wind shifted, and smoke obscured her view.

The wounded came. A young Wolverine arrived first, supported on either side by his comrades. His right leg left a trail of blood. They passed her as they brought him under the tent, and she stilled herself with a deep breath and a quick prayer to Crow.

"Over there," Elora said to the soldiers, who carefully placed the wounded man on a raised platform, then dashed back into the battle. The healer beckoned to Rhia as she slit the side of the soldier's trousers to uncover his wound. Rhia approached the man—scarcely more than a boy, younger than she was by at least a year. She had seen him around the village but didn't know his name or family.

The boy recoiled at the sight of her, which seemed to cause him more pain than the wound itself. She reached for his hand. He squeezed her wrist so hard she feared it would break in his grip. She smoothed dark hair from his soot- and paint-smeared face, enough to gaze into his eyes, pale blue orbs that shone under the dirt and sweat.

Beneath the distant shouts and clangs of the battlefield, she heard...

Nothing. No wings.

"What's your name?" she asked the soldier.

"Sirin."

"Sirin, you're going to be fine."

He leaned his head back in relief, then cried out as Elora flushed the wound. Rhia looked down at his leg, which was sliced nearly in two above the knee, and realized that "fine" was a relative term when it came to battle wounds.

Another Otter gave the wounded boy a drink infused with a painkiller, and he relaxed, his eyes unfocusing. She left him to the healers and rejoined Coranna.

"I heard nothing," Rhia told her. "Felt nothing. He's nowhere near death."

"Savor the silence while it lasts," Coranna said, "for Crow flies low over this battlefield."

They stood side by side and watched the flames devour the wheat field, leaving nothing behind but blackened earth. The fire propelled the fighters to the outskirts of the field as well as back toward the hospital and the wall of archers. It spread too quickly for some to escape, and soldiers on both sides fell, choking and flailing. Rhia's own eyes burned, though the wind now blew the smoke away from her.

A hand gripped her shoulder.

"Distance, Rhia," Coranna murmured. "Each man and woman who falls must be a stranger to you. Though they are within arm's reach, they must seem as if they are standing on the other end of this field. Tell yourself you don't know them."

"I can't do that."

"If you are to do your duty—"

"Doesn't my duty include compassion? Understanding?"

"You must learn to understand their pain without sharing it. Otherwise you will be useless."

Useless. The word burned Rhia's mind like a brand that wouldn't fade.

"They're coming," Coranna said.

Three ponies trotted from the smoke, dragging skids piled with bodies, some writhing in pain, others as still as logs.

Crow's wings rushed through Rhia's mind, louder than she'd ever heard them, blotting out the screams of agony and the pleas for help. Her father led the first pony, coughing, his face already darkened with smoke. She had no time to acknowledge him, but went straight to the skid.

The man on top was already dead, disemboweled to the point where it appeared that more of him was outside than in. When she looked at him, the roar of wings came to a crescendo, then hushed abruptly. With her hand on the dead man's forehead, she quickly murmured the prayer of passage and signaled for Tereus to remove the body. He rolled it to the ground with a thud.

The man who had lain half-under the corpse gasped for breath and clawed at the air in relief. Rhia gripped his hand and stared into dark green eyes, one of which was flooded red with blood from a gash in his head. It was Bolan, one of Arcas's friends, a Horse—no great warrior, just a loyal Asermon willing to give his life.

No, she told herself. He is no one. He has no name, no Animal, no friends. He is pure spirit, either staying or leaving. She looked in his eyes and cleared her mind.

Wings flapped, then faded, leaving only a lingering sound that indicated they might return.

Rhia signaled to the healer who stood nearby. "He can be saved. Quickly now."

Tereus and another man lifted Bolan and carried him under the tent. She turned to the third man on the skid.

He was a Descendant. A dying Descendant.

Crow sounded a thunder of wings, and before Rhia could wonder why the Spirit would take someone who didn't believe in Him, she found herself kneeling beside the man. His mouth opened and closed like that of a fish on dry land.

No blood coated his uniform or armor, and his head looked clear of contusions. What was killing him? she wondered.

He clawed at the front of his shirt, and she pushed it open. A hideous black and purple bruise spread across his chest, which appeared caved in. One of her people must have smashed him with the blunt end of a pole or the hilt of a sword.

The Descendant's eyes flared with pain, and his legs thrashed as if they could run to find air. Though others needed her, she clutched his hand as his mouth begged without words.

"He's coming for you," she whispered. "He's coming."

There were herbs in her pocket to ease his pain, but she couldn't reach them without letting go of the man's hand. Her touch and words of prayer seemed to soothe him, and she felt him stop fighting. In a few moments his eyes stared through her. She forced herself to drop his hand and beckon her father.

"He's dead. Put both the bodies aside."

Tereus reached to touch her arm. She drew it away.

"I need no comfort," she said. "Show me the others."

She repeated the grisly procedure at the next skid. One dead, two injured, one seriously enough to be on the edge of life and death. No sooner had her father and the other two pony leaders disappeared into the smoky battlefield, another three appeared with more wounded.

The bodies became a blur to Rhia—some Asermon, some Descendant, even a Kalindon or two, though all of the archers lived and fought, their task made more difficult by the thick smoke that choked the sky.

The only Kalindon unaccounted for, as far as she knew, was Marek. During one of her brief moments of rest, she scanned the visible edges of the woods for any sign of him.

Her father arrived then with another batch of potential patients. She went to work without hesitation, numb from the death and pain she had witnessed. Response became automatic: yes, no, save her, don't save them, it's too late, it's not too late. The prayer of passage created a constant background hum in her mind, swamped only by the onslaught of Crow's wings. It became easier to distance herself from the sight of oozing red cloths piled high in the corner, from the smell of blood and smoke, and from the sound of wounded warriors calling for their mothers.

Then a battle roar sounded, too close. She looked up from the injured patient at her feet to see a platoon of Descendant infantry charging the wall of archers less than a hundred paces away. The twenty or more soldiers had broken through Asermon defenses in the wheat field. Half a dozen Bears and Wolverines pursued, including Lycas and Nilo, but they were too late.

The archer on the far left was overtaken before he could even react. They were close enough to the hospital tent that Rhia could hear his cry of agony. She stepped out to the edge of the hill to watch the horror as it unfolded.

A Descendant soldier snatched the bow from the dead archer, then knelt on the ground while several of his compatriots shielded him from the arrows now being fired at close range. In a few moments, they parted slightly, and she saw the soldier, still kneeling, aiming an arrow wrapped in something white. A torch-bearing Descendant lit the end of the arrow.

The flaming arrow flew—straight for the hospital. Rhia screamed as it pierced the air over her head and landed on the roof of the tent, which began to smolder. She ran back to the hospital, where the healers had already begun to stack barrels and crates and anything else they could find to reach the roof.

Along with her father and two of the Asermon healers, she climbed the stack of crates. Buckets of water were passed up. At the top of the line next to her, her father dumped the water onto the fire, which was starting to crawl down the seam of the tent. If it spread much farther, the flaming roof would fall onto the patients and healers underneath.

She had just dropped an empty bucket to the person waiting below when she glanced back at the archer's wall from her higher vantage point. The soldier was preparing to shoot another flaming arrow their way even as his defenders were falling before a Wolverine assault.

"Father, look out!" she cried.

A moment before the soldier released the arrow, Lycas pushed aside his last shielder and seized him. The arrow shot, not toward its intended target, but straight up. Before it even reached its zenith, Lycas had torn off the man's helmet and sliced his throat.

The arrow took forever to fall. Like a meteor, its brightness flared as it shoved the air aside on its deadly, indifferent mission. The Descendants, distracted by the arrow's fall and their efforts to avoid its path, proved easy prey for the Bears' swords and Wolverines' knives. The arrow landed harmlessly in the flaming field.

Someone shoved another bucket into Rhia's hands. She passed it on to Tereus, who climbed higher to douse the last few flames on the roof. With the danger averted for now, her attention was drawn back to the battle.

If ever violence could be described as beautiful, her brothers were exquisite. They fought back to back, jabbing and feinting and blocking as one unit, occasionally tossing each other weapons from the arsenal strapped to their chests and hips. The knives themselves seemed connected to their hands, like the long claws of real wolverines.

A Descendant soldier slashed his sword at Lycas's legs, but the natural armor of a second-phase Wolverine resisted the impact of the steel. Rhia closed her eyes and thanked the

Spirits for Mali. In Lycas's first phase, such a blow would have cost him a limb. He laughed at the attempt and dispatched the sword's wielder with a stab to the throat.

Alanka had climbed a small hill behind the wall, providing better aim at the attackers but leaving her unprotected. She fired repeatedly, sweeping her arm back again and again to grab a new arrow. A few Descendants broke off to attack her. Alanka cut down the first two, then reached back—

—and came up empty-handed.

When he saw she was unarmed, the Descendant dropped his shield to run faster. As he approached, Alanka stood stunned, unaccustomed to being the hunted instead of the hunter. Then she turned her bow over, ready to wield it like a club, for it was the only weapon she had. It wouldn't be enough, and she couldn't outrun him. Rhia's knees turned to water.

Just as the Descendant gathered himself to lunge for the Wolf woman, he halted, then tipped forward, as if his feet had caught in a snare. The hilt of a throwing dagger protruded from the base of his neck. Near the archer's wall, Nilo drew his arm back and shouted with victory. Alanka sent him a smile of gratitude, but then her expression changed to one of horror.

Rhia looked at Nilo, whose own face had frozen.

"No!" she screamed, and nearly lost her balance. A hand caught her before she fell.

As Nilo toppled, the Descendant behind him withdrew the sword from his back. Though Lycas was facing the other direction, he staggered as if he had taken the blow himself. He turned, slowly, and saw his brother writhing in the last throes of death.

39

For a moment, Rhia thought Lycas would lie on the burned, bloody grass next to his twin and resign his own life. The earth seemed to tug his body down toward it, as though it wanted to consume their flesh together in a fit meal.

But he was not stopping. He was only gathering and stoking the ultimate source of his magic: rage. Rhia shrank back against her father's legs, unable to look away.

Nilo's killer was headed for the archer's line when Lycas leaped ten paces in a bound and pounced on his back. They tumbled to the ground and rolled until Lycas sat on the man's chest. Rather than draw a weapon, the Wolverine grasped the Descendant's head between his enormous hands and squeezed.

A palm covered Rhia's eyes, and her father said softly, "We must help Nilo."

She turned to him. "It's too late."

"Not for his soul."

Rhia, Tereus and the other healers descended the stack of crates to the ground. Tereus retrieved a pony with an empty skid and led him to the crest of the hill. Rhia followed, though she knew she shouldn't watch.

His hands still drenched in the blood and brains of his brother's killer, Lycas savaged the rest of the dwindling Descendant platoon, stabbing and slicing any flesh he could find. When all of his weapons were embedded in enemy bodies, he attacked the remaining soldiers with his hands and feet, snapping necks and imploding chests. A group of Bears guarded him to ensure he confronted only one opponent at a time, though it seemed he could have easily brought down half a dozen with one blow.

At last he ran out of nearby Descendants to kill, for they had all fled back to their ranks within the field, leaving the area near the archers' wall safe again. Rhia and Tereus hurried toward Nilo, treading carefully to avoid slipping in all that had spilled from the dead and wounded. She told herself that the only difference between this place and the hospital was that the blood was fresher. But here the shrieks of the dying rolled over her, louder even than Crow's wings.

When they arrived at Nilo's side, Alanka was kneeling beside him. She was trying to turn him over, but her hands shook too hard to get a grip on his shoulders. Tereus helped her while one of the young Bears held the pony.

Rhia saw Lycas striding toward the field as if drawn by an invisible rope. She screamed his name against the battle din.

The man that stopped and turned to her was a stranger. Gore caked his hair, which now flew wildly about his shoulders. The green and black war paint from his face ran down his neck and chest. Each weapon sat in its scabbard, awaiting its next brief, warm home.

She stepped back, and he turned away again to honor his brother in the only way he knew how.

"Rhia, we need you," Tereus called.

She watched Lycas disappear into another melee, more than a hundred paces away, then returned to the rest of her family.

Knowing Nilo was dead was one thing; seeing his lifeless eyes gaze at the sky and hearing the silence that came with an alighted Crow…

She sank to her knees at her brother's feet, able to do nothing but stare, as if from afar, at his still figure awash in blood. His heart had been driven through.

Her sturdy walls crumbled, and she scrambled to stand, to move away, to keep from hurling herself on the ground.

"Wait!" Tereus said. "What about the prayer of passage?"

She stopped in her flight and turned to her father.

Tereus's eyes flashed. "What are you waiting for? He deserves that much. He's your brother!"

Her hand reached out, but her feet would not move closer.

"I'll do it," said a firm voice at her side. Coranna had followed them. She slipped to her knees next to Nilo's head.

Rhia's eyes flooded, and she jammed her palms against them. She couldn't cry, couldn't see what was happening. One tear would end her ability to serve Crow with any honor.

But her brother needed her.

"No." Rhia stepped forward. "Let me."

"Are you sure?" Coranna gave her a cautionary look. "You're close to him. It will hurt you."

"Then let it hurt." Rhia knelt beside Nilo across from her

father and Alanka, then took her brother's hand. It was slick with blood.

Scarcely had she murmured the first few syllables when her tears began to flow. She took a deep breath and began again. The more she tried to speak, the more the sobs racked her throat. She was weak. She was failing her brother.

Tereus reached across Nilo's body and cupped her chin in his hand. "It's all right to cry, Rhia. He won't mind."

So she said the prayer of passage through her anguish. The words were garbled and incoherent to human ears, but she hoped—knew—that Crow understood them. She felt a loosening, freeing from Nilo's soul and wished that she could see his face full of life for one more moment before he left.

Another hand grabbed hers, and suddenly Nilo was there, and Coranna, too. They formed a circle in a place of light as they had after Etar's death. Nilo gave Rhia the sly smile she had always loved, the one that said he knew he was secretly her favorite brother. He examined his surroundings, then nodded, as if even the Other Side failed to surprise him.

He was gone.

Rhia opened her eyes to see Tereus looking at her expectantly. The scorching air dried the last tear from her face. "It's done, Papa."

Alanka began to cry. "He died because he was too busy saving me to stay on guard."

Rhia moved to take her sister in her arms. "He died doing what meant most in the world to him."

"You mean killing?" Alanka said bitterly.

"Protecting the people he loved." Rhia stroked her hair. "You should rest a while."

"No!" She pushed out of Rhia's embrace. Before anyone could stop her, she picked up her bow and fled to rejoin the line of archers.

Coranna helped Rhia to her feet. "How do you feel? Can you continue?"

Rhia's bones felt light. Her exhaustion was rapidly dissipating. The sight of Nilo at peace placed a temporary balm on her grief. It would return to shred her later, she knew.

She returned to the hospital with Coranna, leaving Tereus and the young Bear soldier to move the bodies of Nilo and another fallen soldier onto the skid. There were none in the area of the skirmish who weren't past the healers' help.

Water dripped off the roof of the tent as Rhia entered, reminding her to cleanse her hands. She poured hot water from a pitcher into a basin and performed the simple act, which returned her ability to think. "I can keep going," she told Coranna. "I must."

As if in response, another skid arrived, full of lifeless bodies. One of them was Dorius.

Rhia covered her eyes to blot out the vision made real. Part of her had always wondered if her powers had fooled her that day years ago. Now she knew they had seen clearly.

Could she have prevented his death? The sickening thud of her heart said she should have tried. If a warning could have given him a tiny chance—

A hand caught her arm. Elora directed Rhia's attention to an incoming skid. "Some are alive on this one."

They rushed to help the two wounded men. The Kalindon Cougar Adrek grimaced as one of the healers' apprentices helped him into the tent. His foot was twisted at an odd angle, but he appeared otherwise uninjured.

Relieved that at least one case was straightforward, Rhia turned back to the other man.

All sound around her seemed to cease.

It was Arcas.

"No..."

Elora tore his shirt open to reveal a gaping abdominal wound that pulsed with blood. His neck and back curved up in an arch of agony. The Otter pressed the heel of her hand against the wound, and he shrieked.

Rhia covered her ears and closed her eyes. *I can't do it,* she told Crow. *This death will devour me. I'd rather have no magic at all.* There was no answer but the thump of wings, hovering.

Someone called her name. She opened her eyes to see Elora's desperate face looking up at her.

"Tell me now," the healer said. "Can we save him? Is it too late?"

Rhia started to shake her head to say she didn't know.

"Which is it?" Elora's voice pitched up. "No, we can't save him, or no, it's not too late?"

Rhia broke from the healer's gaze and sank to the grass next to Arcas. He saw her now, though his eyes roved the sky beyond her face as if watching someone else approach.

"Hurry, Rhia," Elora said. "There are others coming."

"Arcas..." she whispered. "Don't go with Him. Turn away."

His face seemed too gray.

"No." She spoke to him through gritted teeth. "Fight Him. Stay with us. Don't let Him take you."

He focused on her now. "Rhia...we're winning." His voice caught in a groan.

"I know it hurts," she said. "Crow can take the pain away, but He can't ever bring you back."

"It's so...warm." His head sank to the side, though he kept his gaze upon her. "Tell me you love me."

"No!" She dug her nails into his arm. "Arcas, if you die, I will hate you forever."

He watched her for a few rattling breaths, no doubt waiting to see if she would relent.

Crow hovered.

Rhia turned to Elora. "Save him! Now!"

She watched them carry Arcas into the tent and prayed that she had not dishonored her calling. If Coranna or even Crow wanted to take her to task for it, let them.

The next few groups of wounded and dead consisted of Descendants only, and Rhia noticed that the battlefield had quieted. Perhaps the fighting had dispersed to the surrounding woods due to the flames.

By noon, the field ceased to burn, save for a few smoldering patches. When she looked out upon the blackened ground, the only people standing were Asermons. She could just make out Lycas's hulking figure and black hair. He was kicking the bodies of Descendant soldiers, perhaps looking for signs of life to extinguish. As she watched, he fixated on one random body, driving his boot into the dead man's stomach again and again. Finally Lycas gave a long, curdling shriek to the sky and collapsed. He sat swaying, arms wrapped around his head.

Rhia wanted to run to him. She started toward the field.

A hand touched her shoulder. She turned to see her father.

"I'll go," he said. "You're needed here more than I am. Besides, he could still be dangerous."

She shook her head, not in disagreement but despair. No physical peril mattered anymore. Her mind and soul were shattered, so what good was her body?

Tereus kissed her forehead. "I'm proud of you."

"Papa…" She squeezed her eyes shut. "Please be careful."

He grabbed the halter of a pony with an empty litter and led it onto the smoky field. She turned and entered the tent to see how she could be of use.

Arcas slept on a makeshift bed in the far corner, his abdomen bandaged. When she sat beside him, he shifted and opened his eyes. An uncertain smile crossed his face. "Is it over yet?"

"Should it be?"

"I was wounded by a retreating Descendant. Tried to cut him off, take him prisoner, but slipped in—in someone's blood." He put a hand over his eyes. "I'm not much of a soldier."

"Will they attack again?"

"They might. Rhia, there were so many. Outnumbered us three to one." He paused for several moments to catch his breath. "But when they saw how our soldiers fought—I don't think they knew what we were made of."

"They do now."

"That's the problem. Next time will be worse." His face grew grave. "Have we lost many?" She nodded, unable to speak. "Who?"

"Your uncle Dorius. And—" She forced out her brother's name. "Nilo."

"Ah, no. Rhia, I'm so sorry. And my father, he'll be—" He

cut himself off and looked at her. "You saw it, didn't you? All those years ago, when Dorius was sick."

"Yes." She fought back tears, which she thought had been depleted. "I knew he would die violently, but I didn't know when or how, only that it would happen under the golden oak."

"And you've had to live with that knowledge." Arcas put his hand on hers. "I'm sorry."

"I wanted to warn him, but I couldn't. Crow might have taken him, anyway, if it were his time." She pushed out the words before sobs overtook them. "But at least Dorius would have known, he could have said goodbye to his family. I wish I'd told him."

"No, you couldn't violate your Spirit's trust. You did the right thing. The hard thing."

She cried without shame, tears dribbling onto his blanket. His thumb caressed the back of her hand in sympathy, then stopped. Through bleary eyes she saw that his expression had turned pensive.

She wiped her face to speak. "You want to know if I saw your death."

He looked startled, then guilty. "No, no. Of course not."

"I didn't. Coranna taught me how to prevent the visions. It's too terrible a burden, she says, and she's right."

"Good." He nodded several times, as if to convince himself. "I'm glad."

They sat for several moments, until Elora came to examine Arcas.

"He needs his rest." She gave Rhia a pointed glance, but moved on without a word when she was finished.

"She's wonderful." Arcas watched Elora's retreating figure. "I would have died without her."

"Probably."

"You know of what you speak, right?" A grim smile crossed his lips, then faded. "What about the other Kalindons?"

"Most of the archers survived. I haven't seen Alanka since Nilo died."

"And—Marek?" He stumbled over the name.

Rhia flinched as the worry sliced through her again. "I was hoping you had seen him."

"I'm sorry. To risk his life for people he just met—he was a good man."

"Not *was*. *Is*. He'll come back."

"Of course. Forgive me."

Rhia brushed her hand against his. "I do." She stood. "I'll try to find out what's happening and let you know."

As she crossed the tent, a young Descendant stretched his hand toward her in a plea for help.

She went to him. "What is it?"

"Water...please..."

She fetched a flask and supported his trembling head while he drank. His yellow hair, even caked with sweat and blood, felt soft against her hands. The man's infirmity made him appear even younger than Rhia.

"Thank you," he whispered afterward.

She nodded with what she hoped was an impassionate façade, then turned away.

"Why do you call us Descendants?"

She stopped and said over her shoulder, "Because you descended from us. Why else?"

"You think we're below you. That's the other meaning, isn't it?"

Rhia turned to him. "How dare you accuse us of arrogance, when you invade our lands, planning to crush us under your heels like ants? You underestimated our magic, our determination, our fierceness, and now you're paying the price for your mistake."

His face paled. "I lost my brother out there today."

"So did I." Her statement began as a snarl but ended in a choked cry. She took a step toward him, pity encroaching on her rage. "Why are you here?"

He opened his mouth as if to recite an answer, then his certainty faltered. "I don't know. They tell me to go here, go there, follow my commanders, kill the enemy, whoever they are. I don't question." His chin lifted. "I'm a soldier, like my father, and my brother before me. Like your brother."

"Don't speak of my brother."

"I'm sorry." He regarded the feather around her neck. "What does that mean?"

"It means I serve the Spirit of Crow. He carries people to the Other Side."

"When they die?"

"Yes." It unsettled her to discuss the Spirits with someone who didn't believe in them.

"All people, or just your people?"

"All people, all animals. Every being with a soul." She knew that now, after feeling Crow take the dying Descendants.

"Animals don't have souls."

She almost laughed at the absurd suggestion. "Of course they do."

"You might as well say trees have souls, or rocks."

"Rocks don't scream when you kick them, or trees when you cut them."

He lifted an eyebrow. "Maybe they do, and you just can't hear them."

She examined his expression to determine if he were teasing, then pulled a nearby stool to the side of his bed. "May I ask you a question?"

He gestured to his injured leg. "I can't stop you."

She sat. "Did your ancestors find the White City, or did they build it themselves?"

"It depends who you ask. It was so long ago, no one really knows."

"What do you believe?"

"I believe the gods built it for us, that we were chosen." His brow furrowed. "I could be wrong, though."

She cocked her head at the notion of such a porous faith. "What's your name?"

"Filip."

"Filip, when you speak to your gods, do they answer?"

"Not with words," he admitted, then looked at her with shining eyes. "But we know they're there."

"How?"

"By our success. Their providence makes us rich. They give us strength to overcome our enemies."

"You haven't overcome us."

He shrugged. "Not yet."

Her blood chilled. The young man's voice held simple assurance rather than pride. His assertion was not a boast but a profession of faith. He might as well have declared that the sun would rise in the east tomorrow for all the controversy it stirred within him.

She swallowed and fixed him with a narrow gaze. "I'll die before I let that happen."

His forehead crinkled as if her words had hurt his feelings. "That's sad and unnecessary, but—"

"Enough." She stood abruptly, causing the stool to fall over onto the grass. "May you heal quickly, and leave the same way."

When she reached the other side of the tent, it had grown crowded with anyone who could stand. People pointed at the far end of the field. She slipped through the small gathering until she could see.

Torin and a man who appeared to be the Descendant commander had met in the middle of the field, both on horseback. Someone behind her uttered the word "truce."

"Is it over?" she asked.

"I think so," Coranna said. "Perhaps they're negotiating for an exchange of prisoners."

"We've got Descendants here who aren't well enough to travel," Elora said.

Koli was riding hard toward the hospital tent. When she pulled up, she called out for Coranna and Rhia.

"Torin requests both your presences at the negotiation. Go now. I'm off to find Galen."

Rhia and Coranna hurried down the hill. When they arrived at the conference, Torin motioned for them to step with him out of hearing range of the Descendant commander.

"My opponent, Colonel Baleb, has offered a truce, but one with troublesome terms. I've asked you here," he spoke to Coranna, "as the senior representative of the Kalindon delegation. It concerns one of your people. And you," he said to Rhia, "because it concerns someone close to you. Besides, I believe both of you to be wise, one well beyond her years."

Rhia wanted to acknowledge the compliment but her reaction was muted by dread. Torin said nothing more as he waited for Galen's arrival.

She examined the Descendant colonel, who rode a magnificent golden stallion with a silver-white mane. Unlike most of her people, he sat upon a saddle; the leather of this one was adorned with opulent red and yellow designs, matching the flag carried by the young officer at his side.

Baleb's breastplate gleamed bronze in the late morning sunlight, setting off the deep red of his sleeves, which were embroidered in sharp-angled patterns of gold. For all his defiant posture, the man seemed afraid, specifically of her. He must imagine her to have immense power to compensate for her lack of stature and maturity. If he only knew how little power her exhaustion had left her.

Galen arrived shortly on his own horse.

"What are your terms for a truce?" he asked Colonel Baleb. "If you wish to exchange prisoners, be advised that many of your wounded are being treated by our healers."

"We have taken no prisoners from this battle," growled Baleb. "If our wounded must stay, let them. Your prisoners cannot and will not serve you well in battle, lacking any magic of their own." His greedy gaze lengthened to take in the far end of the field. "Our price for leaving Asermos is five hundred horses."

They cried out in disbelief.

"Five hundred?" Galen gestured toward the village. "We

would be crippled by such terms. All of Asermos has no more than that. We might as well be arming you for another attack."

"Your shortcomings are not my concern."

Torin rode forward and unsheathed his own sword. "We don't need a promise to depart. We have only begun to display our magic. Retreat now while some of you live."

Baleb merely smiled. "In addition to our departure, we will return your spy."

Rhia's heart stopped. Marek.

"Either turn over the horses, or we will kill him." He reconsidered. "But not before examining him, thoroughly."

"He knows nothing of us," Galen said. "He is Kalindon. You'll get no new information out of him."

"Perhaps, but I will enjoy trying." Baleb turned a malevolent gaze on Rhia. Suddenly she knew how to solve the problem, if she dared such a risk.

"How do we know he's even alive?" she asked the colonel, then turned to Galen. "If he's already been tortured, he may not survive. Let me see him so I can determine his chances. If he's dying, they have nothing to offer us, and no right to demand such a ransom."

Galen seemed to search her eyes for signs of insanity.

"Please," she mouthed.

He turned to Baleb. "Bring us this scout, so that we know your word is true."

The colonel shrugged, then waved at one of his soldiers standing at the edge of the woods. The man disappeared into the trees. Baleb motioned to Rhia.

"You and your commander will meet with me and the spy away from the others."

He handed his sword to the nearest Descendant officer. Torin left his own weapon with Galen, who cast a warning glance at Rhia. She shared the Hawk's unease: one miscalculation, and she could forfeit Marek's life and the future of her people.

Rhia followed the two commanders across the field, but the gamble she planned made it seem more like a valley of sleeping hornets.

40

They threw Marek at her feet.

He looked as if he had been left out in the sun for hours without shelter. Every patch of exposed skin—his entire body from the waist up—blistered and peeled where it wasn't dark red from dried blood. His parched lips tried to move as he gazed up at her from the wheat field's scorched grass.

"Rhia…" he mouthed without sound. She sank to the ground next to him, aware that Baleb and Torin were watching.

"They want to trade you for all the horses in Asermos."

"Don't let them," his voice rasped. "I'm not worth it."

Her faith in her plan wavered. Now that Marek was here, she couldn't let him go. She took his hand and whispered, "To me you're worth all the horses, all the people in the world."

Colonel Baleb shouted from his mount. "How long does this take?"

She glared up at him. "It depends. I'm tired from all the people who have died today because of you."

"Hurry up," he huffed.

She returned her gaze to Marek's eyes, one of which was nearly swollen shut from a blow.

He shook his head, so faintly that no one else could see. "Don't."

"How do I choose between you and my people?"

"I am one man. That's how."

A tear fell from her eye, landing on his forehead. He winced as if it burned him.

If she had the strength of a Bear, she could snatch him up and run away. Rhia turned to Torin. His face held the exhaustion of a long battle and the resignation that some would be lost. He would not be so bold as to carry Marek off under the nose of his opponent. She looked around the field and saw no other Asermons close enough to help.

With a breath that twisted her heart, she forced out the lie. "He'll die either way. Not today, but soon. Let there be no ransom."

Baleb let out a sharp gust of air. "I'll have the heads of the idiots who tortured him so." He barked at the soldier who had brought Marek. "Take him away."

"Wait!" She changed her face to that of a mournful lover. "Give me a moment to say goodbye."

"You have wasted too much of my time already." He rode forward as if to grab Marek himself.

She quickly bent close to Marek's ear. "We'll come for you tonight. Do whatever you must to live until then."

A rough hand jerked him away from her. A foot soldier

heaved Marek to the back of Baleb's horse. He moaned when the rough hide scraped his burned skin.

"What of the truce?" Torin said.

Colonel Baleb turned in his saddle. "Consider it fragile."

He rode toward the woods, the foot soldier trailing behind.

When they were out of earshot, Rhia said to Torin, "Who shall we send to rescue him?"

"Rescue?" The general looked down at her with surprise.

Rhia's throat tightened. "We're going to get Marek back." He didn't reply. "Aren't we?"

Torin wiped a sleeve across his forehead and glared at the bright sky. "How do you propose we do that? Storm the Descendant camp? Look at my forces." He waved an arm toward the field, where soldiers sifted through the smoldering grasses to retrieve the dead. "They can barely stand up, much less mount an assault."

"We don't need an assault, only a few people," she said. "We'll go under the cover of nightfall."

"He'll be under guard at all hours. They'll be waiting for us to try." Shaking his head, Torin started to ride across the field toward Galen, who moved to join them. "I won't sacrifice any more of my fighters."

"Then I'll go."

He stopped his horse and turned to her. "Absolutely not. Your gifts are too rare. We can't lose you."

"Lose her how?" Galen approached on foot and looked at Rhia. "What happened?"

"I told Baleb that Marek would die."

"Is it true?"

"Not unless we abandon him." She made another plea to

Torin. "Marek saved Asermon lives by disabling those horses. This is how you thank him?"

"I regret he has to suffer for us. But he understood the danger when he volunteered." The general grimaced. "I won't throw away your life on top of his."

She gave Galen a desperate look, though she knew his answer already.

"No, Rhia. The risks are too great." The Hawk closed his eyes as if in pain. "I am sorry."

She stared at the woods where Marek had disappeared. He would die, and with him a part of her would perish, too. She wanted to lie down on the field of battle and let Crow take her with all the others.

No.

Her simmering rage smothered her ability to speak further with Torin and Galen. She turned toward the archers' wall at the other end of the field. There were still those who believed in loyalty.

The midnight air lay thick and dank over the earth as Rhia, Lycas and Alanka slipped from the cover of one tree trunk to the next, making their slow, secret progress toward the enemy camp. No one, not even Tereus, knew of their mission.

A few trees ahead, Lycas gave Rhia an impatient wave, and she picked up her pace. She longed for her siblings' night vision, now that the yellow crescent moon had dipped below the horizon. Fortunately most of the previous autumn's leaves had decayed to create a soft, noiseless surface on the path. She checked for twigs before taking each step and passed her hand over the freshly sharpened hatchet secured against her trousers with a leather tie.

Alanka scurried back to them. "The camp's just over that ridge, in a large meadow."

"How many guards?" Lycas caressed the sheath of his throwing dagger.

Alanka observed the gesture. "Two at the entrance to the camp and two guarding Marek. You may have to kill."

His grin flashed white in the darkness. This mission had given all three of them a focus, an excuse to delay their grief for Nilo.

Alanka turned to Rhia. "I stayed upwind of Marek so he'd catch my scent. He opened his eyes and looked toward me— not enough to draw attention but enough to show he knows we're here."

Rhia let out a breath. "He's alive."

"The bastards must have thought they could torture more information from him." Lycas gripped his knife. "I'll show them how it feels."

"You have time for nothing but a clean kill," Rhia told him, "and then only when necessary. That was the plan." She hated the idea of cold-blooded slaughter, and didn't want to give the Descendants any excuse to attack again, but taking the guards by surprise was the only way to overcome their disadvantage in number.

Alanka explained the location of the guards and the relative position of Marek.

"Ready?" she whispered. The three of them clasped hands and squeezed. In that moment, Rhia felt Nilo's absence more acutely than ever.

Alanka disappeared to circle around the front of the camp. Lycas and Rhia reached the outskirts and waited in the woods' dense undergrowth. About a hundred paces away, two guards roamed the west side of the perimeter, near an opening large enough for wagons to enter. Many of the camp's tents lay rolled up on the ground, ready for transport. Clearly many Descendants slept a more permanent slumber tonight.

Because of the lack of obstruction, Rhia could see a make-shift pen in the middle of the camp, bordered by two standing torches. A figure lay on its side on the ground, unmoving. Marek.

To their right, an owl hooted twice, then three times—Alanka's signal. Lycas called back in a similar fashion, with a different sound pattern, so as not to raise suspicion.

They were ready.

An arrow thumped a tree on the other side of the guards. One of them gestured to the other to check it out, watching his companion as he disappeared. Lycas moved in a blur of speed and crooked his arm around the second guard's throat. By the time Rhia caught up to him, the Wolverine had inserted his stiletto under the Descendant's ribs, up into his lung, providing a soundless death. No breath would rattle his throat and alert the others.

Her brother removed the blade and laid the dying body quietly on the ground. Rhia stopped as Crow's wings pounded within her mind. She would never get used to that sound.

Lycas touched her shoulder to calm her, then put a finger to his lips and directed her into the camp. He slunk off to find the other guard.

Rhia hurried from one tent to the next, listening for

sounds within before moving toward Marek's pen. Though some men tossed in their bedrolls—no doubt reliving the day's events in their dreams—none seemed to hear her. Outside one tent she felt the presence of Crow alight. Someone within was dying; breath rasped and teeth gritted. She moved on, more quickly.

When she had reached the tent adjacent to Marek's pen, she untied her hatchet and examined the nature of his captivity. A rope led from each of the four corners to one of his limbs. Staked into the ground was a fifth rope, leading to Marek's neck. They were treating him with the contempt they would show a wild beast.

One of his guards watched the surrounding area while the other kept a steady gaze upon Marek's immobile figure. No doubt they knew by now that he could become invisible, and wanted to monitor his movements without blinking.

A soft whinny sounded to her right. Though most of the Descendant horses stood with their heads lowered in a sedated haze, one eyed her with curiosity. Colonel Baleb's gold stallion. He wore nothing but a leather halter, the end of which was looped around a stake outside the largest tent.

When the horse shifted his feet to get a better look at her, he drew the attention of the guard who wasn't watching Marek, a tall, fair-haired man with slumped shoulders. Rhia shrank back behind the tent out of sight. She could no longer see Marek's pen. She strained to hear any sound.

Booted footsteps approached. The Descendant guard must have thought he was walking softly, but compared to most of her people, he was so loud, he might as well have wrapped bells around his ankles. The image—and the fact that her nerves were stretched to the breaking point—almost made her laugh. She clapped a hand to her mouth.

The footsteps halted. Rhia raised her hatchet and thought of the wet, sickening thud it would make in the soldier's flesh.

A mockingbird twittered a familiar tune. Alanka and Lycas were in place on the opposite side of the camp, but the guard was too close for Rhia to answer. Besides, fear had dried her lips too much to whistle even one note.

The footsteps began again. In just a few moments he would discover her. She remembered the gray wolf who had saved her life near the river. If only the wolf could appear again…

There was one animal she could call. But in the middle of the night? And for such a purpose?

Rhia closed her eyes and asked forgiveness, then began a silent prayer of beckoning, the one that would call the crows at a funeral. Her inward recitation was quick and urgent, meant to disturb more than coax.

From a nearby treetop, a rustle came, then an irritated flap of wings.

Please, she added to the prayer. *Help me.*

A soft caw emanated from the branches. The guard's steps halted again, and he murmured a baffled oath. Rhia repeated the prayer, shouting inside her mind, pleading for the crow to wake and fly.

With an indignant *grokkk!,* the bird dropped from the tree. Rhia opened her eyes to see a shadow descend and skim the forest floor. She winced, fearing the daylight-loving bird would fly into a tree trunk. Instead it landed about thirty paces away and rustled within the undergrowth, sounding like an intruder to the enemy camp.

The guard ran past her to investigate and disappeared into the woods. Rhia peered around the tent. The other guard was headed in Alanka and Lycas's direction. Now was her chance.

She ran to Marek's pen and climbed over the side, since it had no gate. His face held a mixture of despair and relief as he held out the rope that bound his neck. She wanted to kneel at his side and salve his wounds with a caress, but there was no time. She planted her foot on the rope between his neck and the stake in the ground, then swung the hatchet to slice the binding clean through. Its impact created a loud thump.

Marek's guard turned at the sound. His mouth opened to yell an alarm, then his body went rigid. He collapsed, an arrow protruding from his back.

She cut the other ropes, Marek pulling each one taut to make it easier. When they were all severed, she turned to him.

His face was etched in horror.

They were surrounded.

41

Guards stood around the pen, swords drawn. A dozen blades pointed straight at Rhia's heart. She dropped the hatchet. It made a dull clang when it hit the ground.

"Leave them alive!"

The Descendant colonel pushed his way past two of the guards and examined Rhia with a grin.

"Our little trap worked. They may not trade their horses for a piece of Kalindon scum, but I'll wager they'll give anything to keep their precious, puny Crow woman."

Rhia looked at Marek. His body drooped as if he were past the point of exhaustion and poised outside death's door. Yet Crow was far from him, which meant his demeanor was an act.

"Tell me, little girl." Colonel Baleb leaned his forearms on the fence as if indulging in casual gossip. "Why go to such lengths to rescue a dead man?" His smile disappeared and he gestured to two of the soldiers. "Tie up the liar and her lover. The rest of you, find the others. Bring any women alive, and the heads of any men. We'll show the Asermons what will remain of our captives if they refuse our ransom."

"No…" Rhia had lost one brother already today. Her knees buckled.

Marek caught her arm and whispered, "When I say, 'now,' climb on my back."

She looked at him in amazement. Did he have the strength to climb the fence supporting her weight, much less while conjuring his power?

All but two of the soldiers dispersed to look for Alanka and Lycas. Soon they would find two of their comrades dead outside the camp entrance and another wandering in the woods after a bumbling crow.

As soon as the pair of soldiers lowered their weapons to climb the fence, Marek bent his knees, whispered, "Now!" and vanished. Rhia clambered on his back and locked her arms around his neck. The outlines of her own body shimmered into nothing.

To the bewildered shouts of the soldiers, Marek vaulted the fence. Rhia nearly lost her grip and slipped several inches before climbing back up. He dodged around Descendants who were flailing the air with sword or knife in search of their captives. His legs began to falter; the Descendants' abuse had taken a toll on his body. He wouldn't be able to remain unseen much longer, and someone would strike them down.

"Behind the colonel's tent," she whispered.

He stumbled past the tent. They came face-to-face with the stallion, who stamped his feet in fear at the smell of invisible humans. Rhia let go of Marek and untied the halter from the hitching post. She let the horse sniff her now-visible hand.

"Come with me," she whispered to the beautiful beast.

Marek boosted her onto the stallion's back, then she reached out her good arm to help him up. From the near-miss of his leap she could tell he was weakening. Marek pressed his body against hers to make her invisible, but it didn't work. Any moment the soldiers would find them.

Rhia convinced the horse to move with a soft click of her tongue. He walked calmly between the tents toward the out-skirts of the camp. She bent low over his neck to hide her profile and wished that Marek could lend his stealth to cover the thump of hoofbeats beneath them.

The colonel's voice rang out. "Where's my horse?" He called even louder. "Keleos!"

The stallion stopped and turned his head toward his master's voice. Rhia urged him on with a whisper.

"You'll never have to fight again." She gave him a light nudge with her heel. "Please."

"Enough of this." Marek grabbed the lead from her and slapped the horse's hindquarters with it. "Go!"

The stallion lurched forward. Rhia steered him toward the opening in the woods using only the halter lead, her legs and her balance. Fortunately, Keleos was as elegant in training as in appearance, and responded to her guidance.

Shouts turned in their direction. Just as they reached the edge of the camp, a soldier leaped from behind the last tent. His sword slashed at Rhia, and she wheeled the horse just in time to avoid the blow.

Marek screamed and became visible again. Blood

poured from behind his right knee, where the sword had struck him.

"Hold on!" she begged him, then urged Keleos to gallop into the woods. Leaves from low branches whipped their faces as they careened among the trees. Her hands twisted in the horse's silver mane, and her injured shoulder throbbed from the effort to stay on the zigzagging horse.

When the cover of trees hid them from the camp, Rhia slowed their pace to a trot. She would ride out a little farther, then circle toward Asermos. If Lycas and Alanka had seen their escape, they would head home as well, she hoped.

She looked back and gasped at the rivulet of blood seeping down the horse's side from Marek's wound. He groaned behind her. With what little power she still possessed, she listened for Crow's wings and heard nothing.

"You'll be all right," she told him. "Just try to stay conscious until we get to—"

Steel whispered against leather on the path ahead of them. The stallion reeled as someone on the ground grabbed for his halter. Marek toppled off with a roar of pain, yanking Rhia with him. They fell to the forest floor with a breath-stealing thud.

Rhia lifted herself on an aching elbow to see one of the soldiers advancing on her, sword drawn. It must have been the one the crow had lured away from the camp. If so, he was alone. She looked at Marek, whose eyes grew wide.

A few steps away now, the soldier halted. "You again."

Though the darkness obscured his face, she would never forget that voice: Razvin's murderer.

The Descendant stepped forward, face set in a snarl.

"Thanks to you I was demoted, left behind on the day of battle to guard vermin like him." His sword pointed to Marek, who tried in vain to stand. "I prayed this day would come." The Descendant smiled slowly. "I guess that means my gods are real."

As long as he was talking, he wasn't killing. "Did you doubt it?" she asked him.

"We all have doubts. Except perhaps you people. You're too simple-minded to ask questions. You might as well expect a dog to ask his master why he should hunt, or lie down or drive the sheep to the left or right."

"I've asked questions," she said. "I've wondered why Crow comes for all people, even those who reject the Spirits."

"I don't believe you."

"It doesn't matter if you believe in them. They still watch over you. Someday Crow will come for you." A movement behind him caught her eye. *Maybe sooner than you think.*

Lycas leaped from the bushes and lunged for the soldier, who turned just in time to deflect his dagger's blow. The clash was so strong, both weapons clattered to the ground. As they fought hand-to-hand, Rhia stepped over the heavy sword to retrieve her brother's knife. It was nearly the length of her forearm, but at least she could lift it, unlike the sword.

At his best, Lycas would have defeated the soldier easily, but his body was worn from battle, while the Descendant had spent the day guarding Marek. Rhia waited for an opportunity to return the knife to her brother.

The soldier slammed the heel of his hand against Lycas's jaw, then gouged a knee into his groin. Lycas dropped to the ground, paralyzed with pain.

The Descendant scanned the ground for his weapon and saw Rhia holding the dagger. His sword lay just behind her feet. He leaped. She raised her hands to protect herself and plunged the knife into the Descendant's gut.

Blood gushed over her hand as she tried to withdraw the weapon. She needed to strike again and again, for he wasn't dead. His eyes grew wide with pain and surprise, but the light in them burned strong and bright.

His hands encircled her neck. She let go of the knife and tried to push him away, but his grip was too tight.

Black spots danced before her eyes. His look of defeat changed to triumph.

"Beast," he whispered as he squeezed.

Steel plunged between them, and the Descendant's hands tightened, then released in a spasm. She backed out of his grip to see Marek materialize beside her. He stood on one foot, the sword in both hands. He twisted it into the chest of the Descendant, who no longer looked superior, only bewildered.

His face pure fury, Marek shoved the sword deeper.

Crow's wings rushed through Rhia's mind, sucking her into blackness.

42

The Great Mourning began.

Asermos filled with chants for the dead, sung by anyone with breath to spare. Word of the Descendant defeat overtook the Asermon refugees on their way to Tiros, and within two days they returned. The wheat field had become a mass burial ground, with no individual graves, for the heat and humidity required immediate internment. Though Rhia understood the reasoning, she longed to know exactly where her brother Nilo lay.

Two evenings after Marek's rescue, she walked through her village, down the main road by the riverside. Nearly every person she passed wore their hair short. With a twinge of guilt, she felt thankful that her mother had not lived to see this day. On the distant shores of the Other Side, Mayra would see Asermos through a thick veil and understand how this battle fit into the Spirits' plan.

Right now it seemed like a terrible plan. But perhaps the Descendants, having witnessed the power of her people's magic, would regain their respect for the Spirits. Perhaps they could all be one people again someday.

Hah, she thought. The dreams of a fool.

She entered Sura the Otter healer's large house, part of which doubled as a hospital. The rooms were jammed with patients, lying side by side on the floor, cushioned by blankets donated by the local villagers, blankets that would likely be ruined by the blood and other fluids that spilled upon them here. She wrinkled her nose at the smells and thought how much worse it must be for a Wolf like Marek.

Sure enough, he sat with his back to the far wall and a piece of cloth tied tightly over his nose and mouth. His eyebrows popped up when he saw her, and he beckoned her over with a bandaged hand.

She picked her way among the sleeping, moaning patients, and tried to cast a soothing glance upon each of them, conveying compassion she was now too numb to feel. Crow's wings were silent; all of these patients would live, despite their suffering.

Marek mumbled something when she stood beside him. She pulled his gag down around his neck. He made a disgusted face. "I said, get me out of here."

She squatted beside him. "How's your leg tonight?"

"Like I need a drink." His mischievous glance quickly faded into soberness. "How are you?"

She looked away. Even he wouldn't understand the wooden despair that lay within her heart.

With the help of a crutch and Rhia's good shoulder, he limped from the healer's house.

"Ah, air," he said when they were outside. "I love air."

He went quiet suddenly and rubbed his neck. For the first time she noticed the red welts across his throat. When she had seen him before, blood or bandages had covered most of his neck. The angry marks must have been caused by the rope with which they had bound him—and probably choked him as well. She wondered if he would ever tell her about his ordeal in the Descendants' camp. Right now it would only stoke the rage that gnawed her inside, devouring her ability to feel anything else.

That night Rhia and Marek slept on the first floor of her home. Tereus gave Elora and Alanka his bed and took the hay-loft himself, since Marek's leg prevented him from climbing.

Marek trembled and flinched in his sleep, emitting small cries of protest. He had always slept quietly; she wondered what dreams or memories plagued his slumber now.

At least he could sleep. Rhia lay staring at the ceiling for hours, waiting for the short summer night to pass. As it did, a certainty within her grew: She could not perform tomorrow's funeral ritual. All feeling—tenderness, sorrow, love—had abandoned her. There was only the numbing, soothing balm of death. She was little more than a shell now, and no one wanted to see a shell perform their people's most sacred ritual. Her friends and family—all of Asermos—needed her comfort, needed her to be whole, which she would never be again.

All the deaths had left her as barren as…

As the second tree.

They rose before her, so vivid, it was as if she were in the glade again with Crow on the night of her Bestowing, but now she stood between the two trees, on the other side of the pool from the Spirit. He watched her across the water, waiting.

The breeze swished through the leaves of the lush tree and rattled the twigs of the barren one. She smelled the green tree's flowers and the black tree's oozing sap. The bitter and sweet scents mixed in the air until she couldn't separate them. She looked across the pool to Crow.

"You must choose," he said.

She put out her hand to the dry branches of the barren tree. Pity coursed through her. No one else understood its pain.

It reached for her. She jerked back her hand and studied the brittle branches. They would clutch her and never let go. But perhaps she would find peace in their dark embrace.

The green tree rustled behind her, whispering of the love that waited in her life to come, if only she would turn toward it. She closed her eyes and heard undertones of the loss that accompanied such love. They reached her ears like a song's faintest harmony, hinting of a tune to come, one whose mournful notes she could not yet imagine.

Crow's deep voice echoed. "It should be a difficult choice. Those who leap easily into the light will quail in the face of darkness."

He was next to her now. "Choose for yourself. Not for Asermos. Not for Marek. Not even for—" His voice cut off. "Not for anyone else."

Her heart felt encased in the bitter wood that tempted

her. Inside such a fortress it would remain impenetrable. Yet there it would also wither and die, long before the end of her days.

For herself, then, if no one else, she would choose the living tree.

For now.

She curled herself around Marek's body, careful to avoid his wounds, and slept without dreams.

The Asermons and Kalindons met in what was once the wheat field under a periwinkle dawn sky. No Descendants would roar out of the far woods today; scouts reported the enemy had departed—how far and for how long, no one knew. Several of their wounded had remained behind. Rhia was curious to see what would happen if they stayed—would they gain magic if they came to believe in the Spirits, or was it lost to them forever because of their ancestors' mistakes?

When she entered the field with Marek, Tereus, Lycas and Alanka, the assembled villagers rose to their feet. Coranna and Galen, along with Berilla, Galen's young Hawk apprentice, waited upon the small hill where they would preside. She joined them as her family took their places near the hill, next to Arcas, who helped Alanka bear Marek's unsteady weight. A look of understanding passed between the two men. Behind them, a mournful Perra stood with her two sons, grieving for Dorius.

Galen and Berilla recited the names of the dead. By the time they finished, the sun had risen, shedding an orange glow across the fresh ruddy soil of the burial ground.

The Hawks stepped aside, and Coranna then began the

chant of the body, low and soothing. Rhia joined in with a soft high harmony. Their voices floated on the thick morning mist. Rhia closed her eyes and slipped into a state of near-trance. Her lingering pains, of both body and spirit, dissolved and dissipated, and she felt the Other Side's sweet beckoning.

"You're off-key, little bird," Lycas said.

Her eyes flew open. Even he couldn't be so unconscionable as to interrupt the chant.

She looked around. No one else had heard him, yet to her the voice of her brother was as loud as if he had been standing next to her. *I imagined it,* she thought, and kept chanting.

"You're still off-key."

Rhia watched Lycas as the voice continued: "Luckily they're too upset to notice."

Her brother had not spoken. He stood with his arm around Mali, weeping into her hair, all traces of the tough warrior washed away.

"Rhia, I'm insulted. You could always tell us apart. And you said I was your favorite."

Her voice failed. *Nilo?*

"That's better."

But you're dead.

"Which makes you…"

Oh.

Pregnant.

"Thank you for singing me home when I died," Nilo said.

I'm sorry I couldn't stop crying.

"It meant more because you did. Besides, brothers love making little sisters cry."

When the chant was finished, everyone sat. One by one,

the people of Asermos praised their fallen heroes. When it was Lycas's turn, he slowly stood and faced the crowd.

"Nilo and I shared a womb, a home, a Guardian Spirit. We always hoped we'd share a grave." His voice shook with bitterness. "That dream was stolen from us, and I—I feel like I've lost the biggest part of me, and the only way to get it back is to kill again and again. But the enemy stole that, too, when they ran away."

Nilo spoke in Rhia's internal ear. "Revenge won't satisfy him. No matter how many he kills, it'll never be enough."

How do you know?

"I have infinite wisdom now."

Then what should he do to fill the space you left behind?

Nilo hesitated. "Perhaps my wisdom's not quite infinite."

Maybe after an infinite amount of time.

"Time. That's it. Only time can ease the pain of grief. Time, and many mugs of ale."

Ale, is that part of the Other Side's infinite wisdom?

"No, it's left over from life. Tell him. But find a more eloquent way to say it."

Rhia spoke her living brother's name. Lycas turned to her.

"Nilo says—" she held his gaze "—not to avenge his death. Only the passing of days and years will ease your sorrow— our sorrow. We will shoulder each other's burdens of grief."

Lycas stared at her. "Are you speaking to him?"

Rhia looked at Coranna to see if she were breaking an unknown code. Her mentor gestured to Lycas.

"Mostly he's speaking to me," Rhia told him.

His eyes widened. "Ask him—ask him if—" He seemed to search for the right words, any words. "Just ask if he's happy."

"Yes," Nilo said.

Rhia nodded. Lycas's face twisted into a smile that was almost a grimace.

"I wish he were as happy now as I am," Nilo said, "but one day he will be. When we're together again on the Other Side."

She repeated her brother's words as they came to her. Lycas staggered back to their family and sat, head in his hands.

Nilo spoke again. "There's a bird here that says I need to leave."

She repressed a plea for him to stay. *I love you.*

"Good luck. Crow tells me you'll need it."

What does that mean?

"I love you, too."

Then he was gone.

She finally gathered the courage to look at Marek. His face bore a quiet smile that held no fear.

Coranna began the calling of the crows, and Rhia joined in a few notes later. From a distance she heard them, as one hears a waterfall—roaring, rushing in the background of the mind. Such a commotion could not be one crow.

The distant horizon darkened, as it had in her dream the night before her death. Now they soared over familiar land-scape, the woods and fields of her home. They came, with voices that both quaked and lifted her soul.

The crowd stood to watch the onslaught. There were too many birds to count, but Rhia was sure that Crow had numbered the souls of the fallen and sent an emissary for each one. They called to one another as they flew, a beauti-ful, terrible chorus.

A chorus of comfort for those left behind.

* * *

"Don't tease the dogs."

Lycas waved off Rhia's concern and continued packing food from her father's kitchen for her return trip to Kalindos.

"I mean it," she said.

"Marek and Alanka asked me to pack ale. I strapped two barrels on each pony, which ought to last you through the summer." He turned to her. "You'll have to come home after that to get more."

"You can always visit."

He seized a loaf of bread so hard, crumbs showered over the table. "Yes, I'm sure the Asermon son of a traitor will be welcomed in Kalindos."

She gently took the bread from him and laid her hand on his arm. "You will if I have any say in it." She wished she could stay in Asermos longer, to grieve for Nilo with her remaining brother, but her new powers required Coranna's guidance.

Lycas moved awkwardly, as though he had been cut in half and was getting used to the new number of limbs. "Mali and I are going to live here for a while. Your father will be lonely without you, and he needs help with the farm."

Rhia understood. The hovel he had once shared with Nilo no doubt had turned into a stranger's home.

Alanka's figure shadowed the doorway. She rushed to Lycas and threw her arms around his neck. "I just got to know you." What was left of her childlike demeanor after Razvin's death had vanished in the smoke of battle.

"Silly Wolf." Lycas stroked the back of Alanka's hair. "I'll come when Rhia has the baby. Save some of that famous meloxa for me."

"I will." She let go of him and looked at the packs on the table. "How much food are we taking?"

"Enough for the journey." Rhia picked up the closest two packs. "If we stop six times a day for meals."

Alanka lifted a pack, which was lighter than she appeared to expect. Her face lit up. "Bread?"

They went outside to where Tereus waited with the Kalindons. A line of ponies stood in the early morning sun, tails shooing flies and mosquitoes. Her father stood close to Elora—closer than friends would, but not as near as lovers. Rhia was glad someone's companionship had eased his loneliness, if only for a short time.

She bid her father and brother farewell and took Marek's hand. He insisted on walking instead of riding, but she knew he'd change his mind once he discovered how much his injured leg slowed the rest of the party. It would be a battle of his pride versus…his pride.

Before they moved into the woods, she took a last look behind her. In the distance the river shimmered blue in the morning light, already dotted with the white sails of boats come to trade at the village port, now returned to peace.

She put a hand to her belly, feeling the power swell within her. As long as new life grew and flourished, like the leaves and branches of a tree, there was hope. Even Crow, death's constant companion, had taught her so. Who better to love life than One who existed on its borders, where He could see all its beauty as a whole and perfect vista?

Coranna wanted Rhia to live in such a way, on the outskirts, merely observing the attachments of others. Perhaps it would ease the pain of her burdens. She turned to look at the Crow woman, whose smile must have had a source besides her false distance from humanity.

Rhia walked on with the Kalindons, her hand in Marek's, until the forest enveloped them in its own lush life.

* * * * *

Follow Rhia on her journey in
VOICE OF CROW,
coming in 2007.

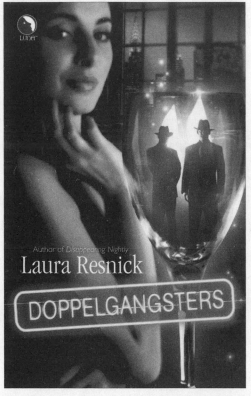